the MONSTRUMOLOGIST

the MONSTRUMOLOGIST

WILLIAM JAMES HENRY

Edited by Rick Yancey

SAGA PRESS

LONDON SYDNEY **NEW YORK** TORONTO NEW DELHI

To Sandy

SAGA PRESS

An imprint of Simon & Schuster

1230 Avenue of the Americas, New York, New York 10020

For information about special discounts for bulk purchases, please contact Simon & Schuster Special Sales at 1-866-506-1949 or business@simonandschuster.com.

The Simon & Schuster Speakers Bureau can bring authors to your live event. For more information or to book an event, contact the Simon & Schuster Speakers Bureau at 1-866-248-3049 or visit our website at www.simonspeakers.com.

Book design by Lucy Ruth Cummins

The text for this book is set in Adobe Jensen Pro.

Manufactured in the United States of America

First SAGA PRESS paperback edition March 2015

10 9 8 7 6 5 4 3 2

The Library of Congress has cataloged the hardcover edition as follows:

Yancey, Rick.

The monstrumologist / Rick Yancey.—1st ed.

p. cm.

Summary: In 1888, twelve-year-old Will Henry chronicles his apprenticeship with Dr. Warthrop, a scientist who hunts and studies real-life monsters, as they discover and attempt to destroy a pod of Anthropophagi.

ISBN 978-1-4169-8448-1 (hc)

[1. Supernatural—Fiction. 2. Monsters—Fiction. 3. Apprentices—Fiction. 4. Orphans—Fiction. 5. New England—History—19th Century—Fiction.] 1. Title.

PZ7.Y19197Mon 2009

[Fic]—dc22

2009004562

ISBN 978-1-4814-2544-5 (mass market pbk)

ISBN 978-1-4391-5261-4 (eBook)

mon•strum•ol•o•gy n.
1: the study of life forms generally malevolent to humans and not recognized by science as actual organisms, specifically those considered products of myth and folklore
2: the act of hunting such creatures

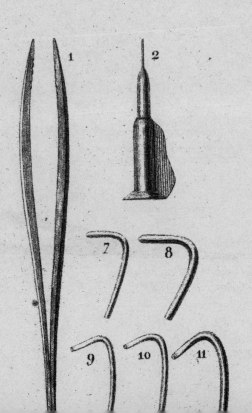

The Androphagi [*Anthropophagi*] have the most savage manners of all. They neither acknowledge any rule of right nor observe any customary law.... [They] have a language all their own, and alone of all these nations they are man-eaters.
—Herodotus, *The Histories of Herodotus* (440 B.C.)

It is said that the Blemmyae have no heads and that their mouth and eyes are put in their chests.
—Pliny the Elder, *Naturalis Historiae* (A.D. 75)

... another island, midway, live people of stature and ugly nature, which have no head and their eyes on the back and mouth, crooked as a horseshoe, in the midst of the breasts. On another island, there are many people without heads, and which has the eyes and head in the back.
—*Wonders of the World* (1356)

Gaora is a river, on the banks of which are a people whose head grow beneath their shoulders. Their eyes on in their shoulders, and their mouths in the middle of their breasts.
—*Hakluyt's Voyages* (1598)

To the west of *Caroli* are divers nations of *Cannibals*, and of those *Ewaipanoma* without heads.
—Sir Walter Raleigh, *The Discovery of Guiana* (1595)

Wherein I spake of most disastrous chances,
Of moving accidents by flood and field,
Of hair-breadth scapes i' the imminent deadly breach ...
And of the Cannibals that each other eat,
The Anthropophagi, and men whose heads
Do grow beneath their shoulders.
—Shakespeare, *Othello* (1603)

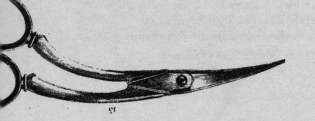

19

PROLOGUE

June 2007

The director of facilities was a small man with ruddy cheeks and dark, deep-set eyes, his prominent forehead framed by an explosion of cottony white hair, thinning as it marched toward the back of his head, cowlicks rising from the mass like waves moving toward the slightly pink island of his bald spot. His handshake was quick and strong, though not too quick and not too strong: He was accustomed to gripping arthritic fingers.

"Thank you for coming," he said. He released my hand, wrapped his thick fingers around my elbow, and guided me down the deserted hallway to his office.

"Where is everyone?" I asked.

"Breakfast," he said.

His office was at the far end of the common area, a

cluttered, claustrophobic room dominated by a mahogany desk with a broken front leg that someone had attempted to level by placing a book beneath it and the dingy white carpet. The desktop was hidden beneath listing towers of paper, manila file folders, periodicals, and books with titles such as *Estate Planning 101* and *Saying Good-bye to the Ones You Love*. On the credenza behind his leather chair sat a framed photograph of an elderly woman scowling at the camera, as if to say, *Don't you dare take my picture!* I assumed it was his wife.

He settled into his chair and asked, "So how is the book coming?"

"It already came," I answered. "Last month." I pulled a copy from my briefcase and handed it to him. He grunted, flipped through some pages, his lips pursed, thick brows gathering over his dark eyes.

"Well, glad to do my part," he said. He held the book toward me. I told him it was his to keep. The book remained between us for a moment as he glanced about the desk, looking for the most stable pile upon which to balance it. Finally it disappeared into a drawer.

I had met the director the year before, while researching the second book in the Alfred Kropp series. At the climax of the story the hero finds himself at the Devil's Millhopper, a five-hundred-foot-deep sinkhole located on the northwest side of town. I had been interested in the local legends and tall tales regarding the site, and the director had been kind enough to introduce me to several residents who'd grown up in the area and who knew the stories of this mythical "gateway to hell," now a state park, presumably because the devil had departed, making way for field-trippers and hikers.

"Thank you," he said. "I'll be sure to pass it around."

I waited for him to go on; I was there on his invitation. He shifted uneasily in his chair.

"You said on the phone you had something to show me," I gently prodded him.

"Oh, yes." He seemed relieved and now spoke rapidly. "When we found it among his effects, you were the first person 1 thought of. It struck me as something right up your alley."

"Found what among whose effects?"

"Will Henry. William James Henry. He passed away last Thursday. Our oldest resident. I don't believe you met him."

I shook my head. "No. How old was he?"

"Well, we aren't really sure. He was an indigent—no identification, no living relatives. But he claimed to have been born in 1876."

I stared at him. "That would make him one hundred and thirty-one years old."

"Ridiculous, I know," the director said. "We're guessing he was somewhere in his nineties."

"And the thing of his you found that made you think of me?"

He opened a desk drawer and pulled out a bundle of

thirteen thick notebooks, tied in brown twine, their plain leather covers faded to the color of cream.

"He never spoke," the director said, nervously plucking at the twine. "Except to tell us his name and the year he was born. He seemed quite proud of both. 'My name is William James Henry and I was born in the year of our Lord eighteen-hundred and seventy-six!' he would announce to anyone who cared to listen—and anyone who didn't, for that matter. But as to everything else—where he was from, to whom he belonged, how he'd come to the culvert where he was discovered—silence. Advanced dementia, the doctors told me, and certainly I had no reason to doubt it . . . until we found these wrapped in a towel beneath his bed."

I took the bundle from his hand. "A diary?" I asked.

He shrugged. "Go on. Open that top one and read the first page."

I did. The handwriting was extremely neat, though small, the script of someone who had had formal schooling, when instruction had included lessons in penmanship. I read the first page, then the next, then the following five. I flipped to a random page. Read it twice. While I read, I could hear the director breathing, a heavy huffing sound, like a horse after a brisk ride.

"Well?" he asked.

"I see why you thought of me," I said.

"I must have them back, of course, when you're finished."

"Of course."

"I'm required by law to keep them, in the unlikely event a relative shows up for his things. We've placed an ad in the paper and made all the necessary inquiries, but this sort of thing happens all too often, I'm afraid. A person dies and there is no one in the world to claim them."

"Sad." I opened another volume to a random page.

"I haven't read all of them—I simply don't have the time—but I am extremely curious to hear what's in them. There may be clues to his past—who he was, where he came from, that sort of thing. Might help in locating a relative. Though, from the little I've read, I'm guessing this isn't a diary but a work of fiction."

I agreed it would almost have to be fiction, based on the pages I'd read.

"Almost?" he asked. He seemed bemused. "Well, I suppose nearly anything is possible, though some things are much more possible than others!"

I took the notebooks home and placed them on top of my writing desk, where they stayed for nearly six months, unread. I was pressed on a deadline for another book and didn't feel compelled to dive into what I assumed to be the incoherent ramblings of a demented nonagenarian. A call that following winter from the director goaded me into unwrapping the frayed twine and a rereading of the first extraordinary few pages, but little progress besides that. The handwriting was so small, the pages so numerous, written on front and back, that I just skimmed through the first volume, noting that the journal seemed to have been composed over a span of months, if not years: The color of the ink changed, for example, from black to blue and then back again, as if a pen had run dry or been lost.

It was not until after the New Year that I read the first three volumes in their entirety, in one sitting, from first page to last, the transcript of which follows, edited only for spelling and correction of some archaic uses of grammar.

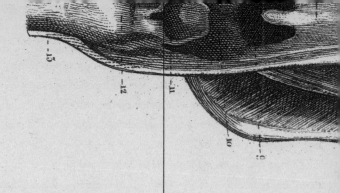

FOLIO I

Progeny

ONE

"A Singular Curiosity"

These are the secrets I have kept. This is the trust I never betrayed.

But he is dead now and has been for more than forty years, the one who gave me his trust, the one for whom I kept these secrets.

The one who saved me ... and the one who cursed me.

I can't recall what I had for breakfast this morning, but I remember with nightmarish clarity that spring night in 1888 when he roused me roughly from my slumber, his hair unkempt, eyes wide and shining in the lamplight, the excited glow upon his finely chiseled features, one with which I had, unfortunately, become intimately acquainted.

"Get up! Get up, Will Henry, and be quick about it!" he said urgently. "We have a caller!"

"A caller?" I murmured in reply. "What time is it?"

"A little after one. Now get dressed and meet me at the back door. Step lively, Will Henry, and snap to!"

He withdrew from my little alcove, taking the light with him. I dressed in the dark and scampered down the ladder in my stocking feet, putting on the last of my garments, a soft felt hat a size too small for my twelve-year-old head. That little hat was all I had left from my life before coming to live with him, and so it was precious to me.

He had lit the jets along the hall of the upper floor, though but a single light burned on the main floor, in the kitchen at the rear of the old house where just the two of us lived, without so much as a maid to pick up after us: The doctor was a private man, engaged in a dark and dangerous business, and could ill afford the prying eyes and gossiping tongue of the servant class. When the dust and dirt became intolerable, about every three months or so, he would press a rag and a bucket into my hands and tell me to "snap to" before the tide of filth overwhelmed us.

I followed the light into the kitchen, my shoes completely forgotten in my trepidation. This was not the first nocturnal visitor since my coming to live with him the year before. The doctor had numerous visits in the wee hours of the morning, more than I cared to remember, and none were cheerful social calls. His business was dangerous and dark, as I have said, and so, on the whole, were his callers.

The one who called on this night was standing just

outside the back door, a gangly, skeletal figure, his shadow rising wraithlike from the glistening cobblestones. His face was hidden beneath the broad brim of his straw hat, but I could see his gnarled knuckles protruding from his frayed sleeves, and knobby yellow ankles the size of apples below his tattered trousers. Behind the old man a broken-down nag of a horse stamped and snorted, steam rising from its quivering flanks. Behind the horse, barely visible in the mist, was the cart with its grotesque cargo, wrapped in several layers of burlap.

The doctor was speaking quietly to the old man as I came to the door, a comforting hand upon his shoulder, for clearly our caller was nearly mad with panic. He had done the right thing, the doctor was assuring him. He, the doctor, would take the matter from here. All would be well. The poor old soul nodded his large head, which appeared all the larger with its lid of straw as it bobbed on its spindly neck.

"'Tis a crime. A bloody crime of nature!" he exclaimed at one point. "I shouldn't have taken it; I should have covered it back up and left it to the mercy of God!"

"I take no stances on theology, Erasmus," said the doctor. "I am a scientist. But is it not said that we are his instruments? If that is the case, then God brought you to her and directed you hence to my door."

"So you won't report me?" the old man asked, with a sideways glance toward the doctor.

"Your secret will be as safe with me as I hope mine will

be with you. Ah, here is Will Henry. Will Henry, where are your shoes? No, no," he said as I turned to fetch them. "I need you to ready the laboratory."

"Yes, doctor," I responded dutifully, and turned to go a second time.

"And put a pot on. It's going to be a long night."

"Yes, sir," I said. I turned a third time.

"And find my boots, Will Henry."

"Of course, sir."

I hesitated, waiting for a fourth command. The old man called Erasmus was staring at me.

"Well, what are you waiting for?" the doctor said. "Snap to, Will Henry!"

"Yes, sir," I said. "Right away, sir!"

I left them in the alley, hearing the old man ask as I hurried across the kitchen, "He is your boy?"

"He is my assistant," came the doctor's reply.

I set the water on to boil and then went down to the basement. I lit the lamps, laid out the instruments. (I wasn't sure which he might need, but had a strong suspicion the old man's delivery was not alive—I had heard no sounds coming from the old cart, and there didn't seem to be great urgency to fetch the cargo inside . . . though this may have been more hope than suspicion.) Then I removed a fresh smock from the closet and rummaged under the stairs for the doctor's rubber boots. They weren't there, and for a moment I stood by the examination table in mute panic. I had washed them the week before and was certain I had placed them under the stairs. Where were the doctor's boots? From the kitchen came the clumping of the men's tread across the wooden floor. He was coming, and I had lost his boots!

I spied the boots just as the doctor and Erasmus began to descend the stairs. They were beneath the worktable, where I had placed them. Why had I put them there? I set them by the stool and waited, my heart pounding, my breath coming in short, ragged gasps. The basement was very cold, at least ten degrees colder than the rest of the house, and stayed that way year round.

The load, still wrapped tightly in burlap, must have been heavy: The muscles in the men's necks bulged with the effort, and their descent was painfully slow. Once the old man cried for a halt. They paused five steps from the bottom, and I could see the doctor was annoyed at this delay. He was anxious to unveil his new prize.

They eventually heaved their burden onto the examining table. The doctor guided the old man to the stool. Erasmus sank down upon it, removed his straw hat, and wiped his crinkled brow with a filthy rag. He was shaking badly. In the light I could see that nearly *all* of him was filthy, from his mud-encrusted shoes to his broken fingernails to the fine lines and crevasses of his ancient face. I could smell the rich, loamy aroma of damp earth rising from him.

"A crime," he murmured. "A crime!"

"Yes, grave-robbing is a crime," said the doctor. "A very

serious crime, Erasmus. A thousand-dollar fine and five years' hard labor." He shrugged into his smock and motioned for his boots. He leaned against the banister to tug them on. "We are coconspirators now. I must trust you, and you in turn must trust me. Will Henry, where is my tea?"

I raced up the stairs. Below, the old man was saying, "I have a family to feed. My wife, she's very ill; she needs medicine. I can't find work, and what use is gold and jewels to the dead?"

They had left the back door ajar. I swung it closed and threw the bolt, but not until I checked the alley. I saw nothing but the fog, which had grown thicker, and the horse, its face dominated by its large eyes that seemed to implore me for help.

I could hear the rise and fall of the voices in the basement as I prepared the tea, Erasmus's with its high-pitched, semi-hysterical edge, the doctor's measured and low, beneath which lurked an impatient curtness no doubt born of his eagerness to unwrap the old man's unholy bundle. My unshod feet had grown quite cold, but I tried my best to ignore the discomfort. I dressed the tray with sugar and cream and two cups. Though the doctor hadn't ordered the second, I thought the old man might need a cup to repair his shattered nerves.

". . . halfway to it, the ground just gave beneath me," the old grave-robber was saying as I descended with the tray. "As if I struck a hollow or pocket in the earth. I fell face-first upon the top of the casket. Don't know if my fall cracked the lid or if it was cracked by the . . . cracked *before* I fell."

"Before, no doubt," said the doctor.

They were as I had left them, the doctor leaning against the banister, the old man shivering upon the stool. I offered him some tea, and he accepted the proffered cup gladly.

"Oh, I am chilled to my very bones!" he whimpered.

"This has been a cold spring," the doctor observed. He struck me as at once bored and agitated.

"I couldn't just leave it there," the old man explained. "Cover it up again and leave it? No, no. I've more respect than that. I fear God. I fear the judgment of eternity! A crime, Doctor. An abomination! So once I gathered my wits, I used the horse and a bit of rope to haul them from the hole, wrapped them up . . . brought them here."

"You did the right thing, Erasmus."

"'There's but one man who'll know what to do,' I said to myself. Forgive me, but you must know what they say about you and the curious goings-on in this house. Only the deaf would not know about Pellinore Warthrop and the house on Harrington Lane!"

"Then I am fortunate," said the doctor dryly, "that you are not deaf."

He went to the old man's side and placed both hands on his shoulders.

"You have my confidence, Erasmus Gray. As I'm certain I have yours. I will speak to no one of your involvement in this 'crime,' as you call it, as I'm sure you will keep mum regarding mine. Now, for your trouble . . ."

He produced a wad of bills from his pocket and stuffed them into the old man's hands. "I don't mean to rush you off, but each moment you stay endangers both you and my work, both of which matter a great deal to me, though one perhaps a bit more than the other," he added with a tight smile. He turned to me. "Will Henry, show our caller to the door." Then he turned back to Erasmus Gray. "You have done an invaluable service to the advancement of science, sir."

The old man seemed more interested in the advancement of his fortunes, for he was staring openmouthed at the cash in his still-quivering hands. Dr. Warthrop urged him to his feet and toward the stairs, instructing me not to forget to lock the back door and find my shoes.

"And don't lollygag, Will Henry. We've work to last us the rest of the night. Snap to!"

Old Erasmus hesitated at the back door, a dirty paw upon my shoulder, the other clutching his tattered straw hat, his rheumy eyes straining against the fog, which had now completely engulfed his horse and cart. Its snorts and stamping against the stones were the only evidence of the beast's existence.

"Why are you here, boy?" he asked suddenly, giving my shoulder a hard squeeze. "This is no business for children."

"My parents died in a fire, sir," I answered. "The doctor took me in."

"The doctor," Erasmus echoed. "They call him that—but what exactly is he a doctor *of*?"

The grotesque, I might have answered. *The bizarre. The unspeakable.* Instead I gave the same answer the doctor had given me when I'd asked him not long after my arrival at the house on Harrington Lane. "Philosophy," I said with little conviction.

"Philosophy!" Erasmus cried softly. "Not what I would call it, that be certain!"

He jammed the hat upon his head and plunged into the fog, shuffling forward until it engulfed him.

A few minutes later I was descending the stairs to the basement laboratory, having thrown the bolt to the door and having found my shoes, after a moment or two of frantic searching, exactly where I had left them the night before. The doctor was waiting for me at the bottom of the stairs, impatiently drumming his fingers upon the rail. Apparently he did not think there was enough "snap" in my "to." As for myself, I was not looking forward to the rest of the evening. This was not the first time someone had called at our back door in the middle of the night bearing macabre packages, though this certainly was the largest since I had come to live with the doctor.

"Did you lock the door?" the doctor asked. I noticed again the color high in his cheeks, the slight shortness of breath, the excited quaver in his voice. I answered that I had. He nodded. "If what he says is true, Will Henry, if I have not been taken for a fool—which would not be the first time—then this is an extraordinary find. Come!"

We took our positions, he by the table where lay the bundle of muddy burlap, I behind him and to his right, manning the tall rolling tray of instruments, with pencil and notebook at the ready. My hand was shaking slightly as I wrote the date across the top of the page, *April 15, 1888.*

He donned his gloves with a loud *pop!* against his wrists and stamped his boots on the cold stone floor. He pulled on his mask, leaving just the top of his nose and his intense dark eyes exposed.

"Are we ready, Will Henry?" he breathed, his voice muffled by the mask. He drummed his fingers in the empty air.

"Ready, sir," I replied, though I felt anything but.

"Scissors!"

I slapped the instrument handle-first into his open palm.

"No, the big ones, Will Henry. The shears there."

He began at the narrow end of the bundle, where the feet must have been, cutting down the center of the thick material, his shoulders hunched, the muscles of his jaw bunching with the effort. He paused once to stretch and loosen his cramping fingers, then returned to the task. The burlap was wet and caked with mud.

"The old man trussed it tighter than a Christmas turkey," the doctor muttered.

After what seemed like hours, he reached the opposite end. The burlap had parted an inch or two along the cut, but no more. The contents remained a mystery and would remain so for a few more seconds. The doctor handed me the shears and leaned against the table, resting before the final, awful climax. At last he straightened, pressing his hands upon the small of his back. He took a deep breath.

"Very well, then," he said softly. "Let's have it, Will Henry."

He peeled away the material, working it apart in the same direction as he had cut it. The burlap fell back on either side, draping over the table like the petals of a flower opening to welcome the spring sun.

Over his bent back I could see them. Not the single corpulent corpse that I had anticipated, but two bodies, one wrapped about the other in an obscene embrace. I choked back the bile that rushed from my empty stomach, and willed my knees to be still. Remember, I was twelve years old. A boy, yes, but a boy who had already seen his fair share of grotesqueries. The laboratory had shelves along the walls that held large jars wherein oddities floated in preserving solution, extremities and organs of creatures that you would not recognize, that you would swear belonged to the world of nightmares, not our waking world of comfortable familiarity. And, as I've said, this was not the first time I had assisted the doctor at his table.

But nothing had prepared me for what the old man delivered that night. I daresay your average adult would have fled the room in horror, run screaming up the stairs and out of the house, for what lay within that burlap cocoon laid shame to all the platitudes and promises from a thousand pulpits upon the nature of a just and loving God, of a balanced and kind universe, and the dignity of man. *A crime*, the old grave-robber had called it. Indeed there seemed no better word for it, though a crime requires a criminal . . . and who or *what* was the criminal in this case?

Upon the table lay a young girl, her body partially concealed by the naked form wrapped around her, one massive leg thrown over her torso, an arm draped across her chest. Her white burial gown was stained with the distinctive ochre of dried blood, the source of which was immediately apparent: Half her face was missing, and below it I could see the exposed bones of her neck. The tears along the remaining skin were jagged and triangular in shape, as if someone had hacked at her body with a hatchet.

The other corpse was male, at least twice her size, wrapped as I said around her diminutive frame as a mother nestles with her child, the chest a few inches from her ravaged neck, the rest of its body pressed tightly against hers. But the most striking thing was not its size or even the startling fact of its very presence.

No, the most remarkable thing about this most remarkable tableau was that her companion had no head.

"*Anthropophagi*," the doctor murmured, eyes wide and glittering above the mask. "It must be . . . but how could it?

This is most curious, Will Henry. That he's dead is curious enough, but more curious by far is that he's here in the first place! . . . Specimen is male, approximately twenty-five to thirty years of age, no signs of exterior injury or trauma. . . . Will Henry, are you writing this down?"

He was staring at me. I in turn stared back at him. The stench of death had already filled the room, causing my eyes to sting and fill with tears. He pointed at the forgotten notebook in my hand. "Focus upon the task at hand, Will Henry."

I nodded and wiped away the tears with the back of my hand. I pressed the lead point against the paper and began to write beneath the date.

"Specimen appears to be of the genus *Anthropophagi*," the doctor repeated. "Male, approximately twenty-five to thirty years of age, with no signs of exterior injury or trauma. . . ."

Focusing on the task of reporter helped to steady me, though I could feel the tug of morbid curiosity, like an outgoing tide pulling on a swimmer, urging me to look again. I nibbled on the end of the pencil as I struggled with the spelling of "*Anthropophagi*."

"Victim is female, approximately seventeen years of age, with evidence of denticulated trauma to the right side of the face and neck. The hyoid bone and lower mandible are completely exposed, exhibiting some scoring from the specimen's teeth. . . ."

Teeth? But the thing had no head! I looked up from the pad. Dr. Warthrop was bent over their torsos, fortuitously blocking my view. What sort of creature could bite if it lacked the mouth with which to do it? On the heels of that thought came the awful revelation: The thing had been *eating* her.

He moved quickly to the other side of the table, allowing me an unobstructed view of the "specimen" and his pitiful victim. She was a slight girl with dark hair that curled upon the table in a fall of luxurious ringlets. The doctor leaned over and squinted at the chest of the beast pressed against her, peering across the body of the young girl whose eternal rest was broken by this unholy embrace, this death grip of an invader from the world of shadows and nightmare.

"Yes!" he called softly. "Most definitely *Anthropophagi.* Forceps, Will Henry, and a tray, please—No, the small one there, by the skull chisel. That's the one."

I somehow found the will to move from my spot, though my knees were shaking badly and I literally could not feel my feet. I kept my eyes on the doctor and tried my best to ignore the nearly overwhelming urge to vomit. I handed him the forceps and held the tray toward him, arms shaking, breathing as shallowly as possible, for the reek of decay burned in my mouth and lay like a scorching ember at the back of my throat.

Dr. Warthrop reached into the thing's chest with the forceps. I heard the scraping of the metal against something hard—an exposed rib? Had this creature also been partially consumed?

And, if it had, where was the *other* monster that had done it?

"Most curious. Most curious," the doctor said, the words muffled by the mask. "No outward signs of trauma, clearly in its prime, yet dead as a doornail. . . . What killed you, *Anthropophagus*, hmmm? How did you meet your fate?"

As he spoke, the doctor tapped thin strips of flesh from the forceps into the metal tray, dark and stringy, like half-cured jerky, a piece of white material clinging to one or two of the strands, and I realized he wasn't peeling off pieces of the monster's flesh: The flesh belonged to the face and neck of the girl.

I looked down between my outstretched arms, to the spot where the doctor worked, and saw he had not been scraping at an exposed rib.

He had been cleaning the thing's teeth.

The room began to spin around me. The doctor said, in a calm, quiet voice, "Steady, Will Henry. You're no good to me unconscious. We have a duty this night. We are students of nature as well as its products, all of us, including this creature. Born of the same divine mind, if you believe in such things, for how could it be otherwise? We are soldiers for science, and we will do our duty. Yes, Will Henry? *Yes, Will Henry?*"

"Yes, Doctor," I choked out. "Yes, sir."

"Good boy." He dropped the forceps into the metal tray. Flecks of flesh and bits of blood speckled the fingers of his glove. "Bring me the chisel."

Gladly I returned to the instrument tray. Before I brought him the chisel, however, I paused to steel myself, as a good foot soldier for science, for the next assault.

Though it lacked a head, the *Anthropophagus* was not missing a mouth. Or teeth. The orifice was shaped like a shark's, and the teeth were equally sharklike: triangular, serrated, and milky white, arranged in rows that marched toward the front of the mouth from the inner, unseen cavity of its throat. The mouth itself lay just below the enormous muscular chest, in the region between the pectorals and the groin. It had no nose that I could see, though it had not been blind in life: Its eyes (of which I confess I had seen only one) were located on the shoulders, lidless and completely black.

"Snap to, Will Henry!" the doctor called. I was taking too long to steel myself. "Roll the tray closer to the table; you'll wear yourself out trotting back and forth."

When the tray and I were in position, he reached out his hand, and I smacked the chisel into his palm. He slipped the instrument a few inches into the monster's mouth and pushed upward, using the chisel as a pry bar to spread the jaws.

"Forceps!"

I slapped them into his free hand and watched as they entered the fang-encrusted maw . . . deeper, then deeper still, until the doctor's entire hand disappeared. The muscles of his forearm bulged as he rotated his wrist, exploring the back of the thing's throat with the tips of the forceps. Sweat shone on his forehead. I patted it dry with a bit of gauze.

"Would have dug a breathing hole—so it didn't suffocate," he muttered. "No visible wounds . . . deformities . . . outward sign of trauma. . . . Ah!" His arm became still. His shoulder jerked as he pulled on the forceps. "Stuck tight! I'll need both hands. Take the chisel and pull back, Will Henry. Use both hands if you must, like this. Don't let it slip, now, or I shall lose *my* hands. Yes, that's it. Good boy. Ahhhh!"

He fell away from the table, left hand flailing to regain his balance, in his right the forceps, and in the forceps, a tangled strand of pearls, stained pink with blood. Finding his balance, the monstrumologist held high his hard-won prize.

"I knew it!" he cried. "Here is our culprit, Will Henry. He must have torn it off her neck in his frenzy. It lodged in his throat and choked him to death."

I let go the chisel, stepped back from the table, and stared at the crimson strand dangling from the doctor's hand. Light danced off its coating of blood and gore, and I felt the very air tighten around me, refusing to fully fill my lungs. My knees began to give way. I sank onto the stool, struggling to breathe. The doctor remained oblivious to my condition. He dropped the necklace into a tray and called for the scissors. *To the devil with him,* I thought. *Let him fetch his own scissors.* He called again, his back to me, hand outstretched, bloody fingers flexing and curling. I rose from the stool with a shuddering sigh and pressed the scissors into his hand.

"A singular curiosity," he muttered as he cut down the

center of the girl's burial gown. "*Anthropophagi* are not native to the Americas. Northern and western Africa, the Caroli Islands, but not here. Never here!"

Gingerly, almost tenderly, he parted the material, exposing the girl's perfect alabaster skin.

Dr. Warthrop pressed the end of his stethoscope upon her belly and listened intently as he slowly moved the instrument toward her chest, then down again, across her belly button, until, back where he began, he paused, eyes closed, barely breathing. He remained frozen this way for several seconds. The silence was thundering.

Finally he tugged the 'scope from his ears. "As I suspected." He gestured toward the worktable. "An empty jar, Will Henry. One of the big ones."

He directed me to remove the lid and place the open container on the floor beside him.

"Hold on to the lid, Will Henry," he instructed. "We must be quick about this. Scalpel!"

He bent to his work. Should I confess that I looked away? That I could not will my eyes to remain upon that glittering blade as it sliced into her flawless flesh? For all my desire to please and impress him with my steely resolve as a good foot soldier in the service of science, nothing could bring me to watch what came next.

"They are not natural scavengers," he said. "*Anthropophagi* prefer fresh kill, but there are drives even more powerful than hunger, Will Henry. The female can breed, but she cannot bear. She lacks a womb, you see, for that location of her anatomy is given to another, more vital organ: her brain. . . . Here, take the scalpel."

I heard a soft squish as he plunged his fist into the incision. His right shoulder rotated as his fingers explored inside the young girl's torso.

"But nature is ingenious, Will Henry, and marvelously implacable. The fertilized egg is expelled into her mate's mouth, where it rests in a pouch located along his lower jaw. He has two months to find a host for their offspring, before the fetus bursts from its protective sac and he swallows it or chokes upon it. . . . Ah, this must be it. Ready now with the lid."

His body tensed, and all became still for a moment. Then with a single dramatic flourish, he yanked from the split-open stomach a squirming mass of flesh and teeth, a doll-size version of the beast curled about the girl, encased in a milky white sac that burst open as the thing inside fought against the doctor's grasp, spewing a foul-smelling liquid that soaked his coat and splattered around his rubber boots. He nearly dropped it, holding it against his chest while it twisted and flailed its tiny arms and legs, its mouth, armed with tiny razor-sharp teeth, snapping and spitting.

"The jar!" he cried. I slid it toward his feet. He dropped the thing into the container, and I did not need his urging to slap on the lid.

"Screw it tight, Will Henry!" he gasped. He was covered head to toe in the blood-flecked goop, the smell of it more pungent than that of the rotting flesh upon the table. The tiny *Anthropophagus* flipped and smacked inside the jar, smearing the glass with amniotic fluid, clawing at its prison with needle-size fingernails, mouth working furiously in the middle of its chest, like a landed fish gasping upon the shore. Its mewling cries of shock and pain were loud enough to penetrate the thick glass, a haunting, inhuman sound that I am doomed to remember to my last day.

Dr. Warthrop picked up the jar and placed it on the workbench. He soaked some cotton in a mixture of halothane and alcohol, dropped it into the jar, and screwed the lid back on. The infant monster attacked the cotton, stripping the fibers apart with its little teeth and swallowing chunks of it whole. Its aggression hastened the effects of the euthanizing agent: In less than five minutes the unholy spawn was dead.

TWO

'His Services Are Indispensable to Me'

Stopping only twice—for another cup of tea around three a.m. and to relieve his bladder near four—the monstrumologist worked through the night and well into the next day, though with noticeably less urgency after the abortion of the abominable creature growing inside the young woman's corpse.

"Upon reaching full term," he explained to me in a dry, lecturing tone, which somehow made the topic more horrific, "the infant *Anthropophagus* bursts from its amniotic sac and immediately begins to feed upon the host, until nothing is left except bones, and those he drills into by means of his needlelike teeth—to suck out the nutrient-rich marrow. Unlike *Homo sapiens*, Will Henry, the *Anthropophagi* develop teeth before practically anything else."

We had separated the bodies with no small effort, for the beast had sunk its two-inch claws completely into its victim. The doctor pulled them out, one rigid digit at a time, using the chisel as a pry bar.

"Note how the claws are barbed," he pointed out. "Like a whaling hook or the forelegs of a praying mantis. Feel the tip, Will Henry—carefully! It is as sharp as a hypodermic and as hard as diamonds. The natives of its natural habitat use them for sewing needles and spear tips."

He pulled the massive arm off the dead girl's chest.

"Their reach exceeds that of an average man by nearly a foot and a half. Observe how large its hand is." He placed his own hand, palm to palm, against the monster's. The creature's hand engulfed the doctor's as an adult's would a child's. "Like the lion, it uses its claws as its primary form of attack, but, unlike the large mammalian predators, it does not attempt to kill its prey before it begins to feed. More like the shark or an insect, the *Anthropophagus* prefers living flesh."

It required both of us to drag its leg off the girl. A bit breathless from the effort, the doctor said, "They possess the largest Achilles tendons known to primates, enabling them to leap astonishing distances, up to forty feet. . . . Note the heavy musculature of the calves and quadriceps. . . . Careful now, Will Henry, or he'll roll off on us."

He directed me to clear a space on the worktable. He took the shoulders of the girl, I took the legs, and together we moved her corpse. She was so light she seemed to weigh no more than a bird. He folded her arms across her chest and gathered the gown around her violated torso. "Fetch a clean sheet, Will Henry," he instructed me, and then he covered her. We stood for a moment before the shrouded figure, neither of us speaking.

At last he sighed. "Well, she is free of it now. If there is any mercy in this, Will Henry, she did not suffer. She did not suffer."

He clapped his hands and turned away, his melancholy vanishing in a wink as he strode back to the examining table, eager to continue his communion with the creature. We pulled it to the center of the table and rolled it onto its back. The black, lidless eyes on its shoulders and the yawning fang-crowded maw in its chest reminded me more than anything of a shark. Its skin was as pale as a shark's underbelly as well, and, for the first time, I noticed the thing was completely hairless, a fact that amplified its nightmarish appearance.

"Like the lion, they are nocturnal hunters," the doctor said, as if he had somehow read my thoughts. "Thus the oversize eyes and the complete absence of melanin in the upper dermis. Also like *Panthera leo*—and *Canis lupus*—they are communal hunters."

"'Communal,' sir?"

"They hunt in packs."

He snapped his fingers, called for a fresh scalpel, and the necropsy began in earnest. While he carved up the beast, I was kept busy, taking dictation, handing him instruments, and scurrying from cupboard to table and back again, filling empty specimen jars with formaldehyde, into which he dropped the organs. Out came one of its eyes, the optic nerves dangling like twisted rope from the back. He pointed out the monster's ears: five-inch-long slits located on either side of its waist, just above the hips.

Then Warthrop opened the chest, just above the leering mouth, using the rib-spreaders to make room for his hand to retrieve the liver, the spleen, the heart, and the lungs, grayish white and oblong like deflated footballs. All the while he continued his lecture, interrupting himself from time to time to dictate measurements and describe the conditions of the various organs.

"The lack of follicles is curious, not something that appears in any of the literature. . . . The eye measures nine-point-seven centimeters by seven-point-three centimeters, perhaps owing to their natural habitat. They did not evolve in temperate climes."

He made an incision a few inches above the monster's groin, plunged both hands into the cavity, and pulled out the brain. It was smaller than I expected it to be, about the size of an orange. He placed it on the scale, and I recorded the weight in the little notebook.

Well, thought I. *That's good at least. With a brain this small, they can't be very smart.*

Again, as if he possessed the ability to read my thoughts,

he said, "Probably the mental capacity of a two-year-old, Will Henry. Somewhere between an ape and a chimpanzee. Though they lack tongues, they can communicate through grunts and gestures, much like their primate cousins, albeit with much less benign intent."

I stifled a yawn. I wasn't bored; I was exhausted. The sun had long since risen, but in this windowless room reeking of death and the acidic stench of chemicals, it was endless night.

The doctor showed no signs of fatigue, however. I had seen him like this before, when the fever of his peculiar passion was upon him. He ate very little, slept even less, all his powers of concentration, which was as formidable as any man's I have ever encountered, focused on the task at hand. Days would pass, a week, a fortnight, without a shave or a bath; he could not even spare a moment to comb his hair or don a fresh shirt, until, for want of food and rest, he began to resemble one of his macabre specimens: bloodshot eyes sunk deep in their sockets, ringed in black; skin the color of coal dust; clothes hanging loosely from his emaciated frame. Inevitably, as night follows day, the flame of his passion would at last exhaust the fuel of his mind and body, and he would collapse, taking to his bed like one suffering from a tropical fever, listless and irritable, his depression made all the more striking by the intensity of the mania that preceded it. All day long and well into the night I would be up and down the stairs, fetching food and drink and extra blankets, putting off callers ("The doctor is ill and can't see any-one right now"), sitting at his bedside for hours while he bemoaned his fate: His work was for nothing. In a hundred years no one would know his name, recognize his accomplishments, sing his praises. I would try to console him the best I could, assuring him the day would come when his name would be spoken in the same breath as Darwin's. Often with disdain these childlike attempts at succor were dismissed. "Oh, you're just a boy. What do you know about anything?" he would answer, turning his head upon the pillow. At other times he would seize my hand, pull me close, look deeply into my eyes, and whisper with frightening intensity, "It is you, Will Henry, you who must carry on my work. I have no family and shall have none. You must be my memory. You must bear the burden of my legacy. Will you promise me that all will not have been in vain?"

And of course I promised him. For it was true: I was all he had. I have always wondered if it ever occurred to him, this man of whom it might be said there had never been another of more towering, awe-inspiring self-absorption, that the opposite was also true—*he* was all *I* had.

His recovery would last a week, sometimes two, and then something would happen, a telegram would be received, a new paper or book about the latest discovery would arrive by post, an important caller would come in the middle of the night, and the cycle would begin again. The spark would ignite the fuel.

"Snap to, Will Henry," he would cry. "We have work to do!"

The spark carried to our door by Erasmus Gray that foggy April morn had, by noon, set the fire roaring to white-hot intensity. All the organs were extracted, examined, catalogued, and preserved; all the measurements were taken; there were hours of dictation and dissertation on the nature of the beast. ("Our friend must be the alpha male of his troop, Will Henry. Only the alpha male enjoys the privilege of breeding.") And after all that, without a moment of respite, there was still the mopping up. The instruments had to be cleaned, the floor scrubbed with lye, every surface sterilized with bleach. Finally, long past the midday hour, unable to stand a moment longer, I sank to the bottom step of the stairs, caring not if he scolded me for my indolence, while I watched him return to the body of the girl, pull back the sheet, and suture the incision in her stomach. He snapped his fingers without looking in my direction.

"Bring me the pearls, Will Henry."

I lurched wearily to my feet and brought him the tray containing the necklace. It had been soaking in alcohol for hours; most of the blood had floated away, turning the liquid a rather pleasant shade of pink. He shook off the excess solvent, undid the clasp, and gently draped the glimmering white strand around her ravaged neck.

"What can be said, Will Henry?" he murmured, dark eyes fixed upon the remains. "What once laughed and cried and dreamed becomes fodder. Fate brought him to her, but if not him, then without question the worm, a no less ravenous beast than he. There are monsters who wait for all of us upon our return to the earth, and so what can be said?"

He flung the sheet over her face and turned away.

"We haven't much time. Where there is one, there must be more. *Anthropophagi* are not particularly prolific. They produce only one or two offspring per year; still, we do not know how long they have gone unnoticed here in the New World. Regardless of the exact number, somewhere in the vicinity of New Jerusalem there is a breeding population of these man-eaters, and it must be found and eradicated—or we shall be overwhelmed."

"Yes, sir," I muttered in reply. My head felt light, my arms and legs heavy, and his face swam in and out of focus.

"What is it?" he demanded. "What's the matter with you? I can't have you collapsing on me now, Will Henry."

"No, sir," I agreed, and then I collapsed upon the floor.

He scooped me into his arms and carried me up the stairs, through the kitchen that glowed with the tender light of the spring sun, to the second floor, and then up the little ladder to my loft, where he laid me upon the bed atop the covers, without bothering to strip me of my blood-spattered clothing. He did pull the hat from my head, however, and hung it upon the peg on the wall. The sight of my tattered little hat hanging forlornly on that peg was too much for me. It represented all that I had lost. To disappoint him in my lack of fortitude and manly stoicism was unthinkable, yet

I could not bear it, the sight of that hat and the memories it represented juxtaposed against the surreal horror of the preceding hours.

I burst into tears, curling into a sobbing ball and clutching my stomach as he towered over me, making no move to comfort or console, but studying me with the same intense curiosity as he had the testicles of the male *Anthropophagus*.

"You miss them, don't you?" he asked softly.

I nodded, unable to speak around my gut-wrenching sobs.

He nodded, hypothesis confirmed. "As do I, Will Henry," he said. "As do I."

He was quite sincere. Both my parents had been in his employ; my mother had kept the doctor's house, and my father, as I would after he was gone, his secrets. At their funeral the doctor had laid a hand upon my shoulder and said, "I don't know what I shall do now, Will Henry. Their services were indispensable to me." He seemed oblivious to the fact that he was speaking to the child left orphaned and homeless by their demise.

It would not be an exaggeration to say my father had worshipped Dr. Warthrop. It would be more than an exaggeration—indeed, it would be an egregious lie—to say my mother had. Now, with the acuity that comes with the passage of many years, I can state unequivocally that the chief cause of friction between them was the doctor, or rather, Father's feelings for him and Father's intense loyalty to him, a loyalty that trumped all others, including any sense of obligation toward his wife or his only child. That Father loved us, I have never had any doubt; he had simply loved the doctor more. This was the root of my mother's hatred for Dr. Warthrop. She was jealous. She was betrayed. And it was that sense of betrayal that led to the most vehement quarrels between them.

Many a night before the fire stole them from me, I had lain awake listening to them through the thin walls of my room on Clary Street, the sound of their voices crashing against the plaster like storm surges smashing against a seawall, the culmination of the conflict that had begun hours earlier, usually when Father arrived late for dinner—late because the doctor had kept him. There were times when Father did not return for dinner, times when he did not return for days. When he at last came home, after my joyful greetings at the door, he would raise his eyes from my adoring ones to the decidedly less than adoring pair belonging to my mother, give a sheepish grin and a helpless shrug, and say, "The doctor needed me."

"What of me?" she would cry. "What of your son? What of our needs, James Henry?"

"I am all he has," was the unwavering reply.

"And you are all *we* have. You disappear for days without a word to anyone about where you are going or when you'll return. And when you do finally drag your thoughtless carcass through the door, you will not say where you have been or what you've been doing."

"Now, do not go on with me, Mary," Father would caution her sternly. "There are some things I can tell you and some things I can't."

"Some things you can? What might those things be, James Henry, for you tell me *nothing!*"

"I tell you what I can. And what I can tell you is the doctor is engaged in very important work and he needs my help."

"But I do not? You force me into sin, James."

"Sin? What sin are you talking about?"

"The sin of false witness! The neighbors ask, 'Where is your husband, Mary Henry? Where is James?' and I must lie for you—for *him*. Oh, how it galls me to lie for him!"

"Then don't. Tell them the truth. Tell them you don't know where I am."

"That would be worse than a lie. What would they say about me—a wife who doesn't know where her husband's gone?"

"I don't understand why it should gall you, Mary. If it weren't for him, what would you have? We owe everything to him."

She could not deny that, so she ignored it. "You don't trust me."

"No. I simply cannot betray *his* trust."

"An honorable man has no need for secrets."

"You don't know what you're talking about, Mary. Dr. Warthrop is the most honorable man I have ever known. It is a privilege to serve him."

"Serve him in *what?*"

"His studies."

"What studies?"

"He is a scientist."

"A scientist of *what?*"

"Of . . . of certain biological phenomena."

"And what does that mean? What 'biological phenomena' are you talking about? Birds? Is Pellinore Warthrop a bird-watcher, James Henry, and you the porter of his field glasses?"

"I will not discuss this, Mary. I will not tell you any more of the nature of his work."

"Why?"

"Because you do not wish to know!" For the first time, Father raised his voice. "I am telling you in truth that there are days when *I* wish I didn't know! I have seen things that no living man should ever see! I have been to places where the angels themselves would fear to tread! Now push no more upon this, Mary, for you do not know of what you speak. Be grateful for your ignorance and take comfort in the false witness it forces you to bear! Dr. Warthrop is a great man engaged in great business, and I shall never turn my back upon him, though the fires of hell itself arise to contend against me."

And that would be the end of it, at least for a time; usually it began again after he put me to bed. Before joining her in the parlor to face her fire, a fire only negligibly less intense than that of hell, he always kissed me on the forehead, always ran his hand through my hair, always closed his eyes with me as I said my bedtime prayer.

My entreaties to heaven complete, I would open my eyes and stare into the kind face and gentle eyes of my father, secure in that tragically naïve way of all children that he would always be with me.

"Where do you go, Father?" I asked him once. "I won't tell Mother. I won't tell anyone."

"Oh, I have been so many places, Will," he answered. "Some so strange and marvelous you would think you were dreaming. Some strange and not so marvelous, as dark and frightening as your very worst nightmare. I have seen wonders that poets can only imagine. And I have seen things that would turn grown men into squalling babes at their mother's feet. So many things. So many places . . ."

"Will you take me with you the next time you go?"

He smiled. A sad and knowing smile, understanding, with the intuitive knowledge of a man who knows his luck is not inexhaustible, that the day would come when he would embark upon his last adventure.

"I'm old enough," I said when he did not answer. "I'm eleven, Father, nearly twelve—practically a man! I want to go with you. Please, please take me with you!"

He laid a hand upon my cheek. His touch was warm.

"Perhaps one day, William. Perhaps one day."

✳

The monstrumologist left me to suffer my sorrow in solitude. He did not go to his room to rest; I heard his footfalls upon the stairs and, after a moment, the faint creak of the door leading to the basement. He would not sleep that day: The fever of the hunt was upon him.

My sobs petered out. A few feet above my head was a little window set in the ceiling, and I could see diaphanous clouds sailing like stately ships across the bright sapphire sky. At the schoolhouse my former chums were in the yard playing stickball, squeezing in the last at bat before Mr. Proctor, the headmaster, called them back inside for their afternoon lessons. Then, at the last ringing of the bell, the excited race for the door, the explosion into the soft spring air, the bedlam of a hundred voices shouting in unison, "Freedom! Freedom! The day is ours!" Perhaps the stickball game would be resumed, mid-inning, the minor distraction of afternoon lessons dismissed with. I was small for my age and not a very good batter, but I was fast. When I left the school for the private instruction of Dr. Warthrop, I was the fastest runner on my team and the holder of the most stolen bases. I had stolen home a record thirteen times.

I closed my eyes and saw myself taking the lead on third, scooting along the baseline, eyes darting from pitcher to catcher and back again, heart high in my chest as I waited for the pitch. Scoot, another foot. Scoot, still another. The pitcher hesitates; he sees me out of the corner of his eye.

Should he whip the ball to third? He waits for me to run. I wait for him to pitch.

And I am still waiting when a voice speaks sharply in my ear.

"Will Henry! Get up, Will Henry!"

I opened my eyes—how heavy the lids felt!—and spied the doctor standing in the opening to my little alcove, holding a lantern, with cheeks unshaven, with hair disheveled, and dressed in the same clothes from the night before. It took a moment for my mind to register that he was covered head to toe in blood. Alarmed, I sprang up with a cry.

"Doctor, are you all right?"

"Whatever do you mean, Will Henry? Of course I'm all right. You must have had a bad dream. Now come along. The hour grows late and there is much to do before dawn!"

He rapped his knuckles against the wall as if to emphasize his point, and disappeared down the ladder. Quickly I donned a fresh shirt. What time was it? I wondered. Above me the stars seared the obsidian canopy of the sky; there was no moon. I felt along the wall, found my little hat on its hook, and put it on. It was quite snug, as I've said, but somehow that brought great comfort to me.

I found him in the kitchen, stirring a pot of noxious liquid, and it took me a moment to realize he was preparing dinner and not boiling flesh off a bone belonging to the *Anthropophagus*. *Perhaps it wasn't blood after all*, I thought. *Perhaps he's covered with my dinner*. He may have been a genius, but, like most geniuses, his brilliance illuminated a very narrow spectrum: The doctor was a terrible cook.

He ladled some of the noxious mixture into a bowl and slapped it upon the table.

"Sit," he said, motioning to the chair. "Eat. We shall not have the opportunity later."

I gave the gruel an experimental stir with my spoon. A grayish-green object floated upon the surface of the thick brown broth. A bean? It was too large for a pea.

"Is there any bread, sir?" I dared to ask.

"No bread," he said curtly. Then he bounded down the stairs to the basement without another word. I rose at once from the table and checked the basket by the cupboard. A single roll, perhaps a week old, lay fermenting inside. I looked about and spied no second bowl, and sighed. Of course he had not eaten. Returning to my soup or stew or whatever the concoction might have been called, I chased down a few swallows with a glass of water and a few anxious words of prayer—not in thanksgiving, but in supplication.

"Will Henry!" floated his call through the open basement door. "Will Henry, where are you? Snap to, Will Henry!"

My prayers were answered. I dropped my spoon into the bowl—it gave a little bounce when it hit the spongy liquid— and hurried down the stairs.

I found him pacing to and fro, from the workbench, where the girl's body rested, to the examining table, now empty and wiped clean. I cast my eye about the room in an irrational bit of panic, as if somehow the thing had risen from the dead and might be lurking in the shadows. I spied it hanging upside down, between the bench and the shelves that housed its organs, the rope suspending it from the ceiling creaking from the enormous weight, and, beneath, a large tub filled with the foul-smelling black sludge of its partially congealed blood. Here was the explanation for the offal on the doctor's clothing: He had been draining the carcass. Later it would be embalmed, wrapped in linen, and shipped by private carrier to the Society in New York, but for now it hung like a slaughtered hog in a butcher's shop, its heavily muscled arms dangling on either side of the tub, the tips of its claws scraping upon the floor as the rope slowly twisted and groaned with its weight.

I looked away; its remaining eye, black and lidless, frozen by death into an unblinking stare, seemed to be gazing directly back at me: I could see my slight frame reflected within that oversized orb.

The doctor stopped pacing upon my arrival and stared at me with open mouth, as if startled by my presence after shouting for me to join him.

"Will Henry!" he said. "Where have you been?"

I started to say, "Eating as you told me, sir," but he cut me off.

"Will Henry, what is our enemy?"

His eyes were bright, the color in his cheeks high, symptoms of his peculiar mania that I had seen a dozen times before. On its face, the answer to his question—barked in a tone more reminiscent of a command—was obvious. I pointed a quivering finger at the suspended *Anthropophagus*.

"Nonsense!" he said with a laugh. "Enmity is not a natural phenomenon, Will Henry. Is the antelope the lion's enemy? Does the moose or elk swear undying animosity for the wolf? We are but one thing to the *Anthropophagi*: *meat*. We are prey, not enemies.

"No, Will Henry, our enemy is *fear*. Blinding, reason-killing fear. Fear consumes the truth and poisons all the evidence, leading us to false assumptions and irrational conclusions. Last night I allowed the enemy to overcome me; it blinded me to the glaring truth that our situation is not as dire as fear had led me to believe."

"It's not?" I asked, though I failed to see the wisdom in his judgment. Did not the beast hanging from the ceiling give the lie to his assertion?

"The typical *Anthropophagi* pod consists of twenty to twenty-five breeding females, a handful of juveniles, and one alpha male!"

He waited for my reaction, grinning foolishly, eyes sparkling. When he saw I did not share in his relief and exultation, the doctor hurried on.

"Don't you see, Will Henry? There could not be more than two or three others. A breeding population in the vicinity of New Jerusalem is impossible!"

He recommended his pacing, incessantly running his fingers through his thick hair, and as he spoke, my presence faded from his consciousness as light fades from the autumnal sky.

"This one fact gave birth to my fear, a fear that aborted all other—extremely pertinent—evidence. Yes, it is a fact that a typical pod has up to thirty members. But it is equally true that *Anthropophagi* are not native to the Americas. There has not been a single sighting of the species on this continent since its discovery; no remains or other evidence of its existence here has ever been found; and there is no corresponding legend or myth about them in the native traditions."

He ceased his circuit and whirled upon me.

"Do you see it now, Will Henry?"

"I—I think so, sir."

"Nonsense!" he cried. "Clearly you do not! Do not lie to me, Will Henry. To me or to anyone else—ever. Lying is the worst kind of buffoonery!"

"Yes, sir."

"We must couple the fact that they are not native to these shores with the fact that they are extremely aggressive. A breeding population could not have gone unnoticed, simply because we are lacking one thing. And what is that one thing, Will Henry?"

He did not wait for my answer, perhaps understanding that I *had* no answer.

"Victims! They must have food, obviously, to thrive, yet there have been no reports of attacks, no sightings, no evidence, direct or indirect, of their presence here beyond *that*." He jabbed a finger at the beast on the hook. "And *that*," he said, swinging the finger round to the covered corpse on the bench. "Hence their numbers are not great, *could not be* great. So you see, Will Henry, how our enemy, fear, makes the impossible possible and the unreasonable perfectly reasonable! No. We have a case of a *recent* immigration, this male and perhaps one—no more than two, I would fathom—breeding females. The great mystery is not in their numbers, but how they came to be here. They are not amphibious; they did not swim here. They don't have wings; they did not fly here. So how did they come to be here? We must answer that question, Will Henry, once tonight's business is transacted. Now, where is the list?"

"The list, sir?"

"Yes, yes, the list, the list, Will Henry. Why do you stare at me like that? Am I a lunatic, Will Henry? Do I speak in tongues?"

"I don't—I haven't seen—you've given me no list, sir."

"We can't lose our focus now, Will Henry. Losing our focus will more than likely cost us our lives. Even one or two females are extremely dangerous. Much like the lion, it is the female to be feared, not the indolent male, who often feeds on the carcass after the females have labored for the kill."

He snatched a piece of paper from the covered chest of the dead girl. "Ah, here it is. Right here, Will Henry, where *someone* laid it." His tone was slightly accusatory, as if he could prove, given enough time and evidence, that it was I who had laid it there. He shoved it in my direction.

"Here, pack it up quickly and put it by the back door. Snap to, Will Henry!"

I took the list from him. His handwriting was atrocious, but I had worked for him long enough to be able to decipher it. I bounded up the stairs and began the scavenger hunt, and a scavenger hunt it was, for the doctor was only a bit more gifted at organization than he was at cooking. It took nearly ten minutes, for example, to find his revolver (it was the first item on the list), which was not in its usual place, the top left-hand drawer of his desk, but on the bookcase behind it. I stuck to it, however, working my way methodically down the list.

Bowie knife. Torches. Specimen bags.

Gunpowder. Matches. Stakes.

Kerosene. Rope. Medical bag. Shovel.

Try as I might to follow the doctor's advice—to focus solely upon the task at hand—the meaning of the list, its import, I found impossible to ignore: We were preparing for an expedition.

And all the while, as I scurried up and down stairs, in and out of rooms, digging through closets and cupboards, cabinets and drawers, the doctor's voice floated from below, shrill and ethereal, "Will Henry? Will Henry, what is taking you so long? Snap to, Will Henry. Snap to!"

At the stroke of midnight I stood by the back door, using a bit of twine to tie a bundle of wooden stakes, to the accompaniment of the doctor's perpetual harangue, "It is not as though I place unreasonable demands upon you, Will Henry. Have I ever placed unreasonable demands upon you?" A sharp rapping upon the door interrupted our tasks, my tying, his upbraiding. "Doctor!" I called softly at the precise moment he appeared at the top of the stairs. "Someone is at the door!"

"Then answer it, Will Henry," he said impatiently. He stripped off his bloody smock and tossed it onto a chair.

Erasmus Gray, the old grave-robber who had called at almost the same hour the previous night, slouched upon the stoop, wearing the same battered wide-brimmed hat. Behind him I spied the same boney nag and rickety cart, half-devoured by the fog. I had the distinctly unpleasant sensation of a dreamer entering for the second time the same nightmare, and for a moment I was sure, absolutely sure, that another grotesque cargo lay in the back of his old cart.

Upon my opening the door he removed his hat and squinted at my upturned face, his rheumy eyes disappearing behind their casing of withered flesh.

"Tell the doctor I've come," he said in a low voice.

There was no need for an announcement. The doctor stepped up behind me, flung wide the door, and pulled Erasmus Gray into the kitchen. And pulling was necessary, for the old man's tread was reluctant; his feet literally dragged across the ground. And who might judge him? Of the three who stood now in that kitchen, only one was looking forward to the hours ahead, and it was not old Erasmus Gray or the doctor's young assistant.

"Load the cart, Will Henry," the doctor directed me, as he, with firm hand upon the old man's elbow, guided—or forced—Erasmus toward the basement steps.

The spring air was cool and moist, the fog a gentle kiss upon my cheeks. When I approached with the first load, the horse dipped its head in acknowledgment, as one beast of burden to its brother. I paused to pat its neck. It studied me with its large soulful eyes, and I thought of the beast hanging upon the hook in the basement, and *its* eyes, blank and dark and filled with nothingness as acute as the space between the stars. Was it merely the emptiness of death that was so unnerving about those eyes—or something more profound? I had seen myself reflected in the dead, soulless eyes of the *Anthropophagus*—how different my reflection seemed in the eyes of this kind and gentle animal before me! Was it merely the difference between the warm look of life and the cold stare of death? Or was my image presented to me as the particular beholder perceived me—to one as companion, to the other as prey?

As I dropped the last bundle of supplies into the cart, the doctor and the grave-robber appeared, bearing the body of the dead girl between them, still wrapped in her makeshift shroud of bed linen. I stepped quickly out of their way and eased toward the warm and comforting light streaming through the open door. A pale hand protruded from the white draping, the index finger extended, as if she were pointing at the ground.

"Lock the door, Will Henry," the doctor called softly to me, though his order was hardly necessary. I was halfway to the door, the key already in hand.

There was no room for me in the little seat in the front of the old cart, so I clambered into the back with the body. The old man's head whipped around, and he frowned at the sight of me huddled next to the shrouded girl. He cast a baleful eye upon the doctor.

"The boy is coming with us?"

Dr. Warthrop nodded impatiently. "Of course he is."

"Begging your pardon, doctor, but this is no business for a child."

"Will Henry is my assistant," the doctor replied with a smile. He gave my head a paternal pat. "A child by outward appearance, perhaps, but mature beyond his years and hardier than he might seem to the unfamiliar eye. His services are indispensable to me."

His tone made clear he would brook no argument from the likes of Erasmus Gray. The old man had returned his gaze to my huddled form as I crouched, shivering, hugging my knees to my chest in the spring chill, and I thought I saw pity in his eyes, a profound empathy for my plight, and not just the immediate plight of being forced to accompany my guardian on this dark errand. Perhaps he intuited the full cost of being "indispensable" to Dr. Pellinore Warthrop.

And as for me, I was remembering my naïve and desperate plea to my father nary a year previously, who, ironically, now shared the same neighborhood as the dead girl lying beside me: *I want to go with you. Please, please take me with you!*

The old man turned away, but with a disapproving cluck and a shake of his ancient pate. He flicked the reins, the cart jerked forward, and our dark pilgrimage commenced.

Now, reader, many a year has passed since the grisly events of that terrible spring night in 1888.

Yet in all those years hardly a day has gone by without my thinking of it with wonder and ever-blossoming dread, the awful dread of a child when the first seeds of disillusionment are planted. We may delay it. We may strive with all our might to put off the bitter harvest, but threshing day always dawns.

The question haunts me still, and will, I suppose, until I join my parents in our final reunion. If the doctor had known what horrors awaited us not only at the cemetery that night, but in the days to come, would he still have insisted upon my company? Would he still have demanded that a mere child dive so deep into the well of human suffering and sacrifice— a literal sea of blood? And if the answer to that question is yes, then there are more terrifying monstrosities in the world than *Anthropophagi*. Monstrosities who, with a smile and a comforting pat on the head, are willing to sacrifice a child upon the altar of their own overweening ambition and pride.

THREE

'It Seems I Must Reconsider My Original Hypothesis'

Old Hill Cemetery lay upon a rise of ground on the outskirts of New Jerusalem, behind black wrought-iron gates and a stone wall designed to discourage the very act that had brought Erasmus Gray to our door the previous night. Laid to rest there were settlers from the earliest days of the colony who had received death's dark embrace in the opening decades of the eighteenth century. My own parents had been buried there, as well as the doctor's clan; in fact, the Warthrop mausoleum was the largest and most impressive edifice on the grounds. It sat at the highest point, at the very top of the hill, visible from every marker and tombstone in the cemetery, a brooding Gothic castle-in-miniature that seemed to lord over the lesser sites like the abode of a medieval prince. And, in a sense, the Warthrops *were* the princes of New Jerusalem. The doctor's great-great-grandfather, Thomas Warthrop, had made a fortune in shipping and textiles and was one of the city's founding fathers. His son, the doctor's great-grandfather, served six terms as mayor. I have no doubt that if not for the labors and hardheaded, tightfisted New England pragmatism of his forebears, Dr. Warthrop would not have had the luxury of abandoning all mundane pursuits to become a "philosopher of monstrumology." He simply could not have afforded it otherwise. His peculiar "calling" was an open secret in town, much whispered about, much maligned by one quarter and feared by the rest. But they left him alone, with few exceptions—owing, I believe, more to the respect afforded by the great, nearly inexhaustible wealth accumulated by his ancestors than to any esteem for his philosophical pursuits. This attitude was perfectly reflected by the cold stone monument that dominated Old Hill Cemetery.

Erasmus Gray drew rein at the iron gates, and we sat for a moment while the old nag struggled to regain its breath after the long, winding climb to the entrance.

"My revolver, Will Henry," the doctor said sotto voce.

The old man watched me pass it to him, and then, with a swipe of his tongue across his lips, he looked quickly away.

"You brought a weapon, I trust," the doctor said to him.

"My Winchester," rejoined Erasmus Gray. "Never shot anything bigger than a grouse with it," he added wistfully.

"Aim for the stomach," the doctor said calmly. "Just below the mouth."

"I'll do that, doctor," Erasmus answered dryly, "if I can

aim true while running in the opposite direction!"

Again, he cast a backward glance at my huddled form.

"What of the boy?"

"I shall manage Will Henry."

"He should stay here at the gates," the old man said. "We'll need a lookout."

"I cannot think of any place worse for him to be."

"He can have my rifle."

"He stays with me," the doctor said firmly. "Will Henry, open the gate."

I hopped from the cart. Before me were the gates, and beyond those was the hill with its row upon row of markers marching upward to the summit, which was hidden behind the boughs of mature oak and ash and poplar. Behind me, completely gripped by the fog, lay New Jerusalem, its inhabitants slumbering in sweet oblivion. Little did they know and less could they suspect that upon that elevated lay of land, that island of the dead rising from the sea of gentle spring mist embracing the living, dwelled a waking nightmare against which all sleep-born nightmares paled in comparison.

Erasmus Gray kept the cart upon the little lane that hugged the wall encircling the grounds. To our right was the wall, to our left, the dead, and above us, the moonless heavens, awash with stars. The night air was still, not a breath of breeze, and quiet beneath the measured *clop-clop* of the horse's hooves, the creak and groan of the wheels, and the low thrum of crickets. The lane was uneven, causing the cart to rock from side to side as we traversed; the corpse beside me swayed back and forth in what struck me as an obscene parody of a babe in its cradle. The grave-robber stared straight ahead, holding the reins loosely in his lap; the doctor was leaning forward, peering anxiously into the trees. At places they crowded the lane, their massive limbs arching over us, and at those places the doctor would throw back his head and stare upward into the foliage.

"Sharp eyes now, Will Henry," he whispered over his shoulder. "They are accomplished climbers. If one should drop, go for her eyes, where she is most vulnerable."

I pulled a wooden stake from the bundle and followed his gaze upward. In the darkness that dwelled between the tangled limbs over my head, my imagination painted humanoid silhouettes with dripping fangs, and enormous arms clinging to the hoary boughs, black eyes gleaming with malevolent intent.

We were nearing the eastern boundary of the cemetery— squinting against the gloom I could make out the intersecting wall looming before us—when Erasmus turned the cart onto a tiny rutted path that twisted through the trees, leading into the heart of the graveyard. Our passing disturbed some woodland creature, perhaps a squirrel or a bird, and as it scrambled and scratched in the underbrush, the doctor swung the revolver around, but there was nothing at which to take aim, only shadows.

"The enemy!" I heard him whisper.

We emerged from the trees into a clearing dotted with tombstones, their silky marble gleaming in the starlight. After a half dozen yards Erasmus brought us to a halt. I rose from my crouch and peered at the closest marker, a large stone emblazoned with the name of the family who owned the plot: BUNTON.

"There it is," the old man said, pointing a gnarled finger at the headstone nearest the path. "That one, Doctor."

Dr. Warthrop hopped from the cart and strode to the grave site. He made a full circle around the plot, scanning the ground, muttering unintelligibly to himself while Erasmus Gray and I remained rooted to our spots, watching him.

My eye was drawn to the stone about which he paced, and the name etched upon it. ELIZA BUNTON. BORN MAY 7, 1872. DIED APRIL 3, 1888. A month shy of her sixteenth birthday when consumed by the indifferent indignity of death's cold embrace, in the first gentle flush of her budding womanhood, only to be pulled into a far less indifferent embrace for a consummation more foul than even the ultimate effrontery of death. In the space of a fortnight, Eliza Bunton had transformed from death's virgin bride to the incubator for a monster's progeny. I turned my gaze from the cold stone to the cold form beneath the white sheet, and my heart ached, for suddenly she was no longer a nameless corpse, an anonymous victim. She had a name—Eliza— and a family who must have loved her, for they had dressed her in the finest raiment and buried her in a necklace of the purest pearls, even arranging her luxurious curls with the utmost care, when all the while her destiny was not to lie in unbroken rest among her brethren, but to be *eaten*.

Erasmus Gray must have sensed my distress, for he laid a hand upon my shoulder and said, "There, there, child. There, there." His tone changed abruptly, from sympathy to indignation. "He shouldn't have brought you. A dark and dirty business is this; no place for any God-fearing Christian, much less a child."

I shrugged his hand from my shoulder. I desired no sympathy from a man of his ignominious profession.

"I'm not a child," I said.

"Not a child, eh? Then these old eyes make a liar of Erasmus Gray! Let me have a closer look . . ."

He lifted my tattered little hat and squinted down at my face, a smile playing on his lips, and, despite myself, so comical was his expression of earnest study, I caught myself smiling back.

"Ack! You're right, not a child—a fine young man, then! D'ye know what I think it is that fooled me, William Henry? It's this hat! It's much too small for a strapping young man such as yourself. A fully grown man should have a man's full-grown hat!"

With one hand he held my little hat, and with the other he dropped his large floppy hat onto my head. It fell over my eyes and nose, much to his delight; his chuckles grew louder, and the cart quivered with the aftershocks of his mirth. I pushed back the hat and saw him looming above me, his spectral frame silhouetted against the velvet sky, my own tiny hat now perched upon his balding head. I found myself giggling right along with him.

"What do ye think, Will Henry? Is it true the clothes make the man? For now I do feel fifty years younger—by Jehoshaphat I do!"

The doctor's impatient call interrupted our revelry.

"Will Henry, fetch the torch and bring the stakes! Snap to, Will Henry!"

"Back to business, Mr. Henry," the old man said with a touch of sadness in his voice. He switched our hats, giving mine a sharp tug once it was on my head, then gently lifting my chin to look me in the eye.

"You watch my back and I'll watch yours, Will Henry. Right, then? Do we have a bargain?"

He offered his hand, which I grasped and pumped quickly before hopping to the ground. The doctor had called, and of course I would go. I reached into the cart and pulled a torch and the bundle of stakes from the stack of supplies. When I joined him at the foot of Eliza Bunton's grave, Warthrop was on his hands and knees, his nose two inches from the freshly turned earth, sniffing like a bloodhound after an elusive quarry. A bit out of breath, I stood before him, unacknowledged, torch in one hand, stakes in the other, awaiting further instruction, while he drew breath to the bottom of his lungs, eyes closed, forehead knotted in concentration.

"I am a fool, Will Henry," he said at last, without lifting his head or opening his eyes. "For a fool takes for granted what a wise man leaves for fools."

He cocked his head toward me without rising an inch, and his eye popped open.

"A *lighted* torch, Will Henry."

Abashed, I turned on my heel, only to turn again upon his barking, "Leave the stakes, light the torch, and bring it back to me. *Snap to, William Henry!*"

Old Erasmus Gray had disembarked and was leaning against the side of the cart upon my breathless return, his Winchester rifle cradled in his arms. Expressionlessly he watched as I fumbled through the supply sack for the box of matches. He drew a pipe and pouch from his pocket and commenced to packing his bowl with tobacco as I with rising panic clawed through the contents of the sack, my memory of picking up the box from the fireplace mantel painfully distinct. *But did I drop the box into the bag, or did I leave it by the back door?*

"What is it you're after, boy?" inquired Erasmus, fishing a match from his pocket and striking it upon the sole of his old boot. I glanced up at him and shook my head, tears welling in my eyes. Of all things to leave behind—the matches! The old man touched the flame to his bowl, and the sweet aroma of his leaf suffused the air.

"Will Henry!" the doctor called.

No more than two seconds passed before I *saw* what I was seeing, and immediately I begged a match from the old man. With shaking hand I lit the torch and trotted back to the doctor, his lecture on panic and fear brought fully home to me: Losing my wits had blinded me to the obvious.

He took the torch from my shaking hand, saying, "Who is our enemy, Will Henry?"

He did not wait for an answer, but turned upon his heel abruptly and repeated his circuit around the grave site.

"The stakes, Will Henry!" he called. "And stay close!"

With the bundle of stakes in hand, I followed him. As he walked, the doctor held low the torch to cast the light upon the ground. He would stop, call for a stake, reaching behind him with outstretched hand, into which I would press a piece of wood. He stabbed it into the earth and then continued, until five were thus planted, one on either side of the headstone and three more in places all roughly two feet from the freshly-turned earth of the grave. I could not tell why he was marking these spots; the ground left unmarked looked identical to that which received a stake. After two more circuits, each several paces farther from the grave, he stopped, holding the torch high and surveying his handiwork.

"Most curious," he muttered. "Will Henry, go and press the stakes."

"Press the stakes, sir?"

"Try to push them deeper into the ground."

I could push none more than half an inch farther into

the rocky soil. When I rejoined him, he was shaking his head in consternation.

"Mr. Gray!" he called.

The old man shuffled over, rifle resting in the crook of his arm. The doctor turned to him, holding the torch high. The light danced upon the codger's weathered features, casting deep shadows into the crevices cutting his cheeks and brow.

"How did you find the grave?" the doctor asked.

"Oh, I knew where the Bunton plot was, all right, Doctor," replied the grave-robber.

"No. I mean, was it disturbed at all? Did you note any evidence of digging?"

Erasmus shook his head. "Wouldn't have bothered with it in that case, Doctor."

"And why is that?"

"I would take it to mean somebody had beaten me to the prize."

Something had beaten him to the "prize," of course, which was the whole point of the doctor's inquiry.

"So you noted nothing out of the ordinary last night?"

"Only when I opened up the casket," the old man said dryly.

"No holes or mounds of dirt nearby?"

Erasmus shook his head. "No, sir. Nothing like that."

"No unusual odors?"

"Odors?"

"Did you smell anything odd, similar to rotten fruit?"

"Only when I popped open the casket. But the smell of death is not so odd to me, Doctor Warthrop."

"Did you hear anything out of the ordinary? A snorting or hissing sound?"

"Hissing?"

The doctor forced air through his closed teeth. "Like that."

Erasmus shook his head again. "It was a normal operation in every way, Doctor, until I opened the casket." He shuddered at the memory.

"And you noted nothing unusual until that point?"

The grave-robber replied that he had not. The doctor turned away to contemplate the grave, the family plot, the grounds beyond, and the line of trees to his right that bordered the lane beside the stone wall, hidden now behind the dense brush.

"Most curious," he muttered a second time.

He shook himself from his reverie, his tone abruptly changing from contemplative to crisp. "The mystery deepens, but doesn't bear upon our errand tonight. Dig it up, Mr. Gray. And you dig with him, Will Henry. We'll return at daybreak and pray our fortunes rise with the sun. Perhaps the light of day will illuminate what evidence the night's shadow conceals! Snap to, Will Henry, and make short work of it."

He abandoned us then, hurrying toward the trees, torch held low, stooping over as he went, swinging the fire left and right and all the while muttering to himself.

"I wouldn't go into those trees if I was him," Erasmus Gray said dourly. "But I'm not the monster hunter, am I?" He clapped a calloused hand upon my shoulder. "Let's snap to it, as your master says, William Henry! Many hands make light work!"

Twenty minutes later, my lower back and shoulders aching and the tender flesh of my palms burning, at only three feet closer to our goal, I thought I could take issue with his proverb, for four hands did not seem that many in this circumstance, and the work proved anything but light. The soil of New Jerusalem, like most of New England, is rocky and unyielding, and despite having been turned the night before by Erasmus Gray in his quest for macabre riches, the soil of Eliza Bunton's grave gave itself up stubbornly to our spades. As I labored, I thought of the enormous male *Anthropophagus*, who, with no tool but his steel-hard claws, had somehow managed to tunnel his way through the hard ground to reach his prey. Like the doctor, I found it most curious that we found no evidence of his invasion and that Erasmus claimed to have found none the night before. Could the old man have missed it in the dark? Had he simply failed to notice it in his lust for booty, and obliterated the evidence in his haste to retreat with his monstrous find?

We could hear Dr. Warthrop in the trees fifty yards away, stomping through the underbrush and the detritus of fallen leaves from the previous autumn, the sound punctuated now and then by soft, incoherent cries of consternation, the first of which caused Erasmus Gray to raise his head in alarm, thinking, no doubt, that the doctor had found—or had been found by—a living specimen of the species hanging in our basement. But they were not cries of panic or fear, I assured the old man; they were the ejaculations of a miner, his pan coming up empty yet again.

Presently the doctor returned and flopped down next to our deepening hole in utter dejection, stabbing the end of the torch into the mound of dirt beside it. He drew his knees to his chest and wrapped his long arms around them, staring glumly at our upraised sweat-streaked faces with the expression of a man who has suffered some irreplaceable loss.

"Well? Did ye find anything, Doctor?" asked Erasmus Gray.

"Nothing!" snapped the doctor.

Erasmus Gray was obviously relieved, and the doctor, just as obviously, was not.

"It defies all logic," the doctor said to no one in particular. "It flies in the face of reason. They are not phantoms or shape-shifters. They cannot float above the ground like pixies or astral project themselves from one spot to another. He must have found her by use of his acute sense of smell, and that is employed by crawling over the terrain, yet there is no evidence of his passing anywhere." A stake lay within his grasp. He reached over and tugged it from the earth, turning it over and over with his dexterous, delicate fingers. "He would have left a breathing hole, yet there is no breathing hole. He would have left a trail, yet there is not so much as one bent blade of grass."

His eyes fell upon our upturned faces. He stared down at us; we stared up at him; and no one spoke for a moment.

"Well, what in God's name are you doing? Dig. Dig!"

He rose and, in his frustration, hurled the stake toward the line of trees, where the deep shadows swallowed it with a muted rattling hiccup of broken branch and fallen leaves.

From the small rutted path behind us came a huffing and a snorting, and all heads swiveled to follow the sound. The old horse, with flaring nostril and rolling eye, stamped its forelegs and gave a low-pitched whinny.

"What is it, ol' Bess?" Erasmus Gray called softly. "What's the matter, girl?"

The beast dropped its head, stretched forth its thin neck, and pawed at the hard ground. The ancient cart creaked and the rickety wheels rasped. I glanced up at the doctor, who was staring at the horse, arms hanging loosely at his sides, his entire being focused on the animal's distress.

"Something's spooked her," said Erasmus Gray.

"Quiet!" breathed the doctor. He slowly pivoted on his heel, scanning the grounds and the path that snaked through the headstones, glimmering sentinels in the starlight, until he stopped, his back to us, peering against the darkness toward the trees. For a long, awful moment there was no sound at all, save for ol' Bess's soft protests and the stamping of her hooves upon the path. The doctor raised his left hand, fingers curling and uncurling, his shoulders drawn back with tension, and a terrible sense of foreboding overcame me. A few more seconds dragged by, during which the animal's agitation grew, corresponding with my own.

And then, on the heels of that ghastly silence, from the trees came the hissing.

Low-pitched. Rhythmical. Faint. Not from one particular spot, but from many. Were they echoes—or replies? Not continuous, but sporadic: *hiss . . . pause . . . hiss . . . pause . . . hissssss . . .*

The doctor turned his head, looking over his shoulder at me. "Will Henry," he whispered. "Did you remember to fill the flash pots with gunpowder?"

"Yes, sir," I whispered back.

"Fetch them at once. Quietly, Will Henry," he calmly cautioned as I heaved myself out of the hole. He dropped his hand into the pocket of his coat where he had dropped the revolver.

"I left my rifle in the cart," Erasmus said. "I'll get the pots. The boy should—"

"No! Stay where you are! Go, Will Henry. Bring as many as you can carry."

"And my rifle if you can manage it, Will!" quavered Erasmus. I heard him whispering urgently to the doctor, "We shouldn't stay, any of us! We'll come back when it's light to return her.'"Tis madness in the devil's own dark to—"

The doctor curtly cut short his plea. I could not make out the words, but I was certain of the gist of his reply. In light of subsequent events, his stubborn refusal to obey the command of our most basic of instincts, which he characterized as "the enemy," exacted a terrible price. There are times when fear is *not* our enemy. There are times when fear is our truest, sometimes *only*, friend.

I dumped the contents of the sack into the bed of the cart and then packed the pots—four tin cylinders roughly the size of coffee cans filled with gunpowder—back into the sack. Bess turned her head in my direction and gave a loud whinny, a pitiful cry of entreaty, the equine equivalent of her master's plea, *We shouldn't stay, any of us!* Urgent though my errand was, I paused to give her slick neck a quick consoling pat. Then back to the grave site, burlap sack in one hand, Erasmus's rifle in the other. How long did seem that return journey to the half-dug hole! Yet upon my arrival it was as if no time had passed. Erasmus still crouched within the hole; the doctor still stood his ground beside it, the torch flickering in its makeshift stand a foot to his left, its light painting his long, lanky shadow across the field. Erasmus grabbed the barrel of the rifle, pulling it from my hand and lowering himself like a soldier in a trench so only the top of his head protruded over the hole's lip.

The hissing had stopped. Now there was silence broken only by the old horse's snorts of fear. If she bolted, what would be our recourse? If they attacked, if we had fewer bullets than beasts, how could we outrun a monster that could leap forty feet in a single bound?

The minutes ticked by. The night was quiet. At last Erasmus called softly from his refuge, "They've gone, thank God. And so should we, Doctor. We'll come back in daylight. I'd rather risk discovery by men than—"

"Quiet, you old fool!" whispered the doctor. "A pot, Will Henry."

I drew a cylinder from the sack and pressed it into his left hand. (His right held the gun.) He touched the fuse to the fire of the torch and with one graceful motion hurled the pot into the trees. It exploded with a white-hot blinding burst of light, like the flash of a photographer's camera. Behind us Bess jerked against her harness, and below us Erasmus Gray gave a startled cry. I saw nothing in the explosive's light. It passed in an instant, leaving the afterimage of the trees impressed upon my eyes, but nothing else, no seven-foot-tall hulking forms with rows of glittering teeth in their chests.

"Most curious," the doctor said. "Hand me another, Will Henry."

"They've moved off, I tell ye." Erasmus Gray's fear had, as fear often does, metastasized into anger. "If they was even here to begin with. Ye hear strange things in the graveyard at night. Take it from me; I've come here often enough! Now, you can stay if ye wish, Dr. Pellinore Warthrop, but me and my horse're leaving. I told ye we shouldn't've come tonight, and I told ye we shouldn't've brought this child. Now I'm leaving, and if you want a ride back to town, you'll come with me."

He laid his rifle at our feet and started to scramble out of the hole.

But Erasmus Gray never got out of that hole.

A massive claw, easily twice the size of a human hand, with a two-inch gray razor-sharp barb on the end of each corpse white digit, burst through the dirt between his feet, followed by the bald muscular arm, flecked with black soil and white stone. And then, like some nightmarish leviathan rising from the deep, the broad shoulders broke the undulating earth, those terrible unblinking black eyes glittering in the glancing glow of the torch, the yawning maw stuffed with three-inch fangs in the middle of the creature's triangular torso snapping as a shark's when excited by the scent of blood in the water. The claw wrapped around the old man's upper thigh; the barbs sunk into his leg. Erasmus flung out his arm in our direction, mouth agape in a high-pitched scream of horror and pain, and to this day that haunts me, the old man's wide-open orifice revealing its pitiful contingent of teeth, an absurd impersonation of the monstrous mouth between his kicking legs.

Instinctively, stupidly, and, no doubt, to the doctor's disapproval and dismay, I caught the old man's flailing wrist. Inside the grave the *Anthropophagus* stuffed Erasmus Gray's captured leg into its snapping mouth, the teeth closed over his jerking calf, the black eyes rolled in their sockets, and I slid two feet forward, until my head and shoulders dipped into the hole and the screams of the old man reverberated like sullen thunder in my ears. The mouth below continued to work, chomping upward as the claw pulled the old man down, his free leg flailing like a drowning man's trying to kick to the surface. I felt the doctor's hands upon my waist, his voice barely audible above the cries of the doomed man.

"Let go, Will Henry! *Let go!*"

But it was not I who held fast with iron grip; it was Erasmus Gray. His fingers were wrapped around my wrist, and he was pulling me into the pit with him. All at once I slid farther in, for Warthrop had released me, and then, out of the corner of my eye, I saw the barrel of the doctor's revolver slam against the old man's forehead.

I whipped my head around, turning my face from the sight as the doctor pulled the trigger, snuffing out the old man's screams of pain and panic in a single explosive instant. Hot speckles of blood and bone and brain splattered in my hair and against the back of my neck.

The fingers around my wrist loosened, and the lifeless arm followed Erasmus Gray's corpse as it collapsed to the bottom of the hole, briefly obliterating the grotesque bloody-mouthed thing beneath him, but I could hear its mouth working, the sickening crunch of teeth pulverizing bone and snapping sinew, the odd grunting like an enormous boar snuffling in the underbrush.

Grabbing the seat of my pants, the doctor yanked me backward and with surprising strength—no doubt the strength born of adrenaline-rich muscles—hoisted me to my feet. He shoved me toward the lane with a single command, a charge that was hardly necessary under the circumstances:

"*RUN!*"

I complied. Unfortunately, so did ol' Bess, who bolted forward with a spring worthy of a mare half her age. As I sprinted toward the cart, it receded from me, pulled by the panicked horse off the lane and onto the rough ground, the frantic animal cutting across the graves and weaving between the tombstones. I dared not look back, but my ears delivered the sounds of the doctor close behind, and harsh, barking calls that seemed to emanate from all directions.

I was swift for my size, as I have said, but the doctor possessed a longer stride, and presently he overtook me. He reached the back of the bouncing cart before I did, threw himself upon it, landed directly atop the body of the girl, and flung his hand toward me.

Was it my imagination, or did I feel something close behind, its hot breath upon my neck, the *thump-thump-thump* of its heavy tread on the hard-packed dirt a mere step or two back? The *humph-humph!* of their calls had grown louder, a frustrated sound infused with rage.

The doctor lay upon his belly beside Eliza's body, his left hand extended toward me. Our fingertips brushed as I strained forward, but the cart was swinging crazily from side to side. Ol' Bess whipped first right, then left, picking her path through the headstones with no goal or finish line in mind, only the blind dictates of her instinct to escape. The doctor screamed something, and though I was but a yard or two from him, I could not make out the words. His right arm swung toward me then, the revolver clutched in his hand and pointed at a spot over my shoulder. He screamed a second time, the gun went off, and the back of my shirt tore away as the monster behind me lunged. My pursuer, it seemed, had not been a figment of my imagination.

The fingers of the doctor's left hand found my wrist. Like Erasmus at the grave he yanked me toward him, though this time toward life, not death, and jerked me into the cart beside him. To my astonishment, he at once abandoned me, shoving the revolver into my shaking hands and hollering into my ear, "I'm going up front!"

And he went, scrambling on all fours toward the seat and the reins that were our sole hope of survival. I had never fired a gun in my life, but I fired it now, until the chamber was spent and the barrel smoked, at the towering forms racing toward us. They came from the trees; they poured out of Eliza's grave, dozens of them, scores, sprinting with arms outstretched and mouths agape, their colorless skin radiant in the starlight, as if every tomb and sepulcher had vomited forth their foul contents.

Clearly we were being outpaced. I watched in helpless horror as the swarm of fiends closed the gap: Ol' Bess's age caught up with her instincts, and her steps began to flag.

Behind me the doctor let forth a string of curses worthy

of a merchant marine, and, with the horrific crunch of shattered wood, the cart came to an abrupt halt, the impact hurling me upon my back, my head saved from cracking open upon the rough boards by the pliant body of Eliza Bunton. I sat up and saw that the old nag had dashed between two huge maple trees; she had managed the passage, but the cart had not. We were wedged tight.

Dr. Warthrop reacted immediately. He jumped over the seat into the cart bed beside me. The *Athropophagi* were a hundred feet away now, and I could *smell* them, an odor unlike any I had ever encountered, a noxious smell I can only liken to that of rotten fruit.

"Out of the way, Will Henry!" the doctor shouted. I scooted backward on my backside toward the front of the cart. He shoved his arms beneath the shoulders of the young girl's corpse and, with a roar as primordial as the things bearing down on us, heaved her off the cart. The dead weight hit the ground with a sickening thud.

"The harness!" he cried. "Undo the harness, Will Henry!"

I grasped his goal, bounded over the seat, and dropped to the ground beside the straining horse. The poor animal was mad with fear, eyes rolling, nostrils flaring, foamy spittle dripping from her mouth. A shape dropped from above on her other side, and I gave an involuntary cry, but it was the doctor, who set about undoing the clasps on the opposite flank.

"Will Henry!" he called.

"Done!" I called back.

He swung himself onto the horse, slid his hand into the pit of my outstretched arm, and hauled me onto her back behind him. Bess needed no goading from us: She leaped forward, guided now by the doctor's sure hand toward the peripheral lane that would bring us to the cemetery's gates and the road beyond. I turned once, just once, and then turned away, pressing my cheek into the doctor's back, closing my eyes as I clung to his waist, willing myself to ignore what I had seen in that last backward glance.

The doctor's desperate gambit had paid off: The pack had abandoned its pursuit and attacked the corpse, tearing it apart in ravenous frenzy, flinging shredded bits of white linen into the air, ripping from her torso her arms, her legs, her head, stuffing chunks of flesh into their snapping maws. The last thing I saw before hiding my face in the doctor's coat was her luxurious dark curls cascading from one of their jaws.

To the main gates . . . and through them. Onto Old Hill Cemetery Road . . . and then toward New Jerusalem. Bess slowed from gallop to trot to exhausted hoof-dragging stride, with bowed head and slick, sweat-dark withers. We relaxed with her, in a quiet made thunderous after our mad flight, and the only thing I can recall the doctor saying on the long ride home that night was this:

"Well, Will Henry. It seems I must reconsider my original hypothesis."

FOUR

"The Hour Grows Late"

Upon our return to the house on Harrington Lane, the doctor sent me upstairs to wash up and change out of my filthy clothes; I was covered from the soles of my feet to the top of my head with dirt and offal, the right side of my face tattooed with the dried blood, skull fragments, and gray bits of brain that had animated Erasmus Gray for more than sixty years. Pebbles and twigs dropped from my tangled hair into the basin and clogged the drain, which rapidly filled with water stained a delicate pink from his blood. Grimacing, I plunged a hand into the fouled water to clear the clog, morbid curiosity drawing my youthful eye to the gray globs of gore floating upon the surface. It was not horror that seized my imagination so much as wonder: sixty years of dreams and desires, hunger and hope, love and longing, blasted away in a single explosive instant, mind and brain.

The mind of Erasmus Gray was gone; the remnants of its vessel floated, as light and insubstantial as popcorn, in the water. Which fluffy bit held your ambition, Erasmus Gray? Which speck your pride? Ah, how absurd the primping and preening of our race! Is it not the ultimate arrogance to believe we are more than is contained in our biology? What counterarguments may be put forth, what valid objections raised, to the claim of Ecclesiastes, "Vanity of vanities; all is vanity"?

"Will Henry!" came the doctor's voice from below. "Will Henry, where the devil are you? Snap to, Will Henry!"

I found him in the library, halfway up the ladder affixed to the floor-to-ceiling shelves, still clad in his traveling cloak and mud-caked shoes; apparently he could not afford the time to change and wash. Without a word he pointed to the shelves on his right, and I rolled the ladder to the spot. Behind us, upon the large table that dominated the room, four stacks of books sat upon the corners of a large map of New Jerusalem and its environs.

"Now, where is it?" he muttered, running his thin finger along the cracked spines in a row of ancient tomes. "Where? Ah, here it is! Catch, Will Henry!" He pulled a large volume from the shelf and let it fall ten feet, where it landed with a heavy thud upon the carpet beside me. I looked up at him as he glared down at me, one side of his face smeared with dirt, his hair falling over his forehead, as matted and filthy as a cur's.

"I told you to catch it," he said in a low, level voice.

"Sorry, sir," I mumbled, scooping the book from the floor

and carrying it to the table. I glanced at the title: *The Histories of Herodotus*. I flipped through the thin pages. The text was in the original Greek. I looked from the book to the monstrumologist.

The doctor scampered down the ladder. "Why are you staring at me like that?"

"Mr. Gray—," I began, but the doctor cut me off.

"We are slaves, all of us, Will Henry," he said, pulling the book from my hand and placing it upon the nearest stack. "Some are slaves to fear. Others are slaves to reason—or base desire. It is our lot to be slaves, Will Henry, and the question must be to what shall we owe our indenture? Will it be to truth or to falsehood, hope or despair, light or darkness? I choose to serve the light, even though that bondage often lies in darkness. Despair did not drive me to pull that trigger, Will Henry; mercy guided my hand."

I said nothing, but swallowed hard, eyes welling with tears. He made no move to comfort me, and I doubt comforting me was his purpose. He cared not whether I forgave him for taking the life of the old man. He was a scientist. Forgiveness mattered not; understanding was all.

"He was doomed the moment the creature struck," he went on. "No more absurd or insidious a precept has ever been laid down than 'Where there is life, there is hope.' Just as the trout is doomed once the bait is taken, there was no hope for him once the barbs were set. He would thank me if he could. As I would thank you, Will Henry."

"'Thank me, sir?"

"If one day I should meet the same fate, I pray you would do the same for me."

Left unspoken but conveyed in his dark eyes was the corollary to his blasphemous prayer: *As you should pray I would for you.* If, in that hole, the monster had seized me instead, no doubt he would not have hesitated to grant me the mercy of the bullet. I did not argue with him, though; I did not have the words to argue. I, at twelve, had only the inarticulate protests of a child whose acute sense of justice has been offended by the pious rationalizations of an authoritarian adult. I did not—only because I could not—argue. So, I nodded. Nodded! Even as my face burned with righteous indignation. Perhaps I was a slave to something he believed to be silly and superstitious: the idea that all life was worth defending and that nothing justified surrender to the forces of destruction. Had I known that night what was to come from deep in the dark belly of the earth, I might have felt less like pummeling his smug countenance with my little fists and more like throwing myself into his arms for the comfort that only one who has trod the dark path can give.

"But enough philosophy! On to more practical and pressing concerns, Will Henry!" he cried, brushing my body aside as casually as he had my troubled soul. He went round to the other side of the long table and peered at the map; already he had drawn a red circle around New Jerusalem. "Obviously the events of this evening prove my original hypothesis incorrect. This is a mature pod of *Anthropophagi*, whose alpha male now hangs in our basement. Twenty to twenty-five breeding females and a handful of juveniles. Perhaps thirty in all, though the circumstances made it difficult to ascertain their exact number."

He looked up from the map. "Did you manage to get a count, Will Henry?" he asked, in all seriousness, as if it were plausible I might have counted them while simultaneously running for my life.

"No, sir," I said.

"But does that seem close to the mark?" he asked. "Twenty-five to thirty? Based upon your observation."

One hundred thirty was closer to the mark based on my observation, but that skill had been tarnished by terror. The cemetery had seemed to overflow with them, pouring from every shadow and from behind every tree.

"Yes, sir," I replied. "I would say twenty-five. Twenty-five to thirty."

"Nonsense!" he cried, slapping his open hand upon the tabletop. The resulting retort caused me to flinch. "Never tell me what you think I wish to hear, Will Henry. Never! I cannot rely upon you if you chose to be a parrot. It is a detestable vice not entirely limited to children. *Always* speak the truth, all the truth in all things at all times! No man ever rose to greatness on the wings of obsequious deceit. Now be honest. You've really no idea whether there were thirty or fifty or two hundred and fifty."

I bowed my head. "Yes, sir," I said. "I could not tell."

"Nor could I," he admitted. "I can only make an educated guess, based on the literature." He picked up the Herodotus from the stack and flipped rapidly through the ancient pages until he came upon a passage and read it quietly to himself in the original Greek. After a moment or two he slapped the book closed, replaced it upon the stack, and returned to the map. He produced a ruler from his pocket, measured the shortest distance between New Jerusalem and the coast, and then proceeded to make calculations in a small notebook, muttering to himself the entire time, while I, so recently the object of his full attention, stood entirely forgotten. His was a concentration more complete and exhausting in its force than that in any other man I have met in my long life. I felt, after the dazzling light of his focus had shifted away, like a person falling into a well, plunging from bright sunlight into utter darkness.

He made several measurements, from the borders of our county to various seaports along the coast, carefully noting each one in his notebook and tracing faint connecting lines along the edge of the ruler. Our town lay but a day's ride from the coast, and soon the parchment was filled with dozens of intersecting lines that reminded me of the intricate design of a spider's web. I was not entirely sure, but thought he had to be trying to discover the route taken by the monsters into New Jerusalem.

It struck me, I confess, as exceedingly odd, after our

narrow escape, that he would be wasting precious time in an interesting but pointless exercise. What did it matter where these things came from or how they had come to be there? Would not our time have been more valuably spent rounding up all the able-bodied men in town for an impromptu hunt? The *Anthropophagi* were loose among us—and clearly hungry. I could not chase from my mind's eye Eliza Bunton's hair spilling from the snapping jaws of the ravenous *Anthropophagi*. Why did we tarry there reading old books, studying maps, and taking measurements while a pack of thirty sojourners from a nightmare roamed the countryside? We should have roused the residents to flee the creatures' onslaught or throw up barricades against the coming siege. The time to unravel the puzzle of their presence in New Jerusalem was *after* their eradication, not then, when our very survival hung in the balance. *Who else,* I wondered, *might perish this night in the same unspeakable manner as Erasmus Gray, while the doctor draws his lines and reads his Greek and jots in his little book? Who else will be sacrificed upon the altar of science?* If such questions occurred to a twelve-year-old boy, surely they occurred to a man of Warthrop's intellect.

I pondered this riddle, remembering his earlier admonitions upon the dangers of fear. Was that it? Was this man, the greatest monstrumologist of his day, overcome by dread, and were these frivolous (to my mind) pursuits at this desperate hour a means of avoiding the stark truth that circumstances had forced upon him? In short, was he, the great Pellinore Warthrop, afraid?

Telling myself it was not for my own selfish comfort, but for my fellow man, I spoke up at last. For those slumbering innocents unaware of the mortal danger in their midst, for the old man asleep in his bed and the tender babe at peace in her crib, I finally spoke.

"Dr. Warthrop, sir?"

He did not pause in his task. "What is it, Will Henry?"

"Should I fetch the constable now?"

"The constable? To what purpose?"

"To—to help," I stammered.

"Help whom? With what?"

"Help us, sir. With the . . . the infestation . . ."

He waved dismissively in my direction, still absorbed in his measurements. "The *Anthropophagi* will not feed again this night, Will Henry," he said. His dark hair fell over his forehead as he leaned over the map, lips pursed in concentration.

I would have dropped the matter had it not been for the folly of his original hypothesis: the predication that there could not have been more than one or two of the man-eaters lurking in the vicinity of New Jerusalem, an error that had cost a man his life, at the time pronounced with the same absolute conviction.

So I pressed him as never before.

"How do you know, sir?" I asked.

"How do I know what?"

"How do you know they won't attack again?"

"Because I can read." A bit of annoyance had crept into his tone. He patted the nearest stack of books. "Two thousand years of observation support my conclusion, Will Henry. Read Herodotus; peruse Pliny, the writings of Walter Raleigh. *Anthropophagi* are gorge eaters, hunting, feasting, and then resting—for days, sometimes weeks—before killing again."

He looked over at me. "What are you suggesting, Will Henry? It is my fault? The blood of the grave-robber is on my hands? Perhaps it is. Was I mistaken about their numbers? Obviously. But it was an estimate based upon all available data, rooted in logic. Given the same facts again, I would take the same gamble, for I deemed time to be of the essence. His discovery forced me into action quicker than I may have liked, and I am certain with more time for careful reflection I would have confronted the possibility that they may have adapted to their new environment in unforeseen ways, which undoubtedly they have. But you must understand, Will Henry, 'possibility' is not 'probability.' It is *possible* the sun will rise in the west on the morrow, but hardly *probable*. I stand by my decision, though I have been proven wrong in the premise that led to it."

And now the monstrumologist laid a hand upon my shoulder, and the force behind his eyes softened somewhat. "I regret his passing. If it brings any comfort to you, remember he was an old man who had lived a long life—a life long in suffering and deprivation, I might add. He fully understood; he fully accepted the danger; and I asked nothing of him that I did not demand of myself. I did not force him to accompany us tonight or ask him to accept any greater risk than I myself was willing to take."

Perhaps he took note of my body quivering beneath his hand, for he followed with this, his gaze becoming flinty again, "And I must say, Will Henry, it is exceedingly curious that you dwell upon the perceived folly and injustice of his end and not upon your own good fortune, the life that would have been forfeit had I not ended his. Do you see? Do you begin to understand why I said he would thank me if he could?"

"No, sir, I don't."

"Then I give you too much credit. I thought you were a clever boy."

I shrugged his hand from my shoulder and cried, "I don't understand! Forgive me, Doctor, but I don't understand at all. We shouldn't have gone there tonight. We should have waited till daylight to bring her back. If we had waited and fetched the constable, he might still be alive!"

"But those are not the facts," he replied calmly. "We did not wait. We did not fetch the constable. You still fail to grasp the essentials here, Will Henry. *James* Henry would have. Your father would have understood—he would not have chided me or judged me. He would have thanked me."

"Thanked you?"

"As you should thank me now, for saving *your* life, Will Henry."

It was more than offensive; it was galling, given what had happened to my father as a result of his unquestioning service to the monstrumologist. He owed his demise, and I the loss of everything I held dear, to this man, and now here this same man stood demanding my gratitude!

"Had I spared him," he went on, "you would not have been spared. I would have lost you, Will Henry, and, as I told the old man, your services are indispensable to me."

What more need I say about this odd and solitary figure, this genius who labored all his life in obscurity in the most obscure of sciences, whom the world would little note nor long remember, but to whom the world owed much, this man who possessed, it seemed, not the slightest shred of humility or warmth, who lacked empathy and compassion and the ability to read men's hearts—or the heart of a twelve-year-old boy whose world had been shattered in an awful instant? To bring up my father in a moment like this! What more may I offer as evidence of my hypothesis that this man's hubris rose to heights—or sunk to depths—rarely seen outside the confines of Greek theater or the tragedies of Shakespeare? He did not equivocate with me. He did not couch his words in comforting bromides or shopworn clichés. He had saved my life because my life was important to *him*. He had saved my life for *his* sake, for the furtherance of his ambition. Thus even his mercy was rooted in his ego.

"Thank me, Will Henry," he said softly, his tone gentle but insistent, the patient teacher to the recalcitrant pupil. "Thank me for saving your life."

I muttered the words, looking down at my feet. Though I spoke barely above a whisper, he seemed satisfied. He patted my shoulder and whirled away, crossing the room quickly with his long stride.

"I shall not forget him!" he called over his shoulder. I thought he was speaking of my father still; he was not. "Though his motives may have been less than pure, his discovery has no doubt saved lives and perhaps brought to light an entirely new species. I shall propose to the Society that it be named in his honor: *Anthropophagi americanis erasmus*."

It seemed to me a trifling recompense, but I held my tongue.

"For if my suspicions are correct, that is precisely what we've uncovered: a generation of *Anthropophagi* that has adapted brilliantly to its new environment, an environment radically different from its native Africa. New England is not the savanna, Will Henry. Ha! Far from it."

As he spoke, he foraged among the shelves for newspapers. The monstrumologist subscribed to dozens of dailies, weeklies, and monthlies, from the *New Jerusalem Gazette* to the *Globe*, from the *Times* of New York and London to the smallest publication from the tiniest hamlet. Every Tuesday a large stack was dropped at our doorstep and carried (by me) into the library, where the papers were sorted (by me) alphabetically and by date of publication. Early on in my apprenticeship it had struck me as odd that for all the papers he subscribed to, I had never seen him read a single masthead. Yet he always seemed thoroughly conversant upon the events of the day, from the portentous to the paltry. He could hold forth for hours, for example, upon the vicissitudes of the stock market or the latest fashion from Paris. He must have, I decided, read them at night after I had retired to my little loft, and for a time I was convinced, based upon this and other evidence, the monstrumologist did not sleep. I had never witnessed it, even during those periods of intense melancholia, which lasted for a fortnight or longer, when he would take to his bed, inconsolable in his malaise.

In the early months of my life at Harrington Lane, sleep had eluded me. I had longed for and dreaded it, for rest I had needed but nightmares I had not, those horrible reincarnations of the night my parents perished. Many dark hours would pass before exhaustion finally overtook me, and occasionally I would creep down the ladder and peek into his room on the second floor, only to find the bed empty. To the stairs I would sneak next, peering down to the main floor, where sometimes the light from the library flooded the hall, or from the kitchen the faint clatter of pots and pans or the clink of silver upon china would rise. Most often, however, the doctor would be in his laboratory, puttering with his vials and specimen jars and drawers full of bones and dried viscera, through the dead hours of the night, until at dawn he would climb the stairs to the kitchen, rising with the sun from that pit of peculiarities and putrefaction to prepare our morning repast (or, as was more common, hastily eat what I had prepared), his smock speckled with blood and bits of tissue and other biological drippings, the nature and origin of which I cared not to speculate about.

There were other times, however, when no nocturnal inquiries were necessary. Always it seemed, well past the witching hour, just as I was finally drifting off into much-needed slumber, hard and fast would come his raps upon the ladder, or, if those failed to rouse me, he would shoot up through the opening and bang his fist against the sloping ceiling, crying in a loud voice, "Up, up, up, Will Henry! Snap to! I need you downstairs at once!" Down the stairs I would drag my weary bones, usually to the place I dreaded the most, the basement, where upon the stool I would prop my fatigued frame while he dictated a letter or the latest paper for the Monstrumologist Society, a task that, to my sleep-deprived brain, could have waited till the morrow.

Sometimes, though, he yanked me from bed for no apparent reason at all. I would sit upon the stool, yawning, while he held forth long after sunrise upon some bit of esoteric knowledge or the latest scientific breakthrough. Though puzzling at the time—and annoying, for he always managed to wake me after a long and bitter struggle with Somnus had been won—it finally occurred to me that the service I was providing was as indispensable to him as any other, perhaps more so than any other, perhaps the most vital service of all: to ease the dreadful burden of his loneliness.

Several circuits he had made between the shelves and the long table, carrying armfuls of newspaper, before I realized he might need my help. But the moment I sprang to action, he rebuked me, ordering me to fetch some stationery and a pen. He continued to scan the papers—particularly the obituary columns—and make notes as he dictated, occasionally setting both newsprint and notebook aside to make a mark upon the map. The dots he deliberately drew began to cluster together, moving generally from west to east, toward the Atlantic coast. The purpose of this plotting was obvious: The doctor was tracing a migration.

The first letter I took down was to the Society, informing it of his discovery and providing a truncated history of the events subsequent to the grave-robber's finding the big male entombed with the remains of Eliza Bunton. He did not mention our mad flight or narrow escape; perhaps he felt it made him appear cowardly, but I suspect it had more to do with protecting his reputation and obscuring the painful truth that he had been completely wrong in his original hypothesis. He appended a postscript informing the Society he would be forwarding his necropsy notes, once transcribed, and the adult specimen, by special post.

He worked methodically as he dictated, jotting in his notebook, dividing the papers into two stacks after perusing them. It was a formidable task, for before him lay nearly three years' worth of reportage. Occasionally he would interrupt himself with a sharp cry or an ejaculation too guttural for me to interpret. Other times he would laugh humorlessly, shaking his head ruefully as he scribbled furiously upon his pad.

"Now another, to Dr. John Kearns, in care of the Smithsonian Institution, Washington, D.C.," instructed the doctor. "Dear Jack," he began, and then stopped, his brow knotted as he chewed on his bottom lip. "Should be Stanley, obviously," he murmured to himself. "Stanley is the real expert, but Stanley is in Buganda. . . . Even if he left immediately, the matter might be over by the time the ship reached Bermuda. . . . But who else, if not Kearns?" He continued his recitation with a hint of distaste. I had never heard of this John Kearns; I assumed he was a fellow monstrumologist or a practitioner in some related field of natural history. I was wrong on both counts. John Kearns was no monstrumologist and no student—at least not of natural history. He was much more and—as I would discover to my sorrow—much less.

Shorter than the missive to his fellow monstrumologists, the letter to Dr. John Kearns read:

Dear Jack,

A potentially new species of Anthropophagi has taken up residence in the vicinity of New Jerusalem. A pod of twenty-five to thirty mature specimens larger and significantly more aggressive than their African cousins. Your inestimable services are required. Can you come at once? Expedition fully financed and all expenses paid.

Hoping this finds you well, etc., etc.

Your Humble Servant,

Pellinore Warthrop

Upon the completion of this letter, the doctor fell silent for several minutes. He leaned upon the tabletop, shoulders rising to nearly the level of his ears as he hunched forward, staring at the map and the cluster of points he had plotted that zigzagged snakelike in its inexorable march toward the sea. Then with a heavy sigh he straightened, pressing his hands into the small of his back, and nervously combed his dark hair with his long, pale fingers. He picked up the notebook and studied his computations, rhythmically tapping the end of his pencil upon the page, as he chewed upon his lower lip, my presence a few feet away again forgotten. I was not unused to this odd isolation in his company, but had yet to become accustomed to the effect it had upon me: There is no loneliness more profound, in my experience, than being ignored by one's sole companion in life. Whole days would pass with nary a word from him, even as we supped together or worked side by side in the laboratory or took our evening constitutional along Harrington Lane. When he did speak to me, it was rarely to engage me in conversation; rather, our roles were rigidly defined. His was to speak; mine was to pay attention. He held forth; I listened. He: the orator; I: the audience. I had learned quickly to not speak unless spoken to; to obey any command instantly and without question, no matter how mystifying or seemingly absurd; to stand ready, as it were, as a good soldier dedicating his sacred honor to a worthy cause, though it was the rare instance when I understood precisely what that cause might be.

The stars were fading from the sky; the night's stubborn grip began to slip at last; and still the monstrumologist labored over his maps and books and newspapers, taking measurements, scribbling in his little notebook, at times whirling from the worktable in intense agitation, wringing his hands and stroking his brow, muttering under his breath and pacing back and forth. He was buoyed by the peculiar pursuit of his passion and the cups of black tea he copiously consumed, his libation of choice during these manic episodes of intense mental exertion. In all the years I knew him, I never saw hard liquor touch his lips. The doctor frowned upon drinking and often expressed wonderment at men who willingly made imbeciles of themselves.

While in the kitchen preparing the fifth pot of tea as dawn approached, I indulged in a few bites of stale cracker to boost my flagging endurance, for all I had had since waking, you may recall, was one or two hurried swallows of the noxious soup prepared by the monstrumologist from ingredients of ambiguous origin. My back ached, and each muscle sang with fatigue as I moved about in a clumsy fog, the adrenaline that had sustained me since our return from the cemetery long since departed, and I was nearing complete exhaustion. Slow of thought and awkward of limb, with the distinctly disconcerting sensation of being an uninvited guest inside the familiar abode of my own skin, I toted the pot into the library, where I discovered the doctor as I'd left him, the silence complete but for the ticking of the mantel clock and his sighing—long, weary, and frustrated. He rifled through the stack of newspapers until he found a particular periodical that he had previously perused. He studied the article circled there for another minute or two, muttered the same word repeatedly, then dropped the paper on top of the stack to study the corresponding colored circle upon the map: Dedham.

"Dedham. Dedham," muttered the monstrumologist. "Now, why is that name familiar to me?" He leaned over the map until his nose came within an inch of the parchment. He tapped the spot with his index finger and repeated the word three times, as his finger fell upon it three times: "Dedham." *Tap*. "Dedham." *Tap*. "Dedham." *Tap*.

He turned the severity of his countenance fully upon me, startling me from my semi-stupor, for suddenly I existed again. I was dead; I was reborn. I was forgotten, and in the blink of an eye—*his* eye—the world remembered me.

"Dedham!" he cried, waving the paper over his head. It snapped in the stultified air of the dusty library. "Dedham, Will Henry! I knew I had heard it before! Quickly—go down to the basement. Under the stairs you'll find a steamer trunk. Bring it to me at once. At once, Will Henry. Snap to, snap *to*!"

The first "snap to" owed to habit; the second was snapped, if you'll forgive me, with barely contained fury, for I did not snap immediately. I had failed to hear the first, for the word "basement" had momentarily deafened me—not by volume, but by import—but only a deaf man would have failed to hear the second "snap."

Quickly I left the library; more slowly did I enter the kitchen; more slowly still did I push open the door to the stairs that plunged into darkness deep, at the bottom of which hung the monster upon the steel hook and stood the glass jar containing the appalling issuance of his loins, pulled whole and slimy and squirming from the belly of the virgin vessel that had borne it, bastard child in the most nightmarish of senses, a headless mass of claws already stained with human blood, with spindly white arms and a chest dominated by razor-sharp fangs that had bitten and snapped and chewed the empty air in its primal rage.

The morning light, streaming with glorious spring abundance through the open windows, flooded down the narrow stairway, yet it seemed as if the darkness at the bottom pushed back or acted as a seawall whereupon the light crashed and broke impotently against its unyielding edifice. The light flooded down; the smell of the dead *Anthropophagus* roiled up, a sickening stench like rotting fruit enmeshed with the unmistakable odor of biological decay. I turned my face away from the open doorway, drew a deep breath, and held it as I descended the steps, one hand covering my nose and mouth, the other trailing along the cool stone wall. The weathered boards creaked and groaned beneath my trembling tread; the hairs on the back of my neck stood up; and my calves felt numb and tingly as imagination overcame cool intellect. With each step my heart beat faster, for in my mind's eye I saw it beneath the stairs, crouching on all fours upon the sweating stone floor, a headless beast with blank black eyes set deep in its shoulders and a mouth overflowing with row upon row of glistening teeth, the lion in the savanna brush, the shark in the reef shadows, and I the grazing gazelle, the juvenile seal frolicking in the surf. It would rise as I descended. It would reach through the open slats and seize my ankle with its three-inch barbs. Once in its unrelenting grip I was doomed, doomed as Erasmus Gray had been doomed the instant the beast in Eliza Bunton's grave had risen from the burial pit in which Eliza had been impregnated. Would the monstrumologist, upon hearing my screams, come running with his revolver and fulfill the promise made but an hour or two before? Would he, as the thing tore apart the rickety stairs to stuff me whole into its snapping maw, show mercy upon me and put a bullet through my brain?

Halfway down, I could will myself no farther. I was dizzy from holding my breath, my heart was pounding, and I was quaking from my toes to the top of my exposed head. (*Where has my hat gone?* I wondered with a flutter of panic. *Did I lose it at the grave site?*) I froze upon the steps, my absurdly long shadow trailing down toward the wall of darkness. I exhaled slowly, and the air was cool enough for my breath to congeal and spin around my head. I gulped a bit of the fetid air—enough, I hoped, to sustain me for the remainder of the journey. *Quickly now, Will Henry!* I scolded myself. *The doctor is waiting!* To return to him empty-handed was unthinkable.

So, pushing aside fear, that enemy common to all combatants, and reminding myself that I had witnessed the creature's partial dismemberment with my own eyes— thus putting beyond all doubt the fact of its lifelessness— I scampered down the remaining steps. I found the trunk beneath the stairs, shoved against the wall and covered in a fine patina of dust, as if it had not been moved or opened in years. It gave a loud protesting screech against the stone floor when I dragged it from its cozy nook, like a creature woken rudely from a long winter nap. Grasping it by its worn leather handles, I lifted the trunk a few inches from the floor: heavy, but not so heavy I couldn't haul it up the stairs. I set it back down and dragged it to the base of the stairs, keeping my eyes focused forward, though out of the corner of my left I could see a shadow blacker than the surrounding gloom common to old basements. The *Anthropophagus.* As I lifted the trunk for the trek upstairs, the voice of my enemy spoke; fear whispered in my ear, echoing the words of Warthrop: *The fertilized egg is expelled into her mate's mouth, where it rests in a pouch located along his lower jaw. He has two months to find a host for their offspring, before the fetus bursts its protective sac and he swallows it or chokes upon it.*

What if he had missed it in the necropsy? What if *another* monster child had rested undetected within the big male's mouth, had subsequently ripped free of its fleshy cocoon and even now was scuttling across the floor toward me? *They are accomplished climbers*, the doctor had said on the cemetery road. What if, by means of its barbed nails, it now clung to the ceiling above me and, in the space of my next breath, would drop on my head, reach down with its pale, thin arms, and tear my eyes from their sockets? I saw myself spinning around the laboratory, blood streaming down from my vacant ocular cavities, as a creature no larger than a fist crawled down my face and silenced my horrified screams by shredding my exposed tongue with tiny tooth and minuscule claw. It was a ludicrous notion, born of panic, but no panic is ludicrous in its particular moment. Panic possesses its own logical integrity. It goaded me up the stairs, gave me unnatural strength and endurance. Unnoticed went the cramping in my fingers, the burning in my shoulders from the trunk's weight, the hard slap of the box against my knees as I climbed, the sunshine that flooded the higher steps bathing me in its luminescent shower of its beneficent light. I dropped the box upon the kitchen floor and slid it into the room, clambered up the final three steps, hopped over the threshold into the kitchen, and slammed the door closed behind me, gasping for air, head spinning, black spots bobbing like dark, dancing pixies before my eyes, feeling as if I had made a narrow escape—but from what? So often the monsters that crowd our minds are nothing more than the strange and thoroughly alien progeny of our own fearful fantasies.

"Will Henry!" called the doctor. "Have you fallen asleep? Are you sneaking something to eat? Time enough for sleep and supper later. Snap to, Will Henry, snap *to*!"

With a deep breath—how sweet the air did taste there above!—I picked up the trunk and carried it down the hall to the library, in the doorway of which the doctor was impatiently waiting. He snatched the box from my hands and dropped it beside the worktable. It landed with enough force to send a shudder through the floorboards.

"Dedham, Dedham," he murmured, falling to his knees before the old trunk. He threw back the brass clasps and heaved open the lid. The hinges of the ancient vessel answered with a protesting screech. I edged closer, curious to discover what this box, which I, despite spending the majority of the past year in that macabre chamber, had never noticed before tucked away in the shadows beneath the stairs, might contain and how its contents related to the particular puzzle presently perplexing the monstrumologist, a conundrum he considered, by all appearances, more urgent than the pressing problem of the *Anthropophagi* running, heretofore unbeknownst, in our midst.

The first object he pulled from the dusty trunk was a human head, mummified and shrunken to roughly the size of a navel orange, the skin turned the color of molasses. The eyes were sewn shut. The mouth, toothless, was frozen open in a silent scream. He set it aside with barely a glance. Sensing my proximity, he glanced up at my face, and something in my startled expression must have amused him. A rare smile, as fleeting as a flash of lightning, crossed his countenance.

"My father's," he said.

My morbid interest metastasized immediately to one of horrified dismay at this confession. I knew him to be strange, yet this was an undreamt-of facet of the unnatural and the bizarre. What sort of man stores beneath his basement stairs the shrunken head of his own father?

He noticed my incredulous reaction to this intelligence, and allowed himself the smallest of smiles again. "Not my father's head, Will Henry. A curiosity collected in his travels."

He returned to unpacking the trunk. Out came stacks of papers, bundles of letters and what appeared to be legal documents, a large package wrapped in fraying twine, a leather pouch filled with things evidently metallic, judging from the clinking sound made as he set it down.

"It is the central mystery of their presence here, Will Henry," he said, referring to the *Anthropophagi*. "Surely it has occurred to you what a truly extraordinary coincidence this is, given the fact that I am the sole practicing monstrumologist within five hundred miles. What are the odds, Will Henry, of a species that is of particular interest to my exceedingly esoteric and uncommon calling appearing within ten miles of the very town in which I practice my craft? An objective observer would conclude that those odds, being astronomically long, give credence to the argument that it is *not* a coincidence, that I must be responsible in some way for their unexpected arrival so proximate to my abode. Of course, I had nothing to do with it; the matter is as mystifying to me as it would be to our hypothetical juror. We cannot entirely rule out the possibility of a truly extraordinary coincidence, of course, for a coincidence it might be, though I doubt it. I doubt it."

A pair of spectacles. A velvet purse containing a man's watch and wedding ring. A weathered pipe, the wood of its bowl rubbed to the color of cream by decades of use. A small wooden box containing a collection of ivory figurines, which the doctor turned over and over, the objects clicking together within his partially closed hand, as he rifled through the few remaining items at the bottom of the trunk.

"There is no university that offers instruction in the science of monstrumology, Will Henry," he said. "The Society regularly hosts seminars, by invitation only, in which the preeminent practitioners of our profession lecture on the finer points of their field of particular expertise. Most, if not all, of us apprentice in the art under the tutelage of a master officially recognized by the Society. Ah, here it is!"

Triumphantly he held aloft a leather-bound book, wrapped in fraying twine, its cover and spine worn to a shiny finish from years of handling.

"Here, Will Henry, take these for a moment," he said, dropping the ivory figures into my hand. He tore the twine from the book as I examined the figurines I now held, still warm from his hand. There were six in total, intricately carved and skeletal in representation, with disproportionally large, grimacing skulls, arms crossed over their rib cages, which were not cylindrical like cigars but flat on the front and back like dominoes. Though he was absorbed in the old book—which appeared to be a diary or daybook of sorts, written in elegant script with an occasional sketch filling in the margins—the doctor must have noted my curiosity, for he said, "Divining bones, from New Guinea. In his later years my father was fascinated by the occult practices of certain shamanistic tribes. Those were fashioned by a priest from the bones of a rival."

Not whale bone, then. Human. The doctor continued, "Though 'fascinated' is too mild a word for it. 'Obsessed' is more accurate. He was terrified of his own mortality; like many, he saw his impending death as an affront to his dignity, the ultimate insult, and his last few years were consumed by his desire to cheat the natural order, or at least wrest from death's icy embrace a scant moment or two beyond his due. The bones in your hand supposedly can predict the future of the one who casts them, like the proverbial roll of the cosmic dice. Interpreting the meaning of how they fall—the various combinations of skull up or skull down—is a complicated business that he never fully mastered, but he spent hours at it; he was anything but negligent in his struggle to do so. I can't recall much of the formulae, though I do remember that rolling six faceup skulls has dire import, imminent death or everlasting damnation or some such nonsense."

He rose suddenly with a celebratory shout. Startled, I fell back a step or two, and the bones slipped from my hand, cascading to the carpet with a rattle and a pop. With trepidation I bent to gather them up, for I feared seeing six grinning skeletons leering up at me. Four up. Two down. I did not know, of course, how to interpret my inadvertent roll, but I was relieved nevertheless. Without thinking, I dropped the bones into my pocket.

"Dedham!" cried the monstrumologist. "I knew I had seen it before! Here it is, Will Henry, in the entry dated November 19, 1871: 'Dedham. I have been to Motley Hill for the last time. I simply cannot bring myself to go there again, to look upon his tortured visage and see in his face perfectly reflected the perfidy of my sin. Upon my arrival he became quite agitated, demanding that I once and for all corroborate his tale of suffering and woe, thus winning him full pardon and possible release, but, by the bitter necessity of the interests of science and of self, I was forced to decline. To relent and make such a confession might have the opposite effect. It might, in all likelihood, ensure his imprisonment for the rest of his days—as well as the rest of my own. This I could not risk, and tried to explain, at which point he threatened me bodily and I was forced to take my leave. . . .

Poor tormented creature! Forgive me, V, forgive me! Thou art not the first to pay for the sins of another! Forgive me for my transgression, neither the first nor the last of many, I fear. I shall see thee again upon the Judgment Day. I shall answer for what I have done to thee. . . .

"'I cannot continue. . . . The witching hour approaches, "When churchyards yawn and hell itself breathes out / Contagion." Though I am sickened to the depths of my marrow, I must answer the dreaded summons. The bell rings, the hour comes, and Christ himself is mocked. . . .'"

Warthrop stopped reading and closed the book upon his finger. Something dark passed over his lean face. He sighed, raised his eyes toward the ceiling, and gently scratched beneath his chin.

"It goes on. More tiresome drivel, more gnawing upon the bone of self-recrimination and blame. In his prime my father had few equals, Will Henry. His intellect was exceeded only by his restless curiosity, his relentless quest for knowledge and truth. Our discipline owes much to the work of his younger years, but as he grew older and the fear of his own mortality began to overwhelm him, he fell farther and farther into the pit of silly superstition and useless guilt. He died a frightened and foolish man, a stranger to the brilliant scientist he once was, consumed by fear, maddened by guilt, borne to his reward upon an ark of fabricated shame."

He sighed again, a much longer, sadder exhalation. "And he died quite alone. My mother had succumbed to consumption twenty years before; I was in Prague; and one by one his colleagues had abandoned him over the years, as he'd slipped into doddering senility and religious mania. I returned to America to settle his affairs, in the course of which I discovered this"—he held up the old journal—"a startling record of my father's slow descent into madness, evidently merely one of many volumes, though this is the only one he did not, for reasons I still do not fathom, choose to destroy. I've long puzzled over the meaning of this particular entry, and until now I was not entirely convinced that it, like many that precede and follow it, might not be the ravings of a once-fine mind crumbling from the onslaught of regret and the debilitating disease called doubt.

"He never mentions Dedham, Motley Hill, or this mysterious V again in this diary, and I have not seen it in any of his published treatises or reports to the Society." He picked up a newspaper from the top of the stack before him. "I've seen no reference to it anywhere, until today, here, in this paper, in my possession for more than three years. Three years, Will Henry! And now I fear the father's sin has come to rest upon the shoulders of the son."

He dropped the newspaper onto the pile and pressed hard his knuckles into his eyes. "If one could call it 'sin,'" he murmured. "A concept foreign to science, though not so much to scientists! For here is the critical, *scientific* question, Will Henry: How many *Anthropophagi* immigrated to these shores? The answer to that is the key to everything, for without it we cannot know how many there now may be, not just here in New Jerusalem, but throughout all of New England. The infestation easily could be more extensive than our encounter in the cemetery indicates."

He studied the map for a few seconds more, then whirled from the table, kicking over the old trunk as he flung himself away, as if he had perceived the Gorgon's eyes in the lines he had plotted, in the article unnoticed for three years, in the tormented calligraphy of a dead man from an autumn long since gone, and was forced to look away lest he be turned to stone.

"The hour grows late," said the monstrumologist. "We have no more than two, perhaps three, days before they strike again. Go now, Will Henry, quickly, and post the letters. Stop for nothing and speak to no one. Straight there and back again. We leave tonight for Dedham."

FIVE

"I Am Quite Lonely at Times"

Less than an hour later, having followed his orders to a T—straight to the post office and back, making no stops along the way, although my route took me past the bakery, where the odors of muffins and fresh bread tempted me with their succulent perfume—I returned to the house on Harrington Lane, where I made straight for the library, expecting to find my master, but finding him not. There was the worktable littered with his research, the tipped-over trunk, its lid yawning like an open mouth, its contents strewn around it, the regurgitated effluvia of his father's life, and the shrunken head resting on its side, its mouth frozen open in the apogee of a scream—but no Pellinore Warthrop. I had entered through the back door, passing through the kitchen on my way to the library, and had not seen him. To the kitchen I returned, hesitated before the half-closed basement door, but no light burned below and no sound rose from its black bowels. Just in case, I softly called his name. No answer returned. Perhaps he had given into the same bone-aching fatigue that now plagued his assistant and had retreated upstairs to his bed, though that possibility seemed ridiculously remote. As I have recorded, the doctor, when spurred to action, seemed unwilling or unable to indulge in the normal human needs for respite and rations. He lived off some hidden reserve unsuspected by a casual observer of his rather lean and angular frame. Nevertheless I trooped upstairs to his room. The bed was empty.

Remembering my irrational dread earlier upon the basement steps—had some spawn of the monster hanging below somehow survived?—I returned hastily downstairs to the half-opened door and again called his name.

"Doctor Warthrop? Doctor Warthrop, sir, are you down there?"

Silence. I turned and trotted down the hall, bypassing the library and entering the study. That favored retreat in times of crisis too was deserted, as was the drawing room and every other room downstairs. Surely if he had left the house, he would have left a note to explain his absence. I returned to the library. As I stood before his worktable, my eyes fell upon the article he had circled, the same article that had sparked his remarkable memory—*I knew I had seen it before!*—and I picked it up to read:

CAPT. VARNER RETURNED TO THE ASYLUM

Yesterday, nearly twenty years to the day of
his incarceration, the General Court of Appeals
handed down its decision in the final clemency
hearing of Capt. Hezekiah Varner. Capt. Varner
was convicted in March of 1865 of blockade-
running and dereliction of duty on the high
seas when his ship, the cargo vessel *Feronia*,
foundered off the coast near Swampscott. At his
original trial, Capt. Varner gave testimony he
had been employed by certain Confederate sym-
pathizers to supply the Rebellion with "goods
and chattel" and that his entire cargo and crew
had been overcome at sea by "creatures not of
this Earth but from the very Bowels of Hell."
At his hearing Capt. Varner, now seventy-two
years old and in poor physical health, spoke on
his own behalf, repudiating his earlier testimony and stating the two days lost at sea after
abandoning his vessel had afflicted him with
a severe case of sunstroke. Capt. Varner produced no other witnesses on his behalf. Dr. J. F.
Starr spoke for the State, giving testimony that
in his opinion Capt. Varner was not in his right
mind. "He was insane twenty years ago, and he
is insane today," said Dr. Starr. Upon the con-

clusion of the Court, Capt. Varner was returned
to Motley Hill Sanatorium, Dr. Starr's private
asylum, in Dedham, where he has been confined
since the conclusion of his original trial.

Creatures not of this Earth but from the very Bowels of Hell. I
thought of the thing hanging on a hook in the room over which
I stood, of the pale, muscular arm bursting through the loose
soil of Eliza Bunton's grave, of the sickening squish of its paw
puncturing the leg of the old man, of the mass of sickly white
flesh and glittering black eyes and drooling mouths laced with
row upon row of triangular teeth glittering in the glow of the
April stars, of huge, hulking, headless monstrosities issuing from
every shadow, leaping and bounding with enormous strides, of
Eliza Bunton's corpse being ripped limb from limb and her
head stuffed into the mouth of a creature that any rational man
would indeed deem from hell. Having read the article and heard
the cryptic entry from the diary, I had no doubt Dr. Warthrop
was correct in his assessment: This Captain Varner (*V,* the elder
Warthrop had called him) had had an encounter with *Anthropophagi.* But that had been twenty-three years before! How had
these bizarre and terrifying predators managed to survive—nay,
thrive and reproduce—undetected for so long?

Thus lost in reverie, I failed to hear the closing of the back door
or the footfalls of the monstrumologist as he strode toward the
room. I was unaware of his return until he appeared in the doorway, cheeks flushed, hair plastered to his head with dirt and grime,

shoes caked in mud, a battered straw hat in his hand. I recognized that hat; it had been placed on my head by an old man whose brains a few hours before I had washed from my hair.

"Will Henry," said the doctor quietly. "What are you doing?"

Feeling the color rise in my cheeks, I said, "Nothing, sir."

"That is obvious," he returned dryly. "Did you post the letters?"

"Yes, sir."

"Straight there and back again?"

"Yes, sir."

"And spoke to no one?"

"Just the postmaster, sir."

"And you mailed both by express delivery?"

"Yes, sir."

He nodded. He fell mute for a moment more, as if his mind had wandered. His gaze was unfocused, and, though he stood perfectly still, agitation seemed to exude from every pore. I noticed a scrap of filthy cloth in his other hand, which at first I took to be a rag, but I quickly realized it was a shredded swatch of Eliza Bunton's burial gown.

"And what are you doing now?" he asked.

"Nothing, sir."

"Yes, yes," he snapped. "So you have told me, Will Henry."

"I didn't know where you were, so I was—"

"Doing nothing."

"Looking for you."

"You thought perhaps I had taken refuge in my father's trunk?"

"I thought you might have left a note."

"Why would I do that?" The notion that he might owe me an explanation of his whereabouts was completely foreign to him.

"You went to the cemetery?" I inquired. Best to change the subject, I thought. When aroused, his temper could be terrible, and I could tell he was already distressed.

My ploy worked, for he nodded and said, "There were at least two dozen distinct sets of prints. Assuming four to five immature juveniles sequestered in wherever their warren may be hidden, a total of thirty to thirty-five. An alarming and extraordinary number, Will Henry."

Seeing the hat in his hand reminded me of my own little cap, my sole possession, lost in our mad flight the night before. Dare I ask him if he found it? He saw my stare, and said, "I've cleaned it up the best I could. Filled her grave. Recovered most of our supplies and scattered the broken pieces of the cart in the woods. With a little luck we may finish this business before we are discovered."

I might have asked why discovery was undesirable in this instance, but everything in his demeanor suggested the answer to that question was obvious. I suspect now the answer had more to do with his discovery of his father's possible involvement than with the hazard of setting off a firestorm of panic. The doctor was more concerned with his father's reputation—

and, by extension, his own—than the public welfare.

Perhaps I judge him too harshly. Perhaps he believed the cost of discovery far outweighed the benefit of adequate warning before the monsters could strike again. Perhaps. Though, after many years to consider the matter, I doubt it. The monstrumologist's ego, as I have noted, like the immeasurable universe, seemed to know no boundaries. Even during those periods of intense melancholia to which he was prone, nothing mattered more to him than his perception of himself, his worthiness as a scientist and his place in history. Self-pity is egotism undiluted, after all—self-centeredness in its purest form.

"I'm going upstairs to wash up," he went on. "Pack up the trunk, Will Henry, and put it away. Saddle the horses and fix yourself something to eat. Snap to, now."

He started down the hall, thought of something, turned, and tossed the old hat and bloody cloth into the room.

"And burn these."

"Burn them, sir?"

"Yes."

He hesitated for a moment, and then he strode into the room and picked up his father's diary from the table. He pressed it into my hand.

"And this, Will Henry," he said. "Burn this, too."

Burn it I did, with the bloody scrap of burial gown and the battered straw hat, and I squatted for a moment before the crackling blaze in the library's fireplace, feeling its heat against my knees and cheeks, the tip of my nose, my forehead, which felt tight from the intense heat, as if the skin were being pulled back from my skull. After the fire that had claimed the lives of my parents, I had imagined I could smell smoke on me for days, in my hair and on my skin. With lye soap I had scrubbed myself until the flesh was red and raw. I had imagined that the smoke lingered about my person like a pall, and it would not be until weeks afterward that the sensation finally abated. For those few weeks, however, I was no doubt the cleanest twelve-year-old boy in New England.

Though I was thoroughly exhausted and very hungry, I was determined to finish in the library before repairing to the kitchen to prepare our repast. I righted the old trunk, emptied of everything but a dozen or so old letters still in their envelopes. Curiosity got the better of me, for upon one I saw his name above the return address: *Pellinore Warthrop, Esq.* Directed to the Dr. A. F. Warthrop of 425 Harrington Lane, the letter was postmarked London, England. The handwriting was clearly the doctor's, only much neater than the specimens I had seen, as if a concerted effort had been made toward legibility. The envelope bore the original wax seal, unbroken, as did the others I examined, a total of fifteen in all, each with the same return address. Having traveled vast distances, these letters from a son to his father had been tossed unread into an old trunk and stored in a dank and dusty corner. Ah, Warthrop! Ah, humanity! Did he know? He had read the diary, had remembered it well enough to find the entry referencing Captain Varner; had he ever noticed, while inventorying this old box, that these letters had never been opened, and would he notice if one should now be?

It was impertinent, disobedient, an outrageous invasion of his privacy. Should I? Dare I? I glanced toward the doorway, holding my breath. No sound but for the ticking of the mantel clock and the roaring of blood in my ears. So much about this man, with whom I shared every waking moment and to whose life mine was now inextricably bound, was a mystery to me. I knew next to nothing about him and absolutely nothing about his past. The letter in my hand would undoubtedly contain clues. *Now or never, Will Henry,* I told myself. *Drop it or open it—now or never!*

I opened it.

The envelope contained a single sheet of foolscap, composed by the same hand that addressed the envelope. Dated March 14, 1865, it read:

Dear Father,

As it has been nearly three weeks since I last wrote, I thought I would write again so you will not think I have been negligent in my thoughts of home. Not much has happened here since last I wrote, except I've developed a very bad cold, with fever and a cough, et cetera, but you would be satisfied to know I have not missed a single day of class because of it. The headmaster says he is very pleased with my progress and went on to say he intends to send you a personal note as to my general welfare, et cetera. Please look for it and, if it isn't too much trouble, extend to him the courtesy of a reply. He thinks a great deal of you, as, of course, do I and all who know you.

I wish you would write to me. Letters arrive every week from America, and I stand in line with the rest of my classmates, and every week I wait for my name to be called, and every week it is not. I am not complaining, Father, and hope you do not take this awkward confession as such. I am quite lonely at times and do not feel entirely at home here. When not in class I mostly keep to my room, and sometimes, like today, when it is cold and cloudy, refusing to rain or snow but remaining dismal withal, as if a shroud lays upon the world, I am very lonely. A letter from you would brighten the gloom, for as you know I tend toward that familial disposition of dourness. I know you are quite busy with your research and your travels. I imagine my letters piling up in the entryway awaiting your return. And of course I worry that something may have happened to you and no one has bothered to send me word. If you do receive this, could you take but a moment or two to jot back a quick reply? It would mean the world to me. I remain, et cetera,

Your Son,

Pellinore

I heard the floorboards creak upstairs. Quickly I folded the letter, stuffed it back into its envelope, and pressed my thumb down hard upon the wax seal, a hopeless act, since it was as hard as a nail after twenty-three years. The flap popped up half an inch. I dropped it into the trunk and scattered a few of its unsullied companions over it.

It would mean the world to me. Apparently, to his father it had not. What the son wrote, the father ignored. Was he indeed away on some adventure during that time when Warthrop was in London, a boy about my age, lonely and bereft of the familiar, longing to hear some news from his far-flung home? If so, why hadn't the elder Warthrop opened these letters upon his return? Why had he kept them at all if he'd cared not for his son? The irony does not escape me that I opened that letter searching for clues, only to deepen the mystery to which I'd sought insight.

But reading it did accomplish one thing. As is so often the case, the insights we seek are not those we find: I could see him clearly in my mind's eye, huddled in his nightshirt upon his little cot, feverishly writing this letter between fits of coughing, a boy not unlike me, torn from his family and friends, with no one and nothing to console him. For the first time I felt something other than awe and fear toward the monstrumologist. For the first time I felt pity. My heart ached for the sick little boy so far from home.

My feelings would be short lived. Barely had I buried the offended missive when the doctor bounded down the stairs and spun into the room.

"Will Henry! What are you doing?"

"Nothing—nothing, sir," I stammered.

"Nothing! Again when I ask what you're doing, you are doing nothing! It seems to be your chief occupation, Will Henry."

"Yes, sir. I mean, no, sir! I'm sorry, sir. I'll stop."

"Stop what?"

"Doing nothing."

"You are no use to me, Will Henry, if every time I give you something to do, you choose to do its opposite. Snap to! It is a good three hours' hard ride to Dedham."

He did not tarry for a response, but fled down the hall toward the kitchen. I heard the basement door slam shut. My face on fire from so close a call, I hurried to finish, tossing the curios and keepsakes back into the trunk, intolerant of my native squeamishness as I unhesitatingly plucked the shrunken head from the floor. It was much lighter than I'd expected. I wondered at the history of this poor fellow of origin undeterminable. Was it another gift to the elder Warthrop from some savage tribal chief befriended in his wanderings, or was there a more personal connection? It was impossible to determine its sex and age, and its race had been erased by the process and the passage of time, that great equalizer that makes a mockery of our temporal distinctions, king and serf; man and woman; hero, knave, and fool. Back into your box, anonymous Yorick, with your sutured eyes and frozen scream! The indignity of your internment is no worse than ours.

I flung the head into the box. It ricocheted against one side before dropping down, rolling onto its side, and coming to rest atop the other items in the trunk. The force of the impact must have dislodged the object tucked inside the hollow of its tiny skull, for I glimpsed protruding from the neck a piece of bright red material. I pulled the head out again, grasped the end of the cloth, and tugged at it until the object to which the other end was tied pulled free of its cadaverous cocoon. It was a key—to what I did not know, but it was too large to belong to the trunk or a door.

"Will Henry!" shouted the doctor from the basement steps.

I dropped the head back into the box and jammed the key into my pocket. I would show it to him later, I decided. He had inventoried the trunk's contents; perhaps he knew all about the key pushed inside the hollowed-out head.

"Horses, Will Henry! Food, Will Henry!"

My descent into the laboratory held none of the terror of my earlier expedition, for the lights blazed below and the doctor was there, standing before the suspended corpse of the male *Anthropophagus*. The doctor turned not as I thumped down the stairs with my burden, but remained with his back toward me, arms crossed, head cocked to one side as he contemplated the beast hanging before him. I shoved his father's trunk beneath the stairs, and then stepped toward him, a bit out of breath.

"Doctor," I called softly. "What would you like to eat?"

He did not turn. He raised his right hand and brushed the air with his fingertips, a dismissive gesture, and said nothing. I thought about mentioning the key, and quickly decided to wait until his mood had improved. I returned upstairs to scrape what sustenance I could from our impoverished larder. I was ravenous.

He burst into the kitchen a half hour later, and though he had washed and changed upon his return from the cemetery, the lingering stench of death below had impregnated his person and now surrounded him in a cloying aerosol. He saw me sitting at the table, took in the steaming bowl before me, and then regarded my bowl's twin at the place setting on the other side of the table, beside it the carefully folded napkin and polished spoon, the teapot and the fresh cup of tea, the aromatic vapor rising from its ebony surface.

"What is this?" he demanded.

"Soup, sir."

"Soup?" As if he had never heard the word.

"Potato soup."

"Potato soup," he echoed.

"Yes, sir. I found two fairly good ones in the bin, and some carrots, and an onion. We had no cream or meat, so I used water and some flour to thicken it."

"To thicken it."

"Yes, sir; flour, sir, to thicken it."

"Flour," he said.

"It isn't bad," I said. "I passed the bakery on my way to the post office, but you told me not to stop, so I didn't, and we've no bread to go with it. You should eat, sir."

"I am not hungry."

"But you said we should eat before—"

"I know what I said," he interrupted crossly. "Few things

are more annoying, Will Henry, than for a person to have his own words thrown back at him as if he were an imbecile incapable of remembering them. *You* are the one who cannot remember what was said, which was that *you* should eat something before we depart."

"But I am eating something, sir."

"Dear God!" he exclaimed. "Are you addled, William James Henry? Do you suffer from some mental defect of which I am not aware?"

"No, sir; that is, I don't think so. I just thought you might like a little soup." I could feel my lower lip quivering.

"A conclusion based upon a false premise," he snapped. "I am not hungry."

I dropped my eyes: The intensity of his gaze was unbearable. His dark eyes glittered with unfathomable fury; his entire being vibrated from its force. What was it? I wondered. Did he perceive my thoughtfulness as its opposite, a willful act of disobedience? Or, having been recently reminded of his cold and strained relationship with his father, was this small act of kindness and devotion mere salt in the wound that, by virtue of his father's now eternal inapproachability, would never be healed?

Though he towered over my hunched and shivering frame, a grown man at the height of his powers, in my mind's eye I saw the sick and lonely boy, a stranger in a strange land, writing to the man whose attention and affections he desperately desired, a man who would reward his filial devotion with the ultimate indignity of paternal rejection: letters unopened, tossed into an old box, forgotten. How marvelously strange, how terribly tragic, the ironic twists and turns of fate! We often take vengeance long after the fact upon blameless surrogates, reprising the same sins of the ones who trespassed against us, and so perpetuate ad infinitum the pain we suffered at their hands. His father rejected his entreaties, so he rejected mine, and I—in the strangest twist of all—was *him*, the isolated and lonesome little boy seeking approbation and acceptance from the one person from whom it mattered most. It offended his pride and doubled his anger: anger at his father for ignoring his need, anger at himself for needing anything in the first place.

"Oh, stop that," he growled. "Stop that insufferable sniveling. I did not take you in to be my cook or my nursemaid or for any reason beyond the obligation I owed your father for his unselfish service. You have potential, Will Henry. You are clever and inquisitive and are not without some mettle in your marrow, indispensable qualities in an assistant and, perhaps, a future scientist, but don't suffer under any illusions that you are more than that: an assistant forced upon me by unfortunate circumstances. You are not here to provide for me; I am here to provide for you. Now finish this fine soup of which you are so inexplicably proud, and get to the carriage house to ready our horses. We leave at nightfall."

SIX

"What of the Flies?"

We rode that night straight through to Dedham, a three-hour journey over rough and isolated roads, stopping once to rest our horses and again, just outside the boundaries of the town, to ease quietly into woods lest we be spotted by an approaching carriage. The night was cool enough for our horses' breath to steam as we dissolved into the deep shadows of the trees. The doctor waited until the hoofbeats and the rattle of the wooden wheels faded before we resumed our journey. We did not slow until we reached the first few houses occupying the town's outskirts. Inside these pleasant cottages lamps warmly glowed, and I imagined the families ensconced inside, in the warmth of one another's company, partaking of the normal intercourse of a Tuesday night, Father by the fire, Mother with her young, with no worrisome thoughts of monsters lurking in the dark except in the minds of the most imaginative of their children. The man riding beside me suffered not from the naïve illusions of well-meaning parents who, with calm voice and gentle touch, extinguished the bright, hot embers of a child's fiery imagination. He knew the truth. *Yes, my dear child*, he would undoubtedly tell a terrified toddler tremulously seeking succor, *monsters are real. I happen to have one hanging in my basement.*

We had not traveled far down the main street of Dedham before Warthrop turned his horse down a narrow lane that wound through a dense stand of poplars, at the head of which a small, inconspicuous sign hung upon a rusting steel pike: MOTLEY HILL SANATORIUM. Trees and tangles of vine and weed crowded upon us as we proceeded, slowly now, up a rise of ground. The woods closed around us; the canopy drooped lower and lower, blotting out the stars, as if we had plunged into a dark and winding tunnel. There was no sound but the steady *clop-clop* of the hooves upon the hard-packed dirt. No chirp of cricket or croak of frog. Nothing disturbed the profound and eerie silence that did not so much descend upon our plunge down this Cimmerian path as slam hard down upon our heads. Our horses became jittery, snorting and stamping as we climbed. The doctor appeared quite collected, but for myself I was not faring much better than my little mare, both our eyes darting in the growing blackness. The trail—it hardly could be called a lane anymore—finally leveled off, the trees drew back, and much to my and my little mare's relief, we emerged into an open, if overgrown, expanse of moonlit lawn.

About a hundred yards directly ahead stood a house of the Federal style, white with black shutters and towering columns guarding the front. The windows were dark and the property had a deserted feel about it, as if its occupants had long ago fled to happier climes. My first thought was that the sanatorium must have been closed and abandoned subsequent to the reinternment of Captain Varner three years previously. I glanced over at the doctor, whose mouth was grimly set and whose dark eyes seemed to glow as if backlit.

"Will Henry," he said softly as we rode toward the house, "you are not to speak. You are not to look anyone directly in the eye. If someone should speak to you, you are to say nothing. Ignore them. Do not address them or respond to them in any way. Not so much as a nod or a wink. Do you understand?"

"Yes, sir."

He sighed. "I think I would rather deal with a dozen *Anthropophagi* than the wretched souls within these walls!"

Upon closer inspection, the house was a shade or two closer to gray than white; it had once been white, many seasons ago, but the paint had faded and begun to peel. Long strips of it hung from the bare, mildewed boards. The windows had not been washed for months. Quivering spiderwebs clung to their corners. Had I a mind of a more metaphysical bent, I would have assumed this house to be haunted, but, like the monstrumologist, I rejected the notion of hauntings and other supernatural phenomenons. There are indeed more things in heaven and earth than are dreamt of in our philosophy, but those things were, like the *Anthropophagi*, quite physical, entirely natural, capable of fulfilling our curious and baffling need for a marauding horror of malicious intent, thank you very much.

The doctor rapped sharply on the door with the head of his walking stick, an exquisite rendering in jade of a snarling gargoyle. There was no immediate answer. Warthrop knocked again, three short raps, a pause, then three more: *rap-rap-rap . . . rap-rap-rap.*

Silence, but for the wind whispering in the trees and the dry rattle of last fall's leaves skittering across the weathered boards of the sagging porch. The doctor rested his hands upon his cane and waited with the patience of the Buddha.

"It's abandoned," I whispered, a bit relieved.

"No," he said. "We are unexpected, that is all."

On the other side of the door I perceived the shuffling footfalls of a painful approach, as if someone very old or lame were coming to answer the doctor's insistent summons. I heard the loud metallic screech and groan of several bolts being drawn back, and then the door opened a crack, the flickering light of a lamp flooded onto the porch, and standing in the half-open doorway was a withered woman dressed in black, the lamp clenched in her gnarled knuckles, holding the lamp high to illuminate our faces.

"No visitors past nine!" the old woman croaked with toothless mouth.

"This is not a social call," rejoined Warthrop.

"No visitors past nine!" she snapped harshly, raising her voice, as if the doctor were hard of hearing. "No exceptions!"

"Perhaps you could make one in my case," said the doctor calmly, holding out his card. "Tell Dr. Starr that Pellinore Warthrop has come to see him."

"Dr. Starr has retired for the evening," she said, "with strict instruction he is not to be disturbed."

"My good woman, I assure you the doctor would not desire that you turn us away."

"The doctor is asleep."

"Then wake him!" the doctor cried, losing patience. "My errand is one of the utmost urgency."

She squinted at the card, her eyes nearly disappearing in the plethora of flesh surrounding them.

"'Dr. Warthrop,'" she read. "Heh! Dr. Warthrop is dead; I know that for a fact. You must be an imposter."

"No, I am his son."

Her mouth moved soundlessly for a moment, and the old eyes darted from the card to his face and back again.

"He never mentioned having a son," she said at last.

"I am certain there are many things of a personal nature he failed to confide in you," said the doctor dryly. "As I have pointed out, I am here on a matter of extreme importance, so if it's not too much trouble, could you, in the most expeditious manner in which one of your advancing years is able, relay to your employer my presence and my earnest desire to speak with him, preferably some time before the night becomes the morrow."

She slammed the door abruptly in our faces. The doctor heaved an exaggerated sigh. As the seconds turned to minutes, he did not move but stood as still as a statue, leaning upon his cane, head bowed, eyes half-closed, as if he were preserving his energy and gathering his wits for an imminent trial.

"Is she coming back?" I said when I could bear it no longer. It felt as if we'd been standing on that porch for hours. He said nothing. I asked again, "Is she coming back?"

"She didn't throw the bolts," he said. "Therefore, I am hopeful."

At last I heard hurried footsteps approach, and the door flew open, revealing an old man—though not quite as ancient as the crone who slumped in the hall a few steps behind him. He had hastily dressed, throwing a dusty frock coat over his nightshirt, but had neglected to address the issue of his bed-matted hair: The wispy white strands hung down nearly to his shoulder, a diaphanous curtain falling over his enormous ears, exposing his mottled scalp. His nose was long and sharp, his rheumy blue eyes small, his chin weak and speckled with stubble.

"Dr. Starr," said the monstrumologist. "My name is Pellinore Warthrop. I believe you knew my father."

"It is a pitiful case," the old man said, lowering his cup with a tremulous hand. The china rattled and a brown tear of tea traced a path down the side of the cup. "Of particular interest to your father."

"Not only to him," said the doctor.

We were sitting in the small parlor just off the front hall. The room was like the rest of the house, chilly, ill-lit, and poorly ventilated. A strange, sickly-sweet odor hung in the air. I had noticed it when we'd stepped inside—that and the indistinct, muffled noise of unseen people somewhere in the shadow-stuffed old house: moans, coughs, screams, cries of desperation, cries of anger, cries of fear, and, floating in faint counterpoint to this cacophony, hysterical peals of high-pitched laughter. Both my master and Dr. Starr ignored the offstage bedlam, acknowledging it only in the minor elevation of their voices. I, however, found myself unnerved to the point of distraction and was forced to dip into the very bottom of my well of stoic fortitude to resist asking the doctor if I could wait outside with the horses.

"So you have taken up his odd profession," ventured the alienist. "I shall be honest with you, Dr. Warthrop: I did not know until this night that he even had a son."

"My father was an intensely private man," offered the

doctor. "He found human intimacy . . . distasteful. I was his only child, and I hardly knew him."

"As is too often the case with a man like your father," observed Starr. "His work was everything."

"I always assumed it owed more to the fact that he didn't like me."

Dr. Starr laughed, and something rattled deep in his chest.

"Excuse me," he said. Producing a stained white handkerchief from his pocket, he spat a copious wad of phlegm into the soiled cloth. He brought it within an inch of his watery eyes and carefully examined the contents. He glanced the doctor's way and gave a rueful smile. "I beg your pardon, Dr. Warthrop. I fear I am dying."

"What is the diagnosis?" Warthrop asked politely. He was the model of forbearance, but his foot tapped rapidly upon the worn carpeting.

"There is none," said Starr. "I didn't say I *am*. I said I *fear* that I am."

"A fear to which all are susceptible from time to time."

"In my case it is nearly constant. Yet my reluctance to seek a diagnosis increases in direct proportion with the fear."

"Interesting," said the doctor without much conviction.

"And unlike your father and, by all appearances, your boy, I have no one to pick up the torch when I am gone."

"Will Henry is not my 'boy,'" Warthrop said.

"No?"

"He is my assistant."

"Your assistant! He is quite young for such an important position, is he not?" The weak eyes fell upon me, and I at once looked away, the doctor's words echoing in my ears: *You are not to look anyone directly in the eye. If someone should speak to you, you are to say nothing.*

"He was pressed upon me by the unfortunate loss of his parents."

"Ah, a charity case."

"Far from it. He may be young, but the boy has potential."

"I am sorry for your loss," Dr. Starr directed at me, but I refused to raise my head or even nod my appreciation for the condolence. *Ignore them*, the doctor had admonished. He had not made an exception for the proprietor of Motley Hill Sanatorium.

"Now, Warthrop," Starr continued. "You wish to speak to Captain Varner."

"I would not presume to ask if the matter were not of the utmost necessity."

"Oh, I've no doubt only an emergency would draw you here at this late hour, unbidden and unannounced! The patient has not kept secret these many years his bizarre tale of cannibalism and murder. If he had, he might be a free man—or a dead one, for no doubt he would have been executed upon conviction."

"My father never spoke of the case," said the monstrumologist. "I stumbled upon a reference to it in his private papers."

"And curiosity brought you to my door."

"A singular curiosity," said the doctor carefully.

"Indeed it must be, my dear Dr. Warthrop! Singularly curious indeed!" His frail form was racked a second time in a fit that lasted a good minute. He repeated the ritual of removing the filthy kerchief and depositing the effluvia into its reeking folds. "But mere curiosity, even an intense or a singular curiosity of the kind to which you confess, could not be construed by even the most lax linguist as a *necessity* or, as you put it to Mrs. Bratton, "a matter of extreme importance.""

"My father apparently believed in the veracity of his claim."

"Well, given his profession, no doubt he would."

"To the extent he felt compelled to come here, as I have tonight. I know the patient is old and not in good health . . ."

"And so you rode three hours from New Jerusalem without making the proper inquiries first, because you were compelled . . . by what precisely?"

"As I have said," replied the doctor carefully, "Varner's condition, the advanced age of the case, and other pertinent factors compelled me to—"

"Ah, yes! That's it! "Pertinent factors." That is what tweaks *my* curiosity, Dr. Warthrop. What, pray tell, might those 'pertinent factors' be?"

The doctor took a deep breath, straightened in his chair, and said tightly, "I am not at liberty to say."

"Then you will forgive me if I take the liberty to say it," said Dr. Starr sarcastically. '*Anthropophagi. Anthropophagi*, yes? Did you think I'd never heard of them? The old salt has repeated his tale for any and all who were willing to listen—even to those who were not! I am not an ignorant man, Warthrop; I know my Shakespeare: "The Anthropophagi . . . men whose heads / Do grow beneath their shoulders.' Oh, yes, I know well enough what has brought you to my doorstep!"

"Very well, then," rejoined the monstrumologist calmly. "May I see him now?"

Dr. Starr cast an eye toward the parlor door, and then back to the doctor: "He is, as you surmised, quite old, and his health is more tenuous than even my own. I may *fear* I am dying; Captain Varner *is* dying. And his mind is nearly spent as well, I'm afraid. Your quest has been in vain, Dr. Warthrop."

"Are you refusing to let me see him?" demanded Warthrop, nearing the end of his patience. "I have come merely to clear up a few lingering questions on an old case of my father's, but I can be content to let them linger. It is of no special interest to me."

"That is not the impression you gave my housekeeper, and it is certainly not the impression you gave me, Dr. Warthrop."

"Nevertheless," growled the doctor. He rose from his chair, shoulders thrown back, hands clinched into fists at his sides. "Come, Will Henry. We are wasting our time here."

"I did not mean to give you that impression," said Starr with a sly smile. "I was only pointing out that your time and the interest of science might be better served by speaking to me about the case. Captain Varner has been, as you know, under my care for twenty-three years. I've heard his story hundreds of times, and I doubt there is a detail of which I am not as conversant as he. I would venture that I am more conversant, given the deterioration of his faculties."

Warthrop said, "I wish to hear it from the captain."

"Though I have informed you he is hardly lucid?"

"I will be the judge of that."

"You certainly are an accomplished fellow, Warthrop. A doctor of psychology as well as a doctor of—what is your so-called science?—*monstrumology*."

Warthrop did not answer. In the pregnancy of that taut moment, I feared he might lose all self-control, leap across the room, and throttle the old man. The ancient alienist did not know the doctor as I did: Though by outward sign Warthrop appeared completely calm and collected, within him a fire burned, as hot as the sun, and only by the supreme effort of his inestimable will was the doctor able to contain it.

Again Starr glanced toward the door, as if he were expecting something. He went on, still wearing that secretive smile. "I mean no offense, Warthrop. My area of expertise is held in no greater regard than yours. I do not mean to mock or ridicule your life's work, for in one way at least it mimics my own: We have dedicated our lives to the pursuit of phantoms. The difference is the nature of those phantoms. Mine exist between other men's ears; yours live solely between your own."

At that point I expected the doctor to invite Starr to New Jerusalem so he could see with his own eyes how phantasmagorical the nature of his life's work was. But he held his tongue, and he, too, glanced toward the doorway. Both men seemed to be waiting for something.

"It is a hard and lonely life," whispered the old man, his tone softening somewhat. "We are, both of us, Warthrop, voices crying in the wilderness. For fifty years I've provided an invaluable service to my fellow man. I have sacrificed, barely subsisting on meager donations and philanthropic grants. I could have taken a steady and certainly more lucrative position at a university, but I chose instead to dedicate my life to helping the poor unfortunates whom fate and circumstance have washed up upon my shore. Mistake me not, I do not complain, but it is hard. Hard!"

Remarkably, the Cheshire grin had fled, and in its place were a quivering lip and a solitary tear trailing down his weathered cheek.

"And this is how I end my days!" he cried softly. "A destitute wretch with hardly enough in his purse to cover the expenses of his burial. You asked for the diagnosis of my affliction, and I spoke truthfully there is none, for I cannot afford the services of a physician. I, a doctor myself, who has sacrificed his well-being upon the altar of altruism, am forced to suffer a humiliating end because I refused to worship the golden calf! Ah, Warthrop, 'tis a pity—but I beg for none! 'Tis pride my undoing—but I would not undo it! I have no regrets. No lungs, either, but I'd rather die honorably poor than dishonorably live."

He dissolved into another raucous coughing spell, pressing his skeletal hands to his collapsing chest. The sleeves of his coat fell to his elbows, exposing his boney arms. He seemed to shrivel before our eyes, to wilt into a quivering mass of withered flesh and oversize yellow teeth.

The doctor made no move. He did not speak. He watched the old fellow repeat the ritual with the handkerchief, saying naught, but his eyes burned with that same disconcerting backlit quality, and his fists remained clenched at his side.

He waited until Starr was still, then quietly stepped forward and dropped a gold coin beside his teacup. The teary old eyes darted to the coin, darted away again.

"I do not require your charity, Dr. Warthrop," the curmudgeon croaked. "You add insult to injury."

"That is certainly not my intention, Dr. Starr," replied the doctor. "This is a loan. You must repay me. The only other stipulation is that you use this to see a doctor."

Dart, dart went the eyes. "My only hope is in finding a specialist."

A second coin joined the first.

"In Boston."

A third. When Starr failed to speak, but sighed loudly in answer to the gentle clink of metal striking metal, Warthrop added a fourth. Starr coughed, and the attendant rattle in his chest sounded like beans smacking about in a hollow gourd. Warthrop dropped a fifth coin onto the pile; Starr sat bolt upright, hands falling to his sides, and cried out in a loud, clear voice, "Mrs. Bratton! Mrs. Braaaat*ton!*"

She appeared in the doorway instantly, the irascible crone who had greeted us at the front door, as if she had been awaiting the summons just out of sight. Her entrance was accompanied by the unmistakable odor of bleach.

"Escort Dr. Warthrop to Captain Varner's room," instructed Starr. He did not attempt to join us. He remained in his chair, sipping the dregs of his tea, holding the cup with a hand markedly steadier than it had been a few moments before. The gold that the doctor had dropped beside the saucer had steeled him.

"Yes, Doctor," answered the old woman. "Follow me," she said to Warthrop.

As we started from the room, Starr called to the doctor, "Perhaps the boy should remain here with me."

"The boy is my assistant," my master reminded him curtly. "His services are indispensable to me." He followed the old woman from the room and did not bid me come, or look behind to see if I would; he knew I would.

Led by the black-clad, chlorine-infused Mrs. Bratton, we mounted the poorly lit narrow staircase leading to the second floor. Halfway up, the doctor murmured into my ear, "Remember what I told you, Will Henry." As we climbed, the eerie moans and cries, which seemed to originate from a twilight region neither wholly fantastical nor altogether human, steadily grew in volume. A guttural voice rose above the din, jabbering a furious monologue peppered with profanities. A woman called desperately, again and again, for someone named Hanna. A man sobbed uncontrollably. And running like a swift undercurrent beneath this unsettled sea of disembodied clamor, the frantic laughter I had heard since entering the sanatorium. Strengthening too as we climbed was the same cloying odor I had noted in the parlor beneath us, its malodorous composition unmistakable as it intensified: a throat-tightening potpourri of unwashed flesh, old urine, and human feces.

Lining both sides of the long second-floor hall were heavy wooden doors, each fitted with iron dead bolts and padlocks the size of my fist, each with a six-inch-wide slot cut into it at eye level, the opening covered by a hinged piece of metal. The old floorboards creaked beneath our feet, alerting the occupants of these barricaded rooms to our presence, and their cries rose to a fever pitch, tripling in volume and intensity. A door shook upon its ancient hinges as the denizen within hurled himself against it. We passed the profane monologist's room, whereat he pressed his lips against the jam and unleashed a string of execrations worthy of the saltiest marine. The shrill, despairing cries for Hanna vibrated in our ears. I glanced up at the doctor's face, seeking some sign of reassurance in this foul Babel of human suffering and misery, but he gave no sign. His countenance was as calm as a man strolling in the park on a warm summer's day.

For me the jittery trek down that dismal hall seemed longer than a mile, and a million more from any pleasant park. When we stopped at the last door, I was out of breath, forced by the stench to breathe shallow gulps through my half-open mouth. Our guide produced a large ring from her apron pocket and commenced to flipping through the dozens of keys hanging from it, an operation apparently more complex than one might imagine, for she bent low over her work, running a crooked finger over the teeth of each key, as if she could identify the proper one by touch. I nearly jumped clear of my clothing when the door directly behind me gave a violent shudder and a rasping voice whispered, "Hello, now, who is this? Who is this?" I heard the sound of someone snuffling as he pressed his nose against the door. "I know you're there. I can *smell* you."

"The patient wasn't awake when last I checked on him," Mrs. Bratton informed the doctor as she caressed her keys.

"Then we shall wake him," said the doctor.

"You won't get much out of him," she said. "He hasn't made a peep in weeks."

Warthrop made no reply. Mrs. Bratton at last found the

key and popped open the old padlock, threw back the three bolts above its clasp, and with her shoulder pushed open the ponderous door.

The room was tiny, hardly larger than my little alcove on Harrington Lane, with no furniture but the rickety bed placed two paces from the door. A kerosene lamp sat on the floor beside it, its smoky flame providing the only source of light. It flung our shadows upon the ceiling and the peeling plaster of the wall opposite the filthy window, beneath which, on the dusty sill, clustered the bodies of desiccated flies. Above them, a congregation of their extant cousins buzzed about and crawled upon glass. My eyes began to water, for the smell of bleach was overwhelming, and I deduced the reason for delaying the doctor downstairs: Mrs. Bratton had needed time to scour and disinfect before our introduction to Captain Varner.

He lay upon the bed beneath several layers of blankets and sheets, the uppermost as white and wrinkleless as a burial shroud, leaving only his head and neck exposed. The bed was not large, but it appeared even smaller due to his enormous bulk. I had imagined him as a frail and shriveled old man, wasted away to a mere husk of humanity after twenty years of confinement and deprivation. Instead, lying before me was a man of monstrous proportions, weighing more than four hundred pounds, I would venture, cradled as it were in a kind of trough created in the mattress by his staggering corpulence. His head was equally huge; in relation to it the pillow upon which it rested appeared to be the size a pincushion. The eyes were lost in folds of grayish flesh; the nose was scarlet and bulbous, rising from the sunken cheeks like a red potato resting upon a parched landscape; and the mouth was a dark, toothless tunnel in which his swollen tongue slithered restlessly over bare gums.

The doctor stepped to his bedside. In her emaciated claws the old woman nervously turned the key ring. The jingling of the keys, the labored breath of the afflicted, and the buzzing of the flies against the window were the only sounds in the tiny, claustrophobic space.

"I wouldn't touch him," she cautioned. "Captain Varner hates to be touched. Don't you, Captain Varner?"

He answered not. Though his eyes were barely visible in their fleshy furrows, I saw they were open. The tip of his tongue, a mottled gray like his skin, wet his lips. His chin, but a knuckle-size knot lodged between his neck and lower lip, shone with spittle.

For a long moment Warthrop regarded this wretched object of his quest, saying nothing, allowing no expression to disclose his feelings. At last he seemed to shake himself from the spell and turned abruptly to the old woman.

"Leave us," he said.

"I cannot," replied she curtly. "It's against the rules."

He repeated the command without raising his voice but measuring the words as if she had failed somehow to understand them.

"Leave . . . us."

She saw something in his eyes, and whatever she saw cowed her, for she at once looked away, furiously shaking her keys, the symbols of her total authority, and said, "The doctor shall hear about this."

Warthrop had already turned back to the beached behemoth upon the bed. The sound of the jangling keys faded down the hall; she had left the door ajar. He directed me to close it. Then, as I pressed my back against its comforting sturdiness, Warthrop leaned over the bed, bringing his face close to the bloated one beneath him, and said in a loud, clear voice, "Hezekiah Varner! Captain!"

Varner did not respond. His eyes remained focused on the ceiling; his mouth hung open; his tongue restlessly swiped the lower lip, then retreated into the shadowy recesses of the toothless maw. From deep within his chest rose a sound somewhere between a hum and a moan. But for the uneasy tongue, he moved not a muscle, if any muscle remained efficacious buried beneath the rolls of fat.

"Varner, do you hear me?" asked the doctor. He waited for an answer, shoulders tensed, jaw tightly set, as behind him the flies fussed against the glass. The room was stifling and reeked of bleach. I breathed as shallowly as I could, and wondered if the doctor would mind if I cracked open the window for a bit of fresh air.

Warthrop raised his voice and fairly shouted into the man's face, "Do you know who I am, Varner? Were you told who has come to see you this night?"

The obese invalid moaned. The doctor sighed and looked at me.

"I fear we may be too late," he said.

"Who . . . ," moaned the ancient mariner, as if to disprove him. "Who has come?"

"Warthrop," the monstrumologist answered. "My name is Warthrop."

"Warthrop!" cried the captain. The eyes, as if loosed by the mention of the name, became as unsettled as his tongue, sliding back and forth in their sockets but refusing to focus upon the doctor's face. They tirelessly traversed the ceiling, where Warthrop's distorted shadow danced, thrown there by the lamp on the floor and looming over Varner like a demon spirit, dark, grotesque, huge.

"You know the name," said the doctor.

The enormous head gave the barest of nods.

"God pity me, I do. I know the name Warthrop," issued the guttural reply, choked in spittle. "'Twas all Warthrop's doing, the devil curse him and all his kin!"

"A curse is one explanation," said the doctor dryly. "Though I lean more toward Darwin's. The evidence is on my side, but time may yet prove me wrong and you right, Hezekiah Varner. Alistair Warthrop was my father."

There was no response but for the odd, strangled, wheezing moans.

"My father," continued the monstrumologist, "who commissioned you sometime in late '63 or early '64, I would guess, to sail to West Africa, perhaps Senegambia or lower Guinea, and return with a special cargo of particular interest to him. Yes? Did he not?"

"No . . . ," murmured the old man.

"No?" echoed the doctor, frowning.

"Not Senegambia or Guinea. Benin," groaned he. "The kingdom of Benin! Home to that godless mockery of royalty, the accursed ruler of that accursed land, the Oba, and I vow there is not to be found a heathen more foul or a libertine more loathsome in the four corners of the world!"

"The Oba of Benin had captured living specimens of *Anthropophagi*?" asked the doctor. He seemed startled by the notion.

"He houses a whole troop of the horrible beasts in a chamber beneath his palace."

"But *Anthropophagi* cannot survive in captivity. They starve to death."

"Not these, Warthrop," gasped the old smuggler. "These monsters were quite fat and happy, thank you! I saw it with my own two eyes, and if I were a braver man, I would pluck them out for the offense!"

"They were fed?" The doctor's tone was incredulous. "How?"

"Children, mostly. Twelve- or thirteen-year-old girls. Girls in the prime of their budding womanhood. Sometimes infants, though, squealing babes hurled naked into the hole. For in the center of the temple is a pit connected by a tunnel to the holding chamber. Into the pit the priests throw her; I have seen this, Warthrop; I have seen it! Cast down twenty feet to the bottom, whereupon she hurls herself against the smooth sides of the sacrificial abyss, scratching and clawing for a handhold, but of course there is none. There is no escape! The head priest gives the signal; the great wooden door rolls up; and they come. You smell it first, a rotten stench like death's decay, then the loud huffing and sharp clicks of their fangs snapping, as the doomed innocent erupts into frenzied screams, crying to her insensible judges above to have mercy. Mercy, Warthrop! They stare down at her with faces set in stone, and, as the beasts burst into the pit, her terror robs her of her last shred of dignity: Her bladder empties; her bowels let go. She collapses into the dirt, covered in her own filth, as they descend upon her in a mad rush, the bigger brutes leaping thirty feet from the tunnel's mouth to where she lays, the sacrificial lamb beneath those pagan lords whose mad whimsy condemned her to a fate unfit for even the most egregious malefactor. But their bloodthirsty gods demand; and so they supply.

"The head is the most coveted prize. The first to reach her seizes it and wrenches it from her neck, and her still-beating heart flushes her blood through that makeshift orifice; a steaming geyser shoots into the air and paints crimson their teeming alabaster bodies. They snarl and snap for a piece of the meat, for meat she be now; human she is no more. Shredded bits of her are flung far over the rim of the pit, spattering the spectators with the bloody remnants of her maidenly form. I lost sight of her in the melee, but 'twas a blindness blessed after the curse of sight. No vision of hell could surpass it, Warthrop. No image or word born in the mind of man could equal what I saw that day!"

(Though I have faithfully recorded here the old man's words, true to my memory of them, they did not flow with any grace, as a casual reading might lead one to believe. Punctuated with the same moans and grunts and unintelligible asides that peppered the entire interview, the foregoing soliloquy lasted nearly half an hour, with some prodding from the doctor, after many a breathy pause and phlegmy snuffle. At times the words were voiced so softly that the doctor was forced to bend low with his ear nearly touching the grayish lips. I have decided, for mercy's sake, to spare the reader these somewhat tiresome and frustrating divagations.)

"Or so I thought," moaned Varner after a moment of ill-settled silence that only the buzzing of the flies disturbed.

"So you thought? What do you mean, so you thought?"

"The king was loath to part with them, for what price do you put upon the heads of your gods?"

"But sell them to you the Oba did," observed the doctor. "He must have."

"Yes, yes, of course. After a fortnight of hard bargaining, he did, but not the number Warthrop desired. He wanted four, a mature pair and two of their infernal offspring. But we sailed with only three in our hold: a two-year-old cub, a young male, and the last . . ." He closed his eyes and took a deep, quivering breath. "The she-devil, the largest of her ferocious troop—larger than the biggest male, and he was near eight feet tall—the one the Benin feared more than any other. We took *that* one. We took *her*." Appalled by the thought after more than twenty years, mortified still, he shuddered beneath the snuggly tucked sheets.

"But why did he want four? Did he say?"

"Dear God, man, he did not say, and I did not ask! I did not even know when I sailed for that damnable country what the bloody things were. Warthrop offered a king's ransom for the work, and I cared not whether he wanted four or fourscore! The war had brought hard times to the *Feronia*. I accepted his offer without question, without a second thought!"

Warthrop turned away from the bed and in two steps was at the window, hands clasped behind his back, studying, in all appearance and of all things, the windowsill. He carefully picked up one of the dead flies, pinching its delicate wings between his thumb and forefinger, and then held it up as if to examine it for the cause of its demise.

The prostrate leviathan on the bed did not watch him. His gaze remained on the ceiling and whatever comfort its yellowed, irregular surface brought him, his enormous body as still as a corpse's beneath the spotless sheets. How long had he lain thus paralyzed, I wondered, unable to move neither head nor limb, forced to stare hour after hour, day after day, upon that blank canvas, and what terrible scenes of hell unleashed, unbounded by the dictates of our Victorian sensibilities, had his imagination painted there in the vibrant colors supplied by his merciless memory? *Poor paralyzed creature, no wonder Warthrop's father abandoned thee!* What succor could he offer to one whose very mind had betrayed the body that sustained it? Even if it so willed, could any intellect be stronger than the horror that freezes the marrow and locks the limbs? Stronger than the thickest dungeon chain is the metaphorical ropes that bound thee, Hezekiah Varner!

"Or so you thought," murmured the doctor, turning the fly in his hand. "Nothing could equal the vision of hell you saw that day . . . or so you thought."

Varner laughed, a sound as thin and crackling as autumn leaves beneath a heavy man's tread.

"Something went terribly wrong on your return passage to America, didn't it?" pressed the monstrumologist.

"He tried to warn me," was the wheezing reply.

"Who? Who tried to warn you?"

"The Oba! The old devil, on the morning we set sail, with a twinkle in his eye and a bright smile lighting his raven cheeks, asked what provisions we had made for them. He told me they can get quite 'tetchy' after several days without their 'victuals,' and offered two of his slaves to tide them over on the voyage. I rebuked the repulsive savage, for king though he called himself, that is what he was, a godless heathen. I am a Christian, I told him. I fear God and his judgment!"

"But you came to regret your rebuke," observed Warthrop.

"I had had assurances," Varner muttered. "I had had strict instructions from the monstrumologist. We reinforced the hold, welded iron bars across the portholes, fastened double locks upon the doors. Two hundred pounds of salt pork we had on board, and in Sapele we took on the livestock in kind and quantity precisely as Warthrop prescribed: twelve goats, five young calves, and seven chimps. 'Try the chimps if all else fails,' he told me. 'They are the closest relative to their preferred prey.' The closest relative! Heaven help us!"

Warthrop let fall the dead fly from his fingertips. It fluttered to the floor, and he pressed the tip of his boot down upon its desiccated carcass.

"Flies," he murmured pensively. "What of the flies?" He watched them for a moment bumping and fussing against the smeared pane before he turned to face Varner. "They refused to feed," he said. It was not a question.

"Aye, refuse they did, as you know, as you know all the rest, and so I will speak no more of it. I know not why you have come here in the dead of night, asking questions the answers to which you already know. I know not why you've come except to torment a sick and dying old man. I know not what pleasure my pain brings you, Warthrop, except it be God's truth you are your father's son! You know already

144 RICK YANCEY

what special order your father had filled and what fate befell the crew of the *Feronia*. What sadistic cause brings you here to my deathbed? To remind me of those awful days of death and the dread thereof, to give the knife your father sank a final twist before I am taken down by the dark angel's last embrace? Have mercy on me! Have mercy on me, Warthrop. Have mercy."

The doctor ignored this diatribe, this anguished plea punctuated by moans and whines. He ignored it and said, "They would kill immediately what you gave them—they are fiercely territorial—but they would not eat it. In a matter of days the ship's hold would reek worse than a slaughterhouse."

"No," whispered Varner, closing his eyes. "No more. I beg you."

"So they managed to escape somehow. There is nothing in the literature to suggest they can swim, so they broke *into* the ship, not *out* of it. And at least two survived until the grounding of the vessel at Swampscott. The adults, I would guess."

Varner sighed, a gravelly exhalation, like a shoe scraping over pebbles. The eyes came open, the mouth yawned, the tongue protruded, the voice escaped. "They ate the little one. It was her own cub, or so the Oba told me. The she-beast ripped him to shreds. With my own eyes—ah, these accursed eyes!—I saw her stuff his beating heart into her damnable mouth. The slender pickings that remained she left for her partner."

"She was the dominant of the two?"

"He was terrified of her; that much was clear."

"Yet she did not turn on him—why?"

Varner did not answer. His eyes had fallen closed again. Perhaps if he closed them, we, like the frightful images playing on the ceiling, would fall away into oblivion. He became so still for a moment that I thought he had stopped breathing.

"You asked why I've come," began Warthrop, returning to his side. "*She* sent me here, Hezekiah, for like you she survived the voyage of the *Feronia*, and her offspring have prospered in their adopted home. Her progeny, perhaps more than thirty strong now, are but a three hours' ride from this very room."

Varner moaned. By now we had endured it so long it had become background noise, like the flies beating themselves against the glass. *What of the flies?* Warthrop had wondered. *What of the flies?*

"My father tortured himself over your fate," he continued. "But showed no concern over the destiny of your peculiar cargo. He was many things, but he was foremost a scientist, and he would not have assumed the *Anthropophagi* had been lost or had perished of starvation at sea. Something or someone had assured him that there was no need to pursue the matter, and there were no witnesses who could do that, save one: the sole survivor of the cargo vessel *Feronia*. Is that why he sought you out after twenty years, to question you again as to its fate?"

Varner's flesh shone sickly gray in the lamplight as he

perspired beneath the mounds of covers, and for the first time I smelled something other than chlorine, the faintest pungent whiff of decay, and I wondered if perhaps a rat had crawled beneath the bed and died. It might have explained the flies. I glanced toward the blackened window. *What of the flies?*

"'Twas two things that doomed the *Feronia*: nature's fickleness and man's folly," Varner groaned, relenting at last to the monstrumologist's demand. "On the nineteenth day at sea, we hit the doldrums. For the next eight days, no wind, just a glassy sea as flat as the Kansas prairie, and the brutal tropical sun beating down upon our heads, day after day, eights days of it, until the crew became restless and bored and nearly always drunk. They took to tormenting them for sport. Placing bets on how long the wretched livestock the men dropped into the hold would last, and which monster would score the kill. Opening the trapdoor and teasing them through the bars, throwing things at them and delighting in the resulting rage. The big one, the female, could leap from the bottom twenty feet below to within a foot of the bars; they bet on that, too, on how close her claws could come without touching them. Wilson, the first mate, invented much of their sport. And it was Wilson who would pay for his folly first."

On the last day before the winds relieved the deadly calm that had stalled their passage, Varner told us, after another hot, indolent, rum-soaked day, Wilson and two of his shipmates decided to butcher one of the calves and offer a bloody slice of it to the *Anthropophagi*. Wilson's drunken reasoning ran thus: *The beasts won't eat what we offer because they know what it is! No self-respecting man-eater will deign to dine on a bloody goat. But if it don't know where it comes from, it might mistake it for man meat and eat it!* The plan was not approved by the captain; he had taken to his quarters with what he suspected might be malaria. His crew slaughtered the squealing sacrifice on deck and hurled its viscera overboard to the waiting sharks, oblivious in their besotted state that the fishes' feeding frenzy was mere prelude, an awful foreshadowing of future events.

Wilson and a roustabout named Smith sliced off a thick piece of the calf's flank and affixed it to a grappling hook. The hook they tied to one end of a thirty-foot coil of rope, and Wilson lowered the bait through the bars, lying on his belly so as to witness the results of his experiment.

It was dusk, a somnolent hour for the *Anthropophagi*, when they burrowed into their bowers of straw, nestlike beds that, the captain informed us, the creatures had spent hours carefully constructing and hours more maintaining. *Anthropophagi* are nocturnal hunters and spend most of the day sleeping, nursing their young, or performing bonding rituals with other members of the troop, the chief—and most bizarre—of which is the practice of picking bits of human flesh lodged in one another's teeth with the tip of their longest nail, the one extending from their middle finger. The operation is a delicate exercise in trust and self-control, for the recipient must remain perfectly still while its companion reaches far into the recesses of its tooth-encrusted maw to clean the back teeth. If it moves, the razor-sharp claw might slice open its gums, causing a reflexive slamming shut of its jaw, thus severing the hand of the one performing this invaluable service.

Wilson could barely see them as they nestled together in the straw at the farthermost corner of the ship's hold. The iron bars welded over the portholes limited the light within even on the brightest day, and now the sun was setting; the monsters were mere darker shadows among lighter shadows, barely discernible from the mounds of straw surrounding them; indeed, none could be certain whether those humped shadows represented their catch or were merely lumps of straw. Wilson swung the rope to and fro, calling softly for them to wake, that dinner was served. It had been more than three weeks since they had last fed, and they had to have been ravenous. His companions, Smith and the navigator, Burns, stood on either side of him, bending low, peering into the gloom, unable to contain their gleeful giggles. They urged Wilson on. "Lower!" they exhorted him. "Swing it closer so's they can smell it!" Into the dark and fetid hole they called, that prison that had once held a thousand pounds of human cargo, chattel for the cotton fields of Georgia and the indigo plantations of Louisiana—for the *Feronia* had been a slaving ship plying the illegal trade in the years prior to the war.

And now it was littered with the rotting carcasses of goats, the unrecognizable remains of the poor little chimpanzees that had followed them to their unthinkable end, and the stinking excrement of the beasts that had torn the animals' bodies apart with the ease of children pulling wings from flies. "Come on now, beasties! Wake thee up and have some dinner!" Their calls went unheeded. Unable to bring the bait within sniffing distance of the sleeping carnivores, Wilson shoved his right arm between the bars, dropping the rope another two feet into the hold. "Be ready to pull me up, lads," he told his companions as he swung the dangling chunk of fattened calf, fresh blood flying from its tip. "You've seen how fast they—"

The thought would never be finished. Wilson, however, in less than thirty terrifying seconds, would be.

Later, before meeting the same awful fate as the foolish Wilson, as he cowered half mad with terror within the captain's cabin behind the makeshift barricade, Burns told Varner what had happened in that horrifying half minute.

Whether she erupted from the straw bedding or from somewhere else, no one could say—Burns because he did not see it, Wilson and Smith because both were dead. Wilson, for fear he might drop it, had wrapped the rope twice around his wrist, so when she struck, her weight upon the hook yanked his shoulder clear through the bars, though he had released his hold in the instant of the attack. The rope unwound from his wrist and dropped to the floor, but Wilson's shoulder was now wedged in the narrow space between the iron bars. In a voice hoarse with rum and heightened by hysteria, Wilson cried for them to pull him up. Did he see her in the murk below? Did her black, soulless eyes, glowing in the light of a dying sun, meet his before the slathering mouth yawned wide and she leaped twenty feet straight up?

The claws that struck punctured clear through the muscle and sinew of his forearm, and, as they raked downward, borne by the creature's enormous girth, she swung her other talon up and latched on to one of the bars, inaccessible to her before Wilson had generously offered her a hand up. His companions recoiled in horror and dismay amid her savage snarls and their foolish companion's cries of fear and pain; his legs jerked; his feet pushed against the weathered planks as he tried to yank himself free, but the drag of her bulk upon his captured arm had wedged him even tighter. He threw back his head, twisting his face from side to side, for the she-beast had released his shredded arm, and now her bloody barbs slashed his face and swiped across the throat he had so considerately exposed. One of her nails must have found his carotid artery, for Burns reported that Wilson's screams abruptly ended in a gurgling report and a veritable geyser of blood, most of which cascaded in a robust stream into the monster's waiting mouth. His head fell forward with a sickening thud onto the metal bars. A final paroxysmal spasm of his legs, and Wilson lay still.

Too late did Smith remember the Colt revolver strapped to his side. By the time he'd freed it from the holster, she had ripped two bars from their heavy bolts, snapping the reinforced boards "as easily as a man snaps a toothpick," the same two bars directly beneath Wilson's lifeless body; his arm was free finally, but too late, and he tumbled into that noisome void to the hold below, where her companion, roused by the bedlam and, no doubt, the acrid smell of fresh blood, waited for him.

Smith fired wildly as she, hanging by one claw, tore out two more bars with the other. Burns could not say if any of the shots found their target; he turned and ran. The boards shuddered beneath his feet. The passage reverberated with the roar of gunfire and Smith's hysterical screams. As Burns scampered up the narrow stairs to the quarterdeck, the gunfire abruptly ended: Either Smith had run out of ammunition or she had heaved herself through the hole, and Smith, like Wilson, was a denizen of the living world no more.

In any case, when the *Feronia* was boarded by Union forces after her grounding, what was left of Smith could have fit, in Varner's words, "into a gunnysack."

At this point in his grim narration Varner paused. All color had drained from his countenance, and his body shook beneath the sheets. Memories can bring comfort to the old and infirm, but memories can also be implacable foes, a malicious army of temporal ghosts forever pillaging the long-sought-after peace of our twilight years. He had begged Warthrop not to make him recall those events he could not forget, for some recollections, as I myself know all too well, remain fresh in the mind whole decades after they are born.

Yet when he fell silent, Warthrop did not press him to go on. Perhaps he understood—as I have come to, much to my regret—that once we set forth upon certain lanes of our memory, there is no turning aside or doubling back. They must be traversed unto their bitter terminuses. It is that same compulsion that forces us to look at the terrible accident or stare with shameful curiosity at the pitiful victim in a circus sideshow. The memories of those dreadful final days aboard the doomed *Feronia* possessed her captain; he did not possess them.

"We stole below, brought up all the food and water we could muster, and sealed off the lower decks," the old man gasped finally. "Posted armed guards around the clock. The weather turned in our favor; with a leeward wind and fair skies, we made good time. The days were quiet, but 'twas an eerie peace, a deceitful calm, for once the sun sank below the foredeck, the pounding began and that infernal, incessant screeching. We could hear them, you see, testing the very boards beneath our feet, knocking and scraping and probing as they searched for weaknesses in the wood. The men drew lots for the night watch, but the winners could sleep no more than an hour or two, and each of those hours seemed longer than a day, and the nights longer than a year. The crew was divided and quarreled bitterly among themselves. Some thought we should abandon ship, take to the lifeboats and pray for rescue. 'We set her alight,' they said. 'Burn her to the waterline!' Others averred that our only hope lay in a surprise assault, attacking them while they slept. "'Tis only a matter of time till they break through,' they said. 'Better to face them at a time and place of our choosing.' I vetoed both these propositions. We were making excellent time; the ship seemed to be holding up under their assault; and by abandoning her we would only be trading the hazard of sharing Wilson's fate for the hazards of sunstroke and starvation. We sailed on."

At first the captain's decision seemed wise, for the enforced truce, like the beneficent weather, held. For a week, then two, until the morning of the forty-first day at sea, when the Bermuda archipelago was sighted to the north. The winds, which had for days blown steadily from the east, abruptly shifted. The southern sky grew as black as coal, and the seas rose a foot in the next hour, then two feet, then four as the sun disappeared behind a shroud of swift-moving clouds; the *Feronia* pitched in the grip of the roiling sea while waves twenty feet high crashed over the rails. The wind began to gust to fifty knots, forcing the crew to lower the sails lest they be ripped from the masts. The rain fell in drenching sheets, a pitiless rain driven by the remorseless gale. For hours the men huddled on deck, exposed to the elements, while the man-eating beasts below stayed warm and dry, an irony not lost on the men, and the debate was born anew. Already a man had nearly been washed to sea by a breaching wave. With each passing hour the storm strengthened; lightning popped and spat around the mainmast; wind drove the rain sideways in blinding sheets, making even the smallest step an exercise fraught with peril; and, as the day aged and the temperature plummeted, there was the danger of hypothermia. All watches and patrols were abandoned. As night fell the crew of the *Feronia* huddled in a single mass of shivering humanity on the quarterdeck, their fear of nature's wrath outweighed by their fear of her insatiable progeny.

"I know not who spied it first," confessed Varner. "Our lamps would not stay lit; the lightning was the only respite we had from the storm's black grip. 'Something's washed onto the deck!' someone cried. We waited all of us with bated breath for the next stroke of lightning, but saw nothing when it came, just shadows stark and a pall of rain. A second flash, then a third, and someone else shouted, 'There, see it there? By the mizzenmast!' They raised their rifles, but I ordered them down—what but the luckiest shot could hit the mark in that maelstrom? In truth I swear to you, I did not think these leaping shadows could be the beasts that roamed below. The man had seen it come over the rail, and what successful passage could one of those things have made up the slick sides of the *Feronia's* hull in a wind fifty knots or more? More than likely it was a fish washed from the bowels of the briny deep, a shark or a sailfish. It was impossible."

"No," said Warthrop quietly. "It is not." He was leaning against the wall beside the headboard, arms folded across his chest, chin down, eyes closed, as he listened. I recalled his warning in the cemetery: *Sharp eyes now, Will Henry. They are accomplished climbers.*

"Through a porthole most likely," ventured Varner. "And then up the side of the ship—but that is only my guess. I had seen a victim's skull in Benin with a crescent-shaped pattern of holes where their nails had broken through the bone; as long as a sloth's they are, Warthrop, and as hard as tungsten steel. Hard to believe now—impossible then—but up the side of the *Feronia* he must have climbed, punching hand-holds as he came, though why he chose to abandon shelter when the risk was greatest I do not know."

"Perhaps hunger drove him forth," said the doctor. "Though I doubt it. Fear, perhaps, either of those meteorological conditions utterly foreign to him . . . or, more likely, fear of his mate. They have that much in common with us: In moments of extreme stress, they have been known to turn upon each other."

"Not that night, Warthrop," groaned Varner. "That night he chose easier victims. Whether hunger or fear compelled him to strike, strike he did, quicker than the lightning itself, leaping forty feet from the deck below, landing square in our midst, and in the hellish racket that ensued—the screams and shouts of my startled crew, the snarls and roars of the attacking beast, the explosions on all sides of rifles and small arms, and the howl of the wind, the crash of the waves, the roar of the thunder—from that bloody bedlam I was shoved down the stairs and dragged to the door of my cabin."

It was the navigator, Burns, the sole survivor of the first attack, who hurled the captain into his quarters and slammed the door, while the battle raged on above them. The captain, still befuddled and weak from his bout of tropic fever, collapsed upon the floor as Burns ripped the heavy wardrobe from the wall and heaved it against the door as a barricade. He returned to the captain's side, whereupon, if he was expecting any thanks for his cool thinking and quick actions under fire, he was summarily disabused. The captain roundly cursed and berated him. He had lost his pistol in the forced retreat, and now they were trapped like rats— a bit drier than the poor rats above, but trapped nevertheless. Burns endured the abuse stoically and without remark, dragging his commander to the bedside and cautioning him to remain rooted to the spot. From this position they had a clear shot at the door and were hidden from sight should anything look through the windows behind the bed.

"In my closet," yelled the captain over the din on the deck directly over their heads. "Quickly, Burns!"

Burns scuttled across the floor—fearing if he walked upright he might attract attention through the windows— to the closet, in which he found an elephant gun and some ammunition. Varner ripped it from his hands and laughed bitterly while he loaded.

"A gift from the king of Ashanti. Never been fired. Let's hope we won't need to test it this night, Burns!"

They sat side by side at the foot of the bed. Lightning flashed through the windows, throwing long, fleeting, hard-edged shadows across the floor. The ship continued to roll and pitch violently at the mercy of the wind-stoked sea as the sound of gunfire gradually dwindled to one or two errant pops. The cries of the crew ceased altogether. It was the smashing sea and the earsplitting thunder and the yowling wind . . . and that was all. They strained their ears for any sound of the men left on deck. Had the men fled the onslaught altogether, scattering to the deck below and finding what cover they could? How many had survived, or had any at all? And what of the monster? Surely it had to be dead or seriously injured. Not even a creature of that immense size and speed could overcome twenty heavily armed men in a close-quarters fight. . . . Or could it? This they asked each other in hushed and breathless whispers, between the dazzling bursts of brilliant white light and its consort, the timber-rattling cannonade of thunder. Their teeth chattering, soaked to their skin, fingers nervously caressing the triggers of their weapons, they pondered and postulated but gave no thought toward what course of action they should pursue. Each moment that passed without incident was a victory; every second that ticked by uneventfully was a triumph.

But those seconds dragged, those minutes crawled, and they fell silent after a while, exhausted by questions to which they had no answers. Neither spoke, until Varner, in a grave and level voice, asked Burns how many bullets he had in his gun.

"I fired twice above, sir," replied the navigator. "So there are four left in the chamber."

"Save two," said Varner.

"Two, sir?"

"Fire twice if you must, but save the last two. One for me and one for yourself, Burns, should it come to that. I do not wish to share in Wilson's fate."

Burns swallowed hard and took a moment to answer. Perhaps he had been trying to frame an argument, an objection appealing to either faith or reason, and, more likely than not, he'd failed, for he said, "Yes, Captain."

"Tell me, Burns, are you a praying man?" asked the captain.

"I am a Christian, sir."

Varner chuckled and shifted the gun lying across his lap. It was quite heavy and was cutting off the circulation to his legs.

"So am I, but the two aren't always the same thing, Burns. Do you pray?"

"Never when I was young," confessed Burns. "More so now, Captain."

"Good," said the captain. "Say a prayer, Burns, and put in a word for your captain."

Dutifully Burns bowed his head and began to recite the Lord's Prayer. He spoke it slowly and with great feeling. When he finished, both men were deeply moved, and Varner asked him if he knew the twenty-third psalm.

"'Tis my favorite," Varner said. "'Though I walk through the valley of the shadow of death . . .' Do you know it, Burns? Say it if you do."

Burns did know it, and Varner closed his eyes as he recited. *The Lord is my shepherd; I shall not want . . .* The words comforted him; they reminded him of his childhood, of his mother and the way she'd held his hand during church, of long carriage rides on warm Sunday afternoons, and the marvelous family dinners that had lasted long into the evening. *He restoreth my soul . . .* How fleeting are those halcyon days of youth! How strange it is that the future seems so far away, yet how upon eagle's wings it arrives! In the batting of an eyelash, the chubby little boy sitting beside his mother in the family pew becomes a middle-aged man cowering in the dark. *Thou preparest a table before me in the presence of mine enemies . . .*

"Good, Burns," he murmured. "Very good."

"Thank you, sir," said Burns. "That's better now."

His legs jerked. His head snapped back against the footboard with a loud report. His eyes rolled in his head, and blood erupted from his open mouth, cascading down his shirtfront, spewing out between his shaking legs. His stomach bulged, expanding like a balloon filling with air. A button flew across the cabin. Then the hand, twice the size of a grown man's, tore through the blood-soaked material, alabaster skin stained crimson, bits of shredded intestines clinging to the three-inch nails. The massively muscled forearm followed, rotated ninety degrees, and the next second found Burns's head buried in the grip of the huge claw. With a sickening pop the beast tore his head completely off his shoulders and yanked it back through the hole punched through his heaving gut.

With a startled cry Varner hurled himself away, dragging the heavy gun with him. He took no time to rise, but swung the weapon toward the headless body of his friend. Shivering uncontrollably, forearm aching from the weight of the gun, struggling to keep his balance while the ship wallowed in the waves, Varner held his breath and willed his raging heart to slow. Light fought with dark; lightning flashed, then in an instant, darkness slammed back down.

But the beast under the bed was patient; she would wait for darkness to win the battle. She would launch her attack when her prey was at his most vulnerable, when his most precious sense was lost to him. A million years of evolution had prepared her for the moment. She was nature's preeminent predator, unlike her prey, whose species had only in the past ten thousand years or so surpassed her kind as lords of the earth. Driven from their ancestral home of savanna and coastal plain, those *Anthropophagi* not killed or captured by tribes like the Benin for sacrificial sport had taken refuge underground or in the vast rain forests of the Congo and the Guinea coast, and her kind had dwindled with the passing years. Even so, humanity's rise had benefited her, and not merely by providing her with an abundance of prey on which to feed: To survive in an ever-diminishing habitat, the *Anthropophagi* had become bigger, faster, stronger. When the pyramids first rose from the Egyptian sands, the average *Anthropophagi* male measured a little more than six feet from foot to shoulder; after a mere five thousand years, a blip in evolutionary time, he now towered more than seven feet. His claws were longer, as were his legs and his powerful arms. His eyes had grown to three times the size of ours, for we had driven him into the night, from his bower in the acacia tree to the cool forest floor or the dank caves of Kinshasa and the Atlas Mountains. Nature may have designed the beast beneath the bed, but the ascent of man had perfected her.

Varner would have but one chance at it: He had abandoned the box of ammunition in his mad scramble across the floor. If he missed, in the next breath she would be upon him. The image of the nude maiden in the pit, her headless corpse flailing in the mud and her own filth, flashed through his mind.

And then, as if that memory were a question, she gave her answer: The monster struck.

The footboard cracked in half as she barreled from her hiding place; it was that thunderous wallop of breaking wood that alerted Varner. He fired; the shot went wild. Something gave his leg a vicious yank: She had sunk her claws into his boot heel. He pounded between her hunched shoulders with the barrel of the gun as she dragged him toward her waiting mouth. He pressed the toe of his boot against the captured heel of the other and kicked hard. His foot slipped from the trap and he scrambled toward his desk, barely keeping his balance in the pitch and roll of the groaning deck.

Years before, he had made the purchase, in Borneo, from a Malayan blacksmith known for his genius in martial metallurgy: a kris, the wavy-bladed dagger that Varner used to open letters or, when nothing more suitable was handy, pick his teeth. Providence smiled on him in that moment, for the room lit up, and the lightning's bright light blazed upon the blade lying on the desk. He grabbed the kris and whirled around, thrusting the knife blindly into the dark.

"I cannot say what it was," wheezed the bedridden old man twenty-three years later. "Chance or destiny. Luck or my guardian angel's guiding hand that brought the blade in blindness thrust into the black eye of the accursed beast. Aye, blind was the jab that blinded her! Louder than the crashing wave and blasting thunder were her roars of fear and pain as she stumbled back, and I heard her fall into the remnants of my bed. Perhaps she tripped over poor Burns; I cannot say. I was already at the door."

Chance or destiny had given him opportunity. Now fear and its beneficent progeny, adrenaline, gave him the strength to seize it: He hurled the wardrobe out of his way, threw wide the cabin door, and dived into the driving sheets of rain.

"I looked neither left nor right," said he. "I cared not if

a rogue wave or an errant bolt took me. I made straight for the lifeboats."

But the rope lashing the boat to the *Feronia* had become hopelessly tangled and twisted by the incessant wind. Crouching in the freezing water that had pooled in the bottom of the raft, Varner squinted against the pounding rain, numb fingers pulling and tugging vainly at the knotted rope.

With head still bowed and eyes still closed, Warthrop said softly, "The knife."

"Aye, Warthrop! The knife. And do you know I worried with those knots even as I bit upon the blade, to keep my teeth from chattering completely from my head? Laughing hysterically at my own folly, wrapped about, as it were, in my own good fortune, I cut the rope and dropped straight down, into the sea."

No one spoke for some moments at the conclusion of his tale. Warthrop remained against the wall, and Varner lay as he had since we'd arrived, as motionless as a corpse, tongue darting between the purplish lips, eyes wandering across the jaundiced ceiling. I stood by the door, where I had stationed myself what seemed like hours before. Had I not seen for myself Eliza Bunton in that obscene embrace, or witnessed firsthand Erasmus Gray's demise, I no doubt would have thought his tale a product of a tortured mind, a delusion borne of an old salt's dementia, worth no more than the stories of mermaids, and leviathans able to swallow a ship and her crew whole. Could there be irony crueler than this? How, upon his rescue, the truth had brought him here, to a house for the mad, for only a madman believes what every child knows to be true: There are monsters that lie in wait under our beds.

"How extremely fortunate," said the doctor, breaking the silence at last. "Not only to have escaped that night, Hezekiah, but to have survived until your rescue."

"I lost them all, every one," responded Varner. "And I have spent the last twenty-three years in this horrid place, the final five years confined to this bed, with only my memories and that hideous key-jingling woman for company. Fortunate indeed, Warthrop! For if life is a question, then I have my answer: There is no escaping it. There is no cheating fate. I was the captain. The *Feronia* belonged to me and I to her, and I betrayed her. I betrayed and abandoned her, but fate cannot be betrayed or abandoned; she can only be postponed. My doom was to be eaten, you see, and though I folded my hand twenty-three years ago, the house has called the bet, and now I must pay up."

Warthrop stiffened. He stared for a moment at the bloated face, the teary, restless eyes, the scurrying tongue. He scooped the lamp from the floor and motioned to me.

"Hold this, Will Henry," he instructed me. "Higher. Now step back."

He grasped the covers with both hands. Varner's eyes slid

in his direction, and the old man whispered, "No," though he did not stir. Warthrop threw off the bedclothes, and I stumbled backward with an involuntary gasp.

Hezekiah Varner lay naked as the day he was born, beneath rolls of gelatinous fat, his body the same grayish hue as his face, a patchwork of gauze swatches hastily plastered in various locations over his colossal anatomy. A more grossly obese human being I had never seen, but it was not the sight that drove me backward or made me gasp; it was the smell. Multiplied tenfold was the cloying stench of rotting flesh I'd detected before, the foul odor I had attributed to a dead rat rotting beneath the bed. I glanced at the doctor, whose expression was grim.

"Up here, Will Henry," he said. "Hold it over him while I have a look at this."

I complied, of course, breathing shallowly through my mouth, but there was a faint taste of it on my tongue, the tingling tartness that accompanies any strong odor. As I held the lamp over the captain's immobile body, the doctor leaned over and gently began to pull back one of the bandages. Varner groaned, but moved not a muscle.

"Don't," he moaned. "Do not touch me!"

Warthrop ignored his plea. "Foolish of me not to see it at once. There could only be one explanation for them, Will Henry."

I nodded, one hand holding the lamp to illuminate his work, the other pressed against my mouth and nose. I nodded, but I did not understand. An explanation for whom? Varner's skin stretched as Warthrop peeled back the gauze. The bandage, like the others covering him, appeared dazzlingly white beside his gray flesh. The dressing was fresh. Mrs. Bratton had been quite busy while Starr had delayed us in the parlor, scrubbing down the room with bleach, stripping Varner of his filthy nightclothes, applying these bandages, piling high upon him the fresh linens, all in an effort to conceal . . . what? Not the bedsores, for they were to be expected on a bedridden man the size of Varner. The answer, of course, buzzed and fretted against the window behind us.

What of the flies?

"Don't touch me," whispered the human fodder beneath us.

The bandage removed by Warthrop had covered most of Varner's right side. Beneath it was a wound roughly the size of pie plate, oval in shape, the edges of which were jagged and enflamed, a weeping cavity bored down to his ribs, which I could see glistening a storm-cloud gray in the flickering lamplight. Bloody pus dribbled over the hole's lip and coursed down a crease formed by two rolls of belly fat toward the mildewed bottom sheet. Mrs. Bratton had not been able to strip it from the bed; Varner was too heavy for that.

Warthrop grunted, bringing his face to within inches of the wound, squinting into the recesses of the suppurating spot.

"No," he murmured, with a shake of his head. "Not here. . . . Ah! Yes, our good Mrs. Bratton missed a few. Do you see them, Will Henry? Look closely; see beneath the second rib there?"

I followed his finger to the spot where they squirmed and twisted in the organic muck of Varner's violated torso: three maggots performing a sinuous ballet in the infected meat, their black heads shining like polished beads.

"Don't . . . *touch* . . . me."

"We are myopic in our perceptions, Will Henry," breathed the doctor. "We populate our nightmares with the wrong carnivores. Consider it: The lowly maggot consumes more raw flesh than lions, tigers, and wolves combined. But what is this?"

He brushed past me to the foot of the bed. I had erred in thinking the captain was completely nude. He was not. He was wearing boots. The leather was cracked; the laces had deteriorated to bits of knotted string. The doctor gently pressed his finger into the swollen red skin directly above the boot on Verner's right foot, and Varner responded with a hoarse cry of pain. Warthrop slid a hand between the heel and the mattress, and that single touch caused the captain to stiffen in agony.

"For the love of God, if there be any mercy in you, Warthrop . . . !"

"The foot is swollen, badly infected, so too the left, I suspect," murmured the monstrumologist, ignoring his plea. "Bring the lamp closer, Will Henry. Stand there, at the foot of the bed. If I only had a sharp knife, I could cut it off."

"Not my boots. Please not my boots!"

Warthrop grasped the decaying shoe with both hands

and gave it a sharp yank. Were these the same boots that had saved his life twenty-three years before? I wondered. Had he lain there all that time, refusing to remove them, in superstitious dread? The muscles in the doctor's neck went taut as he strained to pull the boot off. Varner began to weep uncontrollably. He cursed. He let loose with a string of blasphemies and invectives wrapped in heart-wrenching sobs.

The shoe broke apart in the doctor's hands as it pulled free. The stink of decomposing flesh washed over us in an unwonted, nauseating wave. When the boot came off, the skin encased within came with it, sloughing off in a single, curdled mass, and thick, viscous pus the color of pond scum gushed onto the sheets.

Warthrop stepped back with an expression of disgust and dismay. "God damn them for this," he said in a low and dangerous voice.

"Put it back on!" cried the captain. "It hurts. It *hurts.*"

"Too late," muttered Warthrop.

He looked up into my tear-streaked face. "The infection has spread into his bones," he whispered. "He has only hours, no more than a day."

He dropped the shattered shoe upon the floor and returned to Varner's side. With great tenderness he laid his hand upon the suffering man's forehead and looked deeply into his eyes.

"Hezekiah, Hezekiah! It is very bad. I will do all I can, but—"

"There is only one thing I want," whispered Varner.

"Tell me; I will do all within my power."

With momentous effort, a triumph of human will over inhuman circumstance, the old man raised his head an inch off the pillow and whispered, "*Kill me.*"

The doctor did not answer. He remained silent for a moment, gently caressing the fevered brow, and then straightened slowly with the slightest of nods. He turned to me.

"Will Henry, wait for me outside."

"Out—outside, sir?" I stuttered.

"If you spy her coming down the hall, knock twice upon the door."

He turned back to the dying man, confident, as always, in my immediate obedience. He slid one hand beneath Varner's head and with the other drew from beneath it the pillow. Without turning his head toward me, he said in a thick voice, "Do as I say, Will Henry."

I set the lamp upon the floor, and the shadow thrown over the bed obscured the doctor's face and the man over whom he hovered: a dark shroud for dark business. I left them frozen thus in that melancholy tableau, closing the door behind me, and I sucked the air of the hallway to the very bottom of my starved lungs, like a swimmer breaking the steely clutch of a tide most cruel. I pressed my back against the wall between Varner's door and his neighbor's and slowly slid down, wrapping my arms around my folded legs and pushing my wet face into my closed knees. There was a scratching sound behind the neighbor's door, and the same guttural voice I had heard before spoke again, saying, "Hello again, little one. Are you back to see me? Don't be shy. I know you're there." The person behind the door sniffed a horrid skin-crawling snuffle. "I can *smell* you. Come now, be a good child and open the door. We can *play*. I'll be nice; I *promise*."

I let go my knees and pressed my hands over my ears.

How long I huddled in that miserable hallway while the disembodied voice whispered and pleaded for me to open his door, I cannot say. I was comfortless, inconsolable, haunted by the memories of the maddening buzz and pop of the flies against the windowpane and the gurgling cry of Hezekiah Varner— *Not my boots. Please not my boots!* Time passes differently in places like the Motley Hill Sanatorium. Like during the ill-fated expedition of the *Feronia*, an hour there seemed longer than a day, and the nights longer than a year. What comfort could be taken in the surety that day follows night in a place such as that, when the day is composed of the same tedious routine, a purgatory of selfsame hours? What meaning has an hour when that hour is indistinguishable from any other? A new day dawns, another season comes and goes, a year passes and then another, and another, until twenty-three years have slipped into oblivion. Ah, Hezekiah, no wonder you remember your final voyage as if just yesterday you had thrown yourself upon the mercy of the briny deep! The intervening years are sucked down these acheronian halls like light into a black hole while you helplessly teeter upon the event horizon, where time is measured by the beating of a fly's wing in the stagnant air.

How foolish I now felt to have judged the doctor for taking the life of Erasmus Gray. *No more absurd or insidious a precept has ever been laid down than "Where there is life, there is hope,"* he had averred, and what further proof was required beyond the case of Hezekiah Varner, captain of the doomed *Feronia?* Life he had, but what hope? His fate was no different from that of the fair virgin thrown into the sacrificial pit of the Oba—nay, it was worse, for that savage feeding frenzy lasted but a few seconds, while the maggots' endured for weeks. Could any fate be more hopelessly horrifying than that? To be eaten while cognizant of your own consumption? No doubt Erasmus would have begged as Varner did, *Kill me,* and, no doubt, as the doctor had said, he would have thanked him if he could.

It came as a surprise, then, when the doctor opened the door—his long shadow thrown by the lamplight across the floor and up the opposite wall—lowered himself beside me to assume a similar pose of weary resignation, pressed his fists against his black-rimmed eyes, and said, "I cannot do it, Will Henry."

He laughed humorlessly and added, "I cannot decide which it is, a triumph of will or its failure. Perhaps it is both.

You see why I prefer science to morals, Will Henry. What is *is*. What might be only *might* be. They allowed him to lie in that bed unmoved until his own weight produced the infected sores into which the flies laid their eggs, and now that infection has reached his bones. He is doomed, Will Henry; there is no hope of recovery."

"Then why can't you . . . ?" I whispered.

"Because I do not trust my own motives. I do not know whose hands would hold the pillow, his . . . or mine."

He stood up with a rueful shake of his head and bade me rise. "Come, Will Henry. We've one final piece of business here. The theme of this affair is shaping up to be one of accounting and recompense. *What of the flies* indeed! The maggots that feed upon Varner's body; the worms of doubt and guilt that fed upon my father's soul. There are monsters like the *Anthropophagi*, and then there are the monsters of a more banal bent. What *is* still is, Will Henry, and will always be!"

He strode down the hall without a backward glance. I scurried after him, light-headed with relief that our sojourn there was nearing its end. Down the long hall, in which even at this late hour rang the calls and cries, the screeches and screams of the house's confined "guests," down the narrow, creaking stairs to the first floor hall, where the dour Mrs. Bratton waited, a splotch of white powder on her hooked, witchlike nose. She had donned both an apron and a pained, unnatural-looking smile.

"Are you finished with the patient, then, Doctor?" she asked.

"I am not finished," snapped Warthrop. "Though he nearly is. Where is Starr?"

"Dr. Starr has retired for the evening," she answered stiffly, clearly taking issue with his tone. "It is very late."

The monstrumologist barked a bitter laugh. "Without a doubt, my good woman! What do you keep here for pain?"

A stern frown, much more natural than her smile, appeared. "For pain, Doctor?"

"Laudanum . . . or morphine, if you have it."

She shook her head. "We have aspirin. Or if the patient is particularly uncomfortable, the doctor allows them a sip or two of whiskey."

"Neither will do much good in this case," said Warthrop.

"Is he feeling poorly?" wondered she with a perfectly straight face. "He hasn't complained to me."

"He will not live out the morrow," the doctor said, his cheeks flushed. It took every ounce of his inestimable self-control to keep from seizing her by her scrawny neck and throttling her. "Fetch me the whiskey."

"I can't do that without the doctor's approval," she protested. "And he left strict instructions not to be disturbed."

"You have my permission to 'disturb' him, Mrs. Bratton," snarled Warthrop. "Or I'll have the town constable do it for you."

He turned on his heel and marched back toward the

stairs. My heart sank. I thought our stay, like that night, would never end. As we passed the parlor, Warthrop directed me to grab the small rocking chair by the mantel. I followed him up the stairs, lugging the chair.

"The whiskey, Mrs. Bratton!" he shouted over his shoulder. "And a bottle of aspirin!"

We returned to Varner's room. Warthrop had covered him again, but the smell of human decay still lingered in the air. I placed the chair beside the bed, Warthrop sat down, and the deathwatch began. Mrs. Bratton arrived with the whiskey and the aspirin, refusing to cross the threshold, staring daggers at Warthrop as I took the tray from her.

With casualness bizarre in this dolorous circumstance, she asked, "I've baked a batch of cranberry muffins. Would you or your boy care for one, Doctor?"

"No, thank you," replied the doctor. He swallowed hard. "I'm not hungry."

"As you like," she said archly. "Will you be needing anything else, Doctor?"

He ignored her. She glanced at me. I looked away. She left us.

"Close the door, Will Henry," he said softly. He lifted Varner's head and slipped four aspirin into his half-open mouth. He pressed the mouth of the bottle against his discolored lips. "Drink, Hezekiah. Drink."

For the next hour the captain slipped in and out of consciousness, muttering incoherently whether awake or passed out, groaning and sighing, grunting and moaning, eyes, even when closed, ever moving. Dr. Starr never appeared.

"We've a Hydra in this affair, Will Henry," Warthrop said as he stroked Varner's brow. "For every puzzle solved, two more rise in its place. We now know only two of the creatures were brought to our shores. Given an average birthrate of two off-spring per year and accounting for losses owing to accident and disease—and the occasional male lost during the breed-ing season—it appears both must have survived the ground-ing of the *Feronia*, and the pod we encountered is the sole progeny of the original pair. Thirty to thirty-five individuals, then . . . and no more."

He sighed. "Which raises the question of *why*. Why did my father desire more than one? If he wished to study the species, either in the wild or in the captivity of the Benin, why did he not go to Africa himself? My mother was dead; I was away at school in London; there were no ties to keep him in New Jerusalem. He had shown no hesitation in the past to go wherever his inquiries led him, and was no stranger to hazardous expeditions. He wanted living specimens brought here, and he paid a king's ransom for it. Why?"

He stroked the old man's brow absently as if his minis-trations could coax out the answer. "*Why?*"

Neither the dying man nor I could offer a plausible expla-nation: He was unconscious and I had reached the end of my endurance. I sat upon the floor with my back pressed against the wall, unable to stifle my yawns or keep my heavy lids from drooping. The doctor swam in and out of focus, and the sound of his voice receded into the pooling shadows of the little room. The hum of the flies, the captain's ragged breath, the rhythmic creak of the rocking chair, even the muffled symphony of the afflicted in the hall without—all merged in my ears to a lulling drone. I fell asleep as dawn approached, but not the doctor. With bowed back he bore the burden his father had bequeathed to him. He did not rest; he kept the vigil. Though his body was still, his mind furiously worked on.

I awoke with a stiff neck and a very bad headache. The filthy windowpane filtered the meritorious morning sun, whose light broke like waves against the seawall of dust and grime. In the gloom I could make out the doctor, still sitting in the small rocking chair, fully alert, chin cupped in his hand as he considered with bloodshot eye the immotile form before him. Between the sleeping and the waking, Warthrop had drawn the covers over the captain's head.

Hezekiah Varner was no more.

I rose upon wobbly legs, using the wall behind me for support. The doctor looked not my way, but sighed loudly and rubbed his face. I could hear the palm of his hand scratching against his unshaven cheek.

"It is finished, Will Henry," he said.

I offered meekly, "I'm sorry, sir."

"Sorry? Yes, I too am sorry. All of this"—he gestured toward the bed—"is exceedingly *sorry*, Will Henry."

He pushed himself to his feet and swayed for a moment on legs that did not seem much sturdier than mine. I followed him from the room. Together we walked somnolently down the long hallway, crowded as ever with the calls and cries of the tormented. Mrs. Bratton was waiting for us at the foot of the stairs. She gave the doctor an impassive nod.

"And how is the captain this morning, Doctor Warthrop?" she asked.

"Dead," replied Warthrop. "Where is Starr?"

"Dr. Starr has been called away on urgent business."

The monstrumologist stared at her for a long moment, and then laughed mirthlessly. "No doubt he has!" he exclaimed. "And you will be quite busy in his absence, I am sure. There is much to be done once I've notified the state police, isn't there, Mrs. Bratton?"

She responded stiffly, "I've no idea what you mean, Dr. Warthrop."

"Regrettably that very well might be so," acknowledged the doctor icily. "And all the more appalling if it is! To view your shameful neglect as altogether fitting and humane is beyond deplorable—it is inhuman. You may inform your master that I am not finished here. I am not finished, but Motley Hill is. I shall personally see to it that he is punished to the full extent of the law for the homicide of Hezekiah Varner."

He stepped toward her. She flinched, shrinking back in the fiery face of his righteous indignation.

"And I pray—as he should *not*—that the law shows him—and *you*—the same mercy you have shown these poor souls entrusted to your care."

He brushed past her cowering form without waiting for a reply. He threw open the heavy front door with such force that it slammed into the wall with a reverberating crash. Halfway across the overgrown lawn, the doctor drew rein and turned in his saddle to regard the old house with its peeling paint and sagging roof, brooding in the bright morning light.

"Though Varner himself might argue it about his life," he mused, "it cannot be said about his death, Will Henry. His death shall not be in vain. There will be justice for Hezekiah Varner and all those who suffer inside those accursed walls. I will see to that. By God, I will see to that!"

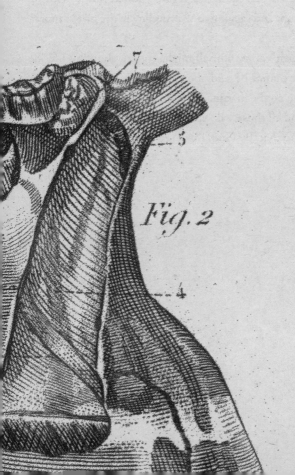

Fig. 2

FOLIO II

Residua

SEVEN

"You Have Failed Me"

I did not know what to expect upon our return to 425 Harrington Lane, beyond something for my empty stomach and a pillow for my weary head. From the curt summons I had posted by express mail the day before, I suspected the doctor intended to await the arrival of John Kearns before proceeding against the *Anthropophagi*, but I dared not ask him, for he had quickly fallen into one of his taciturn moods, growing more uncommunicative with each passing mile.

He left me to stable our horses while he disappeared inside the house. Once they were watered and fed and the dusty miles brushed from their coats, and after a brief visit with ol' Bess, I dragged myself inside, indulging in a tiny, flickering hope that the table might be laid with something of passing palatability. It was a vain hope. The basement door hung open, the lights below burned brightly, and ascending the narrow staircase was a clamor of slamming drawers and heavy objects being dragged or shoved across the stone floor. After a few minutes of this violent upheaval, he came bounding up the stairs, gasping for breath, cheeks ablaze. Ignoring me, he barreled down the hall and into the study, wherein another ruckus of slamming drawers began. When I peeked through the doorway, he was sitting at the desk, rifling through a drawer.

"Must be something," he muttered to himself. "A letter, a bill of lading, a contract for services, *something* . . ."

I jumped when he slammed shut the drawer. He looked up with a startled expression, as if I, his sole companion in life, were the last person he expected to see.

"What is it?" he demanded. "Why are you hovering there like that, Will Henry?"

"I was going to ask—"

"Yes, yes. So ask. Ask."

"Yes, sir. I was going to ask, sir, if you'd like me to run to the market."

"The market? Whatever for, Will Henry?"

"For something to eat, sir. We've nothing in the house, and you haven't eaten since—"

"For the love of God, boy, is that all you ever think about?"

"No, sir."

"What else, then?"

"What else, sir?"

"Yes, what else. Besides food, what else do you think about?"

"Well, I . . . I think about many things, sir."

"Yes, but what are they? That was my question."

He glowered at me, thin fingers drumming on the polished desktop.

"You know what gluttony is, Will Henry."

"Yes, sir. And hunger, too, sir."

He fought back a smile. At least I told myself that; he may very well have been fighting an urge to hurl the handiest heavy object at my head.

"Well?" he asked.

"Sir?" I asked.

"What else occupies your thoughts?"

"I try to . . . understand, sir."

"Understand what?"

"What I am to . . . the purpose of . . . the things you are trying to teach me, sir . . . but mostly, to be honest, sir, for lying is the worst kind of buffoonery, I try not to think of more things than the things I try to, if that makes sense, sir."

"Not much, Will Henry," said the doctor. "Not much."

With a dismissive wave he added, "You know where we keep the money. To the market if you like, but straight there and straight back, Will Henry. Speak to no one, and if anyone speaks to you, all is well; I am busy with my latest treatise, whatever seems most natural to you, as long as it is not the truth. Remember, Will Henry, *some* falsehoods are borne of necessity, not foolishness."

With a much lighter heart I left him to his rummaging. Glad was I for this brief respite—it was not an easy thing, being an apprentice to a monstrumologist of the doctor's temperament—and doubly glad for the very mundanities that most laymen take for granted and even bemoan in their shortsightedness. The simple chores and errands that filled my days were welcome reprieves from the nights' dark business, filled with unexpected callers and mysterious packages, midnight sojourns in the laboratory and pilgrimages to far-flung forgotten regions of the world where the natives had not suffered to be civilized to the point where they forgot to fear what might lurk in the dark. The everyday drudgeries of life were not so to me. After cataloguing the internal organs of a creature from a nightmare, washing the cutlery was a joyous exercise.

So I fairly bounded up the stairs to wash up. I changed my shirt. (It smelled faintly of Captain Varner's room, a peculiar and distinct amalgamation of bleach and decomposition.) But one small item was missing, and before leaving I sought out the doctor. I found him in the library, pulling books at random from the shelves, flipping through the pages before tossing them helter-skelter upon the floor.

"Are you back, then? Good; I need your help," he said. "Start at the far end of that shelf over there."

"Actually, sir, I haven't left yet."

"I beg to differ, Will Henry. You've been gone for some time."

"Only to wash up, sir."

"Why, were you dirty?" He did not wait for a response. "So you've decided you're not hungry after all?"

"No, sir."

"You're not hungry?"

"I am hungry, sir."

"Yet you just said you were not."

"Sir?"

"I asked if you had decided you were not hungry after all, and you replied, 'No, sir.' That is my memory of it, at any rate."

"No, sir. I mean, yes, sir. I mean . . . I was wondering . . . That is, I've been meaning to ask if you found my hat."

He stared at me uncomprehendingly, as if I were speaking an exotic foreign tongue.

"Hat?"

"Yes, sir. My hat. I think I lost it at the cemetery."

"I didn't know you owned a hat."

"Yes, sir. I wore it to the cemetery that night, and it must have fallen off when they . . . when we left, sir. I was wondering if you might have found it when you returned to . . . to tidy things up there."

"I didn't see any hats, except the one I gave you to destroy. Whenever did you acquire a hat, Will Henry?"

"It was mine when I came, sir."

"When you came . . . where?"

"Here, sir. To live here. It was my hat, sir. My father gave it to me."

"I see. Was it his hat?"

"No, sir. It was my hat."

"Oh. I thought perhaps it held some sentimental value."

"It did, sir. I mean, it does."

"Why? What is so special about a hat, Will Henry?"

"My father gave it to me," I repeated.

"Your father. Will Henry, may I give you a piece of advice?"

"Yes, sir. Of course, sir."

"Don't invest too much of yourself in material things."

"No, sir."

"Of course, that bit of wisdom is not original to me. Still, much more valuable than any hat. Have we satisfied your inquiry, Will Henry?"

"Yes, sir. I suppose it's lost for good."

"Nothing is ever truly lost, Will Henry. Unless we are talking about the evidence my father must have left behind regarding this unholy business. Or the reason you remain standing there uselessly while I look for it."

"Sir?" He had completely lost me.

"Either get yourself to the market or help me, Will Henry! Snap to it! I don't know how you manage to draw me into these philosophical diversions."

"I just wanted to know if you found my hat," I said.

"Well, I did not."

"That's all I wanted to know."

"If you're looking for my permission to purchase a new one, get thee to a haberdasher, Will Henry, with the caveat that you do so sometime today."

"I don't want a new hat, sir. I want my old hat."

He sighed. I scampered away before he could fashion a reply. It had seemed a very simple matter to me. Either he had found my hat at the cemetery or he had not. A simple *No, I did not find your little hat, Will Henry* would have sufficed. I did not feel altogether responsible for the circuitous nature of our discourse. There were times when the doctor, despite being America-born and England-educated, seemed flummoxed by the precepts of normal conversation.

I arrived in town hatless but happy. For a few precious minutes, at least, I was free of all things monstrumological. Particularly trying had been the last two days. Had it been only two days since the old grave-robber had appeared at our door with his ghastly burden? It seemed like two times twenty. Hurrying along the cobblestone streets of New Jerusalem's bustling center, breathing deep the crisp, clean air of early spring, I thought, for a fleeting moment, as I'd thought more than once since I had come to live with him (as anyone in my position might think), of escape.

The doctor had not thrown bars over the windows; he did not lock me inside my little alcove like a caged bird by night, or shackle me to a post by day. Indeed, when not in need of my "indispensable" services, he hardly took notice of me at all. If I fled while he wallowed in the malaise of one of his melancholic spells, a month might pass before he realized I was gone. Like the afflicted slave laboring in the cotton fields of the old South, I did not worry about where I would go or how I would get there or what I would do once there. Those concerns seemed but trivialities. The point of freedom, after all, is freedom itself.

Often over the years I have asked myself why I never ran away. What bound me to him beyond the inertia to which all humans are susceptible? I was not bound by blood. Not by oath. Not by law. Yet every time the thought of flight flittered across my consciousness, it disappeared as ephemerally as a will-o'-the-wisp, an ignis fatuus, an elusive glow over the marshland of my psyche. To leave him was not unthinkable—I confess I thought of it often—but to be away from him was. Was it fear that kept me by his side, fear of the unknown, fear of being adrift and alone, fear that I might meet a fate far more frightening than service to a monstrumologist? Was it that an unpleasant "known" is preferable to any unpredictable "unknown"?

Perhaps that was part of it; perhaps it was fear in part, but not in whole. For the first eleven years of my life I had witnessed the esteem—nay, the profound and consummate awe—with which my beloved father had regarded him. Long before I met Pellinore Warthrop in person, I had encountered him countless times in my mind, a towering genius to whom my family owed everything, a looming presence under whose long shadow we dwelled. *Dr. Warthrop is a great man engaged in great business, and I shall never turn my back upon him. . . .* It is no exaggeration to say that my father loved him with an affection that bordered on idolatrous worship, just as it is no overstatement that this same love would lead him to make the ultimate sacrifice: My father died for Pellinore Warthrop. His love for the doctor cost my father his life.

Perhaps, then, it was love that stayed me. Not love for the doctor, of course, but love for my father. By remaining I honored his memory. Leaving would have invalidated his most cherished belief, the one thing that had made service to the monstrumologist—and the terrible cost of that service— bearable: the idea that Warthrop was engaged in "great business" and to be his assistant meant you, too, were part of that greatness; that, indeed, without you his "business" could not even have approached that exalted level. Running away would have been tacit acknowledgment that my father had died in vain.

"Why, bless me, look here who this is!" cried Flanagan, rushing toward the door upon the tinkling of the bell. "Missus, come see what the wind's blown in!"

"I'm *busy*, Mr. Flanagan!" called his wife querulously from the back room. "Who is it?"

The apple-cheeked purveyor of, among other fruits and vegetables, apples, dropped his hands upon my shoulders and peered with sparkling green eyes into my upturned face. He smelled of cinnamon and vanilla.

"Little Will Henry!" he called over his shoulder. "Sweet Mother Mary, I don't think I've seen you in a month," he directed to me, his cherubic features glowing with pleasure. "How have you been, m'boy?"

"Who?" Mrs. Flanagan bellowed from the back.

Flanagan winked at me and turned to shout, "The master of 425 Harrington Lane!"

"Harrington Lane!" she shouted back, and at once appeared in the doorway, a heavy carving knife in her huge red-knuckled hand. Mrs. Flanagan was easily twice the size of her husband and three times as stentorophonic. When she spoke, the very windows rattled in their frames.

"Oh, Mr. Flanagan!" she boomed when she saw me. "It's only Will Henry."

"*Only* Will Henry. Listen to you, Missus." He smiled at me. "Don't listen to her."

"No, sir," I responded automatically. Thinking this might offend his knife-wielding Amazonian mate, I quickly appended, "Hello, Mrs. Flanagan; how are you, ma'am?"

"I would be much better without these constant interruptions," she roared. "My husband, whom my sainted mother *warned* me not to marry, thinks I've nothing better to do than be the brunt of his silly jokes and ridiculous riddles all day."

"She's in a bad mood," whispered the grocer.

"I'm always in a bad mood!" she shouted back.

"Has been since the potato famine of '48," whispered Flanagan.

"I heard that!"

"Forty years, Will Henry. Forty years," said he with a theatrical sigh. "But I love her. I love you, Missus!" he called.

"Oh, stop it. I can hear every word you say, y'know! Will Henry, you've lost weight, haven't you? Be honest, now."

"No, Mrs. Flanagan," I said. "I've just grown a bit."

"That's it, Missus," interjected Flanagan. "It isn't lost; it's just *redistributed*, eh? Right!"

"Oh, nonsense," she rumbled. "These eyes aren't *that* bad yet! Look at him, Mr. Flanagan. Look at his hollow cheeks and bulging forehead. Why, his wrists are no wider round than a chicken's neck. Talk of famine! There's one going on right now in that horrible house on Harrington Lane."

"More than just famine, if the tales I hear have but a smidgen of truth to them," ventured Flanagan with an elevation of an elfish eyebrow. "Eh, Will Henry? You know the stories we hear: mysterious comings and goings, packages delivered in the dark, midnight callers and the sudden, long absences of your master—you know, don't you?"

"The doctor doesn't discuss his work with me," I said carefully, remembering his counsel: *Some falsehoods are borne of necessity, not foolishness.*

"The *doctor*, aye. But what exactly is he a doctor *of*?" barked Mrs. Flanagan, eerily echoing Erasmus Gray.

And I echoed the same feeble reply, "Philosophy, ma'am."

"He's a deep thinker." Mr. Flanagan nodded gravely. "And God knows we need all of those we can get!"

"He's a queer man with queerer habits," she countered, shaking her blade at him. "As was his father *and* his father's father. All the Warthrops were queer."

"I rather liked his father," said her husband. "Much more—oh, what is the word?—*personable* than Pellinore. Very friendly, though in a regal kind of way. Reserved, to be sure, and a bit—oh, what do I need?—*aloof*, but not in any haughty or lordly way. A man of culture and breeding. From good stock, you could say."

"Yes, husband, you could *say* whatever you like, and usually do, but Alistair Warthrop was no different from any of the other Warthrops. Miserly, stuck-up, and standoffish is what he was, a friend to no one save the unsavory transients who oft darkened his door."

"Gossip, Missus," insisted Flanagan. "Gossip and idle rumor."

"He was a sympathizer. That much isn't gossip."

"Don't listen to her, Will," he cautioned me. "She loves to go on."

"I heard that! My ears work as well as my eyes, Mr. Flanagan."

"I don't care whether ye heard or not!" he yelled back.

Nervous now in the presence of this escalating domestic brawl, I grabbed an apple from the bin beside me. Perhaps if

I selected my purchases, the fight might dissipate under the onslaught of commerce.

"They came asking after him," rejoined his wife, her wide face turning the color of the Red Delicious in my hand. "You remember as well as me, Mr. Flanagan."

Flanagan did not answer. The twinkle in his smiling Irish eyes had vanished. His lips were painfully pursed.

"Who came asking after him?" I blurted, unable to help myself.

"No one," growled Flanagan. "The missus is—"

"The Pinkertons, that's who!"

"—stirring tempests in teapots," he finished with a shout.

"Who are the Pinkertons?" I asked.

"Detectives!" she answered. "A whole troupe of them."

"There were two," said Flanagan.

"All the way from Washington," she continued, ignoring him. "In the spring of '61."

"The spring of '62," corrected her spouse.

"With orders from the War Department—from Secretary Stanton himself!"

"No, it wasn't Stanton."

"It most certainly was Stanton!"

"Then it couldn't have been the spring of '61, Missus," said Flanagan. "Stanton wasn't made secretary till January of '62."

"Don't tell me, Mr. Flanagan. I saw the orders myself."

"Why would undercover men for the government show you, a grocer's wife, their orders?"

"What did they want?" I asked. The year (or years) in question nearly coincided with the mission to Benin. Could it have been mere coincidence, the proximity of the two events, the visit from the detectives on behalf of the Union, and the sailing of the *Feronia* but two years later? Had the government somehow learned of the elder Warthrop's plan to bring *Anthropophagi* to America? My heart began to race, for it seemed that this serendipitous encounter might provide the key to unlocking the riddle plaguing the doctor, the answer to the anguished *Why?* at the dying captain's bedside. What would he think if I returned with the answer to that conundrum, after intimating that I had little between my ears; that I was, in essence, a silly, stupid child who could not answer a simple question without becoming befuddled and tongue-tied? How much would my stature grow in his eyes! I might prove myself truly "indispensable."

"They wanted to know if he was a true Union man, which he was, through and through," replied Flanagan before his agitated wife could. "And it really wasn't about him they were asking, if you remember, Missus. It was those two Canadian gentlemen . . . can't recall their names now, but it's been nigh twenty-six years."

"Slidell and Mason," she snapped. "And they weren't Canadian, sir. Rebel spies is what they were."

"The Pinkerton men never said as much," he indicated to me with a wink.

"Both were seen at that house," she said. "That house on Harrington Lane. More than once."

"Doesn't prove anything about Warthrop," he argued.

"It proves he associated with agitators and traitors," she shouted back. "It proves he was a sympathizer."

"Well, you may think so, Missus, and say so, like now, like everyone did back then, but it doesn't necessarily make it so. The Pinkertons left town, and Dr. Warthrop stayed, didn't he? If they had proof of anything, they'd've carted him away. Right? Now you go on about this man—this good man who never did harm to anyone that I know of—but that's all it is. Just going on. It isn't right, Missus, speaking ill of the dead."

"He was a rebel sympathizer!" she insisted. My ears had begun to ring from all her shouting. "He was different after the war, and you know it, Mr. Flanagan. Holed up in that house for weeks at a time, and when he did come out, moped around town like someone who's lost his best friend. Never so much as a 'how do you do' crossed his lips, even when you passed right by him on the street, like he'd been dumbstruck, like a man whose heart's been broken."

"That may be so, Wife," conceded Flanagan with a heavy sigh. "But you can't say it was because of the war. A man's heart is a complicated thing, a little less so than a woman's, I'll admit, but complicated it still is. Perhaps something did break it, as you say, but you can't say what it was that broke it."

I could not say, either, but thought I had a good idea: By the war's end, Alistair Warthrop's hands were stained with blood. Not blood spilled upon the battlefield but poured out by the gallon aboard the *Feronia*—that blood, and the blood belonging to all the future victims of the monsters he'd worked so tirelessly to bring to our soil, all the victims sacrificed upon the altar of his "philosophy."

I found the doctor in his study, sitting in his favorite chair by the window. The blinds were drawn and the room quite dark; I almost missed him when I glanced inside. I had looked for him first in the basement and, finding nothing but overturned boxes and files strewn upon his worktable, checked the library next, which I found in a similar state of disarray, books thrown from the shelves, old newspapers and periodicals scattered pell-mell upon the floor. The study had not fared much better than the library; the contents of every drawer and cabinet lay in jumbled piles on every available surface. The entire house appeared to have been ransacked by bandits.

"Will Henry," he said. He sounded weary beyond words. "I hope you fared better in your quest than I have in mine."

"Yes, sir," I replied breathlessly. "I would have been back sooner, but I forgot to stop by the baker's, and I know how much you like his raspberry scones, so I went back. Got the last one, sir."

"Scones?"

"Yes, sir. And I stopped by the butcher's, too, and Mr. Flanagan's. He sends his regards, sir."

"Why are you gasping like that? Are you sick?"

"No, sir. I ran home, sir."

"You ran? Why? Were you chased?"

"It was something Mrs. Flanagan said." I was near to bursting. His melancholy would soon be swept away by my intelligence, I was certain.

He grunted. "Something about me no doubt. You should not talk to that woman, Will Henry. Talking to women in general is dangerous, but with that one it is a particular hazard."

"It wasn't about you, sir, at least not the important part. It was about your father."

"My father?"

I told him everything in a breathless rush, of Slidell and Mason and the Pinkerton detectives' inquiries around town (confirmed by Noonan the butcher and Tanner the baker), of the generally held belief that his father had been a Confederate sympathizer, of his father's hermetic and heavy-hearted reaction to the South's fall, all of which coincided with the expedition of the *Feronia*. The doctor interrupted only once, to have me repeat the names of the men with whom his father was accused of associating; otherwise he listened with unchanging expression, impassively studying me over his folded hands. I waited with bated breath upon the conclusion of my tale, sure he would leap from his chair, throw his arms around me, and bless me for untying the Gordian knot.

Instead, much to my chagrin, he shook his head and said softly, "Is that it? Is that why you rushed here, to tell me this?"

"Did you already know?" I was crestfallen.

"My father was guilty of many things," he said, "but treason was not one of them. It is possible he met with these men, and it is also possible their errand was of a seditious nature. Perhaps they had some insidious purpose in mind—his peculiar calling was not unknown in certain circles—but any scheme they proposed he would have rejected out of hand."

"But how can you know that, sir? You weren't living here."

He frowned at me. "How would you know where I was living?"

I dropped my head to avoid the intensity of his glare.

"You told me he sent you away to school during the war."

"I don't recall telling you that, Will Henry."

Of course, he had not; I had deduced it from the letter I had purloined from the old trunk. But some lies are borne of necessity.

"It was a long time ago," I offered meekly.

"Well, it must have been, for I have no memory of it. At any rate, the two events being proximate does not mean one is related to the other, Will Henry."

"But it could have something to do with it," I insisted. I was determined to impress him with the elegance of my reason. "If they were Confederate spies, he wouldn't have told anyone or left any record of his contract with Captain Varner. It's why you can't find anything, sir! And it could explain why he wanted more than one of the things brought back. You said they couldn't have been for study, so what were they for? Maybe they weren't for your father at all, but for *them*, Slidell and Mason. Maybe *they* wanted the *Anthropophagi*, Doctor!"

"And why would they want that?" he wondered, watching me hop from foot to foot in my agitation.

"I don't know," I replied. "To breed them, perhaps. To raise an army of them! Can you imagine the Union troops in the face of a hundred of those things, let loose in their ranks in the dead of night?"

"The *Anthropophagi* produce only one or two offspring a year," he reminded me. "It would require quite some time to produce a hundred, Will Henry."

"It took only two of them to wipe out the entire crew of the *Feronia*."

"A lucky circumstance—I mean, of course, for the *Anthropophagi*. They would not have fared as well against a regiment of battle-hardened soldiers. It is an interesting theory, Will Henry, unsupported as it is by any facts. Even if we assume these mysterious callers sought out my father to supply the rebellion with creatures to kill or terrorize the enemy, there are half a dozen he might have procured for them that did not entail the same risk and expense as a breeding pair of *Anthropophagi*. Do you follow, Will Henry? *If* that was their goal, given everything I know about him, he would have rejected it. And even *if* he had accepted, he would not have chosen this particular species."

"But you can't know for sure," I protested, unwilling to drop the matter. I wanted desperately to be right, not so much to prove the doctor wrong, but to be *right*.

His reaction was immediate. The doctor shot up from the chair, his angular face contorted in fury. I blenched: I had never seen him so angry. I fully expected him to strike me across the cheek for my recalcitrance.

"How dare you speak to me like this!" he cried. "Who are *you* to question my father's integrity? Who are *you* to besmirch my family's good name? It's not enough the entire town spreads calumny against me; now my own assistant, the boy to whom I have shown only kindness and pity, with whom I share my house and my work, for whom I have sacrificed my sacred right to privacy, stoops to join in their slanderous conduct! And if that weren't enough, the boy who owes me *everything*, even unto his very *life*, disobeys the one injunction—the *only* injunction—I gave to him! What was it, Will Henry? Do you remember, or were you so distracted by your lust for scones that you forgot? What did I say to you before you left?"

I stammered and stuttered, overcome by the ferocity of

his diatribe. Towering over my cowering frame, he roared, "*What did I say?*"

"Sp-sp-speak to no one," I whimpered.

"What else?"

"And if anyone should speak to me, all is well."

"And what impression do you think you left them with, Will Henry, with these questions about Confederate spies and government detectives and the house of Warthrop? Explain."

"I was only trying . . . I only wanted . . . I didn't bring it up, sir, I swear I didn't! The Flanagans did!"

He spat through his teeth, "You have failed me, Will Henry." He turned his back on me and strode across the room, kicking aside the piles of debris as he went. "And worse. You have betrayed me." He turned back to face me, shouting in the gloom, "And for what? To play the amateur detective, to satisfy your own insatiable curiosity, to humiliate me by participating in the same gossip and backstabbing that drove my father into seclusion and ultimately to his grave a broken and bitter man. You have put me in an untenable position, Master Henry, for now I know your loyalty extends only as far as the bounds of your selfishness, and blind, total, unquestioning loyalty is the one indispensable quality I demand of you. No one asked that I take you into my home or share with you my work. Not even fealty to your father demanded that. But I did it, and this is my reward! . . . What? Did that make you angry? Have I offended you? Speak!"

"I didn't ask to come here!"

"And I didn't ask for the opportunity!"

"There wouldn't have been one if not for you."

He stepped toward me. In the gloaming I could not see his face. A shadow was between us.

"Your father understood the risk," he said softly.

"My mother didn't! *I* didn't!"

"What would you have me do, Will Henry? Raise them bodily from the grave?"

"I hate it here," I shouted at the shadow of the monstrumologist, my mentor—and my tormentor. "I hate it here and I hate you for bringing me here and I hate *you*."

I fled down the hall, flew up the stairs, and raced up the ladder to my little alcove, slamming the door down behind me. I threw myself across the bed and buried my face into the pillow, screaming at the top of my lungs, my being overflowing with rage and grief and shame. Yes, shame, for he was all I had, and I had failed him. The doctor had his work; I had him; and to each what we had was all.

Above me clouds scuddled across the blue vitriol of the April sky, and the sun slumped toward the horizon, painting the clouds' soft bellies golden. When my tears were spent, I rolled onto my back and watched the light seep from the world. My body ached for food and rest, my soul for a more permanent respite. I might eat and I might sleep, but what might I do to ease this crushing loneliness, this inconsolable sorrow, this incurable dread? Like Erasmus Gray hip-deep in the grave, locked in the monster's inescapable grip, or Hezekiah Varner dying in the fermenting stew of his own flesh, had I passed the point of salvation, had all hope already died in the fire that had devoured my parents, as the *Anthropophagi* had devoured Erasmus, as the maggots Hezekiah? Death had brought an end to their misery. Would nothing but a visitation from that same dark angel bring an end to mine?

I waited for sleep, that gentle mockery of death, to take me. I longed for its effacing grace. But its peace eluded me, and I rose from the bed, my head pounding from the salty torrent of my tears and the ache deep in my stomach. I eased open the trapdoor and tiptoed down the ladder. I made straight for the kitchen, where I found the basement door closed. I had no doubt he was down there; it was, like my little alcove, his refuge of choice. Working as quickly and quietly as I could, I set the pot on to boil and prepared a repast worthy of my ravening appetite, featuring two fine lamb chops courtesy of Noonan the butcher. I cleaned my plate with the same rapidity with which I filled it, for a finer meal I had never had, made all the more delectable by virtue of my having cooked it, though the mouthfuls lingered barely long enough upon the tongue for me to taste them.

As I sopped up the juice of the lamb with a chunk of fresh bread, courtesy of Tanner the baker, the basement door opened and the doctor appeared.

"You cooked something," he said.

"Yes," I answered, deliberately omitting the honorific.

"What did you cook?"

"Lamb."

"Lamb?"

"Yes."

"Chops?"

I nodded. "And some fresh peas and carrots."

I carried my plate to the sink. I could feel him watching me as I washed up. I put my cup and plate on the rack to dry and turned around. He had not moved from the basement doorway.

"Do you need me for anything?" I asked.

"I don't . . . No, I do not," he replied.

"I'll be in my room, then."

He said nothing as I walked past him, until I reached the bottom of the stairs, when he stepped around the corner and called from the end of the hall, "Will Henry!"

"Yes?"

He hesitated, and then said in a resigned tone, "Sleep well, Will Henry."

Much later, with the same uncanny ability he had demonstrated in the past to disturb me at the very moment when, after hours of tossing and turning, I was just drifting off to sleep, the doctor began to call for me, his voice high-pitched and ethereal as it penetrated my little sanctuary.

"Will Henry! Will Henreeeee!"

Groggy from the brief sip of sleep's sweet sapor, I slid

out of bed with an acquiescent sigh. I knew that tone; I had heard it many times before. I crawled down the ladder to the second floor.

"Will Henry! Will Henreeeee!"

I found him in his room, lying on top of the bedcovers fully clothed. He spied my silhouette in the doorway and bade me enter with an impatient snap of his wrist. Still smarting from our row, I did not come to his bedside; I took a single step into the room and stopped.

"Will Henry, what are you doing?" he demanded.

"You called for me."

"Not *now*, Will Henry. What were you doing out there?" He waved his hand toward the hallway to demonstrate *out there*.

"I was in my room, sir."

"No, no. I distinctly heard you bumping about in the kitchen."

"I was in my room," I repeated. "Perhaps you heard a mouse."

"A mouse clattering pots and pans? Tell me the truth, Will Henry. You were cooking something."

"I am telling the truth. I was in my room."

"You're suggesting I'm hallucinating."

"No, sir."

"I know what I heard."

"I'll go downstairs and check, sir."

"No! No, stay here. It must have been my imagination. I may have been asleep; I don't know."

"Yes, sir," I said. "Is that all, sir?"

"I am not used to it, as you know."

He fell silent, waiting for me to ask the obvious question, but I was a tired player in this tired drama: He had fallen into one of his frequent black moods, his psyche borne down in the crush of his peculiar proclivities. My role was well defined, and usually I played it with all the pluck I could muster, but the events of the last few days had sapped my spirits. I simply did not feel up for it.

"Sharing the house with someone," he offered when I did not ask. "I have been thinking of soundproofing this room. Every little noise . . ."

"Yes, sir," I said, and pointedly yawned.

"I might have imagined it," he conceded. "The mind can play tricks when denied the proper rest. I cannot remember the last time I slept."

"At least three days," I said.

"Or eaten a decent meal."

I said nothing. If he couldn't come right out and ask, I would make no offer. If he was going to be stubborn, well, so could I.

"Do you know, Will Henry, when I was younger, I could go a whole week with no sleep and a loaf of bread. I once hiked across the Andes with only an apple in my pocket. . . . You're quite certain, then, you were not downstairs?"

"Yes, sir."

"The noise stopped after I called for you. Perhaps you were walking in your sleep."

"No, sir. I was in my bed."

"Of course."

"Is that all, sir?"

"All?"

"Do you need anything else?"

"Perhaps you don't wish to tell me because of the scones."

"The scones, sir?"

"You snuck downstairs for a midnight snack, and you know how much I fancy them."

"No, sir. We still have the scones."

"Ah. Well, that's good."

There was no escaping it. He was not going to go himself and he was not going to ask me. If I simply returned to bed, he would wait until I was on the brink of sleep again, and then my name would echo throughout the house, *Will Henreeee!* until my will was broken. Down to the kitchen, then, I trooped, where I set a pot of water on to boil and plated the scones. I prepared his tea, leaning against the sink and yawning incessantly while it steeped. I loaded the tray and carried it back to his room.

The doctor had sat up in my absence. He leaned against the headboard with his arms crossed and head bowed, lost in thought. He looked up when I set the tray on the small table beside him.

"What is this? Tea and scones! How thoughtful of you, Will Henry."

He waved me toward a chair. With an inward sigh I sat: There was no escaping this, either. If I retreated, in a moment he would call me back to sit with him. If I nodded off, he would raise his voice and snap his fingers and then, with perfect ingenuousness, ask me if I was tired.

"These are quite good scones," he opined after a delicate bite. "But I can't eat both. Have one, Will Henry."

"No, thank you, sir."

"You see, I could consider your lack of an appetite as evidence that you *were* downstairs earlier. Did you see anything, by the way?"

"No, sir."

"It may have been a mouse," he said. "Did you set a trap while you were down there?"

"No, sir."

"Don't go now, Will Henry," he said, though I hadn't moved a muscle. "It can wait till morning." He sipped his tea. "Although to make such a racket, he must have been some mouse! I was thinking that while you were away. Perhaps, like Proteus, he possesses the power to change his form, from mouse to man, and he was whipping up a bit of cheesy sauce for his family. Hah! That is a ludicrous thought, isn't it, Will Henry?"

"Yes, sir."

"I am not mirthful by nature, as you know, unless I'm tired. And I am very tired, Will Henry."

"I am tired too, sir."

"Then why are you sitting there? Go to bed."

"Yes, sir. I think I will."

I rose, bidding him goodnight without much conviction,

for I well knew mine was not the curtain line. I left the room but not the hallway without. I began to count, and by the time I reached fifteen, he called me back.

"I neglected to finish my thought," he explained after waving me back to the chair. "Thinking of our hypothetical mouse brought to mind *Proteus anguinus*."

"No, sir, you mentioned Proteus," I reminded him.

He shook his head impatiently, frustrated by my obtuseness. "*Proteus anguinus*, Will Henry, a species of blind amphibians found in the Carpathian Mountains. And that of course brought to mind Galton and the matter of eugenics."

"Of course, sir," I said, though, of course, I had no idea where I was in the dense thicket of his thoughts: I had never heard of *Proteus anguinus* or Galton or eugenics.

"Fascinating creatures," the monstrumologist said. "And excellent examples of natural selection. They dwell deep in lightless mountain caves, yet retain vestigial eyes. Galton brought the first specimens back to his native England after his expedition to Adelsberg. He was a friend of my father's—and of Darwin's, of course. Father was a devotee was his work, particularly in eugenics. There is a signed copy of *Hereditary Genius* in the library."

"There is?" I murmured mechanically.

"I know they corresponded regularly, though it appears that, like his diaries and practically every letter he received over his lifetime, he destroyed the evidence of it."

Practically every letter. I thought of the bundle of notes to father from son, unopened missives of faded ink on yellowed parchment, at the bottom of an old, forgotten trunk. *I wish you would write to me.*

"When I returned from Prague in '83 to bury him, there was little but his books left. Just his trunk and some notes on various species of particular interest to him, notes that I suppose he could not bring himself to destroy. He destroyed or discarded nearly all his personal effects, down to his last sock and shoelace, and would have the old trunk as well, I'm sure, had he remembered tucking it away beneath the stairs. It is as if in the waning days of his life he sought to eradicate all evidence of it. At the time, I attributed it to that morbid self-loathing to which he had fallen victim in his later years, that corrosive mix of inexplicable remorse and religious fervor. It brought his life full circle, if you will: He was found lying upon his bed one morning by the housekeeper, uncovered, and curled in the fetal position, completely naked."

The doctor sighed. "I was startled by the intelligence. I had no idea how far he had fallen." He closed his eyes briefly. "He was a very dignified man in his prime, Will Henry, quite particular in his appearance, to the point of vanity. The idea that he would end his life in such a demeaning manner was unthinkable. At least, unthinkable to me."

He fell silent, staring at the ceiling, and I thought of Hezekiah Varner, who had had no choice in the matter. "But he was trapped in the amber of my memory; it had been nearly ten years since I'd last seen him, and *that* Alistair Warthrop was a different human being, not the bare shell of one found five years ago."

Warthrop shook himself from his melancholic reverie. He rolled onto his side to face my chair and rested his head on his open palm. His dark eyes glittered in the lamplight.

"Drifted off-course again, didn't I, Will Henry? You must read *Hereditary Genius* sometime. After *Origin of Species* but before *The Descent of Man*, for that is its place both thematically and chronologically. Its influence can be seen throughout *Descent*. The idea that both mental and physical features are passed on to an organism's progeny is revolutionary. Father saw it at once and even wrote to me about it. One of the few letters he ever sent; I still have it somewhere. Galton had shared an early draft with him, and Father believed the theory had applications in his own field of study, an exciting alternative to capture or eradication of the more malevolent species, like our friends the *Anthropophagi*. If desirable traits could be encouraged and undesirable ones suppressed through selective breeding, it could transform our discipline. Eugenics could be the key to saving our subjects from extinction, for the rise of man had numbered their days, unless, Father believed, a way could be found to 'domesticate' them, much as the treacherous wolf was transfigured into the faithful dog."

He paused, apparently waiting for some response from me. When none was forthcoming, he sat up and cried excitedly, "Don't you see, Will Henry? It answers the question of

Why? That's why he desired a breeding pair of *Anthropophagi*—to put Galton's theory into practice, to breed out its savagery and taste for human blood. A daunting enterprise, enormous in scope and staggering in cost, well beyond his means, which may explain why he met with these mysterious agents in '62. That is only a guess, impossible to prove, unless we can find these men, if they still live, or some record of their agreement, if one exists—or ever existed. At any rate, it's the only reason I can think of to explain why he would meet with such men, if he thought their evil cause might advance his just one."

He stopped, again waiting for my reaction. He slapped his hand upon the mattress and said, "Well, don't just sit there. Tell me what you think!"

"Well, sir," I began slowly. The truth was I did not know what to make of it. "You knew him and I didn't."

"I hardly knew him at all," he said matter-of-factly. "Less so than most sons their fathers, I would venture, but the theory fits what I do know about the facts. Only passion for his work could compel him to associate with traitors. It was all he had; he loved nothing else. Nothing."

He fell onto his back, head cradled in his hands, eyes fixed on the blank and ready canvas above him. The possibilities of what might be painted there were bounded only by the limits of his hyperbolic imagination. Our ignorance of our fellows throws wide the gate to our galloping suppositions, even if that fellow is our own father. Into that existential vacuum rushes our wishes and doubts, our longings and regrets, for the father-that-was and the father-that-might-have-been. Though mine had not been a cold and distant man like his, we were brothers in that one instance: Our fathers had bequeathed us nothing but memories. A fire had stripped me of all tangible tokens, save my little hat; Alistair Warthrop had taken most of what had belonged to Pellinore. What remained of them was simply *us*, and when we departed, so would they. We were the tablets upon which their lives were writ.

"Nothing else," the monstrumologist said. "Nothing at all."

I remained at his bedside throughout the night, in a grueling vigil different only in kind from the one the night previous, while the doctor drifted in and out of a light and restless sleep. Inevitably, as I started to nod off, he would jerk awake and call out in a voice bordering on panic, "Will Henry! Will Henry, are you asleep?"

To which I would answer, "No, sir; I'm awake."

"Oh," he would reply. "You should rest, Will Henry. We'll need all our strength in the coming hours. By now he must have my letter, and if I know John Kearns, he will be on the earliest train."

"Who is John Kearns?" I asked. "Is he a monstrumologist?"

He laughed dryly. "Not in the strictest definition of the term, no. By profession he is a surgeon—and a brilliant one, I might add. By temperament he is something altogether different. I would have preferred Henry Stanley, if I knew where to find him. Both have hunted *Anthropophagi* in the wild, and Stanley is a gentleman from the old school, nothing like Kearns."

"He's a hunter?"

"I suppose one might call him that, in a manner of speaking. He certainly has more experience than I, for I have none at all in regard to *Anthropophagi*. I should caution you, Will Henry," he added, his tone becoming grave, "not to tarry too long in the dominion of John Kearns's philosophy. Avoid him if you can."

"Why?" I asked with a child's natural curiosity, tweaked, as is all childlike curiosity, by sober admonition.

"He reads too much," was the doctor's odd reply. "Or not quite enough. I have never been certain. At any rate, steer clear of Dr. John Kearns, Will Henry! He is a dangerous man, but the hour calls for dangerous men, and we must use every tool at our disposal. It's been two nights since they last fed; they will hunt again, and soon."

"What if they already have?" I asked, the thought bringing me fully to my senses. The room seemed to shrink and fill with menacing shadows.

"I assure you that they haven't. The unfortunate Mr. Gray should keep them satisfied, at least for another day or two."

I did not give voice to the objection that immediately leapt to mind: *But what if you're wrong?* I'd tried that tack before, and had paid dearly for it. So I held my tongue. May

God forgive me, I said nothing. Perhaps if I had spoken up, he might have questioned his assumption. Perhaps if I had insisted, perhaps if I had been unrelenting in my doubt and negligent in my trust and deference, six innocent people might not have suffered nearly unimaginable deaths. For, even as he was speaking these soothing words, a family was being slaughtered. While we drowsily whiled away the deadest hours of the night, the beasts were busy imbuing them with blood.

EIGHT

"I Am a Scientist"

Dawn had broken by the time I finally stumbled off to bed. I stripped out of my clothes and crawled beneath the covers, but the hours of sleep I snatched were scant, and teemed with vivid visions of voracious vermin: worms and maggots and the sightless, nameless, colorless creatures that dwell in the dark beneath rocks and wet, rotting logs. I woke feeling more exhausted than when I'd first lain down, with a sour taste upon my tongue and the dead weight of dread in my heart. Above me the midmorning sky was a cloudless, brilliant blue, a joyful spring mockery of my morbid mood. Try as I might, I could not shake the feeling that something terrible lurked just over the horizon. I resolved not to mention my foreboding to the doctor; he would dismiss it with a laugh, followed by a lecture on superstition as echo of our primitive past, when premonitions were efficacious responses to an environment populated by predators only too happy to oblige our apprehensions.

I shuffled downstairs to the kitchen, groggily noting the basement door ajar and the lights on below. I set the water on for tea and leaned against the countertop, wrestling the twin demons of extreme physical and mental fatigue. I may be forgiven by those empathetic souls who, having trod upon a parallel path, may remember how their very thoughts seemed foreign and their bodies commandeered. They will understand how the sharp rapping on the door did not at first grab my attention, as I wavered by the stove, waiting for the water to boil. They will find it not surprising at all the little cry that escaped my lips a moment later, not from the harsh knocking a few feet away but from the doctor's bellowing from the basement beneath me.

"Will Henry! Answer the door! *Answer the door!*"

"Yes, sir!" I returned. "Right away, sir!"

I threw open the door. A tall, thin figure slouched upon the stoop, his head enshrouded in the cloud of sweet-smelling smoke ascending leisurely from his meerschaum pipe, his fragile frame propped precariously upon a cane. The morning sun glinting off the lenses of his pince-nez spectacles, combined with the nearly perfect oval of his face and the bushiness of his mustache, produced a distinctly owlish appearance.

"Ah, so it's Will Henry, then. Good, good!" Constable

Morgan cried in a soft voice, traversing over the transom in a trembling trespass. "Where is Warthrop? I must speak to him!"

The doctor appeared in the basement doorway, his face devoid of expression. The unexpected appearance of the town's chief law enforcement officer seemed not to faze him in the least.

"What is it, Robert?" the doctor asked in a quiet, level tone. His complete calm played counterpoint to the constable's obvious agitation.

"An abomination!" the constable replied. Spittle flew from his lips and clung to the hairs of his mustache. "That's what it is. Horrible! Totally outside the range of my experience."

"Though not, you presume, outside mine."

The constable nodded with a jerk of his head.

"Something has happened," he said breathlessly. "You must come at once."

Within moments we were inside the constable's carriage, dashing pell-mell through the narrow cobblestone streets of New Jerusalem. The two men raised their voices to be heard over the clatter of wheels and the thunder of hooves and the whistling wind streaming through the open windows.

The constable, whose purpose no doubt had been to wrest answers from the doctor concerning the troublesome imponderables of the morning's gruesome discovery, forthwith found himself, as so many who confronted him with similar intent, the object of the intended interrogation. He was pressed, prodded, and pummeled in the flood of the doctor's keen inquisitorial powers. As one having suffered through similar inundations, I was not unsympathetic to the confounding of the constable's purpose. The questions came rapidly, barked in a hammering rhythm.

The doctor: "When was the crime reported?"

The constable: "This morning, shortly after dawn."

"Witnesses?"

"Yes. One—the sole survivor. Until I saw the scene with my own eyes, I thought, as any reasonable man would, he was not only witness but must also be perpetrator. His tale was so outlandish it had to be a lie."

"You arrested him?"

The constable nodded, nervously tapping the tip of his cane upon the boards between his boots. Pressed against him, I could not fail to detect the sickening odor rising like a pall from his clothing, the by now too-familiar smell of death, which the smoldering bowl of his pipe could not completely camouflage.

"And hold him still," said the constable. "For his protection, Warthrop, not for our prosecution. Once I examined the scene . . . No human being is capable of so foul a crime. And I fear what he saw has completely broken his reason."

"What did he see?"

"That tale I'll leave to him, but what *I* saw in that house corroborates his story. It is . . . beyond words, Warthrop, beyond words!"

The doctor said naught. He turned away to face the landscape, awash in the golden light of spring, rolling green hills and lush meadows bursting with blooms. *They've discovered the old man—or what remains of him—and the girl—or what remains of her,* I thought, and wondered if the doctor was thinking the same. *He is taking us back to the cemetery.*

I was surprised when the driver swung upon a little lane that branched from the Old Hill Cemetery Road, taking us past the boneyard—though its western wall remained in sight—slowing our pace as the lane narrowed and the ground rose before us. The maturing sun was warm and the breeze gentle through the open window. Slight as it was, it bore away the sickly stench emanating from my other side. I could smell honeysuckle. Relieved, I breathed in deep.

The respite was short lived. The driver drew rein at the top of the hill. Warthrop leaped from the cab before we could come to a complete stop. More from a sense of duty (my services were, after all, indispensable to him) than eagerness to face what the constable had called an "abomination," I trotted a few feet behind. Before us, at the apex of the hill, were a church and, a stone's throw away, its rectory made of stone and a gable roof, the flower beds bursting with spring bulbs in riots of white, pink, indigo, and gold, as quaint—and ominous—as the house in which poor Hansel and Gretel were nearly roasted alive. At its door two men stood, rifles cradled in their arms. They stiffened upon our approach, their fingers caressing the triggers of their weapons, until they spied the constable struggling up the path behind us. Their demeanor changed again, however, upon recognizing the doctor; dark looks of distrust and fear darkened their faces: Warthrop was not a popular man in New Jerusalem. In another age I've no doubt he would have been accused of consorting with the devil and been burned alive.

"Thank God it isn't Sunday!" gasped Morgan, arriving winded from his hike. "The good reverend's flock would be hard pressed for evidence of the Lord's loving providence upon this unholy day."

Behind his spectacles his eyes, in all ways owlish save one, for they lacked the ethereal serenity of those audacious avian hunters, fell upon my face, and he said, "Though no doubt in his travels Warthrop has seen worse, you are but a child, Will Henry, unaccustomed to such things. You should not go in with us."

"He most certainly will go in with us," the doctor said impatiently.

"But why?" demanded the constable. "What purpose could it possibly serve?"

"He is my assistant," rejoined Warthrop. "He must become accustomed to 'such things.'"

The constable knew the doctor too well to press the argument further. After heaving a heavy sigh and drawing one last time upon the beneficent balm of its bowl, he removed the pipe from his mouth, handed it to one of the nervous deputies, pulled his kerchief from his pocket, and then pressed it against his nose and mouth.

My presence must still have troubled him; he looked down upon my upraised face a moment longer before saying softly, his words muffled behind the cloth, "There are no words, Will Henry. No words!"

He threw open the door over which a sign had been hung, the words etched upon it an ironic preface to the charnel house within: THE LORD IS MY SHEPHERD.

A body lay facedown six feet from the doorway, both arms outstretched, clad in the bloody remnants of his nightshirt. Gone were both his legs. Missing too were five of his fingers, two from the left hand, three from the right. His head lay upon one arm nearly perpendicular to his body, for his neck had been partially ripped from his shoulders, exposing his spinal column, the serpentine tendrils of major blood vessels, and the stringy tendons of the connecting tissue. The back of his head had been smashed in and his brains scooped out, the pulpy remains ringing the wound like grayish curd on the lip of a shattered bowl. During the necropsy, the doctor had informed me, in that dreary, lecturing tone, of *Anthropophagi*'s singular fondness for the noblest of organs, that apogee of nature's design, the human brain.

The room stank of blood, and hanging in the air was the same nauseating stench of rotten fruit I had smelled in the cemetery. The odors did not so much war with each other as mix into a stomach-churning atmosphere that burned the nostrils and set the eyes on fire. No wonder the constable had covered his orifices on the outset of our expedition.

Morgan and I lingered in the open doorway, hesitating, as it were, between the worlds of light and dark, but Warthrop suffered no such disinclination: Rushing to the body, leaving footprints in the tacky blood that pooled round all sides like a shallow moat, he squatted near the head and bent close to examine the gaping wound. He touched it. He rubbed bits of cerebral matter between his thumb and finger.

He remained still for a moment, forearms resting upon his splayed knees, taking in the remains before him. He bent low, barely maintaining his balance, to study the victim's face, or what was left of it.

"This is Stinnet?" he asked.

"It is the reverend," Morgan confirmed.

"And the others? Where is the rest of the family?"

"Two in the parlor: his wife and youngest child, Sarah, I believe. Another child in the hall. A fourth in one of the bedrooms."

"And the child who escaped. That leaves one unaccounted for."

"No, Warthrop. That one is here."

"Where?"

"He is all around you," replied the constable, in a voice thick with revulsion and pity.

And so he was. The reverend, whose body remained more or less intact, had captured our attention as the locus of the slaughter, but all around it, like shards thrown from a grisly centrifuge, upon the walls and floorboards and even the ceiling above our heads, were fragments and scraps of human flesh, unrecognizable effluvia cemented by blood to nearly every surface: tufts of hair, bits of entrails, splinters of bone, shavings of muscle. In some places the walls were so saturated they literally wept with his blood. It was as if the child had been shoved into a grinder and then spewed out in every direction. Lying but a few inches from the doctor's right shoe was the severed foot of the boy, the only recognizable portion left extant by the marauding *Anthropophagi*.

"His name was Michael," the constable said. "He was five."

The doctor said nothing. In a slow circle he turned, hands upon hips, pirouetting to survey the carnage, his expression at once one of fascination and detachment, marveling at the sheer savageness of the attack yet removed from its arrant horror, heart divorced from mind, emotions from intellect, the quintessential scientist, set apart from the very race to which he belonged. Thus he stood, a living temple among ruins crushed in the literal sense of the word, and whatever he was thinking remained hidden within the hallowed halls of his conscious.

Growing impatient, perhaps, with the doctor's disconcerting reticence in this time of utmost urgency, the constable stepped into the room and said, "Well? Would you like to see the others?"

The dreadful tour commenced. First the bedroom where the oldest children had slept. There were the remains of a girl whose name, the constable informed us, was Elizabeth, ripped to shreds like her brother, though her gutted torso was intact, lying upon the remnants of the shattered windowpane. The lace curtains, freckled with her blood, fluttered in the beneficent breeze and, past the jagged glass that still clung to the window's frame, I could see the pleasant meadow of spring grass shimmering in the morning sun.

"The point of entry?" mused Morgan.

"Perhaps," answered the doctor, bending to examine the frame and the shards of glass clustered beneath it. "Though I do not think so. The improvised exit of our witness is my guess."

Next, Morgan led us down the hall, where, upon turning a corner, we found the fourth victim, similarly dismembered and disemboweled, skull crushed and hollowed out, bits and pieces of the vital organs strewn upon the floor and cemented by gore to the walls. And here in this hallway, on the bloody floorboards, we discovered the first evidence of the *Anthropophagi*'s presence: impressions of their passing left in the congealing blood of their prey. The doctor gave an exultant cry at the sight of these footprints, fell to his hands and knees, and spent several excited seconds surveying the find.

"Eight to ten, at the least," muttered Warthrop. "Females, though *this* and *this* may be a juvenile male."

"*Females?* Females, you say? With prints larger than a full-grown man's?"

"A mature female measures seven feet from sole to shoulder."

"A mature female *what*, Warthrop?"

The doctor hesitated for half a breath and said, "A hominid species of carnivores called *Anthropophagi.*"

"*Anthro . . . popi . . .*"

"*Anthro*-po-*phagi*," corrected the doctor. "Pliny named them *Blemmyae*, but *Anthropophagi* is the accepted designation."

"And where in heaven's name did they come from?"

"They are native to Africa and certain islands off the coast of Madagascar," answered the doctor carefully.

"That is a far cry from New England," the constable observed dryly, and waited with narrowed eye for the doctor's response.

"Robert, you have my word as a man of science and a gentleman that I had nothing to do with their appearance here," said the doctor carefully.

"And you have my word, Warthrop, as a man of the law, it is my duty to discover who, if anyone, might be responsible for this massacre."

"I am not responsible," declared the doctor firmly. "I am as shocked as you by their presence here, and I shall get to the bottom of it, Robert, of that you have my word."

Morgan nodded, but his tone was dubious. "It simply

strikes me as exceedingly odd, Pellinore, that such monstrous creatures should appear in the very town where the country's—if not the world's—preeminent expert in these matters resides."

Though spoken in the mildest of manners, the constable's observation caused the doctor to stiffen and his eyes to flash with indignation.

"Are you calling me a liar, Robert?" he asked in a low, dangerous tone.

"My dear Warthrop," replied Morgan, "we have known each other our entire lives. Though you are the most secretive man I have ever met and much of what you do remains a mystery to me, I have never known you to tell a deliberate falsehood. You tell me their presence here comes as a shock to you, and I believe you, but my faith does not change the fact that the coincidence is exceedingly odd."

"That particular irony has not been lost on me, Robert," admitted my master. "One might say oddities are my business, and this case has more than its fair share of them." Then he added quickly, before the constable could press the matter further, "Let's see the others."

We returned down the hall toward the front of the rectory. Here, in the cozy parlor where doubtless the reverend's family gathered round the piano for an evening of convivial song or lounged upon the overstuffed chairs and couches before a cheerful fire while the north wind howled, here we confronted the final, terrible scene: a headless corpse lay in a heap in the middle of the room, clutching the remains of an infant to her chest. Her dressing gown had been white, but was no longer, and lay pooled upon the floor where her legs should have been. One leg we discovered discarded partially shredded beneath the broken window that looked out upon the little lane leading to the house. The other was nowhere to be found—likewise her head, though the doctor had me hunt for it, crawling on my hands and knees to peer under the furniture. He examined the mother's corpse while Morgan lingered in the doorway, his labored breath fluttering the corners of his makeshift mask.

"Both shoulders have been dislocated," the doctor said. He ran his hands down the woman's arms, deft fingers pressing into her still-pliant flesh. "The right humerus has been broken." Now to the fingers locked around the tiny body. "Five fingers broken, two on the right hand, three on the left."

He tried to pry the baby from her hands, his jaw clenching with the effort. Thwarted by the stubborn will of rigor mortis, he relented and examined the baby without removing it from the frozen arms of her mother.

"Multiple puncture wounds and lacerations," he said. "But the body is intact. The baby bled to death or her lungs were crushed. Or she was smothered by her mother's breast. A cruel irony should that be the case.

"How strong is the maternal instinct, Will Henry! Though they tore her shoulders from the sockets and broke the very bones that held it, she did not surrender her child. She held firm. Though they broke her arms and tore off her head, still she held firm. Held firm! Even when she became a cruel imitation of the things that devoured her brood, she held firm! It is a wonder and a marvel."

"You'll forgive me, Warthrop, if I do not consider what happened here in any way marvelous," said the constable with disgust.

"You mistake me," rejoined Warthrop. "And you judge prematurely things unknown to you. Do we judge the wolf or the lion? Do we blame the savage crocodile for obeying the imperatives of nature's design?"

As he spoke, the doctor considered the bloody pietà at his feet, his attitude now wholly introspective and remote, his face an inscrutable, emotionless mask. What tempests, if any, raged hidden beneath the surface of that icy facade? Did the macabre tableau remind him of the words spoken only hours before? *The unfortunate Mr. Gray should keep them satisfied, at least for another day or two.* Words spoken with the characteristic self-assurance that often was mistaken for arrogance—or would it not be a mistake to call it that? I would be less than honest if I said I understood this man to whom I owe so much, this man who took the homeless, orphaned boy I was and sculpted him into the man I became. How oft do they rescue or ruin us, through whimsy or design or a combination of both, the adults to whom we entrust our care! The truth I confess is that I understand him not. Even with the gift of much time and the perspective it grants us, I still do not understand Dr. Pellinore Xavier Warthrop. Did he honestly accept the premise that he was blameless for this horrific slaughter of six innocents? What convolutions and contortions of logic did he employ to ignore the symbolic significance of the Stinnets' blood upon his hands? Or did he look upon the facts, with the same pitiless stare that Eliza Bunton had received, to reach the conclusion obvious to even a twelve-year-old boy? Each possibility was as likely as the other, and neither discernable by his stoic expression. He betrayed nothing, regarding in silence the headless mother and the babe broken against her breast, the two curled at his feet like discarded offerings to a bloodthirsty god.

"Where is the witness?" he asked.

We paused in the yard to clear our lungs of death's foul miasma and for the constable to refill his pipe. His face was flushed, and the fingers holding the match quivered as he lowered the flame to the alabaster bowl.

"I must confess to you, Warthrop, this is wholly outside the range of my experience."

Morgan's gaze strayed to the words etched over the rectory door. *The Lord is my shepherd*. He did not appear comforted. Indeed, he seemed shaken to his spiritual marrow. As the town constable he had witnessed more than his fair share of man's inhumanity to man, from petty thievery to malicious battery. None of it had prepared him, however, for this naked confrontation with gross injustice, this horrific reminder that despite all the honors with which we shower ourselves, we are, ultimately, fodder, mere meat for the inferior, soulless things of which I dreamt the night before, no less than us the Creator's children. It could not have been pleasant, for a man of the constable's limited experience and sensitive temperament, to be confronted with the *Anthropophagi's* savage mockery of our human aspirations, our absurd grandiosities and ambitions, our ever-preening pride.

"He's in the sanctuary," he said. "This way."

We followed him down the gravel path toward the little church that faced the lane leading to Old Hill Cemetery Road. Another guard was stationed there. Without a word he stepped aside to let us pass. The interior was cool and dark. The morning light streamed in broken beams through the stained glass of the windows, shafts of blue and green and red cutting through the dusty air. Our footfalls echoed upon the ancient boards. Two shadowy figures slouched in the front pew. Upon our approach, one rose, a rifle in his arms. The other did not move, did not so much as raise his head.

Lowering his voice, the constable informed the man with the rifle that the hearses would be arriving soon and he should wait outside to help with the removal of the victims. The man did not seem particularly pleased with the assignment, but acknowledged his orders with the briefest of nods before taking his leave.

The guard's footfalls died away. We were alone with our witness. Slumped in the pew, arms folded over his chest, hands gripping tight the edges of the blanket wrapped around his bare torso, he was but a boy of fifteen or sixteen, I guessed, with dark hair and large, bright blue eyes that appeared all the larger owing to the narrowness of his face. Though he was seated, I discerned he was tall for his age; his legs seemed to stretch a mile before him.

"Malachi," said the constable gently. "Malachi, this is Dr. Warthrop. He's here to . . ." The constable paused, as if he were unsure what service the doctor could perform. "Well, help you."

A moment passed. Malachi did not speak. His full lips moved soundlessly, as he stared, like some Eastern mystic, at a space beyond our mortal sphere, looking without but *seeing* within.

"I am not hurt," he said finally, in barely a whisper.

"He isn't that kind of doctor," the constable said.

"I am a scientist," said Warthrop.

Malachi's strikingly blue eyes strayed to my face and remained fixed, unblinking, for a few agonizingly uncomfortable seconds.

"Who are you?" he asked.

"This is Will Henry," answered the doctor. "He is my assistant."

Though Malachi's eyes remained on my face, he had ceased to see it. It was unmistakable, the transition from seeing to not-seeing, the fading of his focus, or, better put, the refocusing to something altogether different, something that only he could see. We warred for his attention with this thing unseen. I knew not what the others were thinking; for myself, I wondered at his condition. His psyche had clearly suffered horrific wounds, yet physically he had emerged unscathed from the ferocious attack. How could that be?

The doctor went to one knee before him. The movement did not distract the stricken lad; his sight remained fixed upon my features, and not so much as an eyelash twitched when Warthrop laid a hand upon his outstretched thigh. In a soft voice the doctor spoke his name, squeezing gently the flaccid muscle beneath his hand, as if calling him back from that faraway, inapproachable place.

"Malachi, can you tell me what happened?"

Again his lips moved and no sound emerged. His other-worldly stare unnerved me, but as one who stumbles upon a terrible accident, I could not tear my eyes away from the awful gravity of his gaze.

"Malachi!" the doctor called quietly, now shaking the limp leg. "I cannot help you unless you tell me—"

"Have you not been there?" cried Malachi. "Did you not see?"

"Yes, Malachi," answered the doctor. "I saw everything."

"Then, why do you ask me?"

"Because I would like to know what *you* saw."

"What I saw."

His eyes, large and blue and as depthless as the spinning

maw of Charybdis, refused to release me from the riptide of their grip. He addressed the doctor, but he spoke to me:

"I saw the mouth of hell fly open and the spawn of Satan spew forth! That is what I saw!"

"Malachi, the creatures that killed your family are not of supernatural origin. They are predators belonging to this world, as mundane as the wolf or the lion, and we are, unfortunately, their prey."

If he heard the doctor, he showed no sign. If he understood, he gave no admission. Beneath the blanket he shivered uncontrollably, though the air was still and the sanctuary warm. His mouth came open and he addressed me now: "Did *you* see?"

I hesitated. The doctor whispered sharply in my ear, "*Answer, Will Henry!*"

"Yes," I blurted. "I saw."

"I am not hurt," repeated Malachi to me, as if he feared I had not heard him before. "I am unscathed."

"A remarkable and extremely fortunate outcome of your ordeal," observed the doctor. Again he was ignored. Snorting with frustration, Warthrop motioned for me to come closer. It appeared Malachi would speak, but only to me.

"How old are you?" he asked.

"Twelve."

"That is my sister's age. Elizabeth. Sarah, Michael, Matthew, and Elizabeth. I am the oldest. Have you any brothers and sisters, Will Henry?"

"No."

"Will Henry is an orphan," Dr. Warthrop said.

Malachi asked me, "What happened?"

"There was a fire," I said.

"You were there?"

"Yes."

"What happened?"

"I ran."

"I ran too."

His expression did not change; the impassive visage remained; but a tear trailed down his hollow cheek. "Do you think God will forgive us, Will Henry?"

"I . . . I don't know," I replied honestly. Being only twelve, I was still a neophyte in the nuances of theology.

"That's what Father always said," Malachi whispered. "If we repent. If we but ask."

His gaze wandered to the cross hanging on the wall behind me.

"I have been praying. I have been asking him to forgive me. But I hear nothing. I feel nothing!"

"Self-preservation is your first duty and inalienable right, Malachi," said the doctor a bit impatiently. "You cannot be held accountable for exercising that right."

"No, no," murmured Morgan. "You miss the point, Warthrop."

He lowered himself into the pew beside Malachi and wrapped his arm around his narrow shoulders.

"Perhaps you were spared for a reason, Malachi," the constable said. "Have you thought of that? All things do happen for a reason. . . . Is this not the foundation of our faith? You are here—all of us—because we are but part of a plan prepared before the foundations of the earth. It is our humble duty to discern our role in that plan. I do not pretend to know what mine or anyone's might be, but it could be you were spared so no more innocent lives might be lost. For if you had remained in that house, you surely would have perished with your family, and then who would have brought us warning? Your saving of your own life will save the lives of countless others."

"But why me? Why am *I* spared? Why not Father? Or Mother? Or my sisters and brothers? Why *me?*"

"That is something no one can answer," replied Morgan.

With a snort the doctor abandoned any pretense of compassion and spoke harshly to the tormented boy. "Your self-pity mocks your faith, Malachi Stinnet. And every minute you wallow in it is a minute lost. The greatest minds of medieval Europe argued how many angels could dance upon the head of a pin, while the plague took the lives of twenty million. Now is not the time to indulge in esoteric debate upon the whimsy of the gods! Tell me, did you love your family?"

"Of course I loved them!"

"Then exile your guilt and bury your grief. They are dead, and no amount of sorrow or regret will bring them back to you. I present you with a choice, Malachi Stinnet, the choice eventually faced by all: You may lie upon the shores of Babylon and weep, or you may take up arms against the foe! Your family was not beset by demons or felled by the wrath of a vengeful god. Your family was attacked and consumed by a species of predators that will attack again, as surely as the sun will set this day, and more will suffer the same fate as your family, unless you tell me, and tell me now, what you have seen."

As he spoke these words, the doctor leaned closer, then closer still to the cowering Malachi, until, with both hands pushing against the pew on either side of him, Warthrop's face came within inches of the boy's, his eyes afire with the passion of his argument. They shared a common burden, though only Warthrop knew it, and so only Warthrop had the power to exorcize it. I knew it too, of course, and now, as an old man looking, as it were, through my twelve-year-old eyes, I can see the bitter irony of it, the strange and terrible symbolism: Upon his own spotless hands, Malachi perceived the blood of his kin, as the man whose hands were literally stained with it berated him to abandon all feelings of responsibility and remorse!

"I did not see everything," came the choked reply. "I ran."

"But you were inside the house when it began?"

"Yes. Of course. Where else would I be? I was asleep. We all were. There was a terrible crash. The sound of glass breaking as they came through the windows. The very walls shook with the violence of their invasion. I heard my mother cry out. A shadow appeared in my doorway, and the room was filled with a horrible stench that closed my throat. I could not breathe. The shadow filled the doorway ... huge and headless ... huffing and sniffing like a hog. I was paralyzed. Then the shadow in the doorway passed. It left; I know not why.

"The house was filled with screaming. Ours. Theirs. Elizabeth leaped into the bed. I could not move! I should have barricaded the door. I could have broken the window not two feet away and escaped. But I did nothing! I lay in the bed holding Elizabeth, my hand over her mouth lest her cries draw them to us, and through the doorway I could see them pass, headless shadows, with arms so long their knuckles nearly dragged on the ground. Before the door two of them fell into a scuffle, with angry grunts and mad hisses, snarling and snapping as they vied for the body of my brother. I knew it had to be Matthew; it was too large to be Michael.

"They tore him apart before my eyes. Ripped him to pieces and tossed his limbless torso down the hall, where I heard it smack the floor, and then the thudding and snarling grew louder as they swarmed around it. It was then I felt Elizabeth go limp against me. She had fainted.

"By now the screaming had all but ended, though I could still hear the beasts in the hall and at the front of the house, their snarls and hisses, their horrible grunts, and the crunching and cracking of bones. Still I could not move. What if they should hear me? They moved so quickly, even if I got to the window, I feared they would be upon me before I could open it . . . and what horror might be lying in wait outside? Were there more patrolling the yard? I strained to rise from the bed, but I couldn't. I couldn't. I couldn't."

He fell silent. His gaze had turned inward again. The constable had risen from the pew while he spoke, and walked with heavy tread to stand before one of the stained-glass windows, his face turned toward the scene of Christ as the good shepherd attending his flock.

"But of course you did rise," prompted the doctor.

Malachi nodded slowly.

"You couldn't get the window open," urged Warthrop.

"Yes! How did you know?"

"So you broke it open."

"I had no choice!"

"And the sound alerted them."

"It must have, yes."

"Yet still you did not flee, though freedom and safety lay but a few feet away."

"I couldn't leave her."

"Back to the bed for her?"

"They were coming."

"You heard them."

"I pulled her into my arms. She was as lifeless as the

dead. I stumbled toward the window, lost my grip, dropped her. I bent to pick her up. Then . . ."

"You saw it in the doorway."

Malachi nodded again, rapidly now, his eyes wide in astonishment.

"How did you know?"

"Was it male or female, or could you tell?"

"Oh, for the love of God, Pellinore!" said the constable in consternation.

"Very well." The doctor sighed. "You abandoned your sister and fled."

"No! No, I would never!" cried Malachi. "I would not leave her to that . . . *for* that . . . I grabbed her arms and dragged her to the window . . ."

"It was too late," murmured the doctor. "The thing was upon you."

"It moved so fast! In one leap it crossed the room, wrapped its claws around her ankle, and yanked her from me as easily as a man might a doll from a baby. It *flung* her upward, and Elizabeth's head hit the ceiling with a sickening thud; I heard her skull shatter, and then her blood rained down upon my head—my sister's blood upon my head!"

He lost all composure then, covering his face with his hands, his body wracked with heart-wrenching sobs.

The doctor endured it for a moment, but only for a moment.

"Describe it, Malachi," he commanded. "What did it look like?"

"Seven feet . . . perhaps more. Long arms, powerful legs, as pale as a corpse, headless, but with eyes in its shoulders . . . or one eye, I should say. The other was gone."

"Gone?"

"Just a . . . a hole where the eye should have been."

The doctor glanced at me. There was no need to say it; we both were thinking it: *Chance or destiny . . . that brought the blade in blindness thrust into the black eye of the accursed beast.*

"You were not pursued," said the doctor, turning back to Malachi.

"No. I threw myself through the broken window, suffering not so much as a scratch—not a scratch!—then I rode as fast as my horse would carry me to the constable's house."

Warthrop placed a hand stained with the family's blood upon Malachi's shuddering shoulder.

"Very good, Malachi," he said. "You have done well."

"In what way?" cried Malachi. "*In what way?*"

The doctor bade me remain in the pew with Malachi while he and Morgan withdrew to debate the best course of action, or so I assumed based on the heated snippets I happened to overhear.

From the constable: ". . . aggressive and immediate . . . every able-bodied man in New Jerusalem . . ."

And the doctor: ". . . unnecessary and imprudent . . . certain to cause a panic . . ."

Malachi regained his composure during their fervent deliberations, his sobs drying to a trickle of tremulous tears, his fear-borne palsy quieting to an occasional quiver, like the small aftershocks of a violent earthquake.

"What a strange man," said Malachi, meaning the doctor.

"He is not strange," I responded, a bit defensively. "His . . . calling is strange, that's all."

"What is his calling?"

"He is a monstrumologist."

"He hunts monsters?"

"He doesn't like them called that."

"Then why does he call himself a monstrumologist?"

"He didn't pick the name."

"I never knew there were such people."

"There aren't many of them," I said. "His father was one, and I know there is a Monstrumologist Society, but I don't think it has many members."

"Not very difficult to imagine why!" he exclaimed.

On the other side of the sanctuary the argument rose and fell like superheated magma bubbling to the surface of a volcanic lake.

Morgan: ". . . evacuate! Evacuate at once! Evacuate everyone!"

Warthrop: ". . . stupid, Robert, stupid and reckless! The mayhem borne of that intelligence would far exceed the benefits. This can be contained . . . controlled. . . . It is not too late . . ."

"I never believed in monsters," Malachi said.

Again his gaze turned inward, and I knew with the genius of a child's intuition that he had lost his grip on the moment and had fallen as swiftly as Icarus down to the bright, bloody memory of that night, where his family now dwelled, like the tortured souls of Dante's dream writhing in eternal torment, forever devoured but never consumed, their death throes replayed endlessly while he, Malachi, lay paralyzed with dread, helpless to halt the slaughter, his dear sister fainted by his side, the one who had sought salvation from him, the one and only one he had had any chance of rescuing, but whom even a brother's love could not save.

The tête-à-tête beneath the fractured light of the stained glass was nearing its crescendo. The doctor punctuated each point with a poke of his finger into the constable's chest, his strident voice echoing in the cavernous confines of the church: "No evacuations! No hunting parties! *I* am the expert here. *I* am the one—the *only* one—qualified to make the decisions in this case!"

Morgan's measured response came quietly yet insistently, in the manner of a parent to a recalcitrant child—or the manner of a frightened object of a madman's attention. "Warthrop, if I had the slightest doubt as to your expertise, I would not have brought you here this morning. You may understand this foul phenomenon better than any man alive; you are, by the nature of your peculiar pursuits, obligated to understand them, even as I am obligated, by virtue of *my* duty, to protect the lives and property of the citizens of this town. And that duty compels me to act with alacrity and without delay."

The doctor mustered every ounce of his forbearance and spoke through gritted teeth, "I assure you, Robert—indeed, I am prepared to stake my reputation upon it—they will not attack again today, tonight, or for many nights to come."

"You cannot assume that."

"Of course I may assume that! The weight of three thousand years of direct evidence supports it. You offend me, Robert."

"That is not my intent, Pellinore."

"Then why in one breath do you acknowledge my expertise and in the next inform me you intend to ignore it? You bring me here to seek my counsel, then rebuff it out of hand. You claim you want to avoid a panic while you make decisions based upon your own!"

"Granted," allowed Morgan, "but in this instance panic might be the most beneficent response!"

The doctor's visage blushed scarlet and he righted himself to stand with his back ramrod straight, his hands clenched into fists, knuckles as white as bleached bone.

"Very well. You reject my opinion. It is a perilous choice, Robert, but of course that too is an opinion. Your duty, as you say, compels you, and therefore the consequences of your compulsion rest solely upon your shoulders. But when that compulsion undoes you, even at the cost of your very life and the lives of your men, I do not expect the judgment to fall upon me. I shan't be held responsible. My hands are clean."

Of course they were not, far from it! Both literally and figuratively, the blood of the *Anthropophagi's* victims was upon his hands. The old grave-robber's, the entire Stinnet clan's, he was soaked through and through with it.

"Come, Will Henry!" cried the doctor. "Our service here was sought but not accepted! Good day, Constable, and good luck to you, sir. If you need me, you know where you may find me."

He strode down the center aisle to the doors, calling in a voice that boomed against the weathered boards, "Will Henry! Snap to!"

I rose from the pew, and when I did, Malachi sat upright and reached for me, his fingers finding my wrist and pulling me back.

"Where are you going?" he demanded. His expression was desperate.

I nodded toward the doctor. "With him."

"Will Hen*reee*!" shouted the doctor.

"May I come with you?" Malachi asked.

The constable had appeared before us. "Fear not, Malachi. You will be staying with me until a more permanent arrangement can be . . ." He searched for the word, and then with a shrug said, "Arranged."

At the door I turned to find the tableau unaltered: Malachi and Morgan against the backdrop of the cross, one slumped in the foremost pew, the other standing, his hand resting upon the boy's shoulder.

Outside, the doctor breathed deep the warm spring air, as a man might take a draft of laudanum to steady his jangled nerves, then, ignoring the two men stationed at the rectory door whose demeanors darkened upon his appearance, he strode straight to the constable's carriage, where the driver loitered, spinning the chamber of his revolver in an attitude of studied boredom.

"Harrington Lane!" the doctor snapped at him, throwing open the carriage door and heaving himself inside. He snapped his fingers impatiently at me, and I clambered in beside him.

We pulled off the narrow lane once to allow three black hearses to pass. We halted a second time for a cart bearing several men with rifles and a pack of hunting dogs, the excited animals barking and straining against their tethers, the attitude of their subdued handlers playing counterpoint to their agitation. The doctor shook his head and muttered derisively under his breath. Through gritted teeth he growled, "I know what you're thinking, Will Henry, but even the tenets of the victims' faith hold a mistake to be no sin. A miscalculation is not negligence, nor prudence a crime. I am a scientist. I base my action or inaction upon probability and evidence. There is a reason we call science a discipline! Inferior minds bolt or build pyres to roast the witches in their midst! It is a false argument to assert that simply because we do not see fairies dancing upon the lawn proves naught as to their existence. Evidence begets theory, and theory evolves as new evidence emerges. Three thousand years of research, direct eyewitness accounts, serious scientific inquiry—was I to abandon all of it upon the doorstep of speculation and doubt? In all crises are we to demand reason's abdication or, worse, champion the coup of our baser instincts? Are we men, or anxious gazelles? An impartial examination of the facts would lead any reasonable man to conclude that I am blameless, that I reacted with prudence and forbearance in the case, and indeed a lesser man might have squandered his energies pursuing those fairies on the lawn, which no one can see!"

He pounded his crimson fist upon his thigh. "So put aside your juvenile judgments, William James Henry. I am no more accountable for this tragedy than the boy who witnessed it. Less so—yes!—if one applies the same cruel criteria to my actions!"

I did not reply to this passionate outburst, for it was not so much directed at me as the peculiar demons that plagued his conscience; I was but a witness to the exorcism. I was keenly aware, as he must surely have been, of the sickening odor rising from our clothing, the toxic tincture of death clinging to our skin and hair, the tart taste of it tingling on our tongues.

Upon our return to Harrington Lane, the doctor descended to the basement, where he stood, motionless, before the suspended corpse of the male *Anthropophagus*. Was this immobility a mere illusion? Below the surface of this calm facade did a cyclone rage? I suspect, like the whole and wholesome sunlight splintered by the shards of colored glass inside the little church, Warthrop's psyche had been split, and though now far away, a part of him was still present at the morning's holocaust, kneeling, as it were, before the hollowed-out skull of the good reverend Stinnet. I could hear him muttering variations of the argument couched in the coach, like a composer struggling with a difficult bridge, seeking to impose melodic balance to the discordant chords of his recalcitrant remorse.

His muttering petered out. For several minutes he did not speak; he did not move. Statue-still he stood, the maelstrom within as well-veiled as the winds of a hurricane seen from space.

"It is she," he said finally, in a tone tinged with wonder. "The matriarch blinded by Varner. By some malevolent twist of fate, she has come here, Will Henry. It is almost as if . . ." He hesitated to give voice to the proposition. It ran counter to everything he believed. "As if she has come looking for him."

I did not ask to whom he referred. I did not need to ask; I knew.

"I wonder," he said pensively, addressing the monster hung before him upon the hook, "if she would be satisfied with his son."

NINE

"There Is Something I Should Show You"

The constable returned to Harrington Lane later that afternoon, his reappearance predicted by the monstrumologist.

"We must to work tidying up, Will Henry," he said. "The good constable will be arriving shortly to petition—or *re*-petition, I should say—for our assistance. When his frustrated hounds give out or his incredulous shooting party gives up, he will call again."

There was a great deal of "tidying up" to do after the doctor's frantic foraging from the previous day. He went to the study while I tackled the library, shelving books, stacking papers, and throwing away the blackened fragments of the old grave-robber's hat and the heat-warped spine of his father's journal, which had escaped the fire. I felt rather like a malefactor cleaning up the scene of a crime, which, in a sense, it was. No sound emerged from the study as I worked. I suspected the reason for this silence, and when I ducked into the room to inform him I was finished, my suspicion was confirmed: The doctor had not been cleaning. He sat in his chair, an island in a sea of rubble, lost in reverie. Without a word I set to work while he watched, his gaze not unlike the inward stare of Malachi Stinnet, seeing me, but regarding something altogether different.

The knock came at a quarter past three. The doctor rose and said, "You can finish later, Will Henry. Just close the door for now, and show the constable to the library."

Morgan had not come alone. Standing behind him was his driver, silver badge gleaming on his lapel, and revolver conspicuously strapped to his side, and Malachi Stinnet, whose dejected countenance noticeably brightened upon my opening of the door.

"Is the doctor in, Will Henry?" asked the constable in a rigid, formal manner.

"Yes, sir. He's waiting for you in the library."

"Waiting for me? No doubt he is!"

They followed me to the room. Warthrop was standing by the long table upon which I had left the marked-up map with its bright intersecting lines and sloppily drawn circles and stars, rectangles and squares. I had neglected in my haste to roll it up, but the doctor seemed unaware of it lying in plain sight, or he did not care.

He stiffened when we entered, and said to Morgan, "Robert, I am surprised."

"Are you?" rejoined Morgan coldly. His attitude was one of barely contained contempt. "Will Henry said you were expecting me."

The doctor nodded toward the deputy and the lone survivor of that morning's massacre. "You. Not them."

"Malachi asked to come. And I asked O'Brien."

The constable tossed something onto the table. It slid a few inches on the slick surface of the map and came to rest beside Warthrop's fingertips.

It was my beloved little hat, the one lost at the cemetery, now found.

"I believe this belongs to your assistant."

Warthrop said nothing. He was not looking at the hat; he was looking at Malachi.

"Will, is that not your initials on the inside band there, W.H.?" asked the constable, though he had not turned his impeaching eye from Warthrop.

"Will Henry, would you take Malachi into the kitchen, please?" said the doctor quietly.

"No one leaves this room," barked Morgan. "O'Brien!"

With a knowing smirk the burly deputy stationed himself in the doorway.

"I think it would be best if Malachi—," began the doctor.

Morgan interrupted him. "I shall decide what's best here. How long have you known, Warthrop?"

The doctor hesitated. Then he said, "Since the morning of the fifteenth."

"Since the . . ." Morgan was aghast. "You have known *four days*, and yet you told *no one*?"

"I did not believe the situation—"

"You did not *believe*!"

"It was my judgment that—"

"Your *judgment*!"

"Based on all the data available to me, it was my judgment and my belief that the . . . the infestation could be addressed with dispassionate deliberation without inciting unnecessary panic and . . . and unreasonable, disproportionate force."

"I asked you this morning," Morgan said, apparently unmoved by the doctor's rationalization.

"And I told the truth, Robert."

"You said you were shocked by their presence here."

"I was . . . and I am. The attack last night certainly did come as a shock, and in that sense I did not lie. Are you placing me under arrest?"

The constable's eyes flashed behind his spectacles, and his mustache quivered. "*You* brought them here," he said.

"I did not."

"But you know who did."

The doctor did not respond. He did not have the chance. At that moment Malachi, who had been listening with growing consternation, who had insisted upon coming in ignorance of the constable's deduction, who now was in the presence of the man whose silence had damned his family, turned not upon the man in the dock, but upon O'Brien. He yanked the gun from the unsuspecting man's holster and threw himself upon Warthrop, forcing him to the floor and pressing the muzzle of the revolver against his forehead. The click of the hammer locking into place was very loud in the stunned silence that followed.

Malachi straddled the doctor's fallen form, brought his face to within inches of Warthrop's, and spat out a single word: "*You!*"

O'Brien lunged forward, but the constable slammed a hand into his chest to stay him and called out to the grief-stricken boy, "Malachi! Malachi, it will solve nothing!"

"I want nothing *solved*!" cried the maddened Malachi. "I want *justice*."

The constable stepped toward him. "It is not justice, boy. It's murder."

"*He's* the murderer! An eye for an eye; a tooth for a tooth!"

"No, it is God's business to judge him, not yours."

Morgan moved slowly toward him as he spoke, and Malachi responded by shoving the end of the pistol hard into Warthrop's skull. The boy's body vibrated with the force of his passion.

"Not another step! I'll do it. I swear I will do it!"

The violence of his tremors caused the gun's muzzle to scrape across Warthrop's forehead, and bright blood welled around the steel that tore through the tender skin.

Without stopping to think—for if I had, I might not have risked both our lives—I brushed past Morgan and went to my knees before them, the tormented Malachi and the prostrate Warthrop, and the boy turned his tear-stained face, contorted with anger and bewilderment, toward mine beseechingly, as if in my eyes he might find the answer to that unspeakable, unanswerable question: Why?

"He took everything from me, Will!" he whispered.

"And you would take everything from me," I answered.

I reached for the hand that held the gun. He flinched. His finger tightened on the trigger. I froze.

"He is all I have," I said, for it was true.

With one hand I grasped his shaking wrist; with the other I eased the firearm from his quivering fingers. In two strides Morgan was beside me, and he snatched the gun from me and handed it to the abashed O'Brien.

"Exercise a bit of care with this next time," he snapped.

I placed my hand, now afflicted with the same palsy affecting Malachi, upon his shoulder. He fell away from the doctor and into my arms, burying his face into my chest, his thin frame wracked with sobs. The doctor struggled to his feet, leaned on the worktable, and pressed his handkerchief against the wound on his forehead. His face was pale, spotted with blood. He murmured, "If I had known—"

"You knew enough," shot back Morgan. "And now you will confess all of it, Pellinore, *everything*, or I *will* arrest you, tonight, without delay."

The doctor nodded. His eyes were upon the miserable Malachi Stinnet, cradled in my arms. "There is something I should show you," he said to Morgan. "But only you, Robert. I believe . . ." He caught himself. "In my judgment . . ." Caught himself again. He cleared his throat. "It would not be in Malachi's best interest to see it."

I knew where they were going, of course, and could not have agreed more with the doctor: It most definitely would not have been in Malachi's best interest to see what hung in the monstrumologist's basement. The beefy O'Brien started to follow them out, but Morgan ordered him to remain with us, and so he lingered in the doorway, looking none too happy about it, glowering across the room at me as if I were somehow responsible for the bloody turn of events. Perhaps I was, in part, and at that moment I certainly felt that way. The shadow of the doctor's guilt stretched long, and though I had questioned him the night of our mad flight from the cemetery, I had not pressed the matter to its utmost. The doctor, after all, hadn't locked me in my room or chained me to a newel. I could have run straight to the constable's that night and sounded the alarm, and I did not. The mitigating factors—my age, my subservient status, my bows to the doctor's superior intellect and the maturity of his judgment—seemed insubstantial in the presence of Malachi's pain, his unutterable loss.

Looking up, my own vision clouded by sorrow for his plight and—I confess—for my own, I made out O'Brien glaring down at me, his upper lip twisted into a derisive snarl.

"I hope he hangs for this," he said.

I looked away, into Malachi's eyes, red-rimmed and wide open. He whispered, "Did *you* know too?"

I nodded. Lying, the doctor had taught me, was the worst kind of buffoonery.

"Yes."

They returned after what seemed like hours, but it could not have been more than a few minutes. All color had drained from Morgan's owlish face, and his locomotion to the chair into which he carefully lowered himself was reminiscent of the stiff and awkward movements of a shell-shocked soldier. With trembling fingers he packed his pipe, and two attempts it took to light it. Warthrop, too, having so recently teetered upon death's black abyss, seemed shaken and stunned, the round wound on his forehead caked in dried blood, perfectly centered an inch above his eyes, like the mark of Cain.

"Will Henry," he said quietly. "Take Malachi upstairs to one of the spare rooms."

"Yes, sir," I replied at once. I helped Malachi to his feet, pulling his arm over my shoulders while he leaned against me, and together we shuffled out of the room, my knees nearing buckling under his weight; he was a good head taller than I. Up the stairs I lugged him, and into the nearest bedroom, the room in which the nude body of Alistair Warthrop had been found five years before. I eased him onto the mattress, where he, like the monstrumologist's father, rolled himself into a miserable ball, until his knees nearly brushed his chin. I closed the door and collapsed into the chair beside the bed to catch my breath.

"I should not have come here," he said.

I nodded in response to this obvious observation.

"He offered to take me to his house," he went on, referring to Morgan. "For I have no place else to go."

"You have no other family?" I asked.

"All my family is dead."

I nodded again. "I'm sorry, Malachi."

"You do everything for him, don't you? Even apologize."

"He didn't mean for it to happen."

"He did nothing. He *knew* and he did nothing. Why do you defend him, Will? Who is he to you?"

"It isn't that," I said. "It's what I am to him."

"What do you mean?"

"I am his assistant," I said not without a touch of pride. "Like my father. After he . . . after the fire, the doctor took me in."

"He adopted you?"

"He took me in."

"Why did he do that? Why did he take you in?"

"Because there was no one else."

"No," he said. "That is not what I meant. Why did he *choose* to take you in?"

"I don't know," I said, a bit taken aback. The question had never occurred to me. "I never asked him. I suppose he felt it was the right thing to do."

"Because of your father's service?"

I nodded. "My father loved him." I cleared my throat. "He is a great man, Malachi. It is . . ." And now my father's oft-spoken words fell from my lips, "It is an honor to serve him."

I attempted to excuse myself. My avowal had reminded me of my place by the doctor's side. Malachi reacted as if I had threatened to throttle him. He grabbed my wrist and begged me not to go, and in the end I could not refuse him. My failure was not entirely owing to a congenital curse (it seemed my lot in life to sit at the bedsides of troubled people); it resulted too from the painful memory of another bereft boy who lay comfortless in a strange bed night after night, consigned to a little alcove, set aside and forgotten for hours, like an unwanted heirloom bequeathed by a distant relation, too vulgar to display but too valuable to discard. There were times, in the beginning of my service to the monstrumologist, when I was certain he must have heard my keening wails long into the night—heard them, and did nothing. He rarely brought up my parents or the night they died. When he did, it was usually to chastise me, as he had the night we'd returned from the cemetery: *Your father would have understood.*

So I remained a few minutes more with him, sitting on the edge of Alistair Warthrop's deathbed, holding Malachi's hand. Clearly he was exhausted from his ordeal, and I urged him to rest, but he wanted to know everything. How had we discovered the creatures that had overcome his family? What had the doctor done in the interim, between the time of our discovery and the attack? I told him of the midnight visit of Erasmus Gray with his nightmarish cargo, of our expedition to the cemetery and the mad flight that followed, of our sojourn in Dedham and the tale of Hezekiah Varner. I omitted the elder Warthrop's involvement in the coming of the *Anthropophagi* to New Jerusalem, but stressed Warthrop's innocence in the matter as well as his efforts to answer the critical questions presented by their presence. Malachi seemed little satisfied with my defense of the doctor.

"If a rabid hound runs amok, what fool looks instead for the creature that made it sick?" he asked. "Shoot the hound first, and then find the source of its madness if you must."

"He thought we had time—"

"Well, he was wrong, wasn't he? And now my family is dead. Me, too, Will," he added matter-of-factly, without a shred of self-pity or melodrama. "I am dead too. I feel your hand; I see you sitting there; I breathe. But inside there is nothing."

I nodded. How well I understood! I gave his hand a squeeze.

"It will get better," I assured him. "It did for me. It will never be the same, but it will get better. And I promise you the doctor will kill these things, down to the last one."

Malachi slowly shook his head, his eyes ablaze. "He is your master and rescued you from the bleak life of the orphanage," he whispered. "I understand, Will. You feel bound to excuse and forgive him, but I cannot excuse and I will not forgive this . . . this . . . What did you say he was?"

"A monstrumologist."

"Yes, that's right. A monster hunter. . . . Well, he is what he hunts."

He fell silent after these damning words, and his eyelids fluttered, drooped, then finally closed altogether. He held tightly to my hand, however, even as weariness bore him down; I had to pry his fingers from mine before making my escape.

I flinched on my way down the stairs, for the evening quiet was shattered suddenly by the banging on the front door and the doctor's bellowing for me to answer it. *What has happened?* I wondered. *Have they struck again?* Night was falling; perhaps another nocturnal rampage had begun—or perhaps word of the Stinnets' demise had leaked out and a party of Warthrop's fellow townspeople had come calling with hot tar and feathers.

He is what he hunts, Malachi had said. I did not believe that but understood how Malachi might judge him, and the rest of the town as well, once it learned of the *Anthropophagi* onslaught.

I did not think the doctor was a monster who hunted monsters, but I was about to meet a man who did—and was.

TEN

"The Best Man for the Job"

He was quite tall, well over six feet, the man standing on the doctor's doorstep, athletic of build and handsome in a boyish way, with rather fine features and stylishly long flaxen hair. His eyes were an odd shade of gray; in the glittering lamplight they appeared nearly black, but later, when I saw them in daylight, his eyes took on a softer shade, the ashy gray of charcoal dust or the hue of an ironclad warship. He wore a traveling cloak and gloves, riding boots and a homburg hat set at a rakish angle. His mustache was small and neatly trimmed, golden like his mane of hair, so diaphanous it appeared to float above his full and sensuous lips.

"Well!" he said with a note of surprise. "Good evening, young man." He spoke with a refined British accent, a leonine purr of a voice, melodic and soothing.

"Good evening, sir," I said.

"I am looking for the house of a dear friend of mine and I'm afraid my driver might be lost. Pellinore Warthrop is his name." With a sparkle in his eye he added, "My friend's name, not the driver's."

"This is Dr. Warthrop's house," I offered.

"Ah, so it's 'Doctor' Warthrop now, is it?" He chuckled softly. "And who might you be?"

"I am his assistant. *Apprentice*," I corrected myself.

"An assistant apprentice! Good for him. And for you, I'm sure. Tell me, Mr. Assistant-Apprentice—"

"Will, sir. My name is Will Henry."

"Henry! Now that name sounds familiar."

"My father served the doctor for many years."

"Was his given name Benjamin?"

"No, sir. It was—"

"Patrick," he said with a snap of his fingers. "No. You are much too young to be *his* son. Or his son's son, if his son had one."

"It was James, sir."

"Was it? Are you quite certain it wasn't Benjamin?"

From within, the doctor called loudly, "Will Henry! Who is at the door?"

The man in the cloak leaned forward, bringing his eyes to the level of my own, and whispered, "Tell him."

"But you haven't told me your name," I pointed out.

"Is it necessary, Will Henry?" He produced a piece of stationery from his pocket and dangled it before my eyes. I recognized the handwriting at once, of course, for it was my own. "I know Pellinore didn't write this letter; compose it, yes; write it, impossible! The man's penmanship is atrocious."

"Will Henry!" the doctor said sharply behind me. "I asked who—" He froze upon seeing the tall Englishman in the entryway.

"It's Dr. Kearns, sir," I said.

"My dear Pellinore," purred Kearns warmly, brushing past me to seize the doctor's hand. He pumped it vigorously. "How long has it been, old boy? Istanbul?"

"Tanzania," returned the doctor tightly.

"Tanzania! Has it really been that long? And what the blazes did you do to your bloody forehead?"

"An accident," murmured the monstrumologist.

"Oh, that's good. I thought perhaps you'd become a bloody Hindu. Well, Warthrop, you look terrible. How long has it been since you've had a good night's sleep or a decent meal? What happened? Did you fire the maid and the cook, or did they quit in disgust? And tell me whenever did you become a doctor?"

"I'm relieved you could come on such short notice, Kearns," said the doctor with that same tightly wound tenseness in his tone, ignoring the interrogatories. "I'm afraid the situation has taken a turn for the worse."

"Hardly avoidable, old boy."

The doctor lowered his voice. "The town constable is here."

"As bad a turn as that, then? How many have the rascals eaten since your letter?"

"Six."

"Six! In just three days? Very peculiar."

"Exactly what I thought. Extraordinarily uncharacteristic of the species."

"And you're quite certain it's *Anthropophagi*?"

"Without a doubt. There's one hanging in my basement if you'd care to—"

At that moment Constable Morgan appeared in the library doorway, his round eyes narrowed suspiciously behind his spectacles. Kearns spied him over the doctor's shoulder, and his cherubic countenance lit up. His teeth were astonishingly bright and straight for an Englishman's.

"Ah, Robert, good," said Warthrop. He appeared somewhat relieved, as if the constable's appearance had freed him from an intolerable burden. "Constable Morgan, this is Dr.—"

"Cory," said Kearns, extending his hand forcibly at Morgan. "Richard Cory. How do you do?"

"Not well," answered the constable. "It has been a very long day, Dr. Cory."

"Please: 'Richard.' 'Doctor' is more or less an honorary title."

"Oh?" Morgan tilted back his chin; his spectacles flashed. "Warthrop informed me you were a surgeon."

"Oh, I dabbled in my youth. More of a hobby now than

anything else. I haven't sliced anyone open in years."

"Is that so?" inquired the constable courteously. "And why is that?"

"Got boring after a bit, to tell you the truth. I am easily bored, Constable, which is the chief reason I dropped everything to answer Pellinore's kind invitation. Bloody good sport, this business."

"It is bloody," rejoined Morgan. "But I would hardly call it sport."

"I'll admit it isn't cricket or squash, but it's far superior to hunting fox or quail. Pales in comparison, Morgan!"

He turned to the doctor. "My driver is waiting at the curb. The fare needs settling up, and I've some baggage, of course."

It took a moment for Warthrop to grasp his meaning. "You intend to stay here?"

"I thought it the most prudent course. The less I'm seen about town the better, yes?"

"Yes," agreed the doctor after a pause. "Of course. Here, Will Henry." He reached into his pocket and pulled out his money clip. "Pay Dr. Kear—*Cory's*—"

"Richard's," interjected Kearns.

"—driver," completed Warthrop. "And take his luggage up to the extra room."

"Extra room, sir?"

"My mother's old room."

"Why, Pellinore, I'm honored," said Kearns.

"Snap to, Will Henry. We'll have a late night of it, and we'll be wanting some tea and something to eat."

Kearns pulled off his gloves, shrugged off his cape, and dropped them and his hat into my arms.

"There are two valises, three crates, and one large wooden box, Master Henry," he informed me. "The valises you can manage. The box and trunks you can't, but the driver may lend a hand if you provide the proper incentive. I would suggest you carry the crates around to the carriage house. The suitcases and the box must go to my room. Be careful with my box; the contents are quite fragile. And a spot of tea sounds spectacularly satisfying. Do you know they had none on the train? America is still an astonishingly uncivilized country. I take mine with cream and two sugars, Master Henry; that's a good lad."

He winked and ruffled my hair, clapped his hands together, and said, "Now, then, gentlemen, shall we get to work? It may have been a long day, Robert, but the night will be longer, I assure you!"

The men retired to the library while I and the driver, once his palm had been properly greased, set to unloading our guest's baggage. The aforementioned wooden box proved to be the most cumbersome item. Though not as heavy as the large crates we carted to the carriage house, the box was at least six feet long and wrapped in a slick silky material that made a good grip difficult. Negotiating the turn of the stairs presented a particular problem, in the end accomplished by easing the box on its end and pivoting it around the corner. The driver cursed and swore and sweated profusely, complaining during the entire enterprise of his back, his hands, his legs, and the fact that he was no beast of burden—he was a driver of them. We both felt cutouts in the wood beneath the silky wrapping that would have made excellent handholds, and he wondered aloud why anyone would bother to wrap a wooden box in bedsheets.

Next I went to the kitchen for the tea and cakes, and at last to the library bearing the tray. As I entered, I realized I had set out only three cups; I would have to go back for another; and then I saw that O'Brien was gone, sent home, perhaps, by Morgan, who may have wanted as few witnesses as possible to the budding of their nascent conspiracy.

The men were leaning over the worktable, considering the marked-up map as Warthrop pointed to a spot of coastline.

"This marks where the *Feronia* went aground. Impossible to say, of course, the precise location where they came ashore, but here"—he picked up the newspaper from the top of the stack—"is a notice of a missing boy who the authorities believed ran off to sea, two weeks later and twenty miles inland. Each circle, here, here, here," he said as he jabbed each spot, "et cetera, represents a potential victim, most of whom were reported missing or were discovered several days or weeks later, their injuries attributed to the foraging of wild animals. I've noted the corresponding dates in each of the circles. As you can see, gentlemen, while we cannot attribute every instance to the feeding activities of our uninvited guests, the record indicates a cone of distribution, a gradual migration that leads here, to New Jerusalem."

Neither in his audience spoke. Morgan sucked on his pipe, long since gone out, and regarded the map through the lower quadrant of his pince-nez. Kearns gave a noncommittal grunt and smoothed his nearly invisible mustache with his thumb and forefinger. Warthrop went on, speaking in that same dry lecturing tone to which I had so often been subjected. He realized it was unlikely that this twenty-four-year migration had occurred without someone discovering the cause of these mysterious disappearances and deaths, but, as there could be no other reasonable explanation, it *must* have happened that way.

At this point Kearns interrupted, "I can think of another."

Warthrop looked up from the map. "Another what?"

"Reasonable explanation."

"I would love to hear it," said the doctor, though it was clear he would not.

"Forgive my cheekiness, Pellinore, but your theory is nonsense. Completely ridiculous, absurdly convoluted, unreasonably complicated balderdash. Our *poppies* no more traveled here on foot than I did."

"And what is your theory? They took a train?"

"*I* took the train, Pellinore. Their mode of transit was undoubtedly a bit more private."

"I don't understand," said Morgan.

"It's perfectly obvious, Constable," Kearns said with a chuckle. "A child could see it. I wager Will does. What do you say, Will? What is your answer to our devilish riddle?"

"My—my answer, sir?"

"You're a bright boy; you must be for Warthrop to employ you as his assistant-apprentice. What is your theory of the case?"

With the tips of my ears burning I said, "Well, sir, I think . . ." All three had turned to stare at me. I swallowed and plunged on. "They're here, obviously, and they must have gotten here somehow, which means they either got here on their own with no one knowing or . . . or . . ."

"Yes, very good. Go on, Will Henry. Or—what?" asked Kearns.

"Or someone did know." I looked to the floor. The doctor's glare was particularly discomforting.

"Precisely." Kearns nodded. "And that someone knew because he arranged their passage, from Africa to New England."

"What are you suggesting, Kearns?" demanded Warthrop, forgetting himself as the course of the conversation veered toward treacherous waters.

"Kearns?" asked Morgan. "I thought his name was Cory."

"Kearns is my middle name," offered the retired surgeon smoothly. "From the maternal side of the family."

"It's as absurd as you claim my theory to be," insisted Warthrop. "To suggest that someone brought them here, with no one being the wiser for it, housed somehow and fed . . . how? And by whom?"

"Again, my dear Warthrop, questions the answers to which are obvious. Don't you agree, Will Henry? So obvious it's comical. I understand your myopia in the matter, Pellinore. It must be quite painful for you to accept, so you have worried and twisted the facts, chewed and gnawed upon the evidence, until up is down, black is white, square is round."

"You offend me, John," growled Warthrop.

"John? But your given name is Richard," objected Morgan.

"A nickname, after John Brown, the agitator. My mother was an American, you see, and quite the abolitionist."

"I am a scientist," insisted Warthrop. "I go where the facts lead me."

"Until your heartstrings tug you back. Come now, Pellinore, do you honestly believe in this claptrap theory of yours? They wander ashore, undetected, and for the next *twenty-four* years manage to feed off the local populace and make little *Anthro-poppies*, leaving behind no direct evidence, no survivors, no eyewitnesses, until they miraculously arrive at the doorstep of the very person who requested the pleasure of their company? You're like the priests in the temple: You strain out a gnat but swallow a camel!"

"It's possible; the facts do fit," insisted the doctor.

"How?"

"Adaptation, natural selection, and some luck, I'll admit that. It's conceivable—"

"Oh, Pellinore," said Kearns. "Really. It's conceivable the moon is made of blue cheese."

"I can't conceive of that," Morgan argued.

"You can't prove it isn't," retorted Kearns. He laid a hand on the doctor's shoulder, a hand the doctor promptly shrugged off. "When did he die? Four, five years ago? Look at your circles there. You drew them yourself; look at them, Pellinore! Look at the dates. See how they cluster there and there? See the gap in time between this circle twelve miles away and this one but a half mile from the cemetery? These here, within this ten-mile radius, beginning in late '83 to the present—these represent true attacks, perhaps; the rest is wishful thinking. They were pulled off that ship, transported here, and kept safe and sound until their keeper could no longer provide them their victuals."

Warthrop slapped him hard across the cheek. The sound of flesh striking flesh was very loud, and no one spoke for a long moment. Kearns's expression hardly changed; he wore the same small, ironic smile he had worn from the moment he'd stepped inside 425 Harrington Lane. Morgan busied himself with his pipe. I fiddled with a teacup. The tea had long since gone cold.

"It's right before your eyes," said Kearns softly. "If you would but open them."

"This John Richard Kearns Cory does have a point, Pellinore," Morgan said.

"Or Dick," interjected Kearns. "Some people call me Dick for Richard. Or Jack for John."

"He would never do such a thing," said Warthrop. "Not the man I knew."

"Then he wasn't the man you knew," Kearns said.

"I mean the reference to opening eyes," corrected the constable. "In terms of what is right before ours. How they got here is not why *we* are here. We must decide, and decide quickly, how to exterminate them."

"I thought that had been decided already," Kearns said. "Or was there some other reason I was invited?"

"In the morning I am contacting the governor's office to request the mobilization of the state militia," pronounced Morgan. "And I am ordering a complete evacuation of the town—of the women and children, at least."

"Completely unnecessary," Kearns said with a wave of his hand. "How many did you say there were, Pellinore? Thirty to thirty-five? An average pod?"

Warthrop nodded. He still seemed shaken by Kearns's argument. "Yes," he muttered weakly.

"I would say no more than five or six of your best marksmen, Morgan. Men who can be trusted to keep their mouths shut, preferably men with a military background, and best if two or three are handy with a hammer and saw. I've made a list of materials to be discreetly acquired; the rest I've brought with me. We can set to it at first light and be done by nightfall."

"Five or six men, you say?" cried Morgan incredulously.

"Have you seen what these creatures are capable of?"

"Yes," said Kearns simply. "I have."

"John has hunted them extensively in Africa," Warthrop allowed with a sigh.

"Jack," said Kearns. "I prefer Jack."

"It cannot wait till morning. We must move against them tonight, before they can attack again," insisted Morgan.

"They will not attack tonight," said Kearns. The constable looked over to Warthrop, but the doctor refused to meet his gaze.

Turning back to Kearns, Morgan demanded, "How do you know?"

"Because they've just fed. In the wild, *poppies* gorge once a month and spend the rest of the time lolling about like indolent lotus-eaters. Satisfied, Constable?"

"No, I am not satisfied."

"It hardly matters. Now, there are some conditions that first must be met before we can proceed."

"Conditions for what?" asked Morgan.

"For my services. Surely Pellinore told you."

"Pellinore chose not to tell me many things."

"Ah. Well, you can hardly blame him, can you? He's already pledged to cover my expenses, but there remains the small matter of my fee."

"Your fee?"

"Five thousand dollars, in cash, payable upon the successful completion of our contract."

Morgan's mouth dropped open. He turned to the doctor and said, "You never said anything about paying this man."

"I shall pay him out of my own pocket," the doctor said wearily. He leaned against the table, his face pale and drawn. I feared he might faint. Without thinking I took a half step toward him.

"Seems only just," said Kearns.

"Please, Jack," the doctor entreated him. "Please."

"Good! So that's taken care of. The one other requirement is something only you can fulfill, Constable: Under no circumstances am I to be held accountable, within the law or outside of it, for any loss of life or limb in the prosecution of our hunt, including any laws I may break or bend in the execution of the same."

"What do you mean, Cory or Kearns or whatever your blasted name is?" barked Morgan.

"It's Cory; I thought I made that quite clear."

"I don't care if it's John Jacob Jingleheimer Schmidt!"

"Oh, Jacob is my baptismal name."

"No matter the arrangements you may have made with Warthrop, I am still an officer of the law—"

"No immunity, no extermination, Robert—or may I call you Bob?"

"I don't care what you call me; I will make no such guarantee!"

"Very well, then. I think I shall call you Bobby. I dislike palindromes."

Now it was Morgan who appeared ready to take a turn on Kearns's cheek. Warthrop intervened before the blow could fall, saying, "We've little choice in the matter, Robert. He is the best man for the job; I wouldn't have brought him here otherwise."

"Actually," said Kearns, "I am the *only* man for the job."

Their discussion lasted late into the night, with a withdrawn Warthrop sitting sullenly in a chair while Morgan and Kearns feinted and parried and circled warily round each other, looking for chinks in the other's armor. Warthrop rarely intervened, and when he did shake himself from his stupor, it was in an attempt to bring the conversation back to the issue that most consumed him: not the *how* of their extermination but the *how* of their presence in New Jerusalem. In the main he was ignored.

Kearns was keen for the constable to grant him total command of the operation. "There can be only one general in any successful campaign," he pointed out. "I cannot guarantee success without full and unquestioning fealty to my orders. Any confusion in this regard practically ensures failure."

"Of course; I understand that," snapped Morgan.

"Which part? The necessity of a clear chain of command or my being at the head of that chain?"

"I served in the army, Cory," said Morgan, who had given up calling Kearns by any of the other names offered. "You don't have to speak to me as if I were a bumpkin."

"Then we are agreed? You will make clear to your men who is in charge?"

"Yes, yes."

"And instruct them to do exactly as I tell them, no matter how bizarre or seemingly absurd the request?"

Morgan wet his lips nervously, and glanced Warthrop's way. The doctor nodded. The constable did not seem comforted. "I feel a bit like Faust at the moment but, yes, I will tell them."

"Ah, a literary man! I knew it. When this is done, Bobby, I would love to spend an evening, just you and me, a snifter of brandy and a cozy fire. We can discuss Goethe and Shakespeare. Tell me, have you ever read Nietzsche?"

"No, I have not."

"Oh, you simply *must*. He's a genius and, not entirely incidentally, a good friend of mine. Borrowed—I shan't say 'stole'—one or two of my pet ideas, but that's a genius for you."

"I've never heard of the man."

"I shall lend you my copy of *Jenseits von Gut und Böse*. You can read German, yes?"

"What is the point of this?" Morgan had finally lost his temper. "Warthrop, what sort of man have you brought here?"

"He told you earlier," Kearns countered, losing in an instant his cheerful facade. The sparkle in his gray eyes extinguished itself, and suddenly his eyes seemed very dark, black in fact, as black and expressionless as a shark's. The face, at all times previous so lively—winking, smirking, alight with jollity—now blank like the eyes, as immobile as a mask, though the impression was the opposite, of a mask falling away to reveal the true character beneath. That personage possessed no personality, neither cheerful nor dour; like the predator whose eyes his now resembled, no emotion moved him, no compunction restricted him. For a telling moment John Kearns allowed the mask to slip, and what lay underneath sent a shiver down my spine.

"I—I mean no offense," stuttered Morgan, for he too must have glimpsed the not-human in the other's eyes. "I simply don't wish to entrust my life and the lives of my men to a mental defective."

"I assure you, Constable Morgan, I am quite sane, as I understand the word, perhaps the sanest person in this room, for I suffer from no illusions. I have freed myself, you see, from the pretense that burdens most men. Much like our prey, I do not impose order where there is none; I do not pretend there is any more than what there is, or that you and I are anything more than what we are. That is the essence of their beauty, Morgan, the aboriginal purity of their being, and why I admire them."

"Admire them! And you claim you aren't defective!"

"There is much we can learn from the *Anthropophagi*. I am their student as much as I am their enemy."

"Are we finished here?" Morgan demanded of Warthrop. "Is that all, or is there more of this drivel to endure before we're done?"

"Robert is right; it's very late," said the monstrumologist. "Unless you have more of your drivel, John."

"Of course, but it can wait."

At the front door Morgan turned to Warthrop. "I almost forgot—Malachi . . ."

"Will Henry." The doctor motioned toward the stairs.

Morgan reconsidered, and said, "No. He's probably asleep. Don't wake him. I'll send someone over for him in the morning." His eye wandered to the wound on the doctor's forehead. "Unless you think—"

"That's quite all right," Warthrop interrupted. He seemed past all caring. "Let him stay the night."

Morgan nodded, and breathed deep the cool night air. "What an odd man this Brit, Warthrop."

"Yes. Exceedingly odd. But particularly suited for the task."

"I pray you're right. For all our sakes."

We bade the constable good night, and I followed the doctor back into the library, where Kearns, having helped himself to Warthrop's chair, sat sipping his cold tea. Kearns smiled broadly and lifted his cup. The mask was back on.

"Insufferable little marplot, isn't he?" he asked, meaning the constable.

"He's frightened," answered Warthrop.

"He should be."

"You're wrong, you know. About my father."

"Why, Pellinore? Because I cannot prove *you* wrong?"

"Setting aside the issue of his character for a moment, your theory is hardly more satisfying than mine. How did he manage to conceal them for such a long period of time? Or sustain them with their gruesome diet? Even granting you the outrageous assumption that Alistair was capable of such gross inhumanity, where did he find victims? How could he, for twenty years, without getting caught or even raising the least bit of suspicion, supply them with human fodder?"

"You overestimate the value of human life, Pellinore. You always have. Up and down the eastern seaboard the cities are seething with trash, the refuge washed up from Europe's slums. It would be no Herculean task to lure scores of them here with promises of employment or other incentives, or, failing that, to simply snatch them from the ghetto with the help of certain men who do not suffer from your quaint romantic idealism. Believe me the world is full of such men! Of course, it is entirely possible—though not, I would say, probable—that he persuaded his pets to adapt their diet to a lower form of life, assuming that was, as you propose, his goal. It is possible they have acquired a partiality to chicken. Possible, though not very probable."

Warthrop was shaking his head. "I am not convinced."

"And I am not concerned. But I am curious. Why do you resist an explanation that makes far more sense than your own? Really, Pellinore, would you care to compute the odds of them migrating here, to your own backyard, by sheer chance? In the back of your mind you must know the truth, but refuse to acknowledge it. Why? Because you cannot bring yourself to think the worst of him? Who was he to you? More important, who were *you* to *him*? You defend a man who barely tolerated your existence." His boyish face lit up. "Ah! Is *that* it? Are you still trying to prove yourself worthy of his love—even now, when it's impossible for him to give it? And you call yourself a scientist!

"You're a hypocrite, Pellinore. A silly, sentimental hypocrite, much too sensitive for your own good. I've often wondered why you even became a monstrumologist. You are a worthy man with admirable attributes, but this business is dark and dirty, and you never struck me as the type. Did *that* have to do with him as well? To please him? So he would finally notice you?"

"Say no more, Kearns." The doctor was so agitated by these barbs set with such exquisite surgical precision that I thought he might strike Kearns again, this time with something harder than his hand, perhaps the fireplace poker. "I did not invite you here for this."

"You invited me here to slay dragons, did you not? Well. That's what I'm trying to do."

I slipped out of the room shortly after this fevered exchange. It was quite painful to watch, and, even now, decades later, to remember in such vivid detail. As I mounted the stairs to the second floor, I thought of soup and of the doctor's words. *Don't suffer under any illusions that you are more than that:*

an assistant forced upon me by unfortunate circumstances. I did not, at the time, know why I should remember those words at that moment. Now, of course, the reason is obvious.

I paused at Malachi's door and peeked inside. He had not moved a muscle since I'd seen him last, and I watched him sleep for a moment before closing the door. Then up the ladder to my loft, to catch or at least chase slumber myself. But an hour later I was up again, for I heard my name being called by a voice shrill with distress. At first, in my groggy condition, I assumed it was the doctor's; however, upon reaching the second floor, I realized the voice emanated from Malachi's room. My route took me by the room now occupied by Jack Kearns, and I paused there, for the door was ajar, and light from within streamed into the darkened hall.

Inside I saw Kearns kneeling before the long wooden box. He had removed the silk covering and the lid, which he had laid on the floor beside him. I noted several quarter-size holes had been drilled into it. Kearns reached into the valise next to him and removed a thin pencil-shaped object that appeared to be made of glass. He flicked it twice with his finger, then bent over the box. His back was to the door, so I could not see more, nor did I wish to. I stepped quickly into Malachi's room and closed the door.

He was sitting up, his back pressed against the headboard, his bright blue eyes shining with apprehension.

"I woke up and you were gone," he said in an accusatory tone.

"I was called away," I said.

"What time is it?"

"I don't know. Very late."

"I was having a dream and a loud noise woke me. I almost jumped out the window."

"You're on the second floor," I pointed out. "You would have broken your leg, Malachi."

"What was the noise I heard?"

I shook my head. "I don't know. I didn't hear anything. It may have been Dr. Kearns."

"Who is Dr. Kearns?"

"He is . . ." In truth I did not know who he was. "He's come to help."

"Another monster hunter?"

I nodded.

"When do they plan to do it?" he asked.

"Tomorrow."

He did not speak for a moment.

"I am going with them," he said.

"They may not let you."

"I don't care. I'm going anyway."

I nodded again. *Me too, I fear,* I thought.

"It was Elizabeth," he said. "My dream. We were in this dark place, and I was searching for her. She called my name, again and again, but I could not find her. I searched, but I could not find her."

"She is in a better place now, Malachi," I offered.

"I want to believe that, Will."

"My parents are there too. And one day I'll see them again."

"But why do you believe that? Why do we believe such things? Because we want to?"

"I don't know' I answered honestly. "I believe because I must."

I stepped into the hall and eased the door closed behind me. Turning to go back to my room, I almost collided with Kearns, who was standing just outside his door. Startled, I stumbled backward. Kearns was smiling.

"Will Henry," he said softly. "Who is in that room?"

"What room, sir?"

"The room you just came out of."

"His name is Malachi, Dr. Kearns. He's . . . It was his family that . . ."

"Ah, the Stinnet boy. First he takes you in, and now another. Pellinore's become quite the philanthropist."

"Yes, sir. I suppose, sir."

I looked away from his smoky eyes, recalling the doctor's words: *Steer clear of Dr. John Kearns, Will Henry!*

"'Henry,'" he said. "I remember now why that name seemed familiar to me. I believe I knew your father, Will, and you're quite correct: His name *was* James, not Benjamin."

"You knew my father?"

"I met him once, in Amazonia. Pellinore was off on

another one of his quixotic quests, I believe for a specimen of that elusive—*mythical*, in my opinion—parasitic organism known as *Biminius arawakus*. Your father was quite ill, as I recall—malaria, I think, or some other bloody tropical disease. We do work ourselves into a tizzy about creatures like the *Anthropophagi*, but the world is chock-full of things that want to eat us. Have you ever heard of the candiru? It's also a native of the Amazon and, unlike the *Biminius arawakus*, not too difficult to find, particularly if you are unfortunate or stupid enough to relieve yourself anywhere near where one is hiding. It's a tiny eel-like fish, with backward-pointing razor-sharp spines along its gills that it unfurls like an umbrella once inside its host. Usually it follows the scent of urine into the urethra, wherein it lodges itself to feed upon your innards, but there have been cases where it enters the anus instead and commences to eat its way through your large intestine. It grows larger and larger as it feeds, of course, and I hear the pain is beyond the power of words to describe. So excruciating, in fact, that the common native remedy is to simply chop off the penis. What do you think of that?" he concluded with a wide smile.

"What do I think, sir?" I quavered.

"Yes, what do you think? What do you make of it? Or of the *Spirometra mansoni*, commonly called a flatworm, which can grow up to fourteen inches long and take up residence in your brain, where it feeds upon your cerebral matter until you are reduced to a vegetative state? Or *Wuchereria bancrofti*, a parasite that invades the lymph nodes, often causing their male hosts to develop testicles the size of cannonballs. What are we to make of them, Will Henry, and the multitudinous others? What lesson is to be gained?"

"I—I . . . I really don't know, sir."

"Humility, Will Henry! We are a mere part of a grand whole, in no way superior, not at all the angels in mortal attire we pretend to be. I do not think that the candiru gives a tinker's damn that we produced a Shakespeare or built the pyramids. I think we just taste good. . . . What is it, Will? You've gone quite pale. Is something the matter?"

"No, sir. I'm just very tired, sir."

"Then why aren't you in bed? We've a long day tomorrow, and a longer night. Sleep tight, Will Henry, and don't let the bedbugs bite!"

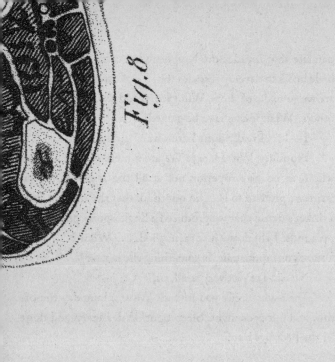

Fig. 8

FOLIO III

Slaughter

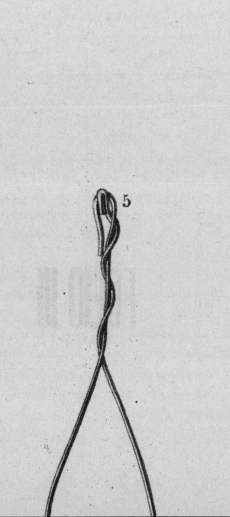

5

ELEVEN

"We Have No Choice Now"

The morning dawned overcast, the glowering sky an unbroken sheet of ruffled gray restlessly rolling, driven by a stiff westerly wind. When I woke from my uneasy nap (it could hardly qualify as anything more substantial), Harrington Lane was quiet but for the sighing of the wind in the eaves and the groaning of the house's hoary frame. Both Kearns's and the doctor's doors were closed, but Malachi's was open, the bed empty. Hurrying downstairs, I found the basement door ajar and the lights burning below. I expected to find the doctor there; instead I discovered Malachi, sitting cross-legged on the cold floor in his stocking feet, contemplating the beast that hung upside down a few feet away.

"Malachi," I said, "you shouldn't be down here."

"I couldn't find anyone," he said without taking his eyes

from the dead *Anthropophagus*. He nodded at it. "It gave me quite a start," he admitted matter-of-factly. "The missing eye. I thought it was *her*."

"Come on," I urged him. "I'll make us some breakfast."

"I have been thinking, Will. When this is over, you and I could run away, the two of us. We could enlist in the army together."

"I'm too young," I pointed out. "Please, Malachi, the doctor will be—"

"Or we could sign on to a whaler. Or go west. Wouldn't that be grand! We could be cowboys, Will Henry, and ride the open range. Or become Indian fighters or outlaws, like Jesse James. Wouldn't you like to be an outlaw, Will?"

"My place is here," I answered. "With the doctor."

"But if he were gone?"

"Then I would go with him."

"No, I mean if he should not survive this day."

I was startled by the notion. It had never occurred to me that Warthrop might die. Considering I was an orphan whose naïve faith in the ever-presence of his parents had been shattered, one might think the possibility would have been foremost in my mind, but I had not contemplated it, until that moment. The thought made me shiver. What if the doctor should die? Freedom, yes, from what Kearns had called this "dark and dirty business," but freedom to do what? Freedom to go where? To an orphanage, most likely, or a foster home. Which would be worse: tutelage under a man such as the monstrumologist, or the miserable, lonely life of the orphan, unwanted and bereft?

"He won't die," I said, as much to myself as to Malachi. "He's been in tight spots before."

"So have I," said Malachi. "The past doesn't promise anything, Will." I tugged at his sleeve to urge him up. I didn't know how the doctor might react if we should be discovered, and I had no desire to find out. Malachi pushed me away, his hand hitting against my leg as he did. Something in my pocket rattled.

"What is that?" he asked. "In your pocket?"

"I don't know," I answered honestly, for I had completely forgotten. I pulled them from my pocket. They clicked and clacked in my hand.

"Dominoes?" he asked.

"Bones," I answered.

He took one and examined it. His bright blue eyes shone with fascination.

"What are they for?"

"For telling the future, I think."

"The future?" He ran a finger over the leering face. "How do they work?"

"I don't really know. They're the doctor's—or his father's, I should say. You toss them into the air, I think, and how they land tells you something."

"Tells you what?"

"Something about the future, but—"

"That's what I mean! The past is nothing! Give them to me!"

He snatched up the five remaining bones, cupped them in both hands, and shook them briskly. The ensuing clatter sounded very loud in the cool, moist air. I could see his hands moving in the big, black blind eye of the *Anthropophagus*.

He tossed the bones into the air. End over end they spun and twisted and turned, and then fell back to earth, scattering willy-nilly on the cement. Malachi crouched over them, eagerly surveying the result.

"All faceup," he murmured. "Six skulls. What does it mean, Will?"

"I don't know," I said. "The doctor didn't tell me."

Thus, buffoon that I was, I lied.

I had managed to coax him into the kitchen for something to eat and was setting the water on the fire to boil when the back door burst open and the doctor barreled into the room, a look of profound anxiety contorting his haggard features.

"Where is he?" he cried.

At that moment Kearns entered from the hall, his countenance as calm as the doctor's was disturbed, his clothes and hair as neat as the doctor's disheveled.

"Where is who?" he asked.

"Kearns! Where the devil have you been?"

"'From going to and fro in the earth, and from walking up and down in it.' Why?"

"We've been loaded up for more than half an hour. They're waiting for us."

"What time is?" Kearns made a great show of removing his pocket watch from his vest pocket and opening it.

"Half past ten!"

"Really? As late as that?" He shook the watch beside his ear.

"We won't be ready if we don't leave now."

"But I haven't eaten anything." He glanced toward me, and then noticed Malachi at the table, ogling him with mouth half-open.

"Why, hullo there! You must be the poor Stinnet boy. My sincere condolences for your tragic loss. Not the usual way we meet our Maker, but whichever way we go, we always get there! Remember that the next time you fancy putting a bullet into Warthrop's brain. I try to."

"There's no time for breakfast," insisted Warthrop, his face growing scarlet.

"No time for breakfast! I never hunt on an empty stomach, Pellinore. What are you making over there, Will? Eggs? Two for me, poached, with a bit of toast and coffee, strong mind you—as strong as you can make it!"

He slid into the chair opposite Malachi and granted Warthrop a glimpse of his dazzling orthodontics. "You should eat too, Pellinore. Don't you ever feed the man, Will Henry?"

"I try, sir."

"Perhaps he has an intestinal parasite. It wouldn't surprise me."

"I'll be outside," said the doctor tightly. "Don't worry with the washing up, Will Henry. The constable and his men are waiting for us."

He slammed out the door. Kearns gave me a wink.

"Tense," he observed. He turned his charcoal eyes upon Malachi. "How close was it?"

"Close?" echoed Malachi. He seemed a bit overwhelmed by the natural force of the hunter's personality.

"Yes. How close did you come to pulling the trigger and blowing his head off?"

Malachi dropped his eyes to his plate. "I don't know."

"No? I'll put it to you this way, then: At that crystalline moment when you pressed the muzzle into his face, when the bullet was a squeeze of your finger away from blasting his head apart, what did you feel?"

"Afraid," answered Malachi.

"Really? Hmmm. I suppose, but did you not also feel a certain . . . oh, how shall I put it? A certain *thrill* in it too?"

Malachi shook his head, shaken, but also, I think, mystified and strangely compelled.

"I don't know what you mean."

"Oh, you must. That euphoric moment when you hold their life here." He held up his hand, palm facing us. "And now *you* are the captain of their destiny, not some ineffable, invisible fairy-tale being. No? Well, I suppose intent has everything to do with it. The *will* must be there. You didn't really intend to blow his brains out."

"I thought I did. And then . . ." Malachi looked away, unable to finish.

"Nice bit of poetic justice if you had. Though I wouldn't hold him entirely accountable. And I do wonder, if he had knocked on your door that night and told you, 'Better get out quick; there's headless man-eaters on the loose!' whether your father would have barred the doors or had him carted away to the nearest lunatic asylum."

"That's a stupid question," said Malachi. "Because he didn't warn him. He didn't warn anyone."

"No, it's a *philosophical* question," Kearns corrected him. "Which makes it useless, not stupid."

The doctor was pacing in the courtyard when we finally stepped outside. O'Brien stood nearby, beside a large wagon already loaded with Kearns's crates, the sight of which caused the English dandy to clap his hands and exclaim, "What's the matter with me? I nearly forgot! Will, Malachi, trot upstairs and fetch my box and bag, the small black bag, that's the one, and step lively! Be careful with them, particularly the box. It's quite fragile."

He had returned the lid and cover, tying down the silken wrap with the same thin rope as before. I set the small black valise on top, and Malachi said, "No, Will; it'll slide off when we go down the stairs. Here, I'll slip it over my arm. . . . It's lighter than I thought it'd be," he said as we hauled the box down the stairs. "What's in it?"

I confessed I did not know. I spoke true; I did not know,

but I suspected. It was macabre; it was well nigh unthinkable, but this was monstrumology, the science of the unthinkable.

We loaded the box beside the crates, alternately goaded and cautioned by Kearns: "Load it up, load it up, boys! . . . Not so rough with it; gently! Gently!" Kearns inspected our packing, nodded briskly, and then craned his neck to study the sky. "Let's hope these clouds clear out, Pellinore. There's an indispensable full moon tonight."

The doctor and Kearns rode with O'Brien in the truck; Malachi and I followed on horseback, he astride the doctor's stallion and I on my little mare. With each inexorable step toward the locus of his family's slaughter, Malachi grew more withdrawn, his eyes assuming that eerie, faraway stare with which he'd first greeted me in the sanctuary of his father's church. Did he know it then, in the subterranean recesses of his soul, the fate that awaited him at the fall of night, in that black, lightless chasm beneath the land of the dead? Did he know, deep in his marrow where wordless verity dwells, what the roll of the bones had presaged, and that he now rode upon that dark road to which Kearns had alluded? If so, he did not turn aside. With his head up, his eyes forward, and his back straight, Malachi Stinnet rode on to his doom.

It was near noon when we rendezvoused with Morgan and his men at the Stinnet house. An argument ensued, the second that day and not the last, between the doctor and

Kearns: Kearns wished to examine the scene of the previous day's carnage, and Warthrop wanted to begin preparations at once for the night's grisly work.

"It isn't a voyeuristic exercise, Warthrop," said Kearns. "Well, not entirely. There may be something you missed that might prove helpful."

"As in?" asked the doctor.

Kearns turned to Morgan, whose drawn features and reddened eyes bespoke of his quality of rest the night before. "Constable, it's your crime scene. May I enter, please?"

"If you feel it's absolutely necessary," answered Morgan testily. "I've agreed to defer to your judgment, haven't I?"

Kearns tipped his hat, winked, and disappeared inside the house. The constable turned to Warthrop and growled under his breath, "If you did not vouch for this man, Warthrop, I would take him for a charlatan. He seems altogether too cheerful for such grim business."

"It's the joy of a man perfectly suited for his work," replied the doctor.

Morgan ordered O'Brien to wait by the door for Kearns, while we joined his deputies inside the church. He had chosen six men for the hunt. They sat on the first pew, the same bench where Malachi had cowered the day before, their rifles at their sides, with expressions stern and stares unflinching, as Morgan introduced the monstrumologist.

"This is Dr. Warthrop, for those of you who don't know him—or of him. He is . . . an authority in these matters."

The doctor nodded gravely to the men, but none spoke and none returned his sober greeting. We waited in gloomy silence for Kearns to complete his gruesome inspection. One of the men picked up his rifle and commenced disassembling it; when he was satisfied with its condition, he methodically put it back together. Beside me Malachi did not stir or speak, but stared at the cross hung high. At one point Morgan glanced our way and whispered to Warthrop, "Surely you don't mean to bring those boys along?" The doctor shook his head and whispered something back that I could not hear.

A half hour later the doors flew open and Kearns strode down the aisle with O'Brien in his wake, pulled along like flotsam in his powerful current. He walked past us without acknowledging our presence, to the front of the sanctuary, where he stood for a moment, his back to our little congregation, contemplating the cross, or so one who did not know him well might think. Morgan endured it as long as he could, then rose from his seat and bellowed, his voice echoing in the cavernous space, "Well? What are you waiting for?"

Kearns crossed his arms over his chest and bowed his head. Another moment he took before turning, and when he did, a small smile he wore, as if he were enjoying some private joke.

"Well, it's *Anthropophagi*, no doubt of that," he said.

"There was never any doubt of that," snapped Warthrop. "Let's get on with it, Kearns."

"My name is Cory."

"All right," muttered Morgan. "I've had enough." He turned to the sharpshooters in the first pew. "Dr. Warthrop has engaged the services of this . . . person who purports to have experience—"

"*Extensive* experience," Kearns corrected him.

"—at killing these things. I would tell you his name, but at this point I'm not sure even he knows what it is, if he has one at all."

"To the contrary, there are more than I care to count." He smiled, but his winsome grin would be short-lived. "Thank you, Constable, for the warm introduction and the ringing endorsement. I shall endeavor to live up to it."

He swung his eyes, which appeared as black as midnight in the ethereal, splintered light of the church, toward the men before him. He reached into his trouser pocket and pulled out a dark gray concave object about the size of a half-dollar. "Can any of you tell me what this is? Pellinore, you're not allowed to answer. . . . No? No one? Then I shall give you a hint: I found it inside the good reverend's house just now. Nothing, not even a guess? Very well. This, gentlemen, is a fragment of temporal bone, from an adult human male approximately forty to forty-five years of age. For those of you whose knowledge of anatomy is a bit rusty, the temporal bone is part of your skull, and not incidentally the hardest bone in your body. Despite its appearance, the large egg-shaped hole you see here in the middle"— Kearns held it up to his eye, looking at his rapt audience as if through a peephole—"was not neatly drilled by a surgical tool, but *punched* by the tooth of a creature whose bite force exceeds two thousands pounds. This is what happens when a ton of pressure is applied to our strongest bone, gentlemen. You can imagine what happens when it's applied to the softer portions of our anatomy." He slipped the piece of skull back into his pocket. "The evolutionary reason for their tremendous bite is that the *Anthropophagi* lack molars. Two rows of smaller teeth ring the outside of the larger, central teeth. Those first rows are for snaring and grasping; the remainder, of which there are approximately three *thousand*, are for slicing and slashing. In short, they do not chew their food; they swallow it whole.

"And we, gentlemen, like the eucalyptus leaves of the gentle koala, make up the entirety of their diet. They are, quite literally, born to eat us. Naturally that fact has created some tension between our species. They need to feed; we would prefer that they not. The advent of civilization and its fruits—the spear and the gun, for example—tipped the scales in our favor, forcing them into hiding and forcing upon them another adaptation of which the brutal assault yesterday is a prime example: The *Anthropophagi* are fiercely territorial and will defend their homestead down to the last little snappy-toothed toddler. In other words, gentlemen, the ruthlessness with which they hunt is exceeded only by the sheer savagery with which they protect their territory.

"And that is precisely where we shall meet them tonight—not on our ground, but on theirs. The time will be of our choosing, but not the place. We shall take the fight to them, and they will give us the fight we ask for.

"And when that happens, gentlemen, you may expect something akin to a two-year-old's temper tantrum, albeit a tantrum thrown by a creature topping seven feet and weighing approximately two hundred fifty pounds, with three thousand razor-sharp teeth embedded in the middle of its chest."

Kearns smiled, his sunny countenance in stark contrast with his words. "Tonight you will witness the stuff of nightmares. You will see things that will shock and appall you, that will freeze you down to your God-fearing marrow, but *if you do everything I say*, you may survive to see the next sunrise, but *only* if you do everything I say. If you are willing to make that pledge now, with no reservations, you'll live to enthrall your grandchildren with the tale of this night. If not, I suggest you take your Winchesters and go home. I thank you for your kind attention, and Godspeed to you."

Silence fell over the little assembly while Kearns waited for their verdict. They had hardly needed the lecture; they all had seen the human wreckage left in *Anthropophagi*'s wake. They understood what they faced. They understood, and none made a move. None accepted the invitation to depart.

One of the men cleared his throat, and growled, "They're not the only ones that defend their own, the bastards. What do you want us to do?"

✳

Kearns put them to work at once constructing two four-by-eight-foot platforms from the load of timber deposited in the front yard. Once completed, the platforms would be transported to the cemetery, raised into position with a system of ropes and pulleys, and attached to the foremost trees of the woods along the cemetery's western border, to a height of ten feet.

"Why ten?" asked the doctor out of earshot of the hammering and sawing crew. "They can easily jump that high."

"Ten is high enough," answered Kearns cryptically. More concerned was he with the weather. He hovered near the back of the truck that contained his crates and the mysterious shrouded box, constantly casting his eye overhead. Around three in the afternoon, as the last nails were being driven, a drizzling rain began to fall, spotting the constable's spectacles, forcing him to yank them off his nose every two minutes for a quick wipe across his vest. The rain dampened his tobacco as well as his spirits; his bowl refused to stay lit.

Kearns took note of it, and said, "When this is over, I'm sending you a pound of the finest perique, Morgan. Far superior to that rabbit dung you smoke."

The constable ignored him. "Pellinore, I'm concerned about the boys." He nodded toward Malachi and me. "I say we either leave them here in the church or send them back to your house. It serves no purpose—"

"To the contrary," interrupted Kearns. "It serves *my* purpose."

"Perhaps you're right, Robert," Warthrop reluctantly acknowledged.

"I will not leave," avowed Malachi angrily. "I am not a boy, and I will not leave."

"I won't have it on my conscience, Malachi," the constable said, not unkindly.

"*Your* conscience?" Malachi fairly shouted. "What of *my* conscience?"

"Absolutely!" Kearns laughed. "You should have stayed in that room so she could rip your head off your shoulders after she was through breaking every bone in your little sister's body. What kind of brother are you?"

With an enraged cry Malachi launched himself at his tormentor. The doctor intercepted him as he swung impotently at Kearns's face, wrapping his arms about Malachi's torso in a fierce embrace.

"Your choice was the right one, Malachi," Warthrop whispered sharply into his ear. "You had a moral imperative—"

"I wouldn't speak of moral imperatives if I were you, Pellinore," cautioned Kearns, his eyes sparkling with delight. "And anyway, this absurd notion of the immutability of morals is a wholly human construct, the fanciful invention of the herd. There is no morality save the morality of the moment."

"I begin to see why you delight in hunting them," said Morgan with disgust. "You've so much in common."

Malachi went limp in the arms of the man whom just the night before he had come within a hairsbreadth of murdering. His knees gave way, and the doctor's arms kept him from collapsing to the wet ground.

"Why, yes, Constable, that's true," agreed Kearns. "We are very much like them: indiscriminate killers, ruled by drives little acknowledged and less understood, mindlessly territorial and murderously jealous—the only significant difference being that they have yet to master our expertise in hypocrisy, the gift of our superior intellect that enables us to slaughter one another in droves, more often than not under the auspices of an approving god!" He turned to Malachi. "So bear up, boy. You'll have your revenge; you'll redeem the 'moral' choice that tears your soul in twain. And tonight, if you meet your God, you can look him straight in the eye and say, 'Thy will be done!'"

He spun on his heel and marched away. Morgan turned his head and conspicuously spat. Warthrop urged Malachi to be calm. Now was not the time to give in to his guilt or indulge in self-pity, he told him.

"You cannot keep me away," he said in reply. "Nothing can."

Warthrop nodded. "And no one will." He looked over the boy's shoulder at the constable, and said, "Give him a rifle and we shall find him a place, Robert."

"And Will Henry? Surely you're not taking him."

I spoke up, hardly believing the words coming from my mouth, as if spoken by a hardier soul, "Don't send me away, sir. Please."

His answer was presaged by a smile, small and sad.

"Oh, Will Henry. After all we have been through, how could I send you away now, at our most critical hour? You are indispensable to me."

The platforms were too large and heavy to transport by wagon, so as the misting rain gave birth to premature twilight, Morgan's men carried them down the long lane to Old Hill Cemetery Road, and then another half mile to the main gates, where the men rested for a moment before the final push to their ultimate destination: the birthplace of this bizarre affair, where its midwife, the old grave-robber, had met his untimely end, dying waist-deep in the very grave he had invaded. The cause of Kearns's mysterious absence that morning became clear upon our arrival, for he was well-acquainted with the lay of the land, had chosen which trees to use as anchors for the platforms, and had carefully drawn out upon a sheet of foolscap the precise dimensions of the place, down to the locations of the tombstones. In the open area between Eliza Bunton's grave and the stand of trees, he had sketched a circle in red and labeled it, in exquisitely ornate script, *The Slaughter Ring*.

The men set to lifting the platforms into position,

pounding the anchoring pins into the trees using hammers whose heads were wrapped in rags, communicating with one another through hand signals and hoarse whispers, for Kearns had issued stern orders before we left the rectory grounds: as little noise as possible, and then no more than was absolutely necessary.

"Though they are sound sleepers—besides eating and copulating, it's their chief occupation—hearing is their most acute sense. Even through several feet of dirt and stone, I daresay they could detect our presence. The rain will be good for one thing, at least. It will soften the ground and hopefully muffle the noise."

While three men hung on to the ropes that kept the backs of the platforms against the anchor trees, the others slid four-by-four braces into place along the front edge. Scrap pieces of wood were nailed into the trunks of the two trees on either end for makeshift ladders. Then Kearns directed O'Brien, Malachi, and me to unload the crates from the truck. "Except my box and my bag. Leave them there for now; I don't want them getting wet. Ah! This accursed weather!"

Warthrop drew him aside, out of earshot of the agitated constable, whose distress seemed to grow by the minute.

"I will probably regret asking this question," he whispered, "but what is in that box?"

Kearns returned a look of mock astonishment at the doctor's ignorance. "Why, Pellinore, you know very well what's inside that box."

He walked over to one of the crates and popped open the lid. Packed into individual compartments within were a dozen dull black canisters, each about the size of a small pineapple, wrapped in straw. Kearns removed one and called softly to me, "Mr. Henry! Catch!" He tossed it underhanded to me; it hit me in the stomach, and I comically juggled it before gaining a grip on its slick hide. "Careful, Will. Don't drop it!"

"What is it?" I asked. It was quite heavy relative to its size.

"What is it? And you call yourself an assistant-apprentice monstrumologist! This is an indispensable tool of the trade, Mr. Henry. It's a grenade, of course. Give that little pin there a pull."

"He's joking, Will Henry," called the doctor softly. "Don't pull it!"

"You're no fun," Kearns chastised him. "What do you say, Will? I'll put you in charge of them. You can be my grenadier! Won't that be grand? Be a good boy now, and once they've that platform secure, you and Malachi can move them up."

He flung open the lid of the second crate. He pulled out a length of sturdy rope with a heavy iron chain attached to one end. A hook was welded to the other end of the chain. Next he reached into the crate and withdrew a metal rod, about four feet long and two inches round, pointed on one end and looped on the other to create an eyehole. It looked like a monstrous sewing needle. The last thing he removed was a large mallet of the size used to drive railroad spikes.

He threw the rope over one shoulder, picked up the hammer and spike, and called for me to follow.

As I trotted after him, I heard the constable whisper, "What the devil is all that for?"

And Warthrop's reply, his voice filled with disgust: "To secure the bait."

Kearns stopped about twenty yards from the tree line, went to one knee on the wet earth, and squinted through the gray mist toward the platform.

"Yes, this should be about right. Hold the stake like this, Will Henry, with both hands, while I drive it. Don't move now! One missed stroke and I'll break your arm!"

I kneeled in the mud and jammed the sharpened end of the stake into the ground. He swung the mallet high over his head and let it fall, the square head hitting the top of the metal loop with enough force to fling tiny pieces of shrapnel in all directions. The impact sent a ringing echo across the cemetery grounds. The men, who were now nailing the cross-braces onto the platform's legs, started at the sound, swiveling their heads around in alarm. Thrice Kearns raised the hammer and thrice let it fall. My arms reverberated with each blow, and I gritted my teeth lest I accidentally bite my tongue in two.

"There; one more should do it," muttered Kearns. "Would you like to give it a try, Will?" He offered me the huge hammer.

"I don't think I could lift it, sir," I replied in all honesty. "It's as big as me."

"Hmm. You *are* quite small for your age. What *is* your age? Ten?"

"Twelve, sir."

"Twelve! I must have a word with Pellinore. He can't be feeding you properly."

"I do all the cooking, sir."

"Why doesn't that surprise me?"

He gave the rod another whack, dropped the mallet, and tugged on the stake with both hands, grunting with the effort.

"Should do it," he said thoughtfully. "How much do you weigh, Will?"

"I don't know exactly, sir. Seventy-five, eighty pounds?"

He shook his head. "The man should be reported. Here." He threaded the chainless end of the rope through the loop and tied it off in a complicated knot. He bade me take the other end—the one with the chain attached—and walk toward the trees until the rope went taut.

"Now give it a hard pull, Will!" he called softly. "Hard as you can!"

He stood, one hand on his hip, the other caressing his nascent mustache, watching the effects upon the metal rod as I strained toward the trees, my feet slipping on the slick ground. He waved for me to stop, picked up the mallet, and gave the rod one last mighty blow. He motioned for me to return to him.

"A bit too long, Will Henry," he said. He untied the knot,

hiked up his pants leg, and removed a bowie knife from the sheath strapped to his calf. He cut off a two-foot section, the blade slicing through the thick rope as if it were a snatch of sewing thread. Then he reattached the rope to the rod. "You'll find three bundles of wooden stakes in the same crate, Will Henry. Be a good lad and fetch them for me, will you?"

I nodded, a bit out of breath from my exertions, and ran back to the truck to comply. Warthrop and Morgan were engaged in a whispering heated argument when I arrived, Morgan emphasizing each point with a jab of his pipe stem into the doctor's chest.

"A full investigation! A thorough inquiry! I cannot be bound by guaranties made under duress, Warthrop!"

As I jogged back to Kearns, he was consulting his soggy diagram and pacing off the dimensions of his "ring of slaughter." He directed me where to jam the stakes into the ground, at four-foot intervals, until a nearly perfect circle had been marked out, around forty feet in circumference, the metal rod marking the center, the circle's western edge coming within fifteen feet of the platform. Kearns admired his handiwork for a moment, and then clapped me on the shoulder.

"Excellent work, Will Henry. The Maori tribe who invented this method could not have done better."

The hunting party had congregated by the back of the truck, each man having armed himself with a shovel. He motioned for them to join us, and they gathered round him, grim-faced, breath high in their chests, their bodies already aching with fatigue. Kearns addressed them in a low, urgent voice, "Night falls sooner than we anticipated, gentlemen. Quickly now. Quickly—but as quietly as you can. Dig, gentlemen, dig!"

Using the stakes as their guide, working in methodical rhythm, the men dug a shallow trench. The rocky, wet soil crunched beneath their biting blades, the sound somewhat muffled by the rain that now fell from the windless sky in a steady thrum, ten thousand tiny drumbeats a second, enough to soak us to our skins and plaster our hair to our heads. Oh, why had I left my hat at home! From the truck several yards away the laboring men looked gray and ghost-like through the opaque curtain of rain.

"Pellinore," said Kearns, "a hand with my box, please."

"Now, then, this box," Morgan muttered as they eased it from the back of the truck. "I would like to know precisely what you've got in it, Cory."

"Patience, Constable, and you'll know precisely what I've got. . . . Easy, Pellinore; set it down easy! Will Henry, grab my bag there, will you?"

He slipped off the silk sheet and pulled off the lid. The doctor stepped back with a sigh of resignation; he had known what was in the box before Kearns had opened it, but knowing and seeing are often two very different things. Morgan stepped forward to peer at the contents, and gasped, all color draining from his cheeks. He sputtered something unintelligible.

A woman lay inside the box, robed in a sheer white dressing gown, reposed as a corpse, eyes closed, arms folded over her chest. No younger than forty, she may have been pretty once; but now her face was fleshy and pockmarked with scars, perhaps from smallpox, her nose enlarged and blushed rose red from the burst capillaries beneath the skin, the result, no doubt, of years of alcohol abuse. Other than the diaphanous gown, she wore nothing, no ring upon her hand or bracelet upon her wrist, except around her neck was a tight band the color of dull copper, a metal ring affixed to the portion beneath her wide chin.

After a few seconds of appalled silence, Morgan found his voice. "*This* is the bait?"

"What would you have me use, Constable?" wondered Kearns rhetorically. "A baby goat?"

"When you asked for immunity, you never mentioned murder," Morgan said indignantly.

"I didn't kill her."

"Then, where did you—?"

"It's a woman of the streets, Morgan," snapped Kearns. He seemed put out by the constable's outrage. "A common tramp with which the gutters of Baltimore are choked to overflowing. A piece of rum-besotted, disease-ridden filth whose death serves a purpose far nobler than any she achieved in her miserable, squandered life. If using her offends your sense of moral rectitude, perhaps you would like to volunteer to be the bait."

Morgan appealed to Warthrop, "Pellinore, surely there has to be another way . . ."

The doctor shook his head. "She is past all suffering, Robert," he pointed out. "We have no choice now: It must be done." He watched Kearns lift her still form from the makeshift coffin, a questioning look in his eye. Her head fell back, her arms slowly slid from her chest to dangle by her sides, as Kearns carried her into the ring of slaughter.

"Will Henry!" he called softly over his shoulder. "My bag!"

All work halted when the men spied his approach. Their mouths fell open; their eyes darted from Kearns to Morgan, who made a motion with his hand: *Dig! Dig!* Kearns gently lowered her to the ground beside the iron stake, cradling her head tenderly in his hands. He nodded toward the rope. I set down the bag beside him and handed him the end attached to the chain. He slipped the hook into the ring about her neck.

"I fail to understand what he's so upset about," he said. "The Maori use virgin slaves—teenage girls, Will Henry, the savage brutes."

He gave the chain a sharp tug. The woman's head jerked in his lap.

"Good enough." He eased her head onto the muddy ground. Then he stood and surveyed the field. I looked to my right, toward the platform, and saw standing there a solitary figure, a rifle cradled in his arms, staring down at us, as still as a sentry on the watch. It was Malachi.

Though the monotonous rain droned on and the gray light heralding night's inexorable arrival seemed to linger, unchanging, still there was a sense of time speeding up, a quickening of the clock, an acceleration of the march to battle. Two large barrels were unloaded from the truck, their contents, a pungent black mixture of kerosene and crude oil, emptied into the freshly dug trench encircling the sacrificial victim. Kearns ordered everyone onto the platform to review what he called the "Maori Protocol."

"I shall take the first shot," he reminded the rain-soaked, mud-spattered men. "You will wait for my signal to open fire. Aim for the area just below the mouth, or the lower back; anywhere else is just a flesh wound."

"How much time will we have?" asked one.

"Less than ten minutes, I would venture, in this weather, more than enough time to get the job done, or this phase of it, anyway, but ten minutes will seem an eternity. Remember, there are only two conditions under which we abandon this platform: when our work is done or if our barrier is breached. Who is on the trench?"

A thin-faced man named Brock raised his hand. Kearns nodded, and said, "Stay by my side and wait for the order— do nothing until I tell you! Timing is everything, gentlemen, once we've marked the scout. . . . All right, then! Any questions? Any last-minute reservations? Anyone who'd like to bow out? Now is your time, for now is *the* time." He raised his face to the weeping sky, closed his dark eyes, and sighed deeply, a smile playing on his sensuous lips. "The bloody hour is come."

We crowded to the edge of the platform, squinting through the gathering gloom, as Kearns knelt beside the body in the center of the circle and dug into the bag I had left there. He bent low over her, his back to us, blocking our view.

"What in the name of all that's holy is he doing now?" wondered Morgan.

"I'm not sure," murmured Warthrop in reply. "But I doubt anything that's holy."

To our astonishment the body jerked in a violent spasm, the legs kicked, the hands gathered mud and bits of grass into their fists. Kearns sat back to observe this phenomenon, and I heard the doctor breathe beside me, "Oh, no." Kearns held his bowie knife casually in his right hand while he pressed the fingertips of his left against the woman's neck.

"Warthrop," Morgan growled. "Warthrop!"

With a single fluid motion of his arm Kearns reached across the thrashing captive's torso and opened up her abdomen with the razor-sharp blade. The piercing screams of agony that greeted this act of heartless barbarity rent the twilight stillness with all the force of a thunderclap. They echoed among the trees and the silent sentinel tombstones.

They filled the silence to overflowing, increasing in volume and intensity with each passing second, and each of those seconds seemed longer than an hour. She rolled in Kearns's direction, flinging out a supplicating arm to the man who had mutilated her, but he was already racing back to us, the bloody blade clutched in his hand. He jammed the knife between his teeth—he must have tasted it then, her blood on his tongue—to clamber up the makeshift ladder and then, once safely aloft, dropped it from his mouth onto the boards. We barely took note, however, for we were riveted by the scene below, frozen in horror, paralyzed with dread. She managed to roll onto her hands and knees and crawl toward us, yowling and squealing like a pig in a slaughterhouse as it chokes on its own blood. The rope played out; the chain attached to her neck grew taut. Kearns snatched up his rifle, tucked the butt against his shoulder, and squinted through the sight, swinging the barrel from north to south and back again, oblivious, it seemed, to our consternation at this unexpected—and horrifying—turn of events, incognizant, apparently, even of the cries of confusion, pain, and fear reverberating all around us.

The author of those cries struggled against her tether only a few feet away, having now raised up to her knees, both arms toward us outstretched, her face contorted in unspeakable agony, her once spotless gown caked in a mixture of earth and blood. The chain that yanked her back snapped and rang with each violent lunge.

"Curse your black heart, Cory!" shouted Morgan. "She's *alive.*"

"I never said she wasn't," replied Kearns reasonably. "Spotters, what do you see? Look sharp! Mr. Henry, you too, look sharp now."

I tore my eyes away from the awful offering and scanned the hunkered markers and rolling grounds for any sign of movement, but a shroud had fallen over the world, and I spied nothing but earth, tree, stone, and shadow. Then, out of the corner of my wandering eye, I saw a dark shape darting between the tombstones, crouched low to the ground, moving in a zigzag pattern toward us. I tugged on Kearns's sleeve and pointed.

"Where?" he whispered. "Ah, good boy! I see it. Easy now, gentlemen, easy; this shot is mine." He stood ramrod straight, legs spread for balance, finger caressing the trigger. "Come, my pet," he murmured. "Dinner is served."

The lone *Anthropophagi* scout hesitated for a moment just outside the trench. The rain glistened on its milky skin, and, even from this distance, in the dying light, I could see its mouth opening and closing—and its teeth gleaming wickedly in its slathering maw. The massive arms were so long its knuckles almost brushed the ground as it stood, a bit bow-legged, at the edge of the trap.

If it was aware of our presence, the beast must have been overcome by bloodlust, or perhaps it simply did not care, for it bounded forward suddenly with a horrible roar, traversing the expanse between it and the wounded woman with stupendous speed. With at least thirty feet still separating them it launched itself into the air, claws outstretched, mouth agape, and at that moment Kearns fired.

The monster twisted in flight, struck by Kearns's bullet an inch below its bulbous eye. It dropped like a stone, its bellowing bawls drowning out the screams of its intended victim. Then it was back on its feet, spitting and snarling, gnashing its fangs as it stumbled stubbornly forward. The woman turned her head at the sound of its inhuman howls, and went stiff for an awful moment before hurling herself toward us. This time, when the chain broke her momentum, her head snapped back with such force I was sure she had broken her own neck. Kearns slammed another bullet into the chamber, rammed the bolt home, and fired a second time, striking the monster in the upper thigh. It stumbled, but came on. Fifteen feet now . . . Ten . . . Kearns reloaded and pulled the trigger. The third shot struck the other leg, and the *Anthropophagus* fell screeching to the ground, writhing in torment, kicking impotently in the dirt. Kearns lowered the Winchester.

Morgan shouted at him, "For God's sake, what are you doing, man? Shoot it again! It's not dead!"

"Fool," snapped Kearns. "I don't want it to be dead."

Below us the woman had completely collapsed. Perhaps she *had* broken her neck, or fainted from fear or loss of blood. The doctor shoved past Kearns and scooped up the bowie knife dropped earlier.

"Will Henry!" he called. "Snap to!"

He swung his legs over the edge of the platform and heaved himself off. I took the longer route, down the improvised ladder, to join him at the woman's side. I looked over his shoulder at the screaming, squirming beast, afraid that it would overcome its injuries long enough to rip our heads from our shoulders with a single swipe of its enormous claw. The doctor evidently did not share my concern; his entire focus was upon the woman. He rolled her onto her back and pressed his fingers below her lower jaw.

"Not too late, Will Henry," he said, raising his voice to be heard over the yowls of the wounded *Anthropophagus* behind him. He cut the rope with one mighty blow, slapped the knife into my hand, and gathered her into his arms. "Follow me!" he called, and we ran, slipping and sliding in the mud, hopping over the oily trench, to the shelter of the platform, directly beneath Kearns and the others. He propped her against a tree trunk and leaned close to examine the wound in her stomach.

Above us I heard Kearns call down, "I wouldn't tarry there too long, Pellinore."

The doctor ignored him. He threw off his jacket, ripped off his shirt—buttons flew in every direction—and then wadded it up, covering the incision with the makeshift dressing. He grabbed my hand and placed it over the shirt.

"A steady pressure, Will Henry. Not too hard."

At the moment he said this I heard Morgan cry out

in a loud, panicky voice: "There! See it? What is that over there?"

The doctor grabbed my shoulder and brought his face close to mine, looking deeply into my eyes. "Can you, Will Henry? *Can you?*"

I nodded. "Yes, sir."

"Here." He pressed his revolver into my free hand and turned to go. He froze, and for a moment I thought we were done for, that one of the *Anthropophagi* had snuck around through the trees and now was upon us. I followed the doctor's gaze and made out a tall, thin form holding a rifle, its bright blue eyes glittering as if in defiance of the gloom.

"I will stay with Will Henry," said Malachi.

Malachi stayed—and the *Anthropophagi* came, answering the cries of pain and outrage of their fallen sister. The earth disgorged them; the graves themselves vomited them up. For months they had been tunneling, expanding their underground warrens to accommodate their growing brood, creating a network of passageways of labyrinthine complexity in the hard New England soil, beneath the sleeping dead. Now, enraged by this encroachment upon their domain, maddened by the howls of their wounded comrade, they came. To the circle's eastern boundary they rushed, crowding into a single hissing and grunting, snapping and snarling milky white mass. They came right to the edge of the circle . . . and stopped.

Perhaps they smelled something they didn't like, or another, deeper sense warned them, an instinct inbred by thousands of years of conflict with their prey, these ambitious bipedal mammals who had had the audacity to evolve from a thick-headed, easygoing primate into hunters themselves, capable of not only defending the human species but of wiping the *Anthropophagi* from the face of the earth. What terrible irony was this: that they needed us to thrive in order to thrive themselves, but at the cost of their own extinction!

I heard Kearns call from above, "Steady, lads, steady. Only on my signal! Brock, are you ready?"

Brock grunted something in reply. Beside me Malachi went to one knee and raised his rifle. I was close enough to hear his ragged breath and smell the damp wool of his jacket. On my other side Kearns's anonymous victim clung to life, grasping my wrist in both her hands as she stared uncomprehendingly at my face.

"Who are you?" she croaked. "Are you an angel?"

"No," I answered. "I'm Will Henry."

I started, for suddenly Kearns's voice rang out. He was shouting at the top of his lungs, "Hullo, hullo, my pretties! Olly olly oxen free! The party's over here!"

The effect upon the milling monsters was immediate: With leaps and bounds, over the trench and into the slaughter ring, they swarmed, two dozen strong, fanning out as they rushed the platform, with black eyes shining and mouths agape, the taunting of Kearns overcoming all cautionary instinct. When the last headless horror had crossed the eastern boundary, Kearns shouted the order to "drop the fire," and Brock hurled a flaming oil-soaked rag into the trench. Five feet high the flame erupted; I felt its heat on my cheeks as it raced around the trench, fed by the fuel of oil and kerosene, sending roiling plumes of acrid black smoke boiling into the atmosphere. The monsters skittered and slid to a panicky halt within the circle of fire, screeching with shock and fear primordial: When man had first tamed fire, it had foreshadowed their doom.

Like the closing of hell's fiery gates, the two lines of flame met on the far side of the trench, sealing the beasts—as well as their fate—inside.

"Fire at will, gentlemen," shouted Kearns over the crackle of the fire, the spitting hiss of the rain, the terrified shrieks of the *Anthropophagi*. Gunfire exploded above us; the boards over our heads rattled and shook violently, to the point where I was certain the entire improvised structure would come crashing down upon our heads. Night had fully fallen, but now the grounds were alight in a smoky orange glow, crowded with spasmodic shadows, choked with the cannonade above and the death cries below. Through the awful din I heard Kearns's delighted cry: "Like shooting bloody fish in a barrel!" An object twice the size of a baseball sailed into the circle, and an instant later the ground shook with the concussion of the grenade's blast, a great blooming ball of flame blossoming where it burst, hurling searing-hot shrapnel in a flesh-rending radius of destruction.

"Can't see, can't *see!*" Malachi muttered in frustration, swinging his rifle to and fro. He scooted forward, as if he actually intended to rush the flames, hop the trench, and take the fight directly to the things that had slaughtered his family. "Just one. Please, God, just one!"

At which point his wish was granted.

Anthropophagi are not born with a taste for human flesh. Neither are they, like the solitary shark or the noble eagle, born hunters. They must, like the wolf or the lion—or the human, for that matter—learn these complex behaviors from their parents or from other members of the group. *Anthropophagi* do not reach full maturity until the age of thirteen, and the interim between birth and adulthood is spent learning from elders. They are allowed to feed only after the kill has been picked over by the older members of the clan. It is a period of learning, of trial and error, of observation and emulation. One startling and rather counterintuitive fact about these creatures is that *Anthropophagi* are actually quite doting and indulgent of their young. Only in the most extreme cases— starvation, for example—would they turn on one of their own.

Such was the case described by Captain Varner that occurred in the hold of the ill-fated *Feronia*, and such a case was probably the genesis of the misconception repeated by Sir Walter Raleigh and Shakespeare that the *Anthropophagi* are cannibals. (So might we humans be fairly called, by that criterion, for, faced with starvation, we have practiced this selfsame unthinkable abomination.) And, like the mother bear with her cub, all members of the group fiercely defend the youngsters when a threat arises: The smallest are sequestered to the remotest corner of the den; the juveniles are consigned to the rear in any assault, whether it be for food or, in the case of that rainy spring night in 1888, in protection of their territory.

A juvenile straggler, then, it had to be, perhaps the same age as I—though two feet taller and several dozen pounds heavier—that had been slow to answer the summons of the one dropped by Kearns's bullet, and had been cut off from the rest by the lighting of the ring of fire. Or perhaps, seized by the impetuousness of youth, he had not followed the herd into the killing zone but had determined to take a more circuitous route to the audacious invader, one that circumvented the fire altogether, bringing him round, unseen in the tumult of battle, to the little woods in which we crouched.

His assault was clumsy and amateurish by *Anthropophagi* standards, owing to his limited experience, to the excitement of the hour, or to a combination of both. Though we did not hear him crashing and stomping through the brush until a few seconds before he sprung from the deep shadows of the trees, those precious seconds were enough for Malachi to react.

He whirled around the instant it emerged from the trees behind us, firing without taking aim, for there was not enough time for that; if he had not fired when he did, I've no doubt Malachi would have succumbed, as would I and my gutted charge. The bullet struck the beast square in the chest, in a spot equidistant between the two black eyes, a mortal wound for a human, but as the doctor had pointed out, the *Anthropophagi*, unlike their human cousins, possess no vital organ between their eyes. The shot barely slowed him, and Malachi had no time to reload. He did not attempt that folly, but flipped the rifle around and rammed the butt into its snapping mouth as hard as he could. The reaction was instantaneous: The jaw clamped down in a violent spasm, shattering the wood with a resounding *crack*, the force of its tremendous bite—more than two thousand pounds, according to Kearns—ripping the rifle from Malachi's hands. Blood poured from the monster's wound, flowing down its heaving chest straight into its mouth, staining its teeth crimson. It lunged for Malachi with arms outstretched as it had seen its elders do, the killing pose, eyes rolling back as the arms came up, the digits of its massive claws splayed, hooked barbs spread wide for maximum effect.

Malachi stumbled backward . . . lost his balance . . . fell. . . . In another half second it would be upon him. But I was only three or four feet away, and a bullet travels far in a half second. It tore into the triceps of the creature's striking arm, throwing off the blow directed at Malachi's head; the tips of its three-inch nails barely grazed his cheek. That was my first shot—as well as my last—for the headless thing abandoned Malachi and turned the full force of its wrath upon me, scrambling in the wet leaves and mud on all fours as it came, like some ghastly man-size spider. Quicker than I could blink, it smacked the doctor's revolver from my hand, wrapped the other claw around my neck, and tugged my head to within inches of its champing mouth. Never have I forgotten, in all my long years, the horrific stench that exuded from its gullet, or its bloody teeth, or the excellent view deep into the recesses of its throat. My view might have been even better if not for Malachi, who had hurled himself onto the monster's back. The doctor's words echoed in my head, and those words saved both our lives.

If one should drop, go for her eyes, where she is most vulnerable.

I yanked the bowie knife from my belt and buried it to the hilt into the closest lidless, lightless eye. The *Anthropophagi* thrashed in agony, its throes throwing Malachi off its back and nearly knocking the blade from my hand. But I held on, giving it a half twist for good measure, before pulling it out and sinking it into the other eye. Blinded now, its blood spurting fountainlike, soaking its contorting torso, soaking *me*, the beast pushed itself to its knees, swaying back and forth while swinging its arms madly in a perverted parody of hide-and-seek.

I had cursed my fate on that seemingly endless night of the necropsy, had been forced, I felt, to endure the doctor's interminable lecture, and witness the gruesome dissection of Warthrop's "singular curiosity." Frightened and weary beyond words, still I had paid attention. *What else occupies your thoughts?* he had asked, implying not much did beyond my appetite. But my answer had been an honest one: I watched; I tried to understand. Like this young *Anthropophagus*, I had learned by observing my elders. I knew, you see, the exact location of its brain.

Holding the hilt with both hands, I drove the knife home with all my strength, into the spot just above its privates. The thrust landed true. Stiff as a board the monster went, arms straight out from its sides, with arched back and open mouth, teetering on the precipice of oblivion before oblivion took him down.

I fell over too then, to lie beside the murdered beast, clutching the dripping knife against my stomach, shuddering in the aftershock of those fleeting, eternal moments of terror. A hand touched my shoulder, and instinctively I raised the knife, but of course it was only Malachi.

His face was streaked with mud; his left cheek bore three bloody stripes where its claws had raked. "Are you hurt, Will?" he asked.

I shook my head. "No, but *it* is. I killed it, Malachi," I added with breathless obviousness. "I killed the damned thing!"

He smiled, and his teeth seemed very bright against the backdrop of his blackened face.

Kearns had been correct in his prediction: It was over in less than ten minutes. The gunfire over our heads dwindled to a few sporadic pops; the fire, having consumed quickly most of its fuel, and suffering from the steady onslaught of rain, petered out, leaving in its wake an undulating black curtain of smoke; and inside the circle itself was heard nothing but the gurgling and muffled grunts of the mortally wounded. The doctor appeared first, and, upon seeing the lifeless young *Anthropophagus* at our feet, his face lit up with surprise and alarm.

"What happened?" he demanded.

"Will Henry killed it," Malachi explained.

"Will Henry!" exclaimed the doctor. He looked at me with wonder.

"He saved my life," averred Malachi.

"Not just yours," Warthrop said. He knelt beside the woman, felt for her pulse, rose. "She has lost consciousness— and a great deal of blood. We must get her to the hospital immediately."

He hurried away to make the arrangements. Malachi picked up the shattered remnants of his rifle and wandered toward the smoking ring, before which Morgan and his men had gathered. I did not see Kearns. The doctor returned after a moment with O'Brien, and with me trotting beside holding the makeshift compress against her stomach, they carried her to the back of the truck.

"What do I tell the doctors?" asked O'Brien.

"The truth," answered Warthrop. "You discovered her wounded in the woods."

We joined the others standing in the no-man's-land between the edge of the platform and the smoldering trench. No one spoke. It was as if we were all waiting for something, but none could say exactly what we were waiting for. The men seemed shell-shocked; their breath was shallow, and the color was high in their cheeks. Morgan lit his pipe with shaking fingers, the match light sparking in his foggy pince-nez. Warthrop beckoned me to follow, and then hopped through the billowing screen of smoke into the killing field. There we spied Kearns, stepping carefully through the tangle of albino limbs and the twisted headless torsos of his victims, their bodies steaming in the warm, moist air.

"Warthrop, lend me your revolver."

I handed it to him. He kicked one of the creatures—a big female—onto her back, and her body jerked in response. A claw swiped feebly at his leg. Kearns jammed the barrel into her abdomen and pulled the trigger. He stepped over to another, poking it in the side with the toe of his boot, then, just to be sure, shot it, too. He cocked his ear toward the ground, listening for any sounds of lingering life. I heard only the hissing trench and the soft, whispery rain. Kearns nodded with satisfaction and handed the gun to the doctor.

"Count them, Warthrop. You, too, Will. We'll compare our numbers."

I counted twenty-eight bullet-ridden, shrapnel-torn corpses. The doctor concurred; he had counted the same.

"My number as well," agreed Kearns.

"There's one more, sir," I said. "Under the platform."

"Under the platform?" asked Kearns, startled.

"I killed it."

"*You* killed it?"

"I shot it, and then I stabbed out its eyes, and then I stabbed out its brain."

"Stabbed out its brain!" cried Kearns with a laugh. "Well done, Mr. Assistant-Apprentice Monstrumologist! Very well done indeed! Warthrop, award this boy the Society's highest honor for bravery!"

His smile faded, and his gray eyes seemed to darken.

"That makes twenty-nine. Assume three, perhaps four immature juveniles tucked away someplace safe, and we are at thirty-two or thirty-three."

"About what we estimated," said Warthrop.

"Yes, except . . . ," began Kearns in a rare moment of gravitas. "We'll fetch a light to make sure, but I can't find a female fitting her description. Warthrop, the matriarch is not here."

Morgan had regained some of his composure when he joined us among the steaming carcasses. Strained to its breaking point by the events of the previous two days, there was not much of his composure remaining for him to regain, but enough for him to reassert—or attempt to, at least—a measure of his authority. His tone with Kearns was stern and uncompromising.

"You are under arrest, sir."

"On what charge?" asked Kearns, blinking coquettishly.

"Murder!"

"She is alive, Robert," Warthrop said. "At least, she was when she left."

"*Attempted* murder! Kidnapping! Reckless endangerment! And . . . and . . ."

"Hunting headless monsters out of season," offered Kearns helpfully.

Morgan turned to the doctor. "Warthrop, I deferred to your judgment in this matter. I relied upon your expert opinion!"

"Well," said Kearns. "The bloody beasts are dead, aren't they?"

"I would suggest you save the self-serving statements for the trial, Mr. Kearns."

"Doctor," corrected Kearns.

"*Dr.* Kearns."

"Cory."

"Kearns, Cory, I don't care! Pellinore, did you know what he intended? Did you know beforehand what was in that box?"

"I wouldn't answer that if I were you, Warthrop," said Kearns. "I know an excellent attorney in Washington. I'll give you his name, if you like."

"No," the doctor said to Morgan. "I did not know, but I suspected."

"I am no more responsible for their diet than I am for them being here," Kearns said reasonably. "But I understand, Constable. This is the thanks I get. You are a man of the law and I am a man of . . ." He let the thought die unfinished. "You hired me to do a job and made certain promises contingent upon my completion of it. I only ask that you allow me to finish it before you renege on our contract."

"We had no contract!" snarled Morgan, and then stopped himself, the import of Kearns's words sinking in. "What do you mean, 'finish it'?"

"There is a strong possibility there are more," said Warthrop carefully.

"More? How many more? Where?" Morgan cast his eyes wildly about, as if expecting another swarm of *Anthropophagi* to leap at us out of the dark.

"That's something we won't know until we get there," Kearns answered.

"Until we get where?"

"Home sweet home, Constable. Be it ever so humble."

He declined to elaborate; instead he summoned the stalwart volunteers, thanked them for their valiant performance under truly extraordinary circumstances, compared them to Wellington's troops at the Battle of Waterloo, and bade them pile up the bodies for disposal. Malachi and I lent our hands to the grisly chore, dragging the body of the young male from beneath the platform to throw onto the pyre. Next the macabre mound was soaked with a half barrel of the oily accelerant reserved for the purpose.

Before striking the match, Kearns said, "*Requiescat in pace.*" He flung the match into the center of the pile. Flames leapt into the night sky, and soon our nostrils burned with the odor of searing flesh, a smell that was not unfamiliar to me. My eyes began to water, not so much from the smoke and smell, but from a memory more vivid at that moment than either.

A hand fell upon my shoulder. It was Malachi, in whose bright blue eyes I could see the flickering flames reflected. A tear coursed down his wounded cheek. The fire was seductively warm, but his anguish was as cold as the graves that surrounded us.

Poor Malachi! What did he think watching those murderous monsters burn, if not of his family, of Michael and his father, of his mother clutching her babe in her broken arms, of his darling sister Elizabeth, who had turned to him as savior and met instead her own demise? Did he feel relief? In his mind, had justice been done? *I am dead too. . . . Inside there is nothing,* he had said to me, and I wondered if he still felt that way, if this conflagration of mangled limbs and tumbled torsos did anything to resurrect his expired spirit.

My empathy toward his suffering was acute, for he and I were fellow sojourners in the forbidding kingdom wherein all roads led to that singular nullity of fathomless grief and immeasurable guilt. We were no strangers to that barren clime, that merciless landscape in which no oasis existed to slake our ravening thirst. What meritorious draft, what magical elixir offered by the art of men or gods had the power to relieve our agony? A year had passed since I had lost my parents; still, the memory and its attendant lords of anguish and rage reigned in the desert sovereignty of my soul, as if no time had expired since that night our house burned to its foundations. Verily, nigh eighty years later, they still smolder in the ruins: the blackened, twisted corpses of my parents. I hear their cries as clearly now as I hear this pen scratch upon the page, or the hum of the fan upon my desk, or the call of the bobwhite outside my window. I see my father in the final moments of his life with the same clarity I see that calendar hanging there on the wall, marking the march of my days, or the sunlight shimmering upon the lawn, where the dragonflies hover and the butterflies dance.

For nearly a week he had lain in bed, wracked by a virulent fever that had swelled and receded like the tides. One moment he was burning hot; the next brought teeth-chattering chills that no amount of blankets piled high upon him could remedy. Nothing would stay in his stomach, and on the third day of his confinement bright red half-dollar-size spots began to appear all over his body. My mother, ignoring his protests ("It's just a bit of fever, that's all"), summoned the family doctor, who diagnosed a case of the shingles and predicted a full recovery. Mother was not convinced: He had recently returned home, having accompanied Warthrop on one of his expeditions to parts unknown, and she suspected he had contracted some rare tropical disease.

Father's hair began to fall out by the fistful; even his beard and his eyelashes dropped like autumnal leaves after the first frost. Alarmed, my mother sent for Warthrop. By this point the rashes had become inflamed dime-size boils with milky white centers, painful to the touch; the lightest brush of his nightshirt against one would send Father into paroxysms of agony. It forced him to lie perfectly still on top of the covers, in helpless captivity to the pain. He could not eat. He could not sleep. He had fallen into a kind of twilight delirium by the time Warthrop arrived, seemed not to recognize him, and was incapable of answering the doctor's inquiries upon his condition.

The doctor examined the festering sores and drew a sample of Father's blood. He shone a light into his eyes and down his throat and collected some of his hair, strands fallen on the pillow and one or two plucked from his balding scalp. He questioned us about the progress of his illness, and pressed us about our own health. He took our temperatures, shone his light into our eyes, and took samples of our blood as well.

"You know what this is," my mother said.

"It could be the shingles," the doctor said.

"But it isn't," she insisted. "You know it isn't. Please, Dr. Warthrop, tell me what's wrong with my husband."

"I cannot, Mary, for I know not. I will have to run some tests."

"Will he live?"

"I think so. Perhaps for a very long time," he added enigmatically. "For now you might try hot compresses, as hot as he can bear. If anything should change, for better or worse, send your boy over immediately. I'll want to see him."

The prescribed treatment did bring temporary respite from the pain. Mother would drop strips of linen into a pot of boiling water, pluck them out with a pair of tongs, and place the steaming cloth over his sores. But once they began to cool in the slightest, the pain would return, accompanied now by an unforgiving, maddening itch.

It was a dreary chore, exhausting for my mother, who trudged from stove to bedside and back again, hour after hour, throughout the day and long into the night, the duty falling to me when finally she could stand it no longer and collapsed into my bed for a few fitful minutes of sleep. My own anxiety, unsustainably acute in the early stages of the illness, resolved itself into a persistent, nagging ache, an undercurrent of care running beneath numbing fatigue and fatalistic dread. A child has little defense against the sight of a parent laid low. Parents, like the earth beneath our feet and the sun above our heads, are immutable objects, eternal and reliable. If one should fall, who might vouch the sun itself won't fall, burning, into the sea?

The fall came during one of those midnight respites of my mother's, after she had retreated to my room to snatch a few minutes of sleep. I had ducked outside to the wood bin to grab another rick for the stove, and stepped back into the kitchen to discover my father out of bed for the first time in days. He had lost twenty pounds since the onset of his illness and seemed wraithlike in his loose nightshirt, with his spindly legs exposed and his pale flesh shining in the lamplight. He was standing unsteadily by the stove, an expression of profound befuddlement in his sunken eyes. He started when I softly called his name, turned his skeletal face in my direction, and hissed softly, "It burns. It *burns*." He stretched one of his emaciated arms toward me, saying, "They won't leave me in peace. Look!" Then, while I watched in mute horror, he ran his fingernail over one of the boils clustered on his forearm, breaking open the swollen white center. A squirming, stringy mass of colorless worms gushed from the wound, each no thicker around than a human hair. "Even my tongue," he moaned. "When I talk, the sores burst open and I *swallow* them." My father began to weep, and his tears were flecked with blood and swam with worms.

Repulsed and dismayed, I remained rooted to the spot.

I had no context in which to understand his suffering, and no power to alleviate it. I did not know then what manner of creature had invaded his body and now attacked him from within. I was not yet under the tutelage of the doctor and had yet to even hear the word "monstrumology." I knew what monsters were, to be sure—what child did not?—but, like all children, when I thought of monsters, I imagined horrible, malformed beasts characterized by a singular trait: their enormous size. But monsters, I now know, come in all shapes and sizes, and only their appetite for human flesh defines them.

"Kill them," my father muttered next, not an imperative directed toward me but a conclusion reached in his own fevered mind. "*Kill them.*"

Before I could react, he flung open the stove's door and with his bare hand reached into its white-hot belly, pulled out a piece of smoldering wood, and pressed the tip of the burning brand against the self-inflicted wound on his arm.

He threw back his head and unleashed an unearthly scream, but a madness greater than the pain guided his hand. The flames licked at the sleeve of his nightshirt, the fabric caught fire, and in a matter of seconds my father was engulfed in a fiery shroud of flame. His searing flesh ripped open, like faults in the earth splitting apart in an earthquake. Curiously bloodless cracks raced from boil to boil, and out of these fissures poured the creatures infesting him. They cascaded from his weeping eyes; they gushed from his nose;

they streamed from his ears; they flooded from his open mouth. He fell back against the sink, and the ravenous fire leapt to the curtains.

I screamed for my mother as smoke and the stench of burning flesh filled the little room. She rushed into the kitchen carrying one of my blankets, which she proceeded to slap at my father's writhing form, all the while screaming hysterically for me to *run*. By now the flames had crawled up the wall to caress the ceiling timbers. The smoke was chokingly thick, and I flung open the door behind me to allow it to escape, but allowing instead a fresh influx of air for the greedy lungs of the fire. Through the opaque screen of smoke and spinning soot, I saw my father lunge for her, and that was the last I saw of my parents while they lived, enfolded in each other's arms, my mother trying in vain to extricate herself from his clutches, as the fire enfolded them in its.

Standing before the seething pile of the immolated *Anthropophagi*, no more than a five-minute walk from their graves, I shuddered at the long-slumbering memory of that night. *What happened?* Malachi had asked me, and I had answered, *I ran.*

And my confession had been true: I did run, and I have been running ever since. Running from the acrid smell of my parents' melting flesh and the pungent stench of my mother's burning hair. Running from the groaning joists as they collapsed behind me, and the bestial roar of the gluttonous flame chomping and chewing everything in its path.

Running, running, ever running. Running still, running to this day nearly thirty thousand days later, always running.

You have heard it said that time heals all wounds, but I have found no succor in its inexorable march, no relief from the crushing burden of my loss. My mother calls my name in the final fiery consummation, victim of a no less ravenous monster than the *Anthropophagi*. Skewered in its scorching jaws, she cries out to me, *Will! Will! Will, where are you?*

And I answer: *I am here, Mother. I am here, an old man whose body time in its mercy has ground down, whose memory time in its cruelty has left pristine.*

I escaped; I am bound.

I ran; I remain.

TWELVE

"The Devil's Manger"

To the bone-weary men gathered round him, against the backdrop of blackened carcasses, with the rain thrumming a subtle timpani, of final descents and dead reckonings, the monstrumologist spoke.

"Our work is not yet done. There is one who has gone into hiding, taking with her the most vulnerable members of her brood. She will defend them to her last breath with a ferocity far exceeding any you witnessed here tonight. She is their mother, the Eve of her clan, and its unrivaled ruler, the most cunning and vicious killer in a tribe of cunning and vicious killers. She has risen to her supremacy through the power of her unerring instincts and indomitable will. She is their heart, their daemon, their guiding spirit. She is the matriarch—and she is waiting for us."

"Then let her wait, I say!" interjected the constable. "We'll seal her off and starve her out. There's no need to go after her."

Warthrop shook his head. "There must be dozens of hidden apertures to their dens. Finding them all would be a hopeless task. Miss one, and our efforts would be for naught."

"We'll set round-the-clock patrols," persisted Morgan. "Sooner or later she must come out, and when she does—"

"She will kill again," finished Warthrop for him. "Those are the odds, Robert. Are you willing to accept them? Now is the time to hunt her down, when she is at her most vulnerable, her full attention focused on protecting her young. We shall have no finer opportunity, no better chance than now, tonight, before she deems it safe to venture above and perhaps move them to another territory entirely. If that should happen, we are doomed to repeat the Maori Protocol all over again."

"Hunt her down, you say. Very well. How? And where? How do you propose we find her?"

Warthrop hesitated in reply, and Kearns stepped into the breach: "I don't know what Pellinore would propose, but I suggest we use the front door."

He turned toward the apex of the burying ground, and our gaze followed his, to the top of Old Hill Cemetery, where the Warthrop mausoleum brooded, its alabaster columns shining like bleached-out bones in the firelight.

We trudged up the hill toward the final resting place of the doctor's antecedents, with bent backs and wary eyes, Morgan's men flanking us on either side, two as lookouts, two as torchbearers, and two as coolies, hauling one of Kearns's crates. Malachi and I walked together, a few steps behind Morgan and the two doctors, who traded heated remarks in a debate that lasted from the smoking ruins of the *Anthropophagi* to the gleaming marble steps of the mausoleum. I could not make out their words, but suspected the doctor had renewed his arguments against Kearns's theory of the case. Upon the portico Warthrop ordered Morgan's men to remain outside; it was clear he thought this a fool's errand and that we would not be long within the tomb.

A central corridor separated the building into two sections. The doctor's ancestors rested behind slabs on either side, their names, chiseled into the hard stone, destined to last long past his forebears' earthly confines. Warthrop's great-great-grandfather Thomas had built this familial temple to serve a dozen generations: whole sections remained to be filled, their compartments empty, their creamy marble facades blank, waiting patiently for a name.

We traversed the length of the echoing sepulcher, pausing briefly when Warthrop stopped before his father's vault and stared silently and without expression at it. Kearns trailed his fingertips along the smooth walls, eyes flicking from side to side, or occasionally dropping to scan the floor. Morgan sucked nervously on his extinguished bowl, the sound, like our footsteps, magnified by the mausoleum's towering walls and arched ceiling.

On our way back to the entrance, Warthrop turned to Kearns and said, unable to disguise his grim satisfaction, "As I said."

"It is the most logical choice, Pellinore," Kearns said reasonably. "Small risk of trespass, well out of sight of prying eyes, a ready excuse if someone should happen to see him. Chosen for the same reason he picked the cemetery for their pen in the first place."

"I've been here more than once; I would have noticed," Warthrop insisted.

"Well, I doubt he would have hung a sign over the door," Kearns replied with a smile. "'Here there be monsters!'"

He stopped suddenly, his eye captured by a shiny brass plaque, embossed with the Warthrops' family crest, riveted into the stone. An ornate silver *W* was attached at the bottom.

"Now, what is this?" Kearns wondered.

"That would be my family crest," answered Warthrop dryly.

Kearns patted his right calf and muttered, "Where is my knife?"

"I have it, sir," I said.

"Right! Christened with *poppy*'s blood; I forgot! Thank you, Will."

He pressed the tip of the blade against one edge of

the plaque, trying to force it between the metal and the cold stone. Thwarted, he tried the opposite edge. Warthrop demanded to know what he was doing, and Kearns made no reply. He regarded the insignia, frowning, rubbing his mustache.

"I wonder . . ." He handed the knife back to me, and grasped the silver *W*. It turned counterclockwise in his hand until it stopped, upside down, and Kearns gave a soft, delighted laugh. "Now it's an *M*! Alistair Warthrop, you clever devil. *W* to *M*, and *M* for . . . Now, what in the world could *M* stand for, hmm?"

He tugged on it gently, and the plaque, hinged on one side, swung outward, revealing a small recessed chamber. Mounted in the back was a clock face, its hands frozen at twelve o'clock.

"Curiouser and curiouser," Kearns breathed as we crowded behind him to peek over his shoulder. "Of all places to put a clock! What do the dead care of the time?"

"What do they care?" echoed Morgan in a hoarse whisper.

Kearns reached into the nook and pushed against the minute hand. He brought his ear close, moving the metal arm slowly to mark a quarter past. He grunted and leaned back to smile at Morgan. "They don't, Constable. It's a letter shy of being a clock."

He rotated the large hand back to the 12, pressed his hands against the marble, spread his legs for balance, and pushed with all his might against the stone.

"This is ridiculous!" cried Warthrop. He had reached the end of even his considerable endurance. Beside him Morgan's mouth moved as he spelled out the word "clock," trying to puzzle out Kearns's enigmatic answer. "We are wasting precious—"

"It would be a number that held some significance to him," Kearns interrupted. "Not an actual time of day. A date, or perhaps a verse from the Bible, a psalm or something from the Gospels." He snapped his fingers impatiently. "Quickly, famous passages!"

"Psalm twenty-three," Malachi offered.

"Not enough hours," Morgan argued.

"Might be military time," Kearns mused. He set the clock to 8:23. This time both he and Malachi, who seemed infected with Kearns's excitement, pushed against the stone, but the huge slab did not budge.

"John 3:16," Malachi guessed next. Still nothing. Warthrop snorted with disgust.

"Pellinore!" called Kearns. "What year was your father born?"

The doctor waved him away. Kearns turned back to the clock face, fingers restlessly caressing his mustache. "Perhaps the year Pellinore was born . . ."

"Or his wife, or his anniversary, or any number of combinations for your clock without a C!" huffed the constable, having decoded Kearns's cryptic phrase at last. "It's hopeless."

Behind us Warthrop said, "The witching hour." I noted the sad expression in his eyes, an acknowledgment of the unacceptable, the recognition of a conclusion unavoidable.

""The witching hour approaches,'" he continued. "From my father's diary: 'The witching hour approaches . . . The hour comes, and Christ himself is mocked.'"

"Midnight?" asked Kearns. "But we tried that."

"The witching hour is an hour past," said Morgan. "One o'clock."

Kearns appeared dubious, but with a shrug tried that combination. Again the great slab would not move, even with all our shoulders pressed upon it.

"What did he say again?" Kearns asked. "The hour when Christ himself is mocked?"

"After his trial he was mocked by the Roman soldiers," Malachi said.

"But what hour was that?"

Malachi shook his head. "The Bible doesn't say."

Warthrop thought for a moment, bringing all his prodigious powers of concentration to bear upon the riddle. "Not mocked by soldiers," he said slowly. "By witches. The witching hour is three a.m., in mockery of the Trinity and a perversion of the hour of his death." He drew a deep breath and nodded decisively. "It's three o'clock, Kearns. I'm sure of it."

Kearns set the hands to three o'clock, the tumblers inside softly clicked, and, before Kearns or anyone else could try his luck, Warthrop reached out and pressed against the nerve-less rock. With a grinding groan the secret door slid straight back, creating an opening on one side through which two men could walk abreast. Neither light nor sound escaped from that dark fissure, only the faintest odor of decay, a smell with which I had, unfortunately, become all too familiar. Like the grave, what lay behind the great marble door was black and silent and reeked of death.

"Well!" Kearns said brightly. "Shall we draw lots to see who goes first?"

Malachi pulled the lamp from my hand. "I will go," he announced grimly. "It is my place; I've earned it."

Kearns pulled the lamp from Malachi's hand. "It is *my* place; I'm being paid for it."

Warthrop pulled the lamp from Kearns's hand. "The place is mine," he said. "I inherited it."

He glanced at Morgan, who misread the meaning of it. The constable dropped a hand onto my shoulder. "I'll look after Will Henry."

Before Malachi or Kearns could protest, Warthrop ducked into the opening. The light of the lamp faded, then disappeared altogether. For several excruciatingly elongated minutes we waited without speaking, straining our ears for any sound to emerge from the stygian darkness that dwelled behind the secret door. The lamp's glow returned at last, attended by the doctor's lean shadow, following next its glow upon his drawn features; I'd never witnessed him wearier.

"Well, Warthrop, what did you find?" demanded Morgan.

"Stairs," replied the doctor quietly. "Descending down a narrow shaft—and a door at the bottom." He turned to Kearns. "I stand corrected, Jack."

"When have you ever known me to be wrong, Pellinore?"

The doctor ignored the question. "The door is locked."

"A good sign," Kearns said, "but a bad circumstance. I don't suppose your father bequeathed you the key to it."

"My father willed me many things," replied the doctor darkly.

Kearns called for the crate to be brought inside the tomb, and he quickly laid out the supplies for the hunt: extra ammunition for the rifles; six of the remaining grenades; a small sack containing a collection of sachets, perhaps two dozen in all, their shape and size reminding me of tea bags; a tight coil of sturdy rope; and a bundle of long tubes with short, fat strings protruding from one end.

"What is that, Cory?" asked Morgan, pointing at the bundle. "Dynamite?"

"Dynamite!" exclaimed Kearns with a slap of his open hand against his forehead. "Now, that is something I should have thought of!" He pulled three canvas bags from the crate and packed each with two grenades, bullets, and a fistful of the little paper packets. He patted the empty sheath strapped to his leg and wondered aloud where his knife had gone.

"I have it, sir," I said, and held out the knife.

"How is it you keep ending up with my knife, Will Henry?" he asked playfully. He flicked the wickedly sharp blade against the twine binding the sticks and distributed them equally into the bags.

"They're long-burning flares, Constable," he informed Morgan. "Bright light for dark work." He slung one of the bags over his shoulder and handed another to the doctor. The last he dangled in the constable's direction. "Bobby—or would you prefer to delegate the duty to one of your brave volunteers?"

Malachi snatched the bag from Kearns. "I am going."

"Your zeal is admirable, but I worry about its effect upon your judgment," Kearns replied reasonably.

"I watched this thing murder my sister," Malachi shot back. "I am coming with you."

Kearns responded with a sunny smile. "Very well. But if your bloodlust gets in the way of my job, I'll put a bullet in your head."

He turned away from the tortured boy, his gray eyes twinkling merrily in the lamplight. "She has every advantage, gentlemen. She is faster, stronger, and what she lacks in intelligence she more than compensates for with her cunning. She knows the lay of the land, whereas we do not, and she can navigate it in darkness as black as pitch, which of course we cannot. We've no choice in the matter, of course, but the light we bring announces our presence; it will draw her to us like a moth to the flame. Her only weakness is the overriding instinct to protect her young, a vulnerability we may be able to exploit, should we be lucky enough to separate them from her maternal care. When threatened in the wild, *poppies* sequester their young in the lowermost chambers of their underground dens. That's our destination, gentlemen, the very bowels of the earth, though we might not reach them; she may meet us halfway, or she may simply wait for us, but the odds we will have the element of surprise on our side are practically nil: We are the hunters—and we are also the bait."

He turned to the constable. "You and your men will remain above, two on patrol of the cemetery's perimeter, two for the grounds, and two on the watch here. She may flee to the surface, but I sincerely doubt it. It isn't in her nature."

"And if she does?" asked the constable, his round, owlish eyes blinking rapidly behind his spectacles.

"Then I would suggest you kill her."

He clapped his hands, beaming with delight at our startled reaction to its echoing retort. "Jolly good, then! Any questions? Fools rush in, you know. Will Henry, be a good lad and grab that rope."

"I thought only the three of you were going," the constable said, dropping his hand upon my shoulder.

"Only as far as the door, Constable," said Kearns. "To save us a trip back up for it. Your concern is touching, though.

Here." With the toe of his boot he pushed the rope across the smooth floor toward Morgan. "You carry it."

Morgan stared at it as if it were a rattlesnake coiled at his feet. His hand dropped from my shoulder. "Well . . . I suppose it would be all right, as long as it's only to the door."

"Touching," repeated Kearns with soft derision. He turned to the doctor as I picked up the rope. "Pellinore, after you."

Now through the black slit in the wall we followed the doctor's dancing light, Kearns first, then Malachi, and finally me, shuffling forward, borne down by the heavy rope draped over my shoulder. A flight of narrow stairs confronted us on the other side of the wall, descending thirteen steps to a small landing, then, after turning sharply to the right, continuing for another baker's dozen to a cramped chamber, six feet long and six wide, its walls and ceiling reinforced by wide wooden planks that reminded me of a ship's decking. Into this claustrophobic space the four of us crowded, our lamps throwing our misshaped shadows upon the weathered timber.

"You said there was a door," Malachi whispered to the doctor. "Where is it?"

"We are standing on it," replied the doctor.

We followed his gaze downward. A trapdoor lay under our feet, hinged on one edge, with a rusting padlock on the opposite side securing it to a clasp bolted into the chamber floor.

"And there is no key?" asked Malachi.

"Of course there's a key," Kearns said. "We just aren't in possession of it."

"No, sir," I spoke up. "I think I have it."

All eyes turned to me, none more astonished than those of the doctor. I had completely forgotten about it in the hurly-burly of events since I'd found it. My cheeks tingling with embarrassment, I reached into my pocket and removed the old key.

"Will Henry—," began the doctor.

"I'm sorry, sir," I blurted. "I was going to tell you, but you were in a foul mood when I found it, so I decided to tell you later, and then I forgot. . . . I'm sorry, sir."

Warthrop took the key, staring at it with wonder. "Where did you find it?"

"In the head, sir."

"The bathroom?"

"The shrunken head, sir."

"Ah," said Kearns, snatching the key from Warthrop. "The constable had it. Will Henry has come to our rescue yet again! Let us see now if fortune smiles . . ."

He knelt beside the rusting lock and slid the key inside. Teeth ground against reluctant tumbler as he forced the ancient gears clockwise. The lock snapped open with a loud *pop!*

"Stand ready," breathed Kearns. "She may be lurking on the other side, though I doubt it."

He grasped the handle of the trapdoor—what bitter irony lay in that name!—and flung it open with a dramatic flourish, like a magician opening a cabinet to reveal its remarkable, heretofore unseen contents. The lid smashed to the floor, a corner nearly catching me in the shin as it came crashing down. From above we heard the constable's consternated cry, "What was that!" and the rumble and clatter of footsteps racing down the stairs. A nauseating wave of putridity rushed through the hole, invading the enclosed space, a profane stench of such profundity that Malachi recoiled with a strangled gasp, retreating to the farthest corner, where he doubled over, clutching his stomach. Morgan and his man Brock appeared above us on the stairs, gripping their revolvers with shaking hands.

"Dear God!" cried the constable, patting his pockets desperately for his handkerchief. "What the devil is *that?*"

"The devil's manger," replied Warthrop grimly. "Will Henry, hand me your lamp."

He knelt on the side of the hole opposite Kearns, and lowered the light the length of his entire arm. The darkness below seemed to resist its glow, but I could see a smooth, cylindrical wall, like the upended bore of an enormous cannon. This chute ran ten feet straight down before it abruptly terminated. What lay beneath it, I could not see.

"Clever," murmured Kearns with frank appreciation. "Drop the victim into the hole, and gravity does the rest." He dug a flare from his bag and lit it. The gloom was banished by brilliant bluish light. He tossed the device down the hole. Down the shaft it dropped, then tumbled into open space, perhaps fifty feet or more, before landing among the jumble of the macabre debris littering the chamber's floor. Morbid curiosity overcame our sense of smell, and we crowded around the hole to peer into the pit.

Below was a jagged landscape of shattered bone that spanned the radius of the flare's illumination, a morass of remains immeasurable in magnitude, thousands of bones, thousands upon thousands, flung willy-nilly in all directions, tiny phalanges and large femurs, ribs and hips, sternums and vertebral columns still intact, rising out of rubble like the ribbed, crooked fingers of a giant. And skulls, some with tufts of hair still attached, skulls small and skulls large, some with mouths frozen open as if the jaw had locked midscream. Into this vile vista of human wreckage we stared, this carnage that human folly and carnivorous frenzy had wrought, our hearts filled with wonder and awe at horror's true face, at once monstrous and all too human.

Beside me Kearns murmured, "'Through me the way into the suffering city . . . Through me the way to the eternal pain . . .'"

"There must be hundreds of them," muttered Morgan, who, having found his trusty handkerchief, spoke now through it.

"Six to seven hundred, I would guess," ventured Kearns dispassionately. "An average of two or three per month for twenty years, if you wanted to keep them fat and happy. It's an ingenious design: The fall would more than likely break their legs, lowering their odds of escape from extremely doubtful to impossible."

He hauled himself to his feet, slung his rifle over one shoulder, and the canvas bag over the other. "Well, gentlemen, duty calls, yes? Constable, if you and Mr. Brock here would hold the rope for us, I think we're ready. Are we ready, Malachi? Pellinore? I'm ready. I'm practically giddy with anticipation: Nothing gets my blood up like a bloody good hunt!" His expression mirrored his words. His eyes shone; his cheeks glowed. "We'll need our lamps lowered to us once we're down, Constable—don't want to waste the flares. So who is going first? Very well!" he cried without waiting for a volunteer. "I will! Hold tight, now, Constable, Mr. Brock; I fancy walking upright like a proper bipedal mammal. Pellinore, Malachi, I shall see you in hell—I mean, at the bottom."

He dropped the rope into the hole, swung his legs over the edge, and scooted on his backside until he teetered on the opening's lip. Taking the rope in both hands, he looked up at me, and for some reason gave me a wink before dropping down. The rope went taut in its human anchors' white-knuckled grips, jerking this way and that as Kearns lowered himself, hand over hand, into the death chamber. I heard the sickening crunch of his landing in the skeletal rubble, and the rope went limp.

"Next!" he called softly. The flare's blue light sputtered and spat, causing his shadow to flitter and lurch over the confusion of bones.

Before the doctor could move, Malachi grabbed the rope. He looked at me and said "I'll see you soon, Will" before disappearing from view.

Now it was the doctor's turn. I confess the words were on my lips, *Take me with you, sir,* but I spoke them not. He would refuse—or worse, agree. Or would that be worse? Were not our fates inextricably bound together? Had not they been entwined since the night my father and mother, embracing, had died in that fire's devouring embrace? *You are indispensable to me,* he had said earlier. Not "your services," as it had always been since I had come to live with him, but "you."

As if he could read my mind, he said, "Wait for me here, Will Henry. Don't leave until I return."

I nodded, my eyes stinging with tears. "Yes, sir. I'll wait right here for you, sir."

He fell out of sight, into the devil's manger.

Their lamps were lowered next, and our anxious vigil commenced. I remained by the opening in the chamber floor, watching the dance of the flare's fire until it died, straining at the feeble yellow glow of their lamps until that too was swallowed up by the dark. Brock sat upon the bottom step and stoically cleaned his fingernails with his pocketknife. Morgan puffed noisily on his empty pipe and obsessively took off and put back on his pince-nez, rubbing the lenses nervously with his handkerchief before shoving them back upon his nose and slapping the kerchief back over his mouth.

After several minutes of this annoying ritual—puff, puff, rub, rub—his restless eyes fell upon me, and he whispered, "There will be a reckoning, Will Henry, I promise you that. Oh, yes. The guilty will answer for their crimes; I will make sure of it!"

"The doctor didn't do anything wrong," I said.

"Well, I beg to differ, boy. He had knowledge, and did nothing. And his inaction resulted in murder, plain and simple. He may tell you and himself his course was prudent, that he was following the dictates of his so-called science, but this was no scientific inquiry or intellectual exercise. This was a matter of life and death, and we both know which he chose! And we both know the *real* reason he tried to keep this abomination secret. To protect the good name of Warthrop, out of misguided loyalty to a man gone clearly mad!"

"I don't think so, sir," I said as politely as I could. "I don't think he believed his father was to blame until we found the hidden door."

"Humph!" snorted the constable. "Even if that's true, it doesn't exonerate him, William Henry. Your loyalty is admirable, if tragically misplaced. I know you, who have lost so much, must fear losing him, too, but I shall personally see to it that you are found a decent home no matter how this horrid business is resolved. You have my word: I will not rest until you are placed in the proper environment."

"I don't want to be placed. I want to stay with him."

"Assuming he survives, where he is going, you cannot follow."

"You're going to arrest him? For what?" I was appalled.

"And that abhorrent Cory or Kearns or whatever his name is. I don't think I've ever encountered a more loathsome human being. He better pray that poor woman survives the unthinkable ordeal he put her through. Why, I believe he actually *enjoyed* doing it. I think seeing her suffer gave him *pleasure*. Well, it shall give *me* the utmost pleasure to see him standing upon the gallows! Let him crack his profane jokes and smirk his damnable blasphemies with the noose around his neck! If it costs my entire allotment of moments, I will gladly spend them to witness the morality of *that* one."

"It was a mistake," I insisted, speaking still of the doctor. I cared little what happened to John Kearns. "You can't arrest him for making a mistake," I pleaded.

"Oh, I most certainly can!"

"But the doctor is your friend."

"My first duty is to the law, Will Henry. And the truth is, though I have known him always, I hardly *know* him at all. You have spent an entire year under his roof, his sole and constant companion. Can you say with any conviction that you know him or understand the demons that drive him?"

It was true, of course, as I have heretofore confessed: I did not know him any better than he had known his own father. Perhaps that is our doom, our human curse, to never really know one another. We erect edifices in our minds about the flimsy framework of word and deed, mere totems of the true person, who, like the gods to whom the temples were built, remains hidden. We understand our own construct; we know our own theory; we love our own fabrication. Still . . . does the artifice of our affection make our love any less real? Not that I ever loved the monstrumologist; I do not say that. I've fealty to neither the man nor his memory, though of the first I have been bereft these many years, and by the second I am admittedly consumed. Not a day passes when I do not think of him and our many adventures together, but that is not evidence of love. Not a night goes by without my seeing his lean, handsome face in my mind's eye, or my hearing the distant echo of his voice in the acoustical perfection of my memory, but that proves nothing. I did not then—nor do I now—nor *ever*—I will say it again—I do not think I protest too much—I never loved the monstrumologist.

"Someone is calling," Brock spoke up, his laconic announcement in counterpoint to the frantic snapping of the rope as someone yanked upon its end. I looked through the opening and saw the doctor standing below, his lamp held high.

"Will Henry!" he called. "Where is Will Henry?"

"Here, sir," I called back.

"We need you. Come down at once, Will Henry."

"'Come down'?" the constable said. "What do you mean, 'come down'?"

"Here, Robert. Lower him down to us immediately. Snap to, Will Henry!"

"If you need an extra pair of hands, Brock can come," Morgan shouted through the hole. Brock looked up from his manicure with a comical expression of surprise.

"No," answered Warthrop. "It has to be Will Henry." He gave the rope another impatient snap. "At once, Robert!"

Morgan chewed on his pipe stem indecisively for a moment. "I won't force you to go," he whispered.

I shook my head, at once relieved and apprehensive. "I have to go," I said. "The doctor needs me."

I reached for the rope. Morgan grabbed my wrist and said, "Go to him, then, but not that way, Will."

He hauled up the rope and tied it twice about my waist. The chute was narrow enough for me to press my back against one side and my feet against the other, and I thought of Saint Nick coming down the chimney. Then all at once I was through, dangling in midair, turning slowly at the end of the twisting tether. At the halfway point I looked up, and saw the constable's face framed in the oval outline of the opening, lamplight glowing in his spectacles, making his eyes appear perfectly round and too large for his face, the most owlish-looking I had ever seen this owlish-looking man.

Then my toes scraped the floor of the chamber, followed by a sickening crunch when my full weight came down among the bones. Death's odor at ground level was chokingly intense, and my eyes filled with tears; I watched the doctor untie me through a watery veil.

"Morgan!" he called softly. "We will need shovels."

"Shovels?" returned the constable. His face, so far above us, was nearly lost in the murk. "How many?"

"There are four of us, so . . . four, Robert. Four."

Warthrop took my elbow and urged me forward, saying quietly, "Watch your step, Will Henry."

The chamber was smaller than I'd anticipated, perhaps only forty or fifty yards in circumference. Its walls, like the walls of the tiny landing over our heads, had been reinforced with wide wooden planks, the boards warped by humidity, bearing dents, gouges, and scratch marks. Remains crowded against the chamber's base, a foot high in some spots, like flotsam washed up by a storm's surge. Not all broke their legs in the fall, as Kearns had surmised. Some must have been ambulatory, and had scrambled to these walls in their frenzy to escape. I pictured them, the poor desperate, doomed creatures clawing and scratching at the impassive wood in the instant before the blow landed from out of the dark—and the teeth smashed their skull apart with the force of a two-ton truck.

I tried to avoid stepping on them—they had been like me once—but it was impossible; there were simply too many of them. The ground was soft, yielding to even my slight weight, and in spots water bubbled around my sole—

water and a reddish-black sludge. Here, where no sun shone and no breeze stirred, their bodily fluids had soaked into the ground and been trapped there. I was walking in a literal swamp of blood.

We stopped at the far end of the chamber. There Kearns and Malachi waited by the mouth of a tunnel, the only other access to the pit that I could see besides the trapdoor. There was no door to this aperture, however: The tunnel's open mouth yawned seven feet tall and six wide.

"At last: our scout," said Kearns, beaming down at me, his lamp casting hard shadows across his soft features.

"The access tunnel has collapsed, Will Henry," the doctor informed me.

"Or been made to," suggested Kearns. "Dynamited would be my guess."

"Follow me," Warthrop instructed. About twenty yards in, a wall of jumbled earth and broken timbers confronted us, a confusion of dirt and rock and the shattered remnants of the huge joists that had once held the ceiling aloft. The doctor squatted at the base and drew my attention to a small opening in the rubble, supported by one of the fallen crosspieces.

"Too small for any of us to squeeze through," he pointed out. "But it appears to go on for a little way at least, perhaps even all of it. What do you think, Will Henry? We must know how wide this wall is . . . if we can dig our way through it with reasonable alacrity or if we must attack the problem another way."

"Dynamite!" exclaimed Kearns. "I *knew* I should have brought some."

"Well?" the doctor asked me. "Are you up for it?"

Of course I would not say no. "Yes, sir."

"Good boy! Here, take the lamp. And here, you might as well take my revolver, too. No, tuck it into your belt there; the safety's on. Careful now, Will Henry. Careful, and not too quick. Come back at the least sign of trouble. There must be several hundred tons of earth above you."

"And if you do make it to the other side, it would be helpful to the cause if you peeked around a bit," put in Kearns.

"Peeked, sir?"

"Yes. Reconnoiter. Get a feel for the place. And, of course, scope out the enemy's position if possible."

The doctor was shaking his head. "No, Kearns. It's too dangerous."

"And scrambling into a hole with tons of rock over his head isn't?"

"You know I would not ask you if there was another alternative, Will Henry," Warthrop said to me.

"I have one," said Kearns. "Dynamite."

"Please," Warthrop said, closing his eyes. "Just . . . shut up, Kearns. For once. Please." He gave my shoulder a pat and a paternal squeeze. "Snap to, now, Will Henry. But slowly. Slowly."

Holding the lamp before me, I crawled inside the cleft. It narrowed almost immediately; my back scraped against the top, and debris rained down and pooled between my hunched shoulders as I inched forward, the lamp offering little guidance in such close quarters. The pathway through the fall was a hazard of arm-size splinters and hard stone, and it continued to shrink as I progressed, until I was forced to lie flat and scoot forward, inch by claustrophobic inch. I could not judge how far I had traveled; pressed on all sides, I could not even turn my head to look behind me. Time crawled along as slowly as I, and the air grew colder; my breath congealed around my head and I lost feeling in the tip of my nose. Now my back rubbed continuously against the top, and I worried I might become hopelessly wedged inside this dread defile. And, if that should happen, how long would I have to remain stuck like a cork in a bottle, until they could dig me out?

My difficulties were compounded by the grade of the defile; it did not cut straight through, but zigged and zagged and rose generally upward, compelling me to force my body forward by pushing with the balls of my feet.

Then all at once I stopped. I laid my cheek against the dirt, trying to catch my ragged breath, struggling to contain my rising panic.

For it appeared I had come to the end of it. A foot before me was a wall of dirt and rock; the way was blocked. I might be a few inches from the other side or I might be several feet; there was no way of knowing.

Or might there be? I wiggled my left arm in front of me and scratched at the dirt gingerly with my fingernails.

If I retreated now, I would have to back my way out, which would prove even more difficult, but a worse prospect by far was returning without the answer the doctor sought. I wanted to impress him; I wanted to confirm his judgment that I was indispensable.

Whether it was by my scratching and scraping against the soil or by my weight pressing down on a particularly unstable spot, the earth abruptly gave way beneath me, and I tumbled down in a torrent of soil and stone, losing the lamp in my helpless fall, rolling head over heels before coming to a jaw-jarring stop upon my bottom.

Fortunately, the lamp survived the fall as well; it lay on its side only a few feet away. I snatched it up and held it as high as my arm could stretch, but I saw no opening or even a hint of one; it had collapsed behind me, and the face of the blockage appeared despairingly uniform in its craggy appearance—I could not tell from whence I'd come.

I paced the length of the wall, anxiously scanning its earthy sides, and spied nothing that might give away the location. I was trapped.

For a moment I nearly swooned with dismay. My companions were far on the other side of the impassable traverse. There was no way to signal my distress, and rescue might not come for hours, if at all, for now I stood between this brooding wall and whatever lay on my side of it—and I *knew* what lay on my side.

Steady now, Will, I told myself. *Steady! What would the*

doctor have you do? Think! You can't go back. Even if you found where you fell through, you dropped a great deal down, and how will you get back up again? You have no choice; you'll have to wait for them to rescue you.

What was that? Did I hear something sneaking up behind me? A scratching sound, a hiss or a huff? I whirled around, the lamp swinging crazily in my shaking hand while with the other I fumbled for the doctor's revolver. A shadow jumped to my left, and I swung the gun toward it, jerking the trigger reflexively, wincing at the expected report that did not follow: I had forgotten to take the safety off. And then, to add to my chagrin, I realized the jumping shadow was my own, thrown by the lamp when I turned.

I took a deep breath and eased off the safety. To steady my jangled nerves I remembered my triumph beneath the platform—how I'd dispatched the young *Anthropophagus* with practically my bare hands—and I shuffled forward, squinting into the gloom.

I was in a chamber roughly the same size as the feeding pit. Small bones—bits of shattered ribs, a spattering of teeth, and other shards and fragments impossible to identify—littered the floor, though not with the same overwhelming abundance found in the first chamber. The floor itself was as hard as cement, packed tight from the tramping of their enormous feet over a span of twenty years. Scattered throughout the chamber—I counted seventeen in all—were gigantic nest-shaped mounds, easily eight feet in diameter, oddly multicolored and glimmering as if encrusted with diamonds. Upon closer examination, I discovered the reason for their strange appearance: The nests were fashioned from tightly woven strips of clothing, blouses, shirts, trousers, stockings, skirts, undergarments. The peculiar glittering points of light had been produced by the reflection of my lamp in the faces of watches and diamond rings, wedding bands and necklaces, earrings and bracelets—in short, nearly every kind of adornment we humans are fond of draping ourselves in. Like the Indians of the Great Plains with their buffalo, the *Anthropophagi* wasted nothing; they had fashioned their nests from the attire of their victims. I imagined them using the bone fragments scattered around the floor to pick our flesh from their teeth.

A high-pitched huffing came out of the darkness behind me. I swung my weapon round, but nothing leaped at me from the shadows, no beast rose from a nest to its full towering, terrifying height. I held my breath, straining my ears and eyes, until, though I saw no movement, I identified the direction of the rhythmical wheezing. The comparison may be absurd in the circumstances, but to my ears it sounded like the rapid respirations of a snoring infant.

I followed the sound, sliding forward flat-footed lest I step on a bone and alert whatever it was to my presence. The huffing led me to the far side of the den, to a mound nestled against the wall. Slowly I raised the lamp to peer over the edge.

Within the bowl-shaped bed lay a young male *Anthropophagus*, surprisingly—at least to me—and almost comically small, perhaps only two or three inches taller than me, though easily fifty or so pounds heavier. The oversize eyes set in its shoulders were not closed in its restless slumber—the creatures have no eyelids—rather a milky white film, a proto-lid, shimmered wetly over its obsidian orbs. Its football-size mouth hung open, exposing the triangular teeth, the smaller gripping ones crowding the forward part of its mouth, a dense thicket of the larger slicing and tearing ones bunched closely behind them.

The juvenile twitched in his sleep. Was it dreaming, and what god-awful sort of dreams do they have? I could hazard a guess. His jerky movement may have been a symptom of something other than a dream, for he was missing a forearm, the knotted flesh around his right elbow a swollen mass of infection. Somehow he had been grievously wounded, and I recalled the bizarre bonding ritual of the species, the reaching deep into each other's mouths to scrape clean the teeth. Is that how he'd lost his arm? A slip of his claw, and the mouth of his elder smashed down, tearing the joint in twain and then swallowing his severed arm whole?

The wound wept yellowish pus; clearly the thing was suffering and likely was not even sleeping. More probably it had slipped into a delirious semiconscious state. Its normally colorless skin was flushed with fever and shone with sweat. It was dying.

That explains it, thought I, kneeling before its bower,

staring at it with morbid fascination. *Why she abandoned him. He would be a pointless burden to her.*

I must confess my feelings were mixed. I had witnessed firsthand the savagery of these monsters, had seen the destruction of which they were capable, had even come close to losing my own life to their ravenous rage. And yet . . . and yet. Suffering is suffering still, no matter what manner of organism suffers, and this particular one suffered greatly, that was clear. Part of me was repulsed. And part was possessed by profound pity for its plight—a much smaller part, to be sure, but a portion nevertheless.

I could not abandon it; I could not leave it to its misery. Practically speaking, it would have been imprudent, for what if he woke and commenced to cry, which might summon his mother to his side and to my certain death? I did not know where she had taken the others, if she lay hidden in a secret antechamber but a dozen yards away, or if she had retreated to the deepest hole of their underground burrow. And my empathy, strange and unnatural as it might have been, compelled me to put an end to the creature's agony.

So I leaned forward, my stomach rubbing the edge of the nest, and leveled the doctor's gun at its groin, at a spot just below its drooling lower lip. It did not occur to me until much later that the sound of the gunshot would far exceed any mewling cry the dying *Anthropophagus* could have produced. *Not close enough,* I decided. I wanted it to be quick and sure, so I brought the barrel within an inch of its glistening pink belly. I cocked the hammer with my thumb, and it was that tiny click, that smallest of sounds, that woke him.

He moved with lightning speed, faster than I could pull the trigger, faster than the beat of a fly's wing. His left arm slapped the gun from my hand as he erupted from his sickbed, snarling and spitting in a delirious rage born of fever and fear. He hurled his body into mine. The lamp flew into the air and smashed down in a burst of flame. We tumbled across the floor in a tangle of flailing arms and legs, his snapping mouth catching upon the tail of my jacket and shredding it to pieces, his left claw swiping at my face while I held on to his wrist, pushing with all my might, with my free hand jabbing at his eyes, which were burning fever-bright now, and by the glow of the fire I could see reflected in them my own face, contorted in fear. Our awkward death dance spun us into the wall; I used its support to bring my foot up and kicked him in the privates as hard as I could. My blow only served to enrage him, and indeed appeared to reinvigorate him: He began to club me about the head with the stub of his right arm. I slipped to one side to dodge the furious blows, and fell backward into empty space.

Our match had taken us to the entrance of a narrow tunnel, and into that steeply downward sloping sluice I now tumbled, carrying him with me. End over end we rolled, like two acrobats at the circus, arms and legs intertwined, falling for what seemed like an eternity before slamming to a stop at the bottom, into a mound of fallen rock and loose soil.

Stunned by the impact, my grip loosened on his wrist for an instant, and that instant was all the monster needed: He pulled my forearm into his powerful jaws and bit down. The pain was explosive, and I howled in anguish, punching him blindly with my free hand, until, in my desperation, I caught hold of his wounded appendage, yanked it to my mouth, and bit down as hard as I could upon the festering wound. Thick viscous pus filled my mouth and poured down my throat; my stomach heaved in protest—in another moment I would vomit copiously over his corpse—but my desperate ploy succeeded. His jaws released my arm and he fell away from me, roaring his anguish. Ignoring my own searing pain, I felt around the floor, my hands (invisible in the pitch black though only a foot from my eyes) falling upon a melon-size stone. I snatched it up, raised it high over my head, and brought it crashing down upon his writhing body. Again and again and again, against soft flesh and hard enamel, against anything that moved, my sobs and screams gradually over-coming his. Blood and stringy bits of tissue flew in all direc-tions, landing in my eyes and my open mouth, soaking my shirt, flowing down the incline and saturating the knees of my britches. His cries died away altogether; he went limp; and still I pummeled him, again and again and again, until all energy was spent and the rock dropped from my rubbery arms. I collapsed on top of his lifeless form, gasping, my sobs gut-wrenching and hysterical, at once loud and wee in the confines of the narrow space. After regaining some of my self-control, I pushed myself up, became sick, then fell back against the tunnel's terminus, clutching my left arm, which now throbbed and burned as if on fire.

I spat several times, trying to clear the foul taste from my mouth. The memory of it was more overwhelming than the lingering flavor, and my stomach rolled. The palm of my right hand was slick with blood. I cautiously explored the bite with my fingertips, counting seven puncture wounds in all, three on top, four on the bottom. My first task was to control the bleeding: The doctor had said their sense of smell was acute. I shrugged out of my jacket, removed my shirt, and wrapped it several times around my arm. Then slowly and clumsily, like a child first learning to dress, I slipped the jacket back on.

So far so good, I told myself, to rally my flagging spirits. *That's two notches in your belt, and all in one night. Now up to the den. You'll find some way back to the others. Courage, Will Henry, courage! You can stay here and bleed to death, or you can pick yourself up and find your way back. Now, which will it be, Will Henry?*

I crawled forward until my hand touched the body of my victim. I hopped over it and then got to my feet and began the ascent, left arm pressed into my stomach, right outstretched to feel the wall. I stepped as lightly as I could, breathing shallowly, forcing myself to take it slow, stopping now and then to bend my ear to the dark, listening for any sound that might betray an *Anthropophagus*'s presence. I had no idea how far I had fallen down the shaft; it seemed, as I've said, that it had taken as long as Lucifer fell. Time passes differently when one of your senses is stripped from you, and all else is magnified by the other senses: every breath is thundering, every scraping, scratching step booms a cannonade. I could smell his blood, and my own. The pain in my arm was excruciating. The taste of his infection burned on my tongue.

On I trudged, on and on, ever upward, yet coming no closer to the goal. At times my right hand slipped into open space, a connecting tunnel or perhaps a natural cleft formed by a more benign force of nature. In the commotion of our fall, had we somehow ended up in a secondary branch of the main thoroughfare, and was I now off-course, blindly proceeding from darkness into darkness, hopelessly lost?

Surely, I thought, coming to a halt, leaning dizzily against the cool, moist rock, surely I would have reached the starting place by now. How much time had passed? How long had I been marching, and what now was I marching toward? The thought paralyzed me. Then I thought, *Well, that might very well be the case, Will, but you're still going up, and up is the direction you want to go.* Perhaps that tunnel led straight to the surface. Was it still raining? I wondered. Oh, to feel the rain upon my face! To breathe the sweet draft of cool spring air to the very bottom of my lungs! The longing was nearly as unbearable as the pain.

So I soldiered on inside that lightless labyrinth, clinging

to the logic of my choice—that moving up meant getting out—and to the memory of rain and sunlight and warm breeze and all such comforting things. Those memories seemed to belong to a different time, to an era long since passed, even to a different person; I felt as if I had absconded with the memories of another boy in another time and place, a boy who was not lost and fighting mindless panic and heart-stopping dread.

For now it was unmistakable: The floor had leveled off. I was no longer moving upward. I *had* somehow taken a wrong turn.

I stopped walking. I leaned against the wall. I cradled my wounded arm. It throbbed in time with my heartbeat. Besides my heightened respirations there was no sound. There was no light. Every instinct urged for me to cry for help, to scream at the top of my lungs. I had no idea how much time had passed since I had stumbled into the den, but surely the doctor and the others had dug their way through the barricade by now. They had to be somewhere, perhaps somewhere close by, around the next bend (if there was a next bend), their lights just outside my range of vision. It would be insanely risky—idiotic, really—to announce my presence, for the odds were just as good that *she* was around the next bend. Or were the odds that good? Kearns had said she would take her young to the deepest part of her lair, and it had been no illusion that, up to now, I had been climbing, not descending. Did not that mean the odds were better that I was closer to my companions than to her? And that the real risk lay in holding my silence, stumbling around in the dark for untold hours until dehydration and exhaustion overcame me, if I didn't bleed to death first?

So the debate raged within, to call for help or to remain silent, and the seconds turned to minutes, and each minute tugged the straitjacket of indecision and paralysis tighter.

My fortitude gave way. I was but a boy, you'll recall; a boy who had been in his share of tight spots and dire straits, to be sure, a boy who had seen things that would make a grown man blanch, but still a boy, still but a child. I slid down the wall and rested my forehead against my upraised knees. I closed my eyes and prayed. My father had not been a particularly religious man; aspects of the divine he had entrusted to my mother's care. She had prayed with me every night and had taken me to church every Sunday, to instill a bit of piety in me, but I had inherited my father's indifference to religion and had gone through the motions of devotion without much conviction. A prayer was mere words repeated by rote. When I arrived at the doctor's house, of course, all churchgoing and prayer had come to an abrupt halt, and I did not pine over the loss.

But now I prayed. I prayed until I ran out of words, and then I prayed with my entire being, a prayer not composed of words but out of the profound, wordless longing of my soul.

It was while I was thus employed, my eyes clenched tightly shut, rocking back and forth in rhythm to the roiling of my harrowed mind, that a voice spoke out of the darkness. It was not, as I first assumed in my distress, the voice of the one to whom we pray. A million miles from it!

"Well, well. What have we here?"

I raised my head and shielded my smarting eyes against the light in his hand. As bright as a thousand suns, it blinded me. He took my elbow and helped me to my feet.

"The little lost lamb is found," whispered Kearns.

As it happened, I had succumbed to despair but a dozen yards from deliverance, a connecting passage that was, Kearns informed me, only a short hike from the *Anthropophagi's* den.

"You're a lucky assistant-apprentice monstrumologist, Will," he informed me with his characteristic playfulness. "I almost shot you."

"Where are the others?" I asked.

"There are two main arteries leading from their nesting chamber; Malachi and Warthrop took one, and I took the other, the same you took, obviously, but what has happened to your arm?"

I related my adventures since my precipitous fall into the heart of their lair. Kearns expressed admiration for my pluck in dispatching the wounded juvenile. He seemed surprised by my grace under pressure.

"Splendid. Absolutely splendid! Bloody good work, Will! Pellinore will be overjoyed. He was quite beside himself when you didn't come back. Positively frantic. I'd never seen a man wield a shovel like that. Digging in another direction, he would have reached China in an hour! But here, let's have a look at that arm."

He unwrapped the makeshift bandage. Tacky with blood, the last bit of fabric stuck to my arm, and I winced from the pain. The bites still oozed blood. He draped the bloody shirt over my shoulder and said, "Best to let it breathe a bit, Will. We don't want to risk an infection."

With a hand on the small of my back, he urged me to the entrance of the tunnel leading out. "Look down," he said. A powdery starburst glowed upon the floor in the light of his lamp.

"What is that?" I asked.

"Crumbs, Will Henry, marking the way home!"

It was the contents of the small paper packets he had packed into their canvas bags, a phosphorescent powder that shone like a tiny beacon in the lamplight.

"You'll find one every twenty yards or so," he instructed. "Keep to the path. Don't turn back. If somehow you get lost, backtrack until you pick it up again. Here, take the lamp."

"You're not coming with me?" My heart began to flutter.

"I've monsters to hunt, remember?"

"But you'll need the lamp."

"Don't worry about me. I have the flares in a pinch. Oh, and I believe you dropped this."

It was the doctor's revolver. He pressed it into my hand.

"Don't fire until you see the black of their eyes." His gray eyes danced merrily at the joke. "Around seven hundred steps in all, Will."

"Steps, sir?"

"Perhaps a bit more for you; your legs aren't quite as long as mine. About four hundred steps, then turn right into the main passage. Don't miss the turn—very important! The way tends downward for a bit, but don't despair. It will start to go up again. When you get back up to the top, tell the constable I miss him terribly. That button nose. That winsome smile. If we haven't come up in two hours, have him and his men come down. These beasties have been busy digging in the dark and we may need the other men's help. Good luck to you, junior monstrumologist. Good luck and God bless!"

With that he turned on his heel and evaporated like a ghost from the lamplight, his footfalls fading fast. He did not seem fazed journeying on in without a light. Indeed, he gave the impression that the prospect delighted him: John Kearns was a man at home in the dark.

How quickly can despair turn to joy! My spirits were brighter than the little light aloft in my hand, my heart higher; I could already smell freedom's sweet fragrance, taste its ambrosial flavor. In the ecstasy attending this answered prayer for deliverance, I forgot to count my steps, remembering too late for counting to do any good, but it hardly seemed important. The trail was well-marked with the glowing powder.

I reached the turn Kearns had marked, the tunnel that would lead me back to the abandoned nests of the *Anthropophagi* and from there to Morgan's "winsome" smile. I paused for a moment in puzzlement, for *two* ways had been marked— one into the intersecting passage and another straight ahead, continuing along the path upon which I trod. *Well*, thought I, *he must have turned right first, went a little ways, then backtracked, finding the way blocked, or perhaps hearing the forlorn cries of a wounded "junior monstrumologist."* His instructions had been explicit. *Don't miss the turn—very important!* So with a shrug I ducked into the opening. If there were seven hundred steps in all and the first leg was four hundred, then this last stretch was three, and I began to count.

The tunnel was narrower, the ceiling much lower; several times I was forced to lower my head or shuffle forward doubled over, the bottom of the lamp scraping the floor. The passage was tortuously serpentine, twisting and turning this way and that, the way sloped and slippery, tending ever downward, as he had promised.

Upon the hundredth step I heard something make a sound behind me—or I thought it was behind me. In those cramped confines it was hard to tell. I stopped. I held my breath. Nothing. Just the falling of dirt and pebbles dislodged by my passing, I surmised, nothing more. I started forward again and resumed the count.

Seventy steps later I heard it again, definitely coming from behind me and almost certainly a portion of the tunnel giving way. I listened carefully, but all I could hear was the soft hissing of the lamp. I checked the safety on the revolver. My nerves were jangled, naturally, from the night's ordeal, and my imagination afire with visions of pale, headless devils dwelling in the dark, yet my good sense was not entirely confounded. Either I was being followed or I wasn't. If I was, confronting my stalker in this claustrophobic circumstance—the tunnel could not have been much more than four feet around by this point— would be folly. If I wasn't, I gained nothing but delay by these fearful halts. Onward!

However had Kearns managed this operose conduit? A grown man would have been forced to crawl, and, if crawling, how had he calculated his steps, when walking was impossible? Forget a grown man—how could a seven-foot-tall hulk of a monster do it without slithering snakelike upon its tooth-encrusted belly? As the walls tightened around me, doubt and fear followed in kind. Surely this could not be the main thoroughfare back to the nesting chamber. I must have misunderstood him or taken a wrong turn . . . but the way had been marked, was *still* marked, though the space between the glimmering sprays had lengthened to far more than twenty feet. And the tunnel continued to go down, not up, as he'd promised, the floor no longer hard packed but spongy, saturated with moisture as it descended into the depths. I inched forward, my progress painfully slow, the lamp illuminating little but the weeping wet walls and the dripping roof, too deep for even the longest roots of the largest trees above to penetrate.

And then I smelled it, a sickly sweet odor like rotten fruit, faintly at first, becoming stronger with each agonizing yard, a nauseating stench that burned my nose and lodged sourly in the back of my throat. I had smelled it before, in the cemetery on the night Erasmus Gray had died; it still clung upon my clothing from the embrace of the juvenile whose delirious slumber I had disturbed. It was the smell of the beast. It was the smell of *them*.

I cannot say I grasped the full meaning of that moment then, the import of the disparate elements, which seems so obvious now: the two pathways marked, one straight and wide, the other crooked and narrow; the tunnel leading downward, ever downward; the sound of something following me; the baring of my wounds to let them 'breathe a bit.' Such profound perfidy is beyond the comprehension of most men, let alone the trusting naïveté of a child! No, I was merely confused and frightened, not suspicious, as I kneeled, lamp thrust before me in one hand while I clutched the gun in the quivering other. The grade was steep and the floor slick. If I turned around now, I would have to crawl slowly or risk sliding back a foot for each I gained. Should I turn back? Or should I ignore the awful smell (perhaps the earth itself had absorbed it like a sponge) and the still, small voice within that whispered, *Turn around! Go back!* Should I press on?

In the end the decision was made for me. A hand reached out of the darkness and tapped my shoulder. With a startled cry I pivoted round, the lamp slapping into the wall as I whirled. Its swaying light lit up in manic flashes his smudged face, the animated eyes and the small, ironic smirk.

"Why, Will Henry, wherever are you going?" he whispered. His breath smelled as sweet as licorice. "Didn't I tell you to keep to the path and not turn back?"

"This isn't the way back," I breathed in reply.

"I had hoped to avoid it," was his cryptic response. "The smell of blood should have drawn her out; I'm at a loss, frankly, why she didn't come."

He gently pulled the lamp from my hand and withdrew a flare from his bag. "Here, take this. Hold it at the base so you won't burn your little hand. Don't let go of it, whatever you do!" He touched the short fuse to the lamp's flame. Smoke curled in the close space; the tunnel burst into dazzling light; darkness fled.

He put his hand on my chest and said with mock sorrow, "I am so sorry, Mr. Henry, but there really is no choice. It is the morality of the moment."

And with those parting words John Kearns shoved me as hard as he could.

My fall was swift, straight, and unstoppable. His crouching form rocketed away from me, dissolving into darkness as I skidded down the grease-slick trough, until a collision with a bend in the wall flipped me onto my back and I slid the remaining few feet digging my heels into the muck in a vain effort to slow my slide into the hole that awaited me at the bottom.

How wondrously strange to an observer below, should he have been standing inside the chamber into which now I fell, to see the virgin darkness, never blessed by light's beneficent kiss, rent by the blinding ember of the flare clutched in my hand, descending like a falling star from heaven's vault. I landed on my back, and the jolt of impact jerked the flare from my hand. For a moment I lay stunned and gasping, the hot, coppery taste of blood filling my mouth: I had bitten the tip of my tongue when I'd hit.

I rolled onto my stomach, spat the blood from my mouth, and had barely gotten to my knees when it came at me with a sibilant screech, arms outstretched, black eyes rolling in its powerful shoulders, slavering mouth agape. I brought up the gun with a foot to spare and yanked the trigger. The young *Anthropophagus* fell at my feet, its body twisting in the stinking muck of the chamber floor. It was a lucky shot, but I had no time to rejoice or wonder at my good fortune, for its brother now barreled toward me from its hiding place. I fired twice, missing both times, shooting as I scrambled backward.

A bullet imploded into the ground scarred by my scurrying retreat, followed the next instant by the rifle's report. It was Kearns, lying on his belly in the tunnel over me, firing through the hole through which I, the bait, had fallen.

My back hit the wall; I thumped down on my backside, legs spread wide; and shot twice more at the advancing form. Both shots went wild, but Kearns's next found its target, striking the beast in its right shoulder, driving its arm into the ground, yet hardly slowing its implacable approach. *They possess the largest Achilles tendons known to primates, enabling them to leap astonishing distances, up to forty feet,* the doctor had informed me in his characteristically matter-of-fact manner. Traversing so great a distance in a single bound might prove a challenge to an immature *Anthropophagus*; fortunately for him, he had a span of only ten feet to cross. He launched himself at me, his left arm extended perpendicular to his body, poised to land the killing blow. I had just one bullet left and one second to decide.

Fortune spared me that awful decision: In midflight he stiffened, shoulders yanked back by the punch of the round landing between them. The second shot struck him in the middle of his back, and dropped him. He lay heaving and mewling at my feet, claws digging impotently in the dirt, before expiring his last breath, and death took him down.

I heard soft satisfied laughter above me and, coming from the far side of the chamber, where the light of the flare could not reach, a familiar voice calling my name.

"Will Henry, is that you?"

I nodded. I could make no other reply. It seemed like years since I had heard that voice, and more times than I could count it had unnerved me, frightened me, filled me with not unreasonable dread and gnawing apprehension. Ah, but now it brought tears of joy.

"Yes, sir," I called to the doctor. "It's me."

The monstrumologist rushed to my side. He grabbed me by the shoulders and looked deeply into my eyes, his own reflecting the intensity of his concern.

"Will Henry!" he cried softly. "Will Henry, why are you here?" He pulled me into his chest and whispered fiercely into my ear, "I told you that you are indispensable to me. Do you think I lied, Will Henry? I may be a fool and a terrible scientist, blinded by ambition and pride to the most obvious truths, but one thing I am *not* is a liar."

He released me with these words and turned aside for a moment, as if embarrassed by his confession. Then he turned back and asked brusquely, "Now tell me, you silly, stupid boy, are you hurt?"

I lifted my arm, and he played the light of his lamp up and down the length of it. Over his shoulder, on the outer edge of the light's reach (for the flare had finally fizzled out), I could see Malachi. He was staring not at our touching tableau but over our heads, toward the hole through which I had fallen.

The doctor carefully brushed the dirt and tiny, scratching pebbles from the wounds, bending low to examine them in the wavering light. "It's a clean bite, and relatively shallow," he pronounced. "A few stitches and you'll be good as new, Will Henry, if a bit battle-scarred."

"There is something up there," Malachi called hoarsely, jabbing his finger toward the roof of the cave. "Above you!"

He swung the rifle to his shoulder and would have pulled the trigger, I've no doubt, if Kearns had not announced his presence and dropped through the hole. He landed on his feet with all the aplomb of a champion gymnast, spreading his arms wide to retain his balance, and he sustained the pose as if to gather us into his metaphorical embrace.

"And so all's well that ends well!" he said heartily. "Or should I say all ends well very nearly near the end. Perhaps 'so far so good' would be better—but here you are, Pellinore, in the nick of time, thank goodness!"

With narrowed eye Malachi returned, "This is very strange."

"Oh, my dear chap, you should have been with me in Niger back in '85. Now *that* was strange!"

"I find it strange too," said the doctor. "Tell me, Kearns: How did Will Henry come to be down here and you up there?"

"Will Henry fell; I did not."

"He fell?" echoed Warthrop. He turned to me. "Is this true, Will Henry?"

I shook my head. Lying was the worst kind of buffoonery. "No, sir, I was pushed."

"Oh, 'fell,' 'pushed'—it's all a matter of semantics," pooh-poohed Kearns. He watched, bemused, as Malachi brought the muzzle of his gun a foot from his chest. "Go on," he urged the enraged orphan. "Pull the bloody trigger, you insufferably melodramatic, semi-suicidal, blubbering bugger. Do you honestly think I care if I live or die? But you may wish to include in your calculations the fact that our work is not finished. *She* is still out there somewhere in the dark, and not very far, I would guess. That said, sir, I would not presume to pass judgment upon the passage of your judgment. Fire at will, sir, and I shall die as I lived, with no regret!" He thrust his chest in Malachi's direction defiantly and grinned ear to ear.

"Why were you pushed, Will Henry?" asked the doctor, barely acknowledging the drama. He had long grown weary of Kearns's theatrics.

"He tricked me," I said, lowering my voice and refusing to look in my betrayer's direction. "I think he found this chamber and he knew they were down here, but he couldn't get off a good shot, so he marked the spot and sent me straight to it. Finding me hurt, he thought the smell of blood might draw them out. When it didn't, he—"

"In my own defense," Kearns said, "I did give you a weapon and I didn't just throw you to the wolves. That was me up there, you know, shooting at them. I don't question the demands of circumstance; I simply obey them. Like Malachi here, abandoning his beloved sister when she needed him the most—"

"Kearns, enough!" admonished the monstrumologist. "Or by God *I* shall shoot you."

"Do you know why our race is doomed, Pellinore? Because it has fallen in love with the pleasant fiction that we are somehow above the very rules that we have determined govern everything else."

"I don't know what he's talking about," Malachi said with unnerving levelness. "But I like his idea. I say we make him bleed and use *him* as bait."

"I would gladly volunteer," rejoined Kearns easily. "But the circumstances no longer, I think, demand it." He grabbed the lamp from the doctor's hand and strode away, his boots squishing in the muddy ground, the heels sinking a good half inch before popping free. When he reached the wall, he turned and gestured for us to join him.

He placed a finger to his lips, then pointed down. A small opening, about twice the width of my shoulders, lay at the base of the wall. He held the lamp close to its jagged mouth while we peered down its murky throat. The passage ran downward at a forty-five-degree angle from the chamber floor. With little jabs of his finger Kearns pointed out the footprints clustered around the wall and the shallow cuts and gouges caused by their nails along the first few feet of the tunnel.

We withdrew to a safe distance, and Kearns said in a soft voice, "Two distinct sets—yes, Pellinore?" The doctor nodded, and Kearns went on. "A cub and a mature female. Two going in and none coming out again. Why she took one and left the others is a curiosity, but undeniably that is what she did. Perhaps these two"—he jerked his head toward the dead *Anthropophagi*—"wandered back up here for some reason, though the prints don't substantiate that scenario. There are only two possibilities as I see it: It may lead to another, deeper chamber or it may be an escape route that eventually returns to the surface; there's only way to find out. Agreed, Pellinore?"

The doctor nodded reluctantly. "Agreed."

"And if they haven't escaped to the surface, the ruckus up here will have alerted her to our proximity. She is, no doubt, expecting us."

"That's fine with me," said Malachi, grimly gripping his gun. "I won't disappoint her."

"You are staying here," said Kearns.

"I don't take orders from you," Malachi sneered.

"All right," Kearns said mildly. "Take them from Pellinore if you wish. We need someone to stay here and guard the exit—and keep an eye on Will Henry, of course."

"I didn't come all this way to be a nursemaid!" cried Malachi. He appealed to Warthrop, "Please. It is my right."

"Really? How do you mean?" interjected Kearns. "It wasn't personal, you know. They were hungry and needed to eat. What do *you* do when you're hungry?"

Warthrop laid a hand upon Malachi's shoulder. "Kearns must go; he is the expert tracker. And I must go, for if anyone has earned the "right," it is I." I remembered the haunting question posed in the basement as he considered her mate hanging before him. *I wonder if she would be satisfied with his son.* "Another must stay, in the event she somehow escapes and returns here. Would you have it be Will Henry? Look at him, Malachi; he's just a boy."

His startlingly blue eyes fell upon my face, and I turned away from the unbearable torment I saw within them.

"I can do it," I offered. "I'll guard the exit. Take Malachi with you."

I was ignored, of course. Malachi watched glumly as the doctor and Kearns doubled-checked their ammunition and supplies. Kearns took two flares and several of the paper sacks used for trail marking from the doctor's bag and dropped them into his, and examined their grenades to be certain they were in working order. The doctor took me aside and said, "There is something that feels wrong about this, Will Henry, though I can't put my finger on it. She wouldn't back herself into a corner—she is far too clever for that. Neither would she willingly abandon two of her young to our mercy. It is exceedingly curious. Keep a sharp eye and call out at once should you see or hear anything out of the ordinary."

He squeezed my arm and added sternly, "And for God's sake, don't wander off this time! I expect you to be here when I return, Will Henry."

"Yes, sir," I said, trying my best to sound brave.

"Preferably alive."

"I will try to be, sir."

With heavy heart I watched him walk with Kearns to the narrow aperture. Something nagged at me. There was something I needed to ask him, something important, something I should remember but was forgetting.

"How long should we wait?" called Malachi.

"Wait for what?" Kearns asked.

"How long should we wait before coming after you?"

Kearns shook his head. "Don't come after us."

At the wall Kearns made a grand, sweeping gesture, extending the honor of going first to the monstrumologist. A moment later they were gone, the gentle glow of their lamp fading quickly as they slid out of sight in pursuit of the matriarch and the last of her brood.

Malachi did not speak for several moments. He walked over to the felled *Anthropophagi* and poked the one shot twice in the back with the muzzle of his rifle. "That's mine there," he said, pointing to the blackened hole in the middle of its back. "The second shot—the killing shot."

"Then you saved my life," I said.

"Do you think it works that way, Will? Now I have only five more for which to atone?"

"You couldn't help them," I offered. "You were trapped in your room. And you couldn't help Elizabeth, either, not really. How could you have saved her, Malachi?"

He didn't answer. "It feels like a dream," he said instead, after a pensive pause. He was looking at the body lying at his feet. "Not this. My life before this, before *them*. You would think the opposite would be true. It's very strange, Will."

He told me what had happened after I'd last seen him

in the passage connecting the devil's manger to the nesting chamber, confirming at least part of Kearns's rendition. They had indeed discovered two main arteries whose directions seemed to tend downward. He and the doctor had taken one and Kearns the other—apparently the one into which the abandoned *Anthropophagus* and I had tumbled. I suspected Kearns, the expert tracker, had noted the signs of our scuffle and knew—but did not tell the others—precisely where I had gone, choosing not to inform them of this intelligence.

The passage, Malachi related, connected to countless others, and at each branch or juncture they chose the downward path. Halfway to this final hiding place, he surmised, the doctor stumbled upon her trail, fresh tracks left in the moist soil, and they followed them until they reached the chamber in which we now waited for the doctor's return.

"It came out over there," he said, pointing to a spot in the shadows directly across from the bodies. "We knew Kearns must have found it first, for we saw the light within and heard the sound of gunfire. But I never expected you would be here, Will."

"Neither did I."

He leaned on his rifle, and his weight forced its butt to slowly sink into the soft soil. He lifted it out and watched water seep into the indenture.

"The ground here is very wet," he observed. "And the

walls weep. There must be an underground stream or river close by."

He was right: There *was* a stream. It ran roughly perpendicular to the cave, twenty feet or so below us, and in the spring it swelled to nearly twice its normal size. Each season its swath widened, as the water cut and chewed its confining walls; every year the very floor upon which we stood became more saturated and unstable. The *Anthropophagi* had discovered it; it was their primary source for freshwater and why their young had no need to venture to the surface in search of that necessity. The path taken by Kearns and Warthrop led directly to a hollow by its banks, where the creatures went to drink and bathe—though they do not bathe in the way we think of bathing. They are not swimmers and are terrified of deep water, but they are compelled, like the raccoon, to wash the gore and offal from their long nails. They also enjoy (if "enjoy" might be used to describe it) sliding on their backs into the shallows, letting the water pour into their open mouths, and then spinning and twisting their bodies, chomping the frothing water like a crocodile in a death roll. The purpose of this odd ritual is not known, but might be, like the picking of one another's teeth, part of their hygienic regimen.

It was to the protected banks of this subterranean stream that she had taken the one-year-old "toddler," the youngest and most vulnerable of her brood. As the doctor had pointed out, her leaving its older siblings behind was exceedingly curious, but I suspect she had meant to return for them, or they, in their confusion and fear, had refused to follow her. Whatever the case, it was this sequestered youngster they found upon the final turn of their final descent, mewling and snarling at the edge of the life-giving water, unable to flee or defend itself. At that age *Anthropophagi*, like their prey of the same age, cannot walk with any efficiency. Kearns went right up to it and killed it with a single shot.

The shot echoed up to us, and Malachi stiffened at the sound, raising his rifle and turning toward the passage's mouth. In the hollow below us the hunters waited, knowing she had to be hiding somewhere close, and certain she would come out.

And they were right; she did come out.

She had returned to fetch her other children. Kearns and the doctor had not encountered her on their way down because she had taken a different path, a path that ran directly beneath Malachi Stinnet's feet.

Behind him the ground burst open in an explosion of water and mud. The floor gave way and he lost his balance, falling forward onto his knees, losing his rifle when he did, the canvas tote slipping from his shoulder as he caught himself from landing face-first in the mud. He slid backward in the muck toward the widening rent in the chamber floor, the expression in his beautiful eyes horribly familiar to me. I had seen it before, in the eyes of Erasmus Gray and in the eyes of my poor father: the grotesquely comical look of the doomed when their damnation is inescapably upon them.

His fingers cut furrows in the wet earth; his legs kicked helplessly. His ankles vanished into the swirling maelstrom in the middle of the muddy whirlpool behind him, and then something caught his boot and *yanked* him. In a trice he was sucked down to his knees.

He screamed my name. His body was spun round like a top, whipping his head about with such force I was certain he must have broken his neck. He was upright now, with only his writhing torso visible, stretching his arms beseechingly toward me as Erasmus had, as my father had, and this soundless supplication broke my paralysis. I lunged forward, reached for him. "Grab hold, Malachi! Grab hold!" He slapped my hand away and gestured violently toward the bag that lay beside me. He sank to his chest in the roiling surface, borne down by the same beast that had punched her fist through the chest of the navigator Burns aboard the *Feronia*, and blood gushed from his gaping mouth. She had rammed her claws into the small of his back and wrapped them around his spinal column, using it as a kind of handle to pull him down.

I had misread Malachi's true desire, which had nothing to do with rescue. Unlike Erasmus and my father, Malachi did not want deliverance. He had never wanted it. It was too late for that.

Again he frantically jabbed his finger at the bag. I picked it up and flung it into his arms, and in mute dismay watched him pull out a grenade. He clutched it to his chest, hooked his finger through the pin, and then with bloodstained teeth Malachi Stinnet smiled triumphantly at me.

He closed his eyes; his head fell back; his expression was one of complete peace and acceptance. He disappeared by degrees, first his arms and chest, then his neck, until for the last time his eyes came open, staring into my mine, unblinking and unconcerned.

"For Elizabeth," he whispered.

He vanished into the bloody froth. I threw myself backward, scrambling away from the spot as fast as I could. The earth heaved, the walls rocked, huge chunks of ceiling shook loose and came crashing down. The concussion of the subsequent blast sent me flying. My fall was broken by, of all things, the body of the juvenile that Malachi's bullet had brought down. Draped over it, I lay stunned for a moment, ears ringing, drenched in water and mud, flecks of flesh and bits of bone. I sat up and rubbed my eyes, the harsh residue of the powder that hung in the air like a fine aerosol burning in the back of my throat. I looked toward the epicenter of the holocaust. The explosion had created a ten-foot crater, in the center of which bubbles lazily ascended to the rosy surface.

Where was the doctor? I turned to my right, peering through the smoky haze, searching for the opening. Had it collapsed? Were he and Kearns now trapped beneath tons of earth? Had the entire structure, weakened by water and ripped apart by the explosion, crashed down upon their heads, crushing them or, worse, burying them alive?

I swayed for a moment upon unsteady legs, took a shuffling step toward the wall . . . and stopped. The smoke had cleared a bit and I could see the opening; it had not collapsed; but it wasn't this welcome sight that gave me pause. It was a sound—the sound of something rising out of the bloody bombed-out crater behind me.

The hairs rose on the back of my neck. The skin between my shoulder blades tingled, the muscles twitched. Slowly I turned my head, and saw her towering form rear up, like an obscene mockery of Venus from the surf, her pale skin pock-marked with shrapnel wounds and painted with her and Malachi's blood, one arm completely gone, torn off by the explosion, her body mangled horribly but her will unbroken. In the cruelest of ironies, Malachi's body had shielded her from the brunt of the blast.

And now she, the matriarch, the mother of the *Anthro-pophagi*, with her one remaining eye spied me standing beside her precious progeny, whom her instincts demanded she defend, as the doctor had said, to her last breath with ruthless ferocity. Her own pain did not matter. The fact that she was herself mortally wounded did not matter. What ani-mated her was as old as life itself, the same irresistible force that the doctor had marveled at in the pastor's parlor: *How strong is the maternal instinct, Will Henry!*

That overriding compulsion now drove her toward the spot where I cowered, frozen in fear's icy grip, wavering in indecisive agony, for even in her injured state she moved with frightening speed and would catch me should I make a run for the passageway—which may or may not still have been open.

The space between us had shrunk by half when I regained my wits, pulled the doctor's revolver from my belt, and took aim, remembering as I started to pull the trigger the thing that had nagged at me before, the thing I should have remembered but couldn't: bullets. I had forgotten to ask the doctor for more bullets. There was but one left.

One bullet. One chance. A wild shot or one that missed a vital organ and it was over. I was bound by the bitter fruit of my own forgetfulness.

She gathered herself for the final, finishing leap. Her extant arm came up. Her mouth came open. Her good eye with merciless malevolence shone. I had to stop her before she made that leap, and I did, though not with a bullet. Instead I turned her mother's love against her.

I flung myself beside the body of her young and jammed the gun against its lifeless side, screaming stupidly at the top of my lungs while praying that no animal instinct told her the child I threatened no longer lived. My feet slipped out from under me, and I landed with a startled grunt upon my backside, my left arm curled awkwardly around its headless shoulders. My desperate gambit had worked, however, for she did not jump but came to a complete and sudden halt. She snuffed the air.

She issued a low, gurgling call, like a cow in the pasture lowing for her calf.

She did not hesitate long, perhaps only a second or two, and then she renewed her charge, leading with the shoulder that held her remaining eye, closing down upon me until I could smell her putrid breath and see the rows of jagged three-inch teeth marching toward the back of her cavernous mouth.

Wait. Wait, Will Henry. Let her get close. You must let her get close! Closer. Closer. Ten feet. Five feet. Three. Two . . .

And when the beast was close enough that I could see my own reflection in its black, soulless orb, when all the world was her rotten stench and her snapping teeth and her slick, glistening, pallid skin, when I reached that instant wherein a hairsbreadth separates life from death, I smashed the muzzle against her groin and pulled the trigger.

THIRTEEN

"You Bear His Burden"

On a May morning of that same year, a month to the day since the old grave-robber's midnight visit that began the singular curiosity of the Anthropophagi affair, as the doctor had taken to calling it, I was bounding up the stairs in answer to his incessant summonses, ignored for too long (I did not appear upon the first shout, in other words) and now shaking the house at 425 Harrington Lane to its foundations.

"Will Henry! Will Henreeeee!"

I found him in the lavatory, straight razor in hand, his half-shaven chin dotted in styptic, the water of his bowl a not unpleasant shade of pink.

"What are you doing?" he demanded upon my breathless entrance.

"You called me, sir."

"No, Will Henry. What were you doing *before* I called you, and why did it take you so long to stop doing whatever it was that forbade you from coming in the first place?"

"I was cooking breakfast, sir."

"Breakfast! What time is it?"

"Nearly nine o'clock, sir."

"I detest shaving." He held out the razor and sat upon the commode while I finished up his chin. "Is it finished?" he asked.

"There's still the neck," I answered.

"Not the shave, Will Henry. Breakfast."

"Oh. No, sir, it isn't."

"No? Why not?"

"I had to stop."

"What happened?"

"You called me, sir."

"Are you being cheeky, Will Henry?"

"I don't try to be."

He grunted. I wiped the blade clean. His eyes followed my hand. "How is the arm, Will Henry? I've not taken a look at it lately."

"Much better, sir. I noticed last night the scars seem to glow in the dark."

"That is an optical illusion."

"Yes, sir. That was my conclusion too."

"What is for breakfast?"

"Potato pancakes and sausage."

He grimaced. The razor raked down his throat. There was a rhythm to it: scrape, scrape, wipe . . . scrape, scrape, wipe. His eyes never left my face.

"Any mail today, Will Henry?"

"No, sir."

"And no mail yesterday. That is unusual."

"Yesterday was Sunday, sir, and the mail doesn't run till ten."

"Sunday! Are you sure of that?"

I nodded. Scrape, scrape, wipe.

"I don't suppose you remembered to pick up a scone or two at the market."

"I did, sir."

He sighed with relief. "Good. I think I shall have one of those."

"You can't, sir."

"And why can't I? Now you *are* being cheeky, Will Henry. I am the master of this house; I suppose I can have anything I please."

"You can't because you ate the last one last night."

"I did?" He seemed genuinely surprised. "Really? I don't remember that. Are you certain?"

I told him I was, and wiped the lathery remnants from his face with a warm towel. He looked in the mirror and gave his reflection a cursory glance.

"A pity," he mused. "A pity squared: first that I have none to eat and second that I can't remember eating one to begin with! Where is my shirt, Will Henry?"

"I think I saw it on your wardrobe, sir."

I trailed behind him into the bedroom. As he buttoned his shirt, I said, "I could run down there now, sir."

"Run down where?"

"To the market, for some scones."

He waved his hand, absently dismissal. "Oh, I'm not really hungry."

"You should eat something, though."

He sighed. "Must we plow that same tiresome row again, Will Henry? What are you doing now?"

"Nothing, sir."

He started to say something, and then apparently changed his mind. "Anything in the papers today?"

I shook my head. One of my duties was to scan the dailies for tidbits that might interest him. Of late there seemed to be only one potentially hazardous matter that concerned him. "Nothing, sir."

"Remarkable," he said. "Not even in the *Globe*?"

I shook my head again. It had been more than a fortnight since he had reported the murder to the authorities, and to date only a brief notice and an obituary had appeared in Dedham's weekly. The police, it appeared, were not taking seriously the doctor's allegations of foul play.

"Damn him," the monstrumologist muttered. I did not know if he referred to Dr. J. F. Starr, the victim, or to Dr. John Kearns, his killer.

Warthrop had promised justice for Hezekiah Varner and those other poor unfortunates suffering behind the heavy padlocked doors of Motley Hill. That promise was kept, though doubtlessly not in the way he had anticipated. Indeed, I do not think that promise was foremost in his mind the morning we arrived in Dedham, three days after the felling of the mother *Anthropophagus*. It wasn't justice he sought; it was answers. Not equity, but exorcism.

"Charming," Kearns commented upon our arrival at the decrepit sanatorium. He had insisted, before taking his leave of New England, on accompanying us. He, too, wanted to verify Warthrop's revised theory of the case—or so he said. "I was committed once. Have I ever told you, Pellinore? Oh, yes, for three long years before I managed to effect my escape. I was all of seventeen. The entire abysmal episode was my dear mother's doing, God rest her angelic soul." He looked down at me and smiled. "She is catalogued with your employer's Society, under *M* for 'Monsters, Maternal.' Four days after my return she fell down the stairs and broke her neck."

"Why did she commit you?" I asked.

"I was *precocious*."

The erstwhile black-clad Mrs. Bratton showed little surprise at our unexpected appearance upon the sagging stoop. The doctor handed her his card and twenty dollars in gold, and presently we were escorted to the little parlor with its odiferous atmosphere and tired trappings, where the ancient alienist huddled in his dressing gown beneath a threadbare blanket, shivering despite the robust fire dancing in the hearth.

There were few preliminary pleasantries. With a gleam in his charcoal eyes, Kearns introduced himself as Dr. John J. J. Schmidt of Whitechapel.

"And what is your area of expertise, Doctor?" inquired the old man.

"Anatomy," answered Kearns.

Warthrop deposited two more coins upon the table by Starr's elbow and immediately inaugurated the interrogation.

"Who were Slidell and Mason?" he asked.

"Madmen," murmured Starr.

"Is that a formal diagnosis?" wondered Kearns.

"No, but I assure you, Dr. Schmidt, madness is *my* area of expertise."

"They were agents of the Confederacy?" pressed the doctor.

"They never claimed to be, Warthrop, at least not to me, but I met them only once, and that briefly. Certainly they were fanatical over 'the cause,' as they called it, the most dangerous kind of fanatics too: fanatics with fabulous sums at their disposal."

"My father introduced you," said the doctor. It was not a question.

The old man nodded, and even that small gesture propelled him into a coughing jag that lasted at least two minutes, at the end of which he produced the same disgusting scrap of cloth and spat into it. Beside me Kearns chuckled, as if something about the ritual delighted him.

"And who did my father say they were?"

"Philanthropists."

Kearns stifled a guffaw. The doctor shot him a look and turned back to Starr. "Philanthropists?"

"Interested—*keenly* interested, in their words—in the advancement of the science of eugenics."

"Fanatical philanthropists," ventured Kearns, still chuckling.

"My father," said Warthrop. "He enlisted their aid in an experiment."

Starr nodded. "As I understood it, it involved the merger of the two species."

"Oh, dear God!" Kearns ejaculated with mock horror.

Warthrop's revulsion was not feigned, however. "*Anthropophagi* with *Homo sapiens*? To what possible purpose?"

"The obvious one, Pellinore," said Kearns. "A killing machine with an intellect on par with its bloodthirstiness. The ultimate predator. The bestial equivalent to Nietzsche's *Übermensch*."

"I don't think he looked at it that way, Dr. Schmidt," said Starr. "*They* might have, Mason and Slidell, but not Warthrop. 'It may be in our power to give a soul to the soulless,' he told me in private. 'Mercy to the merciless. Humanity to the inhuman.'"

"And you agreed," said Warthrop.

"Not at first. I rebuffed the offer outright. I had no desire to play God."

"But you changed your mind. Why?"

Starr stayed silent. His chest rattled in counterpoint to his tortured breath. Warthrop added two more coins to the stack.

"How do you know I changed it?" the geezer croaked.

"You shut up Varner for them. Convinced the court he was insane and locked him away lest anyone ever believe his tale."

"Varner was mad as a hatter."

"And you agreed to the second part of the bargain."

Starr wet his purplish lips. "There was no other part," he insisted. "What is this about, Warthrop? What do you want from me? I am an old man, a *dying* old man, I might add. Why have you come here to badger me about the past?"

Warthrop whirled and, seizing my wounded arm, shoved it under the agitated alienist's nose.

"Because it isn't the past," he growled. He released me and leaned into the old man's face. "You ask what I want. I will answer with the same question: What is it that *you* want, Jeremiah Starr? You have my word as a gentleman I will tell no one what transpires between us this day. You shall not spend the remainder of your miserable little life in prison or end it upon the gallows, though the blood of your countless victims calls to heaven for it! I know most and suspect I know the rest, but I wish to hear it, and there is no one left alive to confess to it but you. You have my word; what else?"

Starr refused to answer, but his greed betrayed him: His rheumy gaze flickered for an instant to the stack of coins at his elbow. Warthrop opened his purse and dumped the entire contents onto the table. The coins clattered, cascaded to the worn carpet. One landed heads-up on top of the old man's throw.

"There!" Warthrop cried. "All I have with me. Tomorrow I'll give you ten times that, only answer the question so the matter can be put to rest once and for all. . . . The creatures in my father's care needed two things to survive during the course of this 'experiment' in eugenics, whatever its true purpose: a safe haven, which no doubt Mason and Slidell funded, and food. Yes? They built the subterranean enclosure and you supplied the meals. Yes? Say 'yes,' you damnable monster."

"Yes," said Starr. A coughing fit doubled him over, and when he sat back, his face was the color of ripe strawberries. Spittle dotted his stubbly chin. Warthrop recoiled in disgust.

"And when the war ended . . . ?"

"He offered to finance it himself," Starr admitted. "He could not let it go."

"Not let it go?" The doctor seemed aghast. "Not let *what* go?"

"He had grown rather fond of them, I think. Rather like his pets or children. I mean no offense, Warthrop. He was very possessive of them."

"And you cared not where the money came from."

"Warthrop," replied Starr in a condescending tone. "Really. These . . ." He waved his mottled claw in the air, searching for the word. "Patients, so-called, they are the dregs of society. They come here because there is literally no place else for them to go. No family, or none that would claim them. All are insane—most criminally so, and those who are not have the intellectual capacity of a turnip root. They are human garbage, discarded by men, toxic to the general populace *and* to themselves, forgotten, unwanted, cruel, comical mockeries of all things that make us human. They could rot here or they could be sacrificed to the higher good."

"With the added benefit that if they vanished, they would not be missed."

Starr nodded, appearing relieved that the doctor understood. "They would not be missed," he echoed.

"And you kept your end of the bargain," prompted Warthrop, his jaw clenched. He would see the truth out whatever the cost. The coins glittered in the lamplight, part of that cost, but not the greatest to him. "Every month, until he died and the money stopped coming, you transported two or three victims to New Jerusalem."

"No, no, no," objected Starr. "Right in the essentials, Warthrop, wrong in the particulars. *I* never brought them over. I had a man for that job. And I didn't stop sending them."

Warthrop was flabbergasted. "What do you mean, you didn't stop?"

"I mean just that, Warthrop. I didn't stop."

Beside me Kearns murmured, "That cannot be true."

The doctor ran his hands through his hair. He collapsed into a chair and rested his elbows on his knees, speaking now to his shoes, "Why didn't you stop?" he managed to ask.

"Your father begged me not to. He established a fund for their safekeeping. He was concerned the experiment had put him in an untenable position: If he cut off their food supply, they would simply look for it elsewhere. I happened to agree with him. The genie was out of the bottle, Pandora's box had been opened; there really was no choice but to continue."

"Otherwise *real* people might die," suggested Kearns. He was nodding and smiling at the wicked old man, as if to say, *We are simpatico, you and I.*

"Yes! That's it exactly." Starr nodded eagerly. "So after he died, nothing changed. Once a month at the stroke of midnight I dispatched Peterson to the cemetery with a load."

"A three-hour journey, putting feeding time at three a.m.," said Kearns. "The witching hour."

Warthrop was shaking his head. "Your story does not match the evidence of the case, Starr. An alpha male was discovered feeding upon a corpse; only *Anthropophagi* pushed to the edge of starvation would resort to that. They had recently dug their way to the surface: unnecessary if you were serving them fresh meat every month. And I do not think the sealing of the tunnel between the nesting and the feeding chambers was the result of any natural phenomenon. You say you never stopped, but you must have stopped."

"Yes, yes, yes," retorted Starr impatiently. "You indicated I must have stopped after your father died, and I said I did not, for he had left funds for my trouble and expense. That money ran out, Warthrop, in December of last year. Their last feeding was on Christmas Day."

Kearns barked a laugh. "O holy night!"

"Then Peterson dynamited the tunnel, sealing off the abominations on the other side."

"Peterson," echoed Kearns.

"Yes, Peterson. I trust him completely; he's been doing the job since the beginning."

"What is his Christian name?"

"Jonathan. Why do you ask?"

Warthrop gave Kearns no chance to respond. "You assumed they would starve to death."

"I thought it the wisest course. It was something your father and I discussed before his death. If it makes you feel any better, Warthrop, he did express morbid remorse from time to time; I don't think the operation gave him any joy.

More than once he mentioned to me the possibility of terminating the experiment—starving them, poisoning them, setting their pens ablaze. But at heart he was an optimist, I think." Starr added, "He truly thought with enough time he could tame them."

"Tame them?" asked Warthrop. "I thought the idea was to interbreed them."

"Oh, he gave up on that after a few years," said Starr with another wave of his splotchy talon. "Every potential mate I sent over they simply tore to pieces."

Kearns laughed. "Not too different from human marriage!"

Warthrop was nodding, but not at Kearns's cynical observation. "That explains all of it, or nearly all. There was no reason to leave the safety of their man-made dens, until their food supply was cut off and hunger drove them to the surface. I had assumed the attack upon the Stinnets was a territorial response brought about by our trespass upon their domain. . . ." The monstrumologist sighed, an exhalation of both relief and painful acknowledgment. "I was wrong. Wrong in my assumption and wrong in my response. But not all questions have been answered, Starr. Why did you let Varner live? Wouldn't it have been safer to discard him in the pit with the other 'garbage'?"

"Dear God, Warthrop, what do you take me for? I may be avaricious, but I am not completely corrupt."

I thought of flies buzzing maddeningly upon a windowpane,

of their repugnant progeny squirming in open sores, of boots filled with liquefying flesh. *I am not completely corrupt.*

"Oh, no," agreed Kearns. He crossed the room to stand before the withered, wheezing old man. With great tenderness he said, "To the contrary, you are a humanitarian, Dr. Starr. Let no one tell you otherwise! An anthropological alchemist, turning lead into gold! The chains that bind most men do not bind you, and in this you and I are brothers, dear Jeremiah. We are the new men of a new and glorious age, free of lies and unbound by any ridiculous rectitude."

He placed his hands on either side of Starr's weathered pate, cupping his face while he bent low to purr into his oversize ear, "The only truth is the truth of the now. 'There is nothing either good or bad, but thinking makes it so.' There is no morality, is there, Jeremiah, but the morality of the moment."

And with that, John Kearns, student of human anatomy and hunter of monsters, with his bare hands gave his victim's head a violent twist, snapping his neck, severing his spine cord, killing him instantly.

Then, brushing past a stunned and speechless Warthrop on his way out of the room, he said this, with no trace of irony: "He will not be missed."

The doctor could barely contain his fury, though by all outward signs he appeared perfectly collected; but I knew him too well. He held his tongue until we had turned off the narrow lane to the house on Motley Hill, and then he turned on Kearns.

"It is murder, Kearns, plain and simple."

"It was a mercy killing, Warthrop, simple and plain."

"You've given me no choice."

"One always has that, Pellinore. May I ask a question? What would happen should the old coot's heart suddenly spring to life and he makes a deathbed confession to his crimes? Would you not like to continue your life's work? . . . Sorry, that was two questions."

"I have a better question," retorted Warthrop. "What is my choice if staying silent allows you to continue *your* life's work?"

"Why, Pellinore, you wound my feelings. Who is to say whose work is more worthy of approbation? 'Judge not, lest you be judged.'"

"They say no one knows the Bible better than the devil."

Kearns laughed merrily, reined in his mount, and turned back toward town.

"Where are you going now?" demanded the doctor.

"To and fro in the earth, my dear monstrumologist, walking up and down in it! Look for me upon the rising of the moon; I shall return!"

He spurred his horse and rode off at a full gallop. Warthrop and I watched him until he disappeared behind the crest of the last hill. The doctor was chewing his bottom lip anxiously.

"Do you know where he's going, sir?" I asked.

He nodded. "I think so." He sighed, and then laughed long, softly, and bitterly. "'John J. J. Schmidt'! Do you know, Will Henry, I don't think Kearns is his real name either."

He kept his word, though, whatever his true name was. An hour after our dinner, as the full moon lifted her silvery head above the treetops, he returned, retreating to his room without a word for either of us, only to clump down the stairs again in fresh clothing, draped in his traveling cloak, bags in hand.

"Well, Pellinore, I'm off," he announced. "Jolly good fun this, but I don't wish to overstay my welcome, which I suspect I might have by at least a day."

"More than one, John," replied Warthrop dryly. "What have you done to Jonathan Peterson?"

"Who?" He seemed genuinely bewildered. "Oh! The old codger's lackey. Yes. Him. Why do you ask that?"

"Where is he?"

He shook his head sadly. "No one seems to be able to find him, Pellinore. It is a sad case."

Warthrop said nothing for a moment, and then, gravely: "I still intend to inform the authorities."

"Right, and really I can't blame you for it, so I will make no more appeals to your good sense. It's rather like God switching the covenant to the insects." He giggled into the doctor's stony countenance. "Do you know why I like you so much, Warthrop? You're so bloody *earnest*."

He turned to me. "And you, Will Henry! No hard feelings, I hope, about that unfortunate incident in the caves; it really couldn't be helped. Not that I would, but if I ever told anyone of *your* bravado in battle, I would be taken for a liar. You shall make an excellent monstrumologist someday, if you can survive the tutelage of Warthrop here. Goodbye, Will."

He shook my hand and tousled my hair. The doctor asked, "Where are you off to next, Kearns?"

"Oh, really, Pellinore, you threaten to turn me in and then ask for my whereabouts? I'm not a complete fool, no Bobby Morgan, after all. By the way, however did you convince him not to throw you in jail?"

Warthrop stiffened, and said, "Robert is an old friend of mine. He understands the importance of my work."

"Keeping you on the hunt keeps New Jerusalem safer? Tell that to the good reverend Stinnet and his clan."

"I thought," the doctor said evenly, "that you were leaving."

"So I am! In all seriousness, though, I do think I need a nice long holiday. A more leisurely kind of hunt, a less daunting quarry to tax me, particularly since I shan't have the indispensable services of Master Will Henry here."

"Another matter I haven't forgotten," the doctor replied darkly. "You should leave, Kearns, before I begin to dwell too long upon it."

He took the doctor's advice, taking his leave at once, and the next morning Warthrop kept his promise, reporting the murder to the authorities, though nothing, to my knowledge, ever came of it. One notice appeared in the papers regarding the mysterious disappearance of Jonathan Peterson, but to my knowledge, nothing else; his body was never found.

We did not speak much of Jack Kearns after that spring of '88. The topic seemed to subject the doctor to moral dilemmas with which he did not care to be burdened.

But in the late fall of that year the subject did come up in a roundabout way. I was in the dining room polishing the family silver when I heard a loud cry from the library and the sound of something heavy falling to the floor. Alarmed, I rushed to the room, expecting to find the doctor collapsed in a heap. (He had been working very hard for days without sleep or sustenance.) Instead I discovered him wearing a path back and forth on the carpet, incessantly running his hand through his hair, long overdue for a trim, muttering angrily to himself. He stopped when he spied me in the doorway and watched silently as I scurried to pick up the small table he had hurled down in his consternation. Next to the table was the front section of the *Times* of London. The headline under the masthead blared: RIPPER STRIKES AGAIN/WHITECHAPEL KILLER CLAIMS FOURTH VICTIM.

Whitechapel. I had heard that name, in the parlor of the house on Motley Hill six months before: *Dr. John J. J. Schmidt of Whitechapel.*

The doctor said nothing as I read the gruesome article, remained silent for a few seconds when I looked up at him, and it was I who at last broke that awful silence.

"Do you think . . . ," I asked. There was no need to finish the question.

"What do I think?" he said rhetorically. "I think Malachi should have taken him up on his offer."

After dressing and picking over the profoundly disappointing potato pancakes (he left the sausage untouched), the doctor summoned me to the basement. It was time for my bimonthly checkup.

I sat upon the tall metal stool. He shone a bright light into my eyes, took my blood pressure and temperature, measured my pulse, examined the back of my throat. He drew a vial of blood from my arm. I watched, quite accustomed to the ritual by this point, as he squirted a small amount of iodine solution into the tube and swirled the concoction for a few seconds. *You will have to know how to do this, Will Henry,* he had told me. *We will not be together forever.*

"Eyedropper," he said, and I pressed the implement into his open palm. He squeezed a drop of the bloody mixture onto a slide, placed another slide on top of the first, and then slid the sample under the microscope's lens. I held my breath as he bent to examine the outcome. He grunted, motioned for me to have a look.

"See those oblong black specks?" he asked.

"Yes, sir, I think so."

"Yes you do or yes you think you do? Be precise, Will Henry!"

"I see them. Yes, sir."

"Those are the larvae."

I swallowed. The shapes resembled tiny obsidian orbs, thousands of dead little black eyes, swimming in a single drop of my blood.

The doctor removed his gloves and said matter-of-factly, "Well, it appears the population has remained more or less stable." He flipped open the file beside the microscope, marked *Subject: W. J. Henry/ Diag: B. arawakus Infestation* and scribbled a sloppy note under the date.

"Is that a good thing?" I asked.

"Hmm? Yes, it is a good thing. No one knows why in some cases *arawakus* maintains perfect symbiosis with its mammalian host, giving the host unnaturally long life, and in other cases overwhelms the body with the sheer volume of its numbers. Singularly curious is your case, Will Henry, for it falls in the former category, whereas clearly your father's did not. There is a theory much too complex for me to explain adequately in all its elegant detail, from an excellent paper written by one of my colleagues at the Society, which, briefly put, postulates that what happened to your father was a means of propagation, a way for the parasite to find a new host."

"A new host," I echoed. "Me."

He shrugged. "I doubt it happened the night of the fire. You weren't near him when they made their ill-timed exit. It is only a theory; the method by which they infest a host is not known."

"But it was an accident, wasn't it?"

"Well, I doubt your father infected you on purpose!"

"No, that is not what I . . . I mean, sir, what happened to my father. It *was* an accident, wasn't it?"

He frowned. "What are you asking, Will Henry? Are you suggesting your father was intentionally infected?"

I made no reply, since no reply was necessary. The doctor placed his hand on my shoulder and said, "Look at me, Will Henry. You know I do not lie. You know that about me, yes?"

"Yes, sir."

"I am not the midwife to your affliction, if affliction and not boon it turns out to be. I do not know how or when your father picked up this contagion, though undoubtedly it was a by-product of his service to me. In that sense, I suppose, it was no accident what happened to him and what is now happening to you. You are his son, Will Henry, and as his son you bear his burden." He looked away. "As do all sons."

Later that same afternoon, the doctor retreated to his study to prepare a paper he intended to present at the annual congress of the Society, cautioning me he was not to be disturbed. The week before he had received by post an early draft of a monograph to be delivered by a fellow monstrumologist—the chief presiding officer of the Society, no less—forwarded to him anonymously by a concerned colleague, who urged Warthrop to compose a public reply.

I vouch it is no hyperbole to aver that the very future of our discipline is at stake, wrote his friend. *And I can think of no better man to contest our esteemed president's alarming and dangerous disquisitions.*

After perusing the draft of the venerable Dr. Abram von Helrung, Warthrop found himself in complete agreement with his colleague on both counts: The president's paper was dangerous and there was no better man to avert the anticipated catastrophe than Warthrop himself. He set about the task with his usual single-mindedness. On that particular afternoon, he was working on the twelfth version of his reply to von Helrung.

While he toiled away in the vineyard of his considerable intellectual acumen, I retreated to my little loft to change for a quick trip to town. My purpose was simple: to pick up some raspberry scones from the baker's, for I knew he would ask for one when he awoke on the morrow and would not be able, for the life of him, to understand why the scone-less condition persisted despite my having knowledge of the deficiency.

I did not notice it at first in my haste (the baker's would be closing in less than an hour). I had changed and was reaching for my little hat upon its peg, when I happened to glance down and see it hanging on the bedpost: It was a brand-new hat, noticeably larger than the tattered, mud-stained cousin now in my quivering hand. What was this? I picked it up, turned it over, and saw embroidered on the inner lining, in golden thread, my initials: *W.J.H.*

For a moment I remained there, frozen to the spot, my heart for some reason pounding as if I'd raced up a steep hill, holding in one hand my little hat, which still smelled faintly of wood smoke from a fire long since quenched, and in the other the new one that seemed to have appeared out of nowhere, but of course did come from somewhere—from *someone*.

Bareheaded, a hat—one old, one new—in either hand, I trooped back downstairs. From the library I heard the sound of a heavy object hitting the carpet, and I dashed into the room to investigate. I had assumed Warthrop was still in his study.

The doctor was sitting on the floor before the hearth, stoking the fire. Beside him sat his father's old trunk. If he noticed my appearance, he gave no sign of it, as he threw open the lid and, one by one, began tossing the contents into the crackling conflagration. The flames leaped and spat with each addition (the smell of the shrunken head's hair was particularly pungent). I came to his side and sat down. He barely took notice.

The heat intensified upon our faces. He tossed in the old letters, one by one. If he noticed one had been opened (*I am quite lonely at times and do not feel entirely at home here*), he gave no sign. In fact, his face betrayed no emotion at all, neither sorrow nor anger, regret or resignation. He might have been engaged in a mundane chore rather than the destruction of the sole remaining evidence of his father's existence.

"What have you got there, Will Henry?" he inquired without taking his eyes from the purifying pyre.

I looked down at the two hats lying side by side in my lap. I raised my head and studied his face, turned away from my own, turned toward the fire. Upon his angular profile shadow warred with light, the obscured visible, the hidden revealed. His father had named him Pellinore in honor of the mythical king who quested after a beast that could not be caught, an act of thoughtless cruelty, perhaps; at the least a fateful portent, the passing on of a hereditary malady, the familial curse.

"My hat, sir," I answered.

"Which one, Will Henry? That is the question."

The fire popped and crackled, snapped and growled. *That is it*, thought I. *A fire destroys, but it also purifies.*

I tossed my old hat into the center of the flames. Warthrop gave merely the slightest of nods, and in silence we watched the fire consume it.

"Who knows, Will Henry," he said after it had been reduced, like the effluvia of his father's life, to ashes. "Perhaps this burden you bear will prove a blessing."

"A blessing, sir?"

"My colleague nicknamed *arawakus* the 'Fountain of Youth Contagion.'"

"Does that mean I'll never grow up?"

He lifted my new hat, his first gift to me, from my lap and dropped it upon my head. "Or that you will live forever—to carry on my work. Talk about turning burdens into blessings!"

The monstrumologist laughed.

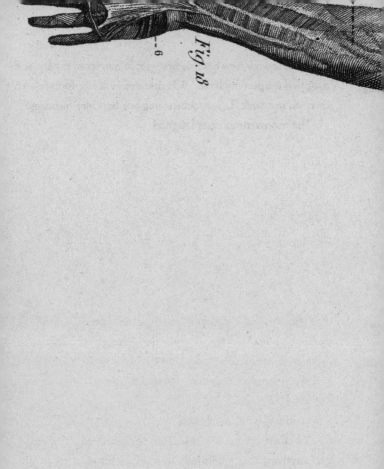

Fig. 18
- 6

EPILOGUE

May 2008

One hundred and twenty years after the conclusion of the "Anthropophagi Affair," I called the director of facilities to tell him I had finished reading the first three volumes of William Henry's remarkable journal.

"And?" he asked.

"And it's definitely fiction."

"Well, of course it is." He sounded annoyed. "You didn't find anything that might help us identify him?"

"Nothing substantial."

"His hometown . . . ?"

"He calls it 'New Jerusalem,' but there's no such town, at least not in New England."

"He changed the name. He has to be from *somewhere*."

"Well," I said, "he mentions two towns, Dedham and

Swampscott. Those are actual places in Massachusetts."

"What about family? Brothers, sisters, cousins . . . anyone?"

"I've only read the first three notebooks," I answered. "But he indicates his only relatives were his parents." I cleared my throat. "I guess the police ran his prints when they found him?"

"Yes, of course. No matches."

"He was given a full physical when they brought him in, right?"

"That's standard, yes."

"Did they—Do you normally run any kind of blood test?"

"What do you mean, like DNA?"

"Well. That too, but as part of the physical, do you guys perform a full workup on a person's blood?"

"Of course. Why do you ask?"

"And there wasn't anything . . . unusual about the sample?"

"I'd have to pull the file, but I'd remember if the doctor had told me there was. What are you getting at?"

"What about an autopsy? Is that SOP?"

"Not unless there's suspicions of foul play or the family requests it."

"Neither of which applies to Will Henry," I said. "What was the cause of death?"

"Heart failure."

"He wasn't sick right before he died, though? No fever, or maybe a rash?"

"He died peacefully in his sleep. Why?"

"He kind of gives an explanation for his age. Must have made it up, like everything else."

He agreed. "Well, thanks for taking a look at them."

"I'm not finished," I said. "And I'd like to, if that would be okay. Do you mind if I keep them for a little while longer? Maybe I'll run across something that'll help."

He said he didn't mind; nobody had answered the ad, and all his inquiries, like mine, had yielded nothing. I promised to call back if I found something useful. I hung up, relieved: I was afraid he might have demanded the return of Will Henry's journal before I could finish the remaining volumes.

Over the next few months, whenever I had the time to devote to it, I trolled the Internet, mining for any nugget of information that might lend credence to the journal's authenticity. Of course I found many references to the mythical creature described in the preceding transcript, from Herodotus to Shakespeare, but nothing about an American invasion in the late nineteenth century. Nothing about a Monstrumologist Society (or "monstrumology" for that matter—apparently it was part of a lexicon invented by Will Henry), and nothing to indicate a person named Pellinore Warthrop had ever existed. I found a reference online to a turn-of-the-century sanatorium in Dedham, though it wasn't called Motley Hill, and its proprietor was not named Starr. I found no reference to a cargo vessel called *Feronia* grounding near Swampscott in 1865. There was no record of *any* ship wrecking there that year.

I perused several sources on the all-too-real personage of Jack the Ripper, but found no mention of the alias John Kearns or any theory that might support Will Henry's startling claim that he had hunted monsters when he wasn't hunting human beings. A very kind employee of the British Museum finally returned my calls regarding the personal papers of Sir Francis Galton, the father of eugenics, whom Warthrop claimed had been a close friend of his father's. As I suspected, no mention of an Alistair Warthrop or anyone who remotely resembled him was contained in any of Galton's letters.

I couldn't find anything on *Biminius arawakus*, either. There is no myth—and, of course, nothing in the scientific literature—about a parasitic organism that somehow extends the natural life span of its host.

At times, immersed in this ultimately fruitless research, I would laugh at myself. Why was I wasting my time trying to find some shred of proof in what was so obviously a work of a demented man's imagination? I felt pity for him. Maybe that's a part of it. I don't think Will Henry would have called it a work of imagination. I think he actually *believed* it was all true. It was fiction, obviously, but not a deliberate fiction.

Nearly four months after our conversation, I called the

director again and asked where William James Henry was buried. The municipal cemetery turned out to be less than ten minutes from my house. I found a small stone marker there, etched with only his name, if that was his name, just another pauper's grave among the scores of indigents' plots. I wondered what the procedure was for requesting an exhumation of the remains. Standing at the foot of his grave, I was struck by the absurdity of the idea—why in the world would I want *any* of his strange story to be true?

On a whim, I squatted down and scratched at the ground with a stick, digging down four or five inches into the sandy topsoil. A recent thunderstorm had saturated the ground, and water immediately began to seep into my little hole.

I saw it after a minute or two, a tiny wormlike creature, not some fat night crawler or chubby grub, but something long and very thin squirming on the surface of the dark water. *No thicker around than a human hair*, Will Henry had said, describing the things that infested his father.

I fished the anonymous invertebrate from the hole with the end of my stick and held it up, squinting at it in the gloaming of that late summer's day. I remembered Warthrop's words from the journal—*the method by which they infest a host is not known*—and I flung the stick away in a moment of mindless panic.

Get real, I told myself, trying to laugh it off, and that brought to mind something else Will Henry had written. The words followed me as I beat a hasty retreat to the car and, beyond that, to my modern life in a world where room for monsters shrinks by the hour.

Yes, my dear child, monsters are real. I happen to have one hanging in my basement.

BE AFRAID OF THE DARK.

Turn the page for a look
at the second chilling
book in Rick Yancey's
Monstrumologist series.

RICK YANCEY

NEW YORK TIMES BESTSELLING AUTHOR

THE CURSE
OF THE WENDIGO

THE MONSTRUMOLOGIST

When you look too deep in the darkness, the darkness looks back at you

I do not wish to remember these things.

I wish to be rid of them, to be rid of *him*. I set down the pen nearly a year ago, swearing I would never pick it up again. Let it die with me, I thought. I am an old man. I owe the future nothing.

Soon I will fall asleep and I will wake from this terrible dream. The endless night will fall, and I will rise.

I long for that night. I do not fear it.

I have had my fill of fear. I have stared too long into the abyss, and now the abyss stares back at me.

Between the sleeping and the waking, it is there.

Between the rising and the resting, it is there.

It is always there.

It gnaws my heart. It chews my soul.

I turn aside and see it. I stop my ears and hear it. I cover myself and feel it.

There are no human words for what I mean.

It is the language of the bare bough and the cold stone, pronounced in the fell wind's sullen whisper and the metronomic *drip-drip* of the rain. It is the song the falling snow sings and the discordant clamor of sunlight ripped apart by the canopy and miserly filtered down.

It is what the unseeing eye sees. It is what the deaf ear hears.

It is the romantic ballad of death's embrace; the solemn hymn of offal dripping from bloody teeth; the lamentation of the bloated corpse rotting in the sun; and the graceful ballet of maggots twisting in the ruins of God's temple.

Here in this gray land, we have no name. We are the carcasses reflected in the yellow eye.

Our bones are bleached within our skin; our empty sockets regard the hungry crow.

Here in this shadow country, our tinny voices scratch like a fly's wing against unmoving air.

Ours is the language of imbeciles, the gibberish of idiots. The root and the vine have more to say than us.

I want to show you something. There is no name for it; it has no human symbol. It is old and its memory is long. It knew the world before we named it.

It knows everything. It knows me and it knows you.
And I will show it to you.
I will show you.

Let us go then, you and I, like Alice down the rabbit hole, to a time when there still were dark places in the world, and there were men who dared to delve into them.

An old man, I am a boy again.

And dead, the monstrumologist lives.

He was a solitary man, a dweller in silences, a genius enslaved to his own despotic thought, meticulous in his work, careless in his appearance, given to bouts of debilitating melancholia and driven by demons as formidable as the physical monstrosities he pursued.

He was a hard man, obstinate, cold to the point of cruelty, with impenetrable motives and rigid expectations, a strict taskmaster and an exacting teacher when he didn't ignore me altogether. Days would pass with but a word or two between us. I might have been another stick of dusty furniture in a forgotten room of his ancestral home. If I had fled, I do not doubt weeks would have passed before he would have noticed. Then, without warning, I would find myself the sole focus of his attention, a singularly unpleasant phenomenon that produced an effect not unlike the sensation of drowning or being crushed by a thousand-pound rock. Those dark, strangely backlit eyes would turn upon me, the brow would furrow, the lips tighten and grow white, the same expression of intense concentration I had seen a hundred times at the necropsy table as he flayed open some nameless thing to explore its innards. A look from him could lay me bare. I spent many a useless hour debating with myself which was worse, being ignored by him or being acknowledged.

But I remained. He was all I had, and I do not flatter myself when I say I was all that he had. The fact is, to his death, I was his sole companion.

That had not always been the case.

He was a solitary man, but he was no hermit. In those waning days of the century, the monstrumologist was much in demand. Letters and telegrams arrived daily from all over the world seeking his advice, inviting him to speak, appealing to him for this or that service. He preferred the field to the laboratory and would drop everything at a moment's notice to investigate a sighting of some rare species; he always kept a packed suitcase and a field kit in his closet.

He looked forward to the colloquium of the Monstrumologist Society held annually in New York City, where for two weeks scientists of the same philosophical bent met to present papers, exchange ideas, share discoveries, and, as was their counterintuitive wont, close down every bar and saloon on the island of Manhattan. Perhaps this was not so incongruous, though. These were men who pursued things from which the vast majority of their fellows would run as fast as their legs would carry them. The hardships they endured in this pursuit almost necessitated some kind of Dionysian release. Warthrop was the exception. He never touched alcohol or tobacco or any mind-altering drug. He sneered at those he considered slaves to their vices, but he was no different—only his vice was. In fact, one might argue his was the more dangerous by far. It was not the fruit of the vine that killed Narcissus, after all.

The letter that arrived late in the spring of 1888 was just one of many received that day—an alarming missive that, upon coming into his possession, quickly came to possess him.

Postmarked in New York City, it read:

My Dear Dr. Warthrop,

I have it upon good authority that his Hon. Pres. von Helrung intends to present the enclosed Proposal at the annual Congress in New York this November instant. That he is the author of this outrageous proposition, I have no doubt, and I would not trouble you if I possessed so much as a scintilla of uncertainty.

The man has clearly gone mad. I care as little about that as I care for the man, but my fear is not unjustified, I think. I consider his insidious argument a genuine threat to the legitimacy of our vocation, with the potential to doom our work to oblivion or—worse—to doom us to sharing space in the public mind with the charlatan and the quack. Thus, I vouch it is no hyperbole to aver that the very future of our discipline is at stake.

Once you have read this offensive tripe, I am certain you will agree that our only hope lies in delivering a _forceful_ Reply upon the completion of his Presentation. And I can think of no better man to contest our esteemed president's alarming and dangerous disquisitions than you, Dr. Warthrop, the leading Philosopher of Aberrant Natural History of his generation.

I remain, as always, etc., etc.,

Your Obt. Servant,

A Concerned Colleague

A single reading of the enclosed monograph of Abram von Helrung convinced the doctor that his correspondent was correct in at least one regard. The proposal did indeed pose a threat to the legitimacy of his beloved profession. That he was the best—and obvious—choice to refute the claims of the most renowned monstrumologist in the world required no convincing on anyone's part. Pellinore Warthrop's genius included the profound insight that he happened to be one.

So everything was put aside. Visitors were turned away. Letters went unanswered. All invitations were declined. His studies were abandoned. Sleep and sustenance were reduced to the barest minimum. His thirty-seven-page monograph, with the rather unwieldy title, _Shall We Doom the Natural Philosophy of Monstrumology to the Dustbin of History? A Reply to the Hon. President Dr. Abram von Helrung upon His_

Proposal to Investigate and Consider as Possible Inclusions into the Catalogue of Aberrant Species Certain Heretofore Mythical Creatures of Supernatural Origin at the One Hundred Tenth Congress of the Society for the Advancement of the Science of Monstrumology, went through multiple revisions and refinements over that frantic summer.

He enlisted me in the cause, naturally, as his research assistant, in addition to my duties as cook, maid, manservant, laundryman, and errand boy. I fetched books, took dictation, and played audience to his stiff, overly formal, sometimes ludicrously awkward presentation. He would stand ramrod straight with his lanky arms folded stiffly behind his back, eyes focused unerringly upon the floor, chin tilted downward so that his otherwise compellingly dark features were lost in shadow.

He refused to read directly from his paper, so he often "went up" in the parlance of the theater, completely losing track of his argument, thrashing like King Pellinore, his namesake, in the dense thicket of his thoughts in search of the elusive Questing Beast of his reasoning.

At other times he fell into rambling asides that took the audience from the birth of monstrumology in the early eighteenth century (beginning with Bacqueville de la Potherie, the acknowledged father of this most curious of esoteric disciplines) to the present day, with references to obscure personages whose voices had long been stifled in the Dark Angel's smothering embrace.

"Now, where was I, Will Henry?" he would ask after one

of these extended extemporaneities. It never failed that this question came at the precise moment when my mind had wandered to more interesting matters, more often than not to the current weather conditions or the menu for our long-overdue supper.

Unwilling to incur his inestimable ire, I would fumble a reply, blurting the best guess I had, which usually included somewhere in the sentence the name of Darwin, Warthrop's personal hero.

The ploy did not always work.

"Darwin!" the monstrumologist cried once in reply, striking his fist into his palm in agitation. "Darwin! Really, Will Henry, what does Darwin have to do with the native folklore of the Carpathians? Or the mythos of Homer? Or Norse cosmology? Have I not impressed upon you the importance of this endeavor? If I should fail in this, the seminal moment of my career, not only will I go down in humiliation and disrepute, but the entire house will fall! The end of monstrumology, the immediate and irrevocable loss of nearly two hundred years of unselfish devotion by men who *dwarf* all those who came after them, myself included. Even me, Will Henry. Think of that!"

"I think it was . . . You were talking about the Carpathians, I think . . ."

"Dear Lord! I *know* that, Will Henry. And the only reason *you* know that is I just said it!"

As hard as he threw himself into the task of his oral presentation, more assiduously still did he labor over his written reply, composing at least twelve drafts, each of them in his nearly illegible scrawl, and all of which fell to me to transcribe into readable form, for, if the reply had been delivered to the printer's in its original state, it would undoubtedly have been wadded up and hurled at my head.

Upon the conclusion of my hours of toil, hunching over my desk like a medieval monk with aching ink-stained fingers and itching, burning eyes, the monstrumologist would snatch the product from my quivering grip and compare it to the original, hunting for the slightest error, which, of course, he would invariably find.

At the end of this Herculean effort, after the printer delivered the finished product and there was little left to do (and little left of the monstrumologist, for he must have lost more than fifteen pounds since the project had begun) but wait for that fall's convocation, he fell into a profound depression. The monstrumologist retreated to his shuttered study, where he brooded in a gloom both actual and metaphysical, refusing to even acknowledge my halfhearted attempts to alleviate his suffering. I brought him raspberry scones (his favorite) from the baker's. I shared with him the latest gossip gleaned from the society pages (he held a strange fascination for them) and the local doings of our little hamlet of New Jerusalem. He would not be comforted. He even lost interest in the mail, which I arranged for him, unread, upon his desk, until the desk's surface was covered as thickly as the forest floor by the leaves of autumn.

Near the end of August, a large package arrived from Menlo Park, and for a few moments he was his old self again, delighting in the gift from his friend. Enclosed with it was a brief note: *All my thanks for your help with the design, Thos. A. Edison.* He played with the phonograph for the space of an hour, and then touched it no more. It sat upon the table beside him like a silent rebuke. Here was the dream made real of Thomas Edison, a man who was destined to be lauded as one of the greatest minds of his generation, if not in all history, a true man of science whose world would be forever changed for his having lived in it.

"What am I, Will Henry?" the doctor asked abruptly one rainy afternoon.

I answered with the literalness of a child, which, of course, at the time I was.

"You're a monstrumologist, sir."

"I am a mote of dust," he said. "Who will remember me when I am gone?"

I glanced at the mountain of letters upon his desk. What did he mean? It seemed he knew everyone. Just that morning a letter had arrived from the Royal Society of London. Sensing he meant something deeper, I answered intuitively, "I will, sir. I will remember you."

"You! Well, I suppose you won't have much choice in the matter." His eyes wandered to the phonograph. "Do you know it was not always my desire to be a scientist? When I was much younger, my great ambition was to be a poet."

If he had stated that his brain were made of Swiss cheese, I would not have been more flabbergasted.

"A poet, Dr. Warthrop?"

"Oh, yes. The desire is gone, but the temperament, you may have noticed, still lingers. I was quite the romantic, Will Henry, if you can imagine it."

"What happened?" I asked.

"I grew up."

He placed one of his thin, delicate fingers upon the ceresin cylinder, running the tip along the pits and grooves like a blind man reading braille.

"There is no future in it, Will Henry," he said pensively. "The future belongs to science. The fate of our species will be determined by the likes of Edison and Tesla, not Wordsworth or Whitman. The poets will lie upon the shores of Babylon and weep, poisoned by the fruit that grows from the ground where the Muses' corpses rot. The poets' voices will be drowned out by the gears of progress. I foresee the day when all sentiment is reduced to a chemical equation in our brains—hope, faith, even love—their exact locations pinned down and mapped out, so we may point to it and say, 'Here, in this region of our cerebral cortex, lies the soul.'"

"I like poetry," I said.

"Yes, and some like to whittle, Will Henry, so they will always find trees."

"Have you kept any of your poems, Doctor?"

"No, I have not, for which you should be grateful. I was horrible."

"What did you write about?"

"What every poet writes about. I fail to understand it, Will Henry, your uncanny gift for seizing upon the most tangential aspect of the issue and drubbing it to death."

To prove him wrong, I said, "I will never forget you, sir. Ever. And neither will the whole world. You'll be more famous than Edison and Bell and all the rest put together. I'll make sure of it."

"I will pass into oblivion, to the vile dust from whence I sprung, unwept, unhonored, and unsung. . . . That is poetry, in case you're wondering. Sir Walter Scott."

He stood up, and now his countenance shone with the profundity of his passion, at once terrifying and strangely beautiful, the look of the mystic or the saint, transported from the constraints of ego and all fleshy desires.

"But I am nothing. My memory is nothing. The work is everything, and I will not see it mocked. Though the cost be my very life, I will not let it pass, Will Henry. If von Helrung should succeed—if we allow our noble cause to be reduced to the study of the silly superstitions of the masses—so that we jibber-jabber on about the nature of the vampire or the zombie as if they sat at the same table as the manticore and the *Anthropophagus*, then monstrumology is as dead as alchemy, as ridiculous as astrology, as serious as one of Mr. Barnum's sideshow freaks!

"Grown men, educated men, men of the highest sophistication and social refinement, cross themselves like ignorant peasant when they pass this house. 'What que unnatural goings-on in there, the house of Warthrop!' W you yourself can attest that there is nothing queer or unnat ral about it, that what I deal in is altogether natural, that if it weren't for me and men like me, these fools might find themselves choking on their own entrails or being digested in the belly of some beast no more queer than the lowly housefly!"

He drew a breath deeply, the pause before the start of the next movement in his symphony, then suddenly he became very still, head cocked slightly to one side. I listened, but heard nothing but the rain's gentle kiss upon the window and the metronomic *tick-tick* of the mantel clock.

"Someone is here," he said. He turned and peered through the blinds. I could see nothing but the reflection of his angular face. How hollow his cheeks! How pale his flesh! He had spoken boldly of his ultimate fate—did he know how close he seemed to that vile dust from whence he came?

"Quickly, to the door, Will Henry. Whoever it is, remember I am indisposed and can't receive visitors. Well, what are you waiting for? Snap to, Will Henry, snap to!"

A moment later the bell rang. He closed the study door behind me. I lit the jets in the front hall to chase away the preternatural shadows lying thick in the entryway, and threw wide the door to behold the most beautiful woman I have ever seen in all the years of my exceedingly long life.